TEMPTING THE NEIGHBOR

MOUNT MACON BOOK 2

ASHLEY MUÑOZ

Cover Design: Amanda Simpson from Pixel Mischief Designs
Editing: HEA Author Services: Kimberly: Jessica Snyder Edits
Proofing: Tiffany Hernandez

❀ Created with Vellum

To anyone who has ever been told they were too much or not enough.

Live your very best life knowing they are missing all the best parts of yours.

TEMPTING
the
Neighbor

PROLOGUE

Nora

Three Years Ago

MY CAR MADE A SAD, pathetic sound when I pulled the parking brake. Normally I'd have been a bit gentler, but time was of the essence. I was already flinging the strap out of the way, unbuckling as if the seat belt were trying to strangle me. I winced when it slapped against the glass.

"Shit, shit, shit," I chanted, grabbing my bags and slamming the door shut with my foot. I ran up the stairs to the house and barreled through the front door.

"Jason, are you ready?" I called, tossing my school books onto the couch and slinging my leather bag over the back of the chair.

Bounding up the stairs, I charged into the master bedroom, finding my boyfriend sitting on the bed, staring at his cell.

"You're ready, right?" I veered for the walk-in closet, hitting the light while I grabbed my duffle. "Because I'm not and we're already so freaking late."

His silence was a little too loud as I piled my clothes into the bag and exited the closet.

"Hey…" I tried again, a bit slower and less panicked, he continued to stare at his phone making my anxiety spike. Either he was ignoring me, or an alien had stolen his body.

I wore insecurity like a second skin when it came to relationships, which was why I had turned Jason down the first three times he'd asked me out. We dated for six months before he asked me to move in with him and we celebrated our one-year anniversary last month. Part of me wondered if a proposal was on the horizon, but I didn't want to get my hopes up. It made me nervous to think about getting married, but I loved Jason and the idea of being his wife made my stomach flip with excitement, not fear.

I gently nudged him with my foot, and that seemed to do the trick.

"Hey…sorry, I was just thinking," he finally replied, giving me a half smile.

But it felt different from any look he'd ever given me.

He stood and grabbed for his duffle, and I let out a sigh of relief.

"No worries." I gave him a warm smile in return and turned toward the dresser. "If we leave within the next fifteen minutes, we can make it to my parents' before dark."

My back was to him, but I watched in the mirror as he bent down to put on his shoes and I removed my earrings. When he shoved his arms into his coat, I turned.

"You have something thicker that you're bringing, right? Because it gets really cold in Macon…and we have to go tree hunti—"

"Nora."

I paused. Uncertainty rattled in my chest like a bottle of prescription pills.

Dipping his head and tucking his hands into his pockets, he explained.

"I'm not going to your parents', Nora…I'm going home to mine."

Feeling my face fall with confusion, and a tiny tendril of worry flicker in my core, I calmly asked, "Why, what's going on?"

We'd already agreed to go to my parents' house for Christmas. I had met his family at Easter, and when he had suggested we spend the holidays in Macon, a part of me thought he'd want to talk to my dad about asking for my hand in marriage. Not that he had to, it was an ancient tradition anyway, but my dad was old-school.

He shifted, revealing a pained expression. "I can't do this anymore."

Bending to grab his bag, he continued, "Can you have your stuff moved out by the end of Christmas break?"

"Move out?" My lungs wanted to close. It wasn't like I'd been physically active and yet, my chest felt like I'd run up a hill at a breakneck speed. We'd been together for a year, how could he just—

"I don't want to fight, Nora..." He sighed dramatically, walking over to our dresser. He opened the top drawer and dug around.

My gaze narrowed and blurred as I processed what he'd grabbed. "Wait...so you're not coming with me, but you're taking condoms with you on break?"

What the fuck was happening?

He didn't respond, his face flushed red as he stashed the rubbers in his duffle.

"Just hang on for a second, explain what's going on." I sat down, putting my hand to my head.

It was spinning as unease unfurled inside me like a balloon.

Stepping closer, with his bag completely zipped and the evidence that he planned to move on tucked away, he softly replied. "I know this isn't easy...I'm not trying to hurt you, but...it's over."

Tears stung my eyes as I looked up, and he met my gaze with an indifferent stare. As if I were a stranger, he politely asked me to vacate his home. I hated that he'd had time to adjust to this ending, slowly building up all the reasons in his mind as to why he wanted it to end.

"But *why*, what in the hell happened? Was it something I did?"

"It's what you don't do, Nora." His hand dropped, like he was exasperated with this conversation. "It's just, you know how your parents fix all your problems? I've recently realized how involved in our lives they'd be if I stayed with you...I need someone a little more independent."

"No...that's not..." I shook my head, tears trailing my cheeks. "My parents aren't that involved..."

They weren't. It was the normal amount of involvement...his mom called plenty. They always sent him money, they bought him a car. This was normal. I was an only child, and had recently left home…it was an adjustment, that's all.

Jason stepped closer and the green in his eyes shone bright as the sun shifted, breaking through the bedroom windows. "I called your dad three weeks ago, and do you know what he said when I asked for your hand in marriage?"

Emotions clogged my throat as I considered that maybe this was all a very confusing and backward way of him proposing. He'd asked for my hand! That had to mean something…it had to mean—

"Your dad told me I wasn't good enough for his little girl. He reminded me what it would take to care for you, he went on and on about how you can't do things on your own, how you'll be a kept woman one day and you needed someone who would be able to provide that."

My face twisted in confusion as I stood. "What are you even talking about?"

Jason shook his head with a scoff. "He told me that you needed someone who would care for you, and honestly, I'm just not looking for someone who needs to be catered to like that. I'm looking for someone who wants to take care of herself."

He stepped back, giving me one long look.

I followed after him, all the way down the stairs, feeling a fire to defend myself rage in my chest.

"I'm not that girl, that's not me. You know me."

He stopped, turning on his heel, suddenly cupping my face with tenderness. "Don't you get it, Nora? That *is* you…you rely on your parents for everything and have since I met you. You want them involved in every aspect of your life. You may not think you want that life, but I know that you do."

Pity lined every crevice of his face as he leaned forward and pressed a gentle kiss to my forehead. His lips were only there a brief second before he was moving down the stairs again.

I hated myself for going after him again. He'd torn me wide open, and I was tossing salt into the wound.

I called after him as he opened the front door and walked out. He didn't stop.

"You can't just end this without letting me defend myself..." I cried.

Tossing his bag into the back seat, he slammed the door and exhaled evenly.

"There's nothing to defend, don't be upset. This is a good thing. Your parents will help you get into a new place...you'll find someone they like who can give you the life you want."

He didn't let me say anything else before ducking into his car and driving away. I watched him go, feeling like my heart had been ripped from my chest, but the hands responsible belonged to more than just Jason.

My father's prints were all over the shattered pieces he had no business touching.

1

NORA

FRIDAY NIGHTS USED to be my absolute favorite.

All my life, I would do mental gymnastics thinking of the countdown to the end of the week. I'd plan movie nights, epic sleepovers with my best friend, complete with new nail colors and a fresh tin of cheddar popcorn. Occasionally, my parents would plan big weekend trips, where after school we'd rush to pack the car so we could get an early start.

Friday used to be fucking magical.

Now, as a grown-ass adult...Fridays were pure garbage.

Shuffling in through my back door, the wood wobbled in my arms as the snow created an ice-like slickness under my snow boots. I froze mid step. I nearly whimpered as my back locked into an agonizing position, and I considered how being frozen to the floor would be ten times better than slipping and breaking something vital...like my back or my face.

The howling wind flew in like a vortex behind me through the open door, tossing my hair into my face while I stood like a statue in the entry-way. I briefly recalled removing the rug out of my laundry room because I wanted to clean off all the mud that I had tracked in. Only, I had never put it back.

Fuckity-Fuck.

If I took a single step, I knew I was going to fall, and with my back already aching from cutting the miniscule amount of wood in my arms, if I fell, I'd just stay down. I wouldn't even get up, in fact, I was fairly sure I had a bag of nuts in my coat pocket. I'd be fine until morning. Maybe if I slipped out of my boots first, it would be fine.

With the idea in mind, and exhilaration hitting my chest because my boots were loose and untied, I slid my left foot free. Sweet Jesus, it worked.

Once that foot was out, I did the same with the other and while my socks would be wet, at least I wasn't going to fall. Once clear of the thick boots, I kicked the door shut and let out a relieved sigh. This homeowner shit was getting old really fast.

No one told me that I'd have to cut wood all winter to keep my living room warm, because I had overlooked the fact that there were no heating vents anywhere on the left half of the house. The bedrooms were all fine, thankfully, but if I wanted to be comfortable in my living room while I binge watched Vampire Diaries, then I'd have to become comfortable cutting wood. For the record, I was not. My logs all looked odd, like I hit the wedge at the wrong angle, or tried to mangle the lumber to death.

With the pile still in my arms, I walked with sopping wet socks into the living room and dumped it into the cute box my best friend Rae had purchased for me as a housewarming gift. She wanted to cheer me up as soon as it became clear that this would be my lot in life once winter hit. We had gone to a home décor show back in November, thinking the cutesy box would make cutting and gathering wood somehow more manageable. In the grand scheme of things, it seemed ridiculous to pay fifty dollars for a bin that contained firewood.

I could be using a cardboard box for how much easier it's made my life.

But I had thought with winter coming, it would be cute.

Cute.

Winter was not cute in any capacity, let me be clear.

Maybe I once thought it was, but as an adult homeowner who didn't get to walk inside and magically have hot cocoa waiting for me, I detested the entire season. Honestly, it could officially melt into the ozone for all I cared, and never show itself again. To hell with droughts, and the world ending, and fucking all of it.

Now came the fun part of my night, when I kneeled in front of my gaping, cold hearth for eternity, trying to start a fire. I swear if my life actually depended on lighting a fire, I would die. Plain and simple. I had even watched a myriad of YouTube videos on how to set the wood up in a triangle, tepee shape, while stuffing kindling and paper inside. But every single time, the entire thing would topple, and the spark would go cold. How is it that I signed the papers for this house, got my keys, and all the powers at be seemed perfectly fine with the idea that I had never once dealt with how to build a fire, or how to buy a hot water heater, or what to do if the pipes froze.

No one would send a reminder to blow out my sprinklers or turn off the water to the hoses before they freeze and potentially flood the house. And no, I didn't learn these lessons along the way, most of this information was picked up from varying episodes of some PBS special where four old men helped distressed homeowners, like myself, fix their mistakes.

I started taking notes, and all I've learned so far is that I needed elderly men in my life to come assess my home and teach me how to fix it.

"Finally," I said, once the fire ignited. I sank to the floor, rolling onto my back.

This was supposed to be easier. This was supposed to be the start of something amazing and wonderful for me, and all it proved was that I, Nora Petrov, was spoiled.

Spoiled. Spoiled. Spoiled.

My parents, who were second-generation immigrants from Europe, had made their own way in this town, owning not one but two businesses here in Macon, Oregon. Peter and Lilly Petrov were two pillars in this small community and have created a wonderful life for me, and I took every opportunity the privilege provided.

I had purchased this house myself, like my car and the design business I launched. So, it wasn't as though I hadn't taken steps to be free of my parents' umbrella of safety, but living here in Macon with them, it was far too easy to call my dad to have him fix all the things for me. Which was exactly what I wanted to do. I wanted him to come and cut enough wood to last me the rest of winter. I wanted him to figure out why my pipes groaned when I turned on the water, and why it took forever to heat said water up.

I wanted him to fix it all, but they were leaving, and it wasn't like I had anyone else to rely on.

I had to start handling this stuff myself.

Which was why I didn't call either of them when the wind picked up. Or while I knew my father's right-hand man lived right next door, I didn't walk over in the middle of the night to ask if this amount of wind was normal…or if the swaying of the trees was any indication that I should be worried. What even constituted being worried? How did other homeowners know when to panic?

Out of sheer anxiety, I ended up curled up on my couch, hugging a pillow to my chest.

Sleep came and went, as dreams of loud thunder and cracking wood pranced along my consciousness.

After an entire night of rattling shutters and branches scratching at windows, I finally woke to a bleary room and a horrific crick in my neck.

Lying twisted in the thin blanket and half curled into the couch, my breath clouded in front of me. Glancing over at the cold hearth where last night's fire had burned out, I registered that I shouldn't have slept in the living room. A major miscalculation on my part.

Dammit.

Tugging the blanket over my shoulders and slowly twisting to the side of the couch, I barely let my thick socks hit the floor before a hiss came through my clenched teeth.

The wood floor was frigid.

Shivering under the thin throw blanket, I walked to the newer eco-friendly thermostat I had put in. Usually I could control the temperature directly from my phone, but at the moment I had no idea where my phone was.

Gasping while I tiptoed across the floor, I stopped cold when I saw that the screen was completely dark, indicating it was offline.

Shit.

That would mean that the power had gone out at some point during the night…which meant I was in a world of homeowner hell.

Once a-fucking-gain.

Miserable, I traded the blanket for my winter coat and then tiptoed to the back door to pull on my snow boots. With my fingers still trembling, I pulled on a beanie and some gloves as well. Once my body regulated, and I didn't feel like an ice cube, I had to see if something had happened outside to cause the power outage.

As early dawn broke open across the sky, I trudged down the steps, watching as my feet disappeared into the deep snow. After I was clear of the stairs, I narrowed my eyes at the sky, realizing a little too late the significant amount of it that I didn't normally see.

What in the—

Oh. My. Gosh.

My jaw literally dropped as I stared in shock at what lay in front of me. And as my mind spiraled out of control about what to do, I heard my neighbor's back door slide open and his clunky work boots hit his porch.

Closing my eyes and exhaling slowly, I decided to face this head-on.

Right as I turned on my heel, I heard his deep voice call over the fence. "Did you know a tree fell in your yard?"

My surly, obnoxiously hot neighbor stood there on his porch, already dressed for work, staring over the brim of his coffee mug at me. My face caught fire as his eyes leisurely perused my bed head, a coat that made me look fifty pounds heavier, and thanks to the tourist surge in the area, the world's ugliest snow boots.

If Colson Hanes were just a neighbor, a mere man, I wouldn't care... but to my utter mortification and dismay, I had a rather complicated obsession with said neighbor. I dreamed of marrying the man at night, but during the day—it was all stabby sensations and petty insults.

The snow crunched underfoot as I stepped toward his side of the fence.

"No shit, Sherlock." It was too early to be mature and dodge his annoying comments that always seemed to dig at me in ways that shouldn't.

He sipped from his cup of coffee, the steam billowing from the top of the mug. "Figured since you're staring at it like it will just get up and go back into the ground, you weren't sure."

I hadn't missed the massive pine sprawled out in the middle of my yard, its nose barely touching the edge of our shared fence. I just couldn't process that it had actually fallen. Furthermore, I truly could not, *would not*, think of how the hell one got rid of a fallen tree in their yard. What sort of winter fuckery was this?

I chose to turn my anger on the man who was currently caffeinating.

"And instead of offering a helpful hand or any empathy at all, you chose to be a dick?"

He clicked his tongue, keeping his eye on the massive pine tree that lay like the bridge to Terabithia to our two worlds.

"You could start with an axe...you do know what an axe is, yes?"

Okay, so he wanted to hurl petty insults before I had a chance to caffeinate.

His funeral.

Hands on my hips, my eyes narrowed, and mouth primed with a bitchy retort, I watched as his jaw set in a firm line, as though he was expecting exactly this response from me. I let out a gust of hot air instead. He wasn't worth it. Not today anyway.

Stepping closer, so I had a better view of him, I attempted to be civil.

"Look, do you have any advice, or any tips at all on how I might go about handling this tree?"

Up close, Colson Hanes resembled a winter deity, with blond hair tucked under his beanie and those crystal blue eyes, his normal surfer appearance looked that much better with winter gear. Now he could be a model found in a snowboarding magazine. I hated that I had fallen for him, and when I say fall, I mean down a dirt hill, into a rocky river.

I had actively worked to hate him since then.

Colson's eyes moved, traveling from the pine in my yard to my face, and down to my boots.

I felt judged.

Very judged.

He probably had an actress model girlfriend tucked away in what I assumed was a massive bed, covered in silk and feathers. I had no idea why that image was the one that popped up when I thought of Colson and sex, but it wouldn't budge.

"Well, you need to call the power company to come and take care of the downed wires, and then I guess you'll need to chop up the tree…or call a tree removal service to do it."

"Now if only I had a helpful neighbor who also happened to own a chainsaw." I rolled my eyes, annoyed that he hadn't already offered to help. I knew what our relationship was—a bunch of insults and bullshit. But deep down, I had always assumed if I actually needed help, he'd offer it.

Guess I was wrong.

Dipping his head, he made an exasperated sound, while a muscle feathered along his jawline. For two seconds, I thought he'd give me a break and say he was just giving me a hard time, but he only proved where we were in this neighborly relationship.

"Maybe try the neighbor on that side." He lifted his mug, his eyes moving past me. "The one on this side has an early meeting. Good luck with everything."

His lips twisted into a smug smile, and then he turned to leave.

Anger made the tops of my cheeks heat, but I wouldn't show him. I wouldn't even call after him or beg him to leave his cup of coffee behind. I narrowed my eyes at where he disappeared into the house, deciding I had finally hit my breaking point.

2

COLSON

SEVEN YEARS OLD

Dear Cole,
Go to the garden after school, Martina says there's a
surprise for you. – Love, Mom

DEAR MOM,
   Dad says the grden is not where I shuld be and I need to stop gowing in there…when are u coming home? – Luv Cole

Dear Cole,
I'm sorry your father said that. I'll talk to him. I am coming
home soon; I'm feeling much better. Eat some berries for me. –
Love Mom

Dear Mom,

Dad says u had a bad week agin...so I will wach ur grden for you. I found the bunnies, I named one after you. – Luv Cole

I NEEDED A FUCKING STRESS BALL.

My grip strangled the steering wheel as I drove away from my neighbor, and the mess she'd once again seemed to find herself in. How the hell had she not woken up when the tree had fallen?

Honestly, the way Nora Petrov slept and essentially existed through life was something that needed to be studied by an entire team of experts because it was baffling. Fucking baffling. The woman had dug up half her garden, transplanting them into various pots, and while I had watched her do it, I had never asked her why. Could be because once again, she had been out there in that tiny robe that barely covered her ass, and Nora Petrov had an ass that was incredibly distracting.

Another time, I watched as she used a barstool to hang patio lights from her gutter, only to have them fall a thousand times until finally, the whole fucking gutter came down, taking her with it. She had tried mowing once, and a rock flew through her kitchen window, and don't even get me started on her weed-whacking skills...or lack thereof.

She had a way of getting into trouble while ignoring all the obvious signs that would usually warn someone away from attempting something. I had a feeling she knew those trees were bad in her backyard, but instead of having them inspected before winter set in, she ignored it. Just like she had when it had fucking fallen overnight.

My insults hurled across the fence had gotten old for both of us. So, I did the only thing I could do and ignored her as often as possible. Which wasn't easy, considering how often she liked to saunter around in practically nothing. Seeing her today covered from head to toe in winter gear was a welcome sight.

As callous as I was toward her, I wasn't a complete monster. Which was why I had already planned to take care of her tree problem. But first, I wanted to make her sweat a bit...see if she could, in fact, come up with a solution all on her own. It was doubtful, but there was always a chance she'd surprise me.

Grateful for the distraction of an early morning meeting, I pulled into the small coffee shop near the edge of town. The coffee shop was made mostly of brick and reclaimed barnwood with a chimney stack and a curl of smoke jutting from the roof. On the outside, there were about a hundred twinkle lights strung up, and a large red sign boasting of serving the best mocha in town. Only one other car shared the parking lot and that belonged to my boss, Peter.

Although Macon nestled up against a massive mountain peak, the townspeople acted as though they'd grown up on the beach for how often they seemed to leave their homes. I suppose it could be due to the howling winds that got upward of forty miles per hour, or the negative temperatures, but as a kid who'd visited and even lived here for a time, I couldn't get enough of it.

"Colson, oh good, you're here. I already started your order." Peter waved me over as I dusted my boots on the rug.

Settled in the most popular spot in the whole coffee house, my boss had secured the two armchairs that faced the fireplace. Seeing that it was already roaring and warm, I took off my layers and settled into the armchair across from him.

Peter Petrov had just turned sixty-two and looked it, with slightly graying hair and a recent transition to glasses, but he had the work ethic of someone in their twenties, which was a big reason why I enjoyed working for him. He was passionate, determined, and knew the value of hard work. I grew to respect him over the past year, and it was because of him that I finally realized what I wanted out of life.

"Cold out there today..." Peter sipped his coffee, keeping his eyes on an email that had popped up on his phone.

That was something I appreciated about my boss. He didn't ask me pointless questions like how my morning was, or how I was doing. No one ever gave a shit, so why ask? But the weather, on a cold as fuck day like today? That was worth a comment or two.

Setting his cell to the side, he reclined back into his chair, flicking his gaze my way. "The wind made a mess of the town last night, have you seen how many trees were downed?"

The waitress arrived with my coffee, placing it next to me on the side table. I thanked her and took a long sip before replying.

"I woke up and noticed that Nora had one fall last night…has she called you yet?"

I liked to tread carefully where his daughter was concerned because Peter Petrov loved two things in this world and only two things.

His wife and his daughter.

Nora was the spoiled only child to Peter and his wife Lilly, who both happened to be prominent business owners in Macon. Lilly, Nora's mother, owned a local tourist shop, selling all sorts of goods from the area. Like my boss, his wife wanted to retire, so she put the store up for sale and it was purchased by my friend Davis recently. I knew that both Peter and Lilly were planning something since they were both selling their businesses, but I wasn't sure where Nora fit into all of it.

Peter set his mug down mid sip and shook his head.

"That girl…I wish she had just gotten an apartment or rental. She isn't ready to be a homeowner."

I sipped my coffee, thinking that over. He wasn't wrong…Nora was only twenty-three, and had recently graduated from college, so in a way, he was right. She was young and inexperienced, but for some reason I was feeling defensive of her. Even if in my own mind she was a disaster, I didn't like that anyone else might think that.

"Did you get her squared away, or do I need to go over there?" Peter's brow puckered as if I owed him an explanation.

"I had this meeting…" I nodded toward him as though he were just now realizing we'd set this up. "I barely saw her come outside before I left."

"So, she has no power, and you just left?"

Hold up…*was he angry with me?*

Setting my mug aside, I rumbled off a weak excuse. "I'm sure she doesn't want my help…" Explaining that I had planned on helping when it worked for me would only make this worse and make him think I had ulterior motives with Nora. I was damned either way.

"Colson, she's a single woman, living alone in the middle of winter…
it's not about her preferences, or yours…you need to help her."

It was mid-December, not even technically winter yet, but okay.

We hadn't broached this topic in over a year, and our relationship had
been smooth, undisturbed by any Nora-related issues. So why was he
acting like I'd abandoned his daughter in her time of need?

"Colson, I need to know that someone will be here to help her…she
needs someone to take care of her until she settles down. Her mother and I
are leaving sooner than she even knows. That's why I wanted to meet with
you."

My stomach felt like it had been tossed off the tallest building and then
set on fire. I had been waiting for Peter to explain his plans for me and his
retirement for weeks. He had been dropping hints left and right, trailing off
about retirement and possibly selling. In case he was serious about any one
of the scenarios he had prattled on about, I had been practicing my business
pitch. Because if Peter was planning to sell his company, I wanted it.

It was just a construction company, and in the grand scheme of life and
achievements, it wasn't that significant, but in my small…carefully crafted
world, it mattered. I knew after the first day I returned home with calluses
on my fingers and dust in my hair that I wanted every day to end that way.
My muscles ached, my body was sore…but I felt filled in ways I had never
experienced in my life. For once, there wasn't anyone to give me what I
wanted merely based on my last name. No one tried to kiss my ass here, no
one cared that my father was about to make his first billion…no one cared
that our family had graced the covers of magazines, television shows, and
had even attended movie premieres.

No one in Macon cared about anything that I had left behind in Malibu.

The feeling was addictive, and I carved a place for myself here, outside
of my family's shadow. A completely unexpected haven where they'd
never dare look. It was work I could do honestly, with my own hands, not
tainted by my father's money…Peter's company had freed me, and if he
sold it to someone else, there was no guarantee that I would continue to
live this way. So, it became my dream.

My hope.

My salvation.

Peter edged forward in his seat. "Colson, you've been more than a right-hand man this past year, you've single-handedly finished more projects and grown the company beyond anything I ever imagined it would be. I want to know if you would consider…"

His pause nearly made me shake him.

Consider taking it over? Buying it?

Fuck.

Gathering himself, he cleared his throat and tried again. "Would you consider being the one that watches out for Nora?"

I waited for him to continue, but he brought his cup to his mouth and was now waiting for my response.

Had he really just asked me that…

I didn't even know what to say…or how to veer this conversation back to me purchasing his company.

"Peter…I'm honored, but I'm not sure I'm the right person…"

Peter shook his head. "You're the man for the job…I'll be looking over a few offers and proposals for the company, and if you're wanting to throw your hat in the ring, this would give you a considerable leg up."

For a second, I stared at him because I did want the leg up. I had wanted him to pick me since the day I realized how satisfying it was to see a completed project from the comfort of my truck… I had never had anything that was just mine…I'd never had anyone that was either, which was why this entire offer was so bittersweet.

"Of course, to be clear, you'd be taking on a brotherly role. Just like we discussed before."

Right…before. How could I forget?

Feeling the surge of frustration burn under my skin, I dipped my head to gather my bearings. I had never done well being told no, or that I couldn't have something… but if there was a good reason for it, then I would honor it. Peter's aversion to me being anything more than a friend to his daughter had no grounding…other than the mere fact that I worked for him and anyone who did was completely off-limits from dating his daughter. He'd also mentioned once that I was way too old for her. Five years was not too old, but the fucker was trying to make a point.

But, I listened and blew up the bridge that led to her ensuring zero chance in hell she'd ever look at me as more than a blustery, annoying neighbor. So, what did I have to lose?

"I can watch out for her, sir."

His gray eyes narrowed on me intensely.

"I will make my decision by Christmas…show me you can be there for her in the way we discussed. Show me that I don't have to worry about my little girl once I leave, and I'll give you a fair deal and the first chance to bid."

His hand shot out for me to shake, and while this seemed like the strangest fucking deal I had ever made, I thrust my hand out and shook, feeling his firm squeeze as a silent warning. It was one I knew I'd heed.

3

NORA

"WHY ARE you calling me so early, we're still sleeping," my best friend whined into my speaker.

I balanced the phone on the small chair next to the sliding glass door while I used my fingers to test the handle.

"Rae, can you be less whiny and more supportive please? I'm doing my first B&E and thought I'd have you tag along."

After a pause, a burst of loud laughter interrupted my covert operation.

I grabbed the phone, whisper yelling into it, "You're going to wake Davis, shh."

"Why can't he wake up?" she asked, her voice still light with laughter.

I rolled my eyes as the glass door slid open with ease.

"Because he's friends with Colson, he'll text him and alert him to what's going on here."

I tried to keep the annoyance out of my voice, but my best friend's boyfriend had developed a bromance with my neighbor, and I didn't like it.

Not one bit.

"To be clear, he'll tell Colson that you're currently breaking into his house?"

"My heat and power are out, a tree fell in my backyard, and Colson stood from his porch and didn't offer to help. So, yes. I decided to steal a little coffee and heat from the man."

Rae let out a sigh and mumbled something about going back to sleep.

"How come your mountain man isn't up yet? I thought they woke with the dawn or something."

She laughed, and more shuffling happened before she explained. "The snow sort of put a stop to everything, so we're snuggling under the blankets and sleeping in. Or at least we were."

Wincing, I walked across Colson's gorgeous hardwood floors and expensive rugs into his kitchen. "Sorry about that."

"It's fine, want me to ask if Davis can chop up your tree?"

Oh, that's right, her boyfriend chopped wood on the regular.

I lit up. "Yes, please, but only if I can pay him."

"No need, I'm sure he'll do it for free. But call the power company, okay?"

I didn't like getting things for free, even from my best friend's boyfriend, but I also wasn't so stubborn that I'd push the issue. "Okay, I will as soon as they open."

"Don't stay too long."

"I won't." I promised and hung up, marveling at the space I'd infiltrated.

I let out a sigh, seeing that Colson had an old-school coffee system set up. Thankfully, about a cup remained in the pot, and it was still warm.

"Small miracles."

Pouring myself a cup, I wandered around and took in the small effects of his house. No sign of a girlfriend or any roommates. Another small miracle.

Obviously still a bachelor pad, with the way he had magazines spread out along the coffee table and empty coffee mugs everywhere.

"No coasters." I clicked my tongue as I bypassed the mess.

Colson Hanes was the vice president of my father's construction company, and after a year of having to see him on my father's work sites, and being around him at different functions, I was finally getting an inside look at his life.

After foolishly tripping over myself more than once where the man was concerned, I was feeling hives break out on my arms as I walked around. He'd already made it abundantly clear that he didn't want me in his life. He barely looked at me, and when he did manage to let that azure gaze stray in my direction, his face would go pale as if he'd been caught stealing.

I had made it a point to avoid the man as often as possible, but being inside his home, and invading his space…I had to cling to my reasons with the grip and tenacity of a toddler stealing a cookie.

I continued to walk through, my arms crossed over my chest, as I noticed a few photos scattered along different surfaces. Edging near the side table, I saw one frame was of him with two other guys his age, maybe younger, holding surfboards. They all looked so happy and free with sand and wave-swept hair.

Another photo was centered on his mantel, it featured the same people, only snowboarding. Then one on his bookshelf of a wedding, all the guys from the previous photos were in it, along with several more family members by the looks of it. Colson stood in a beautiful black suit next to a man who was probably his father. He had Colson's eyes, but lighter hair and much less of it.

I had heard of the Hanes', everyone on the West Coast had. They were supposedly millionaires, and the fact that Colson was here, working for my father was insane and didn't make any sense. Even if they did once vacation here or something similar, it didn't really matter since they were now in Malibu or somewhere swanky and warm.

If I were honest with myself, I hadn't ever thought past my crush on Colson long enough to consider what it would be like to be connected to a family like that. I didn't think I could do it, if in some magical dimension, Colson actually wanted me the way I wanted him—it would never work out.

I wandered the rest of the house, taking my coat off as I went and stepping out of my shoes. My fingers trailed over his cream walls as I sauntered down the hall, peering into each room. He had two nice-sized bedrooms, vaulted ceilings, and natural wood trim that matched the flooring in the hall. The rooms had a cream-colored carpet that blended well with his walls. His house was beautiful and nicely designed.

At the end of the hall was a closed door, which of course I opened because what if Colson was secretly hiding dead bodies. If more people would be nosy, I was positive more crimes would be solved.

But as soon as that door cracked, my eyes rounded, and my jaw hung loose.

It wasn't the massive king-size bed, with no feathers or silk in sight, that got me. It wasn't his elaborate record collection or his deep-set leather chair that faced his backyard, or the billion-inch television mounted on the wall. No, what had me fully arrested was the soaking tub in his bathroom, complete with jets and a soft pillow neck rest.

The urge to relax and let the stress of the morning slip away was too strong to resist.

I let out a sigh, tugged off my shirt and whispered, "Come to Mama."

THE MAN HAD shower gel that I used as bubble bath, it smelled woodsy with a blend of spice that made me groan, and I managed to find exactly three candles under his bathroom sink. They were a part of an emergency kit, but whatever. With the few candles, bath gel, and steaming hot water, I stripped. The warm air was like velvet against my bare skin as I tossed my pajamas to the side.

Once the tub was full, I turned off the faucet and hissed as my toe plunged into the water.

"Perfect."

I sighed, lowering the rest of my body into the steam.

As I soaked, I closed my eyes and began a deep breathing routine. This was what I needed, regardless that I had to steal it…it felt good. Now I could think over what to do while I waited for Davis to come and cut up the tree.

I hated that Colson had witnessed me finding it, and obviously being so out of depth regarding what to do. I did not like it when other people observed my shortcomings, and Colson Hanes had a front-row seat lately with my new venture into homeownership.

I could feel myself getting worked up once more, the anxiety coming back full swing as I tried to sort out my thoughts, so I held my breath and ducked under the water. This was something I used to do as a kid when taking baths, mostly because it was fun to pretend I was a mermaid, but also because it was the best way to quiet my anxiety when it roared a little too loudly.

I counted slowly, feeling my lungs expand and wisps of my hair float around my head. I didn't usually like getting my curls wet, but it also felt too good not to plunge under. Right as I counted to eighteen, I shoved back through the surface of the water.

"What. The fuck. Nora?!" a loud, angry voice boomed from somewhere off to my left.

My heart flipped inside my chest; my lungs still burned from holding my breath. My eyes were still closed because I hadn't rubbed the water out of them yet, but now I was apprehensive about opening them.

I didn't need to see, to know it was Colson standing there, witnessing me taking a bath in his house. Naked.

Oh. My. God.

I was currently naked.

I let out a small animalistic sound and ducked back under the water, as if that could hide me. Until I realized most of the bubbles had dissipated because shower gel was not bubble bath.

Fuck.

I resurfaced right as I heard him speak again.

"Do you want to explain to me what in the hell you're doing here?"

Finally, I pressed my fingers into my closed eyes to wipe away the water and slowly slid my gaze to the mirror, which reflected a menacing form. Leaning against the door frame, with crossed arms and a scowl on his handsome face, Colson glared. Keeping his eyes locked on mine, not perusing my body, he waited for me to respond.

But what would I even say? How did I come back from this?

A horrible realization snapped into focus, making me go back a year to another instance when Colson had walked in on me nearly naked by accident. He'd misunderstood something my dad had said, or at least that's what my father had explained afterward. But the nitty-gritty of the humiliating situation was that Colson had innocently walked into a room, completely unaware that I had claimed it as my changing area. When he came face-to-face with me in just my bra and panties, he acted horrified and blurted out that he had a girlfriend, which was only cemented weeks later when he saw me in the grocery store and stopped mid stroll, turned his cart around, and went in the other direction.

This man had never once led me on. I knew he was likely dating someone…which made this whole situation infinitely worse.

"Look…" I swallowed thickly, keeping my eyes on him through the mirror. My arms were crossed over my breasts, and I brought my knees up for extra coverage. "If you feel the need to press charges, please let me explain myself first."

His hand came up, tunneling through his messy blond hair. The beanie he'd worn earlier was gone, so were his shoes and jacket, now he stood in thick jeans and a soft T-shirt. I hated how badly I wanted to run my fingers along the stretchy material and rub it against my face when he wasn't looking. It looked so soft.

"I never said anything about pressing charges, Nora. All I asked was for you to explain yourself, so please…" He held his hand out as if I should continue.

Right.

My sopping curls frizzed as I sat in the water, watching him in the mirror.

"I have no power at my house…no coffee or way to make breakfast…" I was totally hoping for empathy from him, but his face was made of stone, completely unmoving, so I pushed on. "I just planned to steal a little heat and some coffee, but then I saw your tub."

His head tilted the slightest bit. "And how is it that you found my tub?"

I puckered my brow at the reminder of his closed door.

"Yeah, about that…why leave your door shut when no one else lives here?"

He inclined his head as if to challenge me.

"Why would you assume that no one else lives here?"

Oh, shit…why would I assume that? What if his girlfriend was at the gym this morning…or already at work…had I been that wrong about who came and went…how had I missed an extra vehicle? Maybe that meant I wasn't nearly as obsessed with noticing when he came and went as much as I thought.

"Colson, I'm so sorry. I have no idea what came over me, let me just get up and I'll leave."

I was about to let my arms free, bracing my hands on either side of the tub, but Colson stood there staring...it seemed as though he was lost in thought. Maybe he was considering what to do with me...maybe he wanted to call the cops. I wouldn't blame him, especially if he didn't live alone.

A churning sensation took place in my stomach as I considered how bad this was, and how this would change our neighborly relationship forever. My face was overheating, I knew he could see it, especially as his eyes narrowed on my reflection.

This moment mimicked the previous one last year, way too closely. He hadn't outright said he'd had a girlfriend this time, but he sort of implied it, which made me want to jump off the nearest bridge.

"I'll be waiting out here for you..." he finally turned and left the bathroom so I could escape.

With quick, jerky movements, I blotted my legs and arms with the soft towel I'd found in his small storage area next to the shower. I tugged on my panties and pajama pants, then threw my hoodie over my head. My boots were by the back door but were easy to slip on. My dark curls hung in heavy tangles down my back, practically screaming for product so that my hair didn't frizz, but that wasn't going to happen anytime soon.

Slowly exiting Colson's bedroom, I had a moment where I stared at the front door longingly, wondering how painful it would be to run outside barefoot and hope he'd toss my snow boots over the fence later. He'd probably throw them *away* at this rate. With a heavy sigh, I gave up on the idea and walked into the living room.

He was in the kitchen, a dishtowel tossed over his shoulder while he stirred something in a pan.

"Do you want toast with your eggs?"

Frozen in place, my socks pressing into his plush white carpet, I stared at his muscular back.

I must have waited too long because he moved, turning toward me, not smiling...but not frowning either.

"Toast?"

"Yes…please." He was feeding me after I broke into his house? Ok.

I slowly walked to the barstool tucked under the lip of his counter and dragged it free. He worked effortlessly, stirring scrambled eggs, turning to smear butter on the toast, then he added a dash of salt and pepper. I hated that I'd be storing this image away for later when I carefully pulled it free and tried to recreate it on my wedding inspiration board.

"You need milk with your coffee?" he asked, his eyes barely lifting up to meet mine before dashing away again.

"No…I can drink it black, thank you."

Was he messing with me? I swear, I was about to be punked…the sheriff was going to walk in, or worse, my father.

Flipping the burner off, he plated the eggs, and then handed me mine. The yellow eggs were fluffed to perfection, with cream cheese mixed in and spinach. My mouth watered instantly. The toast had melted butter and raspberry jam, and he'd added blueberries and strawberries on the side. For some reason it all made me teary-eyed.

Why was he being so nice to me?

He'd never been this nice to me.

"Thank you…I—" How did I even begin to apologize?

Colson cut off my apology.

"I don't blame you for breaking in…" Colson started, his deep voice cutting through my thoughts. He stood at the counter across from me, picking at a few berries as he talked.

"I should have told you to come in before I left. I guess I was trying to see if you'd figure something out before then…either way, I realize you had no power, and it was shitty of me to just leave."

Wow…had he just…

A huff of air left my chest as I asked, "Did you just apologize?"

His blue eyes narrowed, while taking a large bite of egg. His jaw moved, and I was mesmerized by how sexual it looked.

I copied, chewing while I stared, enraptured by his presence.

We stayed like that, engaged in some weird staring contest where I definitely won, when he finally let out a sigh and placed his empty plate in the sink.

"Is me seeing you naked going to be an issue?"

I happened to be sipping coffee when he asked that question, so of course I sputtered and coughed within seconds. Once I finally recovered, I shook my head.

"Not for me."

Totally for me. I would hoard the fact that he saw my nipples and pretend he was wildly obsessed, even harboring a crush of his own that he only indulged in at night.

"Then we're good. I have a few errands to run, then I'll get started on your tree. Stay here, watch TV...relax. If you take another bath, please shut the door, maybe use the lock that's there."

Flames pranced under my skin, burning my face like wildfire.

"Obviously, I don't plan on taking a bath again...and I appreciate the offer, but I'm good to go home now. I just wanted a little coffee." And a soak in your tub, but like hell was I saying that. Instead, I moved toward my boots and unlaced them.

"Nora, you don't have any power. Stay put until I can get over there and sort out what's going on."

"No, thank you." I muttered politely while lacing up my boots.

"I'm not asking. Stay here...stay warm, I'll be back in an hour..."

I stood up straight, surprised by his terse tone.

We hadn't even talked about the break in, or anything for that matter. He'd fed me and was now telling me to stay put. What the hell had gotten into him? Where had my asshole neighbor gone?

Giving me one last nod toward the couch, I decided to play his game and set aside my pride. Settling into his sofa, I was handed a blanket, a remote, and instructions on how to work the varying apps. Apparently, he had all of them, which was a far cry from me still using my parents' Netflix subscription, and occasionally catching episodes of that dragon show while at the gym.

"Stay put," Colson said one last time as if I were a Golden Retriever he was leaving for the day. The second his truck left the driveway, I bolted up and found my boots.

Like hell would I stay put, and for fuck's sake, I wasn't a damn dog.

4

COLSON

NINE YEARS OLD

DEAR MOM,

I'm sad u didn't come home for XMAS...I miss u. Dad says u arnt getting better. That scares me. Plz get better. — Love, Cole

Dear Cole,
I am doing my best darling, but do Mommy a favor and practice writing to me as much as you can, your letters make me the happiest. Also, please check on Mommy's garden. — Love Mom

DEAR MOM,

Yur garden is sad I think because there's not much sun...what should I do?
— Love Cole

Dear Cole,

Thank you for checking on it. In the winter, there isn't much to do but ensure leaves don't crowd their space, a garden sleeps in the winter but it doesn't mean they don't need to be cared for. You just have to pay extra careful attention to it. Talk to them while they sleep. Pull out the weeds, and leaves, be sure to check on it every day. – Love, Mom

THIS FUCKING DAY.

What the hell had I gotten myself into? I'd gone to three different places to find a chain saw because while I worked in construction for a living, I didn't in fact own one. Then I had to find gas because all the electric choices were out of stock. On my way to the different stores, three different people had slid off the road, so I helped tow them to safety. Then I stopped at the store to get Nora some provisions for her house, assuming whatever was in her fridge had gone bad. By the time I had gotten back, it was close to dark. Hopefully she'd helped herself to the food in the kitchen and was nice and warm by the gas fire.

The image of her on my couch, drinking cocoa while watching television, had nestled nice and tight in my mind. It wasn't an unpleasant picture and for once it wasn't one that I tried to undo the second it popped in there. Instead, I allowed it to linger…and unfold.

Was she still in her pajamas? Had she decided to take another bath?

Shit, I'd be thinking of her in my house, using my bath, for the rest of my life. It took all my strength not to go to where she was and trace the rivulets of water that trailed down her skin and revel in how smooth she felt under my touch. Then she popped up, and I realized I wasn't angry she'd invaded my space, it felt more like I'd been waiting for her to arrive. So, I would have a reason to keep her in it.

Dismissing those intrusive thoughts, I parked and hopped out of my truck, taking a few bags in with me. Once I was inside my house, I called out.

"Hey, I grabbed us some dinner if you're hungry."

I had purchased that dinner for her to eat at her house, *alone*…so the fact that I was now acting as though it was for us both was a problem.

So was the fact that she wasn't responding to me.

Walking down the hall with my wet boots, I searched the room but didn't see her, so I called out.

"Nora?"

The couch still had the blanket draped across the back, but the television was off, and her boots were gone.

Shit.

It wasn't even that she hadn't listened to me and left regardless, but it was the fact that my boss had tasked me with this one thing to prove myself, and I'd already fucked it up.

Putting the food away, I headed back outside.

Her car was still stuck behind a massive wall of snow from the plow that had cleared our street. Only those who'd ventured out and shoveled were able to leave. Something she hadn't done yet.

With a dark house, and no smoke coming from her chimney, I had no reason to believe she was inside, but the idea that she was in there being stubborn and freezing to death meant I had to check.

Pounding my fist against her door got me nowhere, so I pulled a page from her book and went around back.

The back door was locked too, but I happened to know where she kept her spare key.

The waning daylight was stripped to pink and orange, illuminating a cotton candy sky. It was enough light to swipe at the snow surrounding her small garden gnome.

Unlocking and pushing through her back door, I tried calling again.

"Nora?"

The power was still out, so the house was freezing. Her fireplace hadn't been touched all day by the looks of it.

She wasn't home, but without a car, where would she have gone?

Probably her parents' but fuck if I wanted to call my boss after he'd specifically asked me to prove that I could watch out for his daughter. So, I decided to cross her best friend off the list first.

Shooting a text to Davis confirmed Nora wasn't up at their place, but my friend relayed a message from Rae that Nora had just shared a funny TikTok with her, so she wasn't worried. I asked if she could give me her number, but I never got a reply.

Shaking my head, I pocketed the device and took a chance she was out for a walk or something. As cold as it was outside, it wouldn't surprise me in the least for Nora to bundle up and brave it.

Giving the house one more turn, I left through the front door, down the steps, and over to my side of the fence.

WITHIN THE SPAN of ten minutes, I had covered our neighborhood and the entire block. The streets were plowed, the sidewalks were shoveled, and the moon was out, making the night clear enough to see by. Not to mention, our town currently looked like Christmas had claimed every lamppost, store window, and traffic light.

Twinkle lights, pine wreaths, garland, and bulbs seemed to hang everywhere, which helped to add extra light to the darkened town. There wasn't a soul out walking in the twenty-degree temperatures. I kept going, heading closer to Main Street and to the center of town.

I considered how stupid I was for not having Nora's cell number and how that was on me. She'd tried to give it to me once, saying it was for the party she was planning for her dad. But I'd crumpled the paper in my palm and tossed it into the garbage, explaining that I wouldn't be in town. At any turn where Nora was concerned, I dodged and maneuvered away from her and now it was biting me in the ass.

If my boss found her first, fuck, it wouldn't be good.

I rolled down another street, still not seeing her.

Finally, when I was about to turn my truck around and head to her parents' to admit defeat, I saw through the frosted diner window those brown curls that distracted me far too often.

Parking right there in front of the small café, I hopped out and pushed the glass door open. I eyed the two other customers that were tucked away on the opposite side of the diner, and a few more that were scattered along barstools at the counter, before focusing on the loner in the back. Smiling at Roger, the owner, I walked past a few empty booths until I stopped next to the girl who'd had me running all over town.

Peering down at her, I inhaled the coffee scent that permeated the air and tried to get Nora's attention. She never once looked up, which meant this was going to take a bit more coaxing.

Sliding in across from her, I watched as she pulled her sweater down over her hands, and once our eyes met, I could see that hers had gone wide. She had these curls that were usually tamed into relaxed waves but catch her on a busy day or after she worked out, and you could see when her curls spiraled, cascading down the middle of her back. She didn't have a stitch of makeup on, which left her big aqua eyes more vibrant.

I pushed down what it did to see her like this, imperfect and undone.

"Hello, Colson." Nora reached forward for her mug.

I waited a second, observing her movements, trying to understand why she was here of all places, and why she'd left my house, trading it for a weathered booth at Mac n Millie's, right after the dinner rush.

Snow had begun falling outside, and there were white Christmas lights strewn up inside the diner windows, creating a nice warm ambiance. I could see the appeal, regardless of how quaint the town dressed up for the holidays, it was cozy. Very unlike Malibu, or anything I had experienced over the past several years.

"Hello, Nora. Would you like to explain to me why you left my house?"

Picking at her nail, she furrowed her delicate brows and sighed.

"I didn't like being told to stay as if I were a puppy in training."

Tugging at a sugar packet, I toyed with it as I considered her behavior.

"It's close to six at night, you're sitting here alone in a diner, where I'm assuming you ate dinner, and are now biding your time, staying warm until Roger closes up... am I right?" I raised my brow in question, trying to piece together her night.

Her eyes flicked away for a brief second, landing on Roger, then swung back to the cup in front of her.

"Why not go to your parents'?"

She shrugged her shoulder, which made the wide neck of her sweater shift the smallest bit, revealing a patch of tan skin. I only allowed myself the standard three seconds of indulging in how soft her skin looked before I looked away.

"My car was blocked in."

No, that wasn't it.

Leaning forward, I whispered, "Bullshit. You could have easily shoveled it...it's not like you don't know how."

There was something deeper here...something she wasn't saying.

"Why not call your dad?"

She spun her mug back and forth, refusing to look up.

The sound of classic Christmas music played overhead from the small speakers in the room, while Roger bustled around the diner, laughing with a group of older men who'd come in for coffee and pie.

Nora finally met my stare, but still didn't expand about not calling her dad, so I switched tactics.

"So, you were going to walk home, and then what?"

She shrugged again, this time glancing outside. "I guess start a fire, sleep close to it tonight. The power company said they could get a guy to come out first thing, there were just too many people without power today to get to everyone."

I had heard that too, so I nodded, then pulled on the edge of the sugar packet, thinking over what I was about to offer.

"Well, you're not sleeping in your house when there's no heat. You'll sleep at mine. I have a guest room, or a couch, whichever you prefer, but at least they'll both ensure you don't have frostbite by morning."

She swung her eyes up, her lips parting the smallest bit like she couldn't believe I had offered what I did. I waited for her to accept, because I knew she would. This was Nora, after all, she liked to be taken care of.

I had watched for a year how her father did everything for her, hell he'd probably bought her house for her too. The one she didn't know how to fucking take care of.

Her staring led to a disgruntled scoff.

"Uh…no. Hell no." She shook her head like she couldn't believe I had offered her refuge for the night. "And also, can you leave so I can enjoy the rest of my evening? Roger and I were discussing trivia questions before you rudely barged in."

Roger took that moment to add, "Did you know that bamboo is the fastest growing plant in the entire world? Nora here says it can grow thirty-five inches in a single day!"

My gaze swung back to the woman in front of me, who was now smirking.

Shit, she wasn't making this easy.

"Okay, how about I start over?" I lifted my hands in an act of surrender.

She sipped the last of her drink, then lounged into the booth, waiting for me to finish.

Leaning closer, I set my hands in front of me, leveling her with a stare. "I'm worried about your safety…so would you please just accept my help and sleep in my guest room?"

Crossing her arms, she mirrored my posture by leaning over the table. "No. I have a home and enough wood to stay warm."

This girl was aggravating my nerves, more so than she had over the past year.

We stared for several breaths, challenging one another…but when she raised her dark brow, I backed off.

"Okay…would you at least keep me company while I drive back?"

Lifting her chin in defiance, I mentally prepared to throw her over my shoulder and make the decision for her because she wasn't fucking walking home in these temperatures. But she surprised me when her pink lips fell and her shoulders slumped.

"Fine."

Letting out a silent, relieved breath, I slid out of the booth and held out my hand for the cup she had been drinking from. Once she handed it over, I dropped the sugar packet inside and walked it over to Roger, who took it from me along with a five-dollar bill to cover her coffee and tip.

She had emerged from the booth and stood with her arms linked across her chest, waiting for me.

Why the hell did I like that she was waiting for me?

I blinked, filing that image away, like I had for every Nora-related thing that had acted as a splinter in my conscious… Digging, weaving, accessing places she had no right to.

She held the glass door open, then followed me to my truck.

I walked past her and opened the door, not offering to help her inside. Then rounded to my side.

Once I settled in the seat, I glanced over at her to steal another image for later. She looked so natural sitting in my truck, settling into the seat, placing her purse on the floor and pulling the strap over her chest. With a flip of her curls, and a quick glimpse over at me, I could feel that splinter work further, on the verge of ruining something vital.

It took less than five minutes to pull into my driveway, and even less time to notice that she still smelled like me. An image of her sitting in my tub, surrounded by dissipating foam from my body wash, surfaced and made me smile.

Rounding the hood, I opened her door and held it as she hopped down.

"Thank you for the ride." She muttered quietly, tucking a few curls back while pulling her purse across her chest.

She stepped away, heading to her side of the fence, not giving me a second look.

I followed.

At her porch, she turned. "I'm good from here if you want to head home."

"I am…but first I'm making your fire."

With her hand on the doorknob, she opened her mouth to argue, but decided against it with a low, muttered curse.

Good, we were finally getting along.

Once she opened her door, I sidestepped her and headed to the hearth. She had a decent amount of wood stacked in a small rectangular box, painted black with white lettering that spelled out "Firewood."

"What is this?"

Pulling a few blankets off the couch, she wrapped it around her shoulders and sunk to the floor next to me.

"It's a box for holding firewood."

Reaching for a few logs, I set up the fire and grabbed some tinder while shaking my head.

"Right."

The fire crackled as we perched in front of the growing flames.

"It's dumb, I know…Rae got it for me as a housewarming gift." Nora said, sounding a little embarrassed.

Peering over my shoulder, her blushing cheeks confirmed that I had insulted her.

"It's nice…I mean, you design for a living, right? Makes sense."

She didn't reply, just stared at the amber glow.

It was difficult not to indulge in how domesticated this felt…blinking, I finally forced myself to move.

"You need more wood, so I'll go get—"

"No need, I'll get it." Nora jumped up, rubbing her hands together.

Fuck all with this girl, I had no idea what to expect from her.

"Nora, sit by the fire. I'll get it."

She shook her head, already pulling on her coat. "It's my house, my fire…I'll do it. You can head home now."

Putting my hand on her arm, I stopped her. "I *know* I can head home, but I *want* to get your wood, so go fucking sit and let me get it."

She stared at my hand, and for a few seconds we stood there, closer than we'd ever been. This somehow felt bigger…more intense than any other moment we'd shared.

That splinter in my chest, with her name on it, wiggled further in. Daring me to drop my hand to the dip of her waist.

She pulled away first. "Fine, knock yourself out."

I walked out through the back where the glow from her porch light illuminated the dark as I grabbed more wood from her dwindling pile. My eyes scanned the fallen tree taking up the expanse of her yard, still covered in snow…she could pay someone to come and take care of it. My boss wouldn't care one way or another…her power would be back on by tomorrow. But…that fucking splinter had moved so goddamn deep that I already knew I'd chop the fucker up with that chain saw I had purchased, and I'd do it tonight so she could wake up to one less problem.

This wasn't a good idea. I should go…leave the wood on her steps and walk home.

But, fuck.

Stalking back inside, and stomping the snow from my boots, I returned to the little designer box she had set up and dropped the armful of wood into it. Nora had changed into a pair of sweats, a hoodie, and thick wool socks. And with her ass pointed at me, it looked as though she was in the process of pulling cushions off the couch.

"Here." I moved to help, moving cushions until she had a small bed in front of the fireplace. Her aqua eyes flicked to mine in surprise, then darted away.

Staying quiet, she disappeared down the hall, using her cell phone as a flashlight so she could see. She returned with a pile of blankets bulging from her arms. I watched as she tossed them on the bed of cushions and rearranged them.

I stared longer than I probably should have, but I liked looking at her… and it was so rare that I ever had an excuse to.

"Do you have more blankets you want me to get?"

"Why are you doing this?" she asked, pausing her movements and watching mine instead.

"What?" I paused with my hand on the iron poker.

Fluffing out the first blanket, she laid it out over the cushions and then reached for the second one, flicking her gaze toward me and then returning it to her makeshift bed.

"You haven't cared one way or another about me for over a year. You've done everything to keep your distance…and then all the sudden you're telling me to stay in your warm house and then chasing me down at the diner?"

Trying to seem unfazed by her behavior, I shook my head.

"I have no idea what you're talking about. I—"

"The fuck you don't. Did you forget the dinner party, or the petty insults you've hurled at me every chance you've had?"

The way her tone slipped into hurt made my head turn. My actions wounded her…and while I had my reasons for each and every barb, it still didn't feel good to hear that it hurt her.

Swallowing around that feeling surging in my chest, I said, "Well, maybe I realized how much of a prick I've been and wanted to make up for it."

Her face flushed pink, and I assumed maybe she hadn't considered that.

"So that's it, you're just trying to do better?"

It wasn't a complete lie.

Stalling and gently securing the poker, I smiled and said, "Well, maybe be a friend too."

She seemed to consider that, while getting inside her little bed and pulling the blankets over her.

"Okay, well, I don't buy it, but I'll see you tomorrow." She put on a pair of white headphones and clicked a few buttons on her phone until her eyes closed and she nestled into her blankets.

Dismissed by pulling on a pair of headphones, and all I could think of was what it would feel like to crawl in behind her on that little couch raft.

Some carnal and raw part of me wanted to do just that, grip her chin, make her understand how badly I wanted her. She needed to stay warm, and what better way than body to body heat? Fuck.

Pushing all that down, I added a few more logs and made sure her doors were locked. But right before I let myself out, I heard her mutter.

"Thank you, Colson."

I paused, hand on the door, watching her track my every move. I didn't know why it felt like she was peeling back a layer of mine, invisible it seemed to everyone but her, but I had to get out of there.

Dipping my head, I replied quietly, "You're welcome."

Then I left.

5

NORA

MY BACK ACHED like I'd been clinging to the edge of a cliff all night, and because I literally had clung to the edge of a cushion, I barely slept. Unfortunately, I didn't have time to wallow in self-pity because according to the text I received, my best friend was at my front door. Swinging open the door and ignoring how numb I felt from the cold, I tried to give her a smile, but it came out more like a wince.

"It's so bright." I whined, ducking back inside.

"Did someone shovel your drive?" Rae asked annoyingly loud before bypassing me and walking inside.

"No, why?" I yawned, slamming the door shut.

She walked over to the fire and stuck her hands out to warm them. "There's a huge space cleared around your car, and the windshield is all scraped clean."

Too cold not to be in my nest of blankets, I burrowed back inside them while asking, "Who do you think did it?"

A quick slap landed on my leg through the thick blanket. "No, who do *you* think did it?"

"The Boy Scouts?" I glared up at her.

How was she so awake and alive? It was barely seven in the morning.

"Well, whoever it was, I'm glad your car is finally free. Now, get up.

We have to head to the coffee shop and talk business." Rae made it sound like *bizzness*, with extra *z*'s.

"I hate driving in the snow." I whined, pulling the covers back over my face.

She snatched them away from me.

"I hear you, but everything is plowed. There's no reason not to drive. Now come on."

Begrudgingly, I rolled out of my blankets and made my way down the hall.

"I can see my breath, Nora, this is madness." Rae yelled from the living room while I traded my sweats for real clothes.

I was still too tired to comment, or add anything cute to the conversation, so I let her continue to talk.

"How did you not die last night?"

Finally dressed and marginally warm, I sauntered back down the hall and muttered. "The only time it's okay to be this cold is if you landed on some alien planet and happen to be the mate to one of the locals."

Rae squealed, trailing me into the kitchen. "Did you start the *Ice Planet Barbarian* series? OMG, I told you that you'd love it."

"I do love it, which is probably why I've been imagining Colson's face on a massive blue alien, with a dick that's twelve inches long." I pulled on the string to the blinds hanging over the sink to look at the backyard.

Rae stopped, her mouth gaping as a lilt of laughter bubbled in her chest. "I'm sorry, what?!"

We had no secrets. She knew I had an unacceptable and incurable crush on my father's right-hand man, and she also knew that he did not return the sentiment in any capacity, so I felt rather pathetic about all of it.

"Totally had Colson's face, and was like seven feet tall…" I admitted jokingly.

"Did his thing have that extra barb thing on it, like in the books?"

Shaking my head, I walked around her. "I didn't look that closely. I focused on his face, and his glowing eyes, and the undying love he confessed to me."

Rae snorted.

I pulled open the back door and traipsed out. The yard remained the same as it was yesterday, like I'd seen in the window, the tree had been covered in snow. Every green branch was concealed, but the bulk of where the tree should have been was…

"Gone." Rae breathed my sentiments.

I searched the yard as though I could literally place a missing fallen tree but came up empty. The fresh snow that had fallen overnight must have covered any debris from it being cut or moved.

"Who would have…" I turned in a circle, my eyes still raking over the whitewashed yard.

"Oh my gosh, Nora." Rae moved toward the side of my house, where the garage connected.

I followed her, crunching some of the older snow as I went.

"He chopped it all and stacked it for you."

I snapped my head in her direction. "Who?"

Did she assume my father had done this, because he would not have had the time.

Rae twisted toward me, a secret smile on her face. "Colson, the Ice Barbarian, of course."

I didn't even mean to laugh, but it bubbled up out of me like an over-flowing pot of hot water.

"He most certainly did not."

"He did!" She argued, pushing my shoulder.

"But why would he, I mean he…"

I paused, thinking over last night and how he'd started my fire and given me a ride home.

"Why would he do this?" I asked, walking the length of the pile. It would have taken him all night to chop and stack it.

"He texted Davis last night asking if you were up at our place," Rae said, standing shoulder to shoulder with me.

"He asked me to stay in his house." I explained, while rubbing the stress out of my forehead.

Right as Rae was about to reply, someone interrupted us.

"There you are!"

We both spun toward the small alley between my garage and front yard. Mr. Scholler, my neighbor, was standing there, fuming with a red face.

"Hi Mr. Sch—"

"Don't start with pleasantries." The older man warned, grabbing for his hat with aggression.

Rae bit her lip, likely holding back a laugh. The man was clearly upset, but why?

"Did I do something to upset you, Mr. Scholler?"

His scoff echoed. "You ran a chainsaw all night! Wendell, Harris, and Leroy down the way all heard it too. Now, there's a right way and a wrong way to handle things like tree removal."

His hands came out, ready to break it down for me.

Rae had to duck her face because she was cracking up.

We had to get out of there before she lost it completely and made him any angrier.

"I'm so sorry, Mr. Scholler, it will never happen again. I promise." I yanked on Rae's hand, forcing us away from his angry tirade.

We could hear him yelling at our backs while we both broke into laughter. I didn't think it was funny that Colson had used a chain saw all night, but I did find it humorous that Mr. Scholler believed it was me who had used it.

"Come on, let's get you some coffee." Rae hugged my shoulder and guided me back toward the house.

"OKAY, here are the plans for the community center." Rae laid out a few pieces of paper in front of me. Dark lines made up the image of a floor pattern, another page made up different rooms with dimensions. We'd come here after I had called the power company and then promptly left the frozen house for the safety of the warm café.

Rae spread the plans, her black nails pointing to a few different blank spaces.

"This is going to be a tricky job because we need you to help draw up design plans before they start construction."

I had vaguely accepted this job when Rae had been asked to spearhead the project by the mayor. After she saved failing businesses in Macon, breathing life back into our tiny town, City Council was desperate to keep the momentum going, and they figured something for the community would be the way to do that.

"Okay, so what do you need from me right now?" I tugged the image closer.

"I need you to plan the space. We'll need a reception area with a desk. I'm hoping to have it right here in the front, to provide an extra safety measure for kids when they're here. I want to have a place where people can look for jobs, and other community assistance. If they need help paying their power or water bill, I want them to have a private area they can go and talk to someone where they won't feel embarrassed. Then there's the larger area here, where we can host meals for the homeless, and different religious groups can use it for whatever they want. Yoga classes can be held there, bingo nights...the space needs to be fluid and interchangeable." She moved her finger to another section. "Here's where I want classes offered."

My eyes tracked as she talked through each space, as each area came alive in my head.

"This will be a joint Macon effort, meaning several businesses are going to give back and donate materials and things needed for the project. I want the aesthetic we created in the town to be used throughout the center, and for it to feel like an extension of the town. So, the artwork should be mountain vibes, wood, and rustic charm. Davis already agreed to supply you with whatever fixtures and things you might need for the completion."

I nodded my head, loving that she was dating one of the best iron workers in the area, and that she'd thought to include that feature in the building.

"Okay, when do you need the first outline by?"

Rae bit her lip, and that's when the barista came out to check on us.

"You guys good, need anything else?"

This girl was new, which was a testament to my friend's achievement with the town. The small coffee shop had already increased their profits enough to hire extra help. Three other tables were occupied, and at least five people had been in and out for to-go orders.

"We're good, thank you, Susan."

I pulled my cell out and saw that it was getting late, and I still needed to go to a few stores.

"I'm hoping to have the first draft by the end of the week, if possible."

I snapped my eyes to hers and laughed. "Rae, that's not—"

"Just hear me out." She held her hands out as if to calm me down. "I don't need it detailed, I just need a rough sketch. An idea where you might place things, and where you'd put the classrooms, and how the general flow will look."

"Rae, I do interior design for homes and offices, I'm not—"

My best friend leaned forward and grabbed my hands. "Nora, you're the one. You are. You have such an amazing vision for stuff like this, please."

Relenting a bit, I let out a sigh. "Fine...but why the rush?"

Rae set back and seemed to take a calming breath. "The contractors around here are booking up insanely fast. The only way I can get a bid in is if I have a rough blueprint ready for them so we can discuss an estimate. Since we're renovating an older building, it'll go significantly faster."

Looking over the solid lines that framed the space, I pictured where I would put things. Already, an itch under my skin enticed me to sit down at my desk and begin sketching.

"Okay, I'll get started."

Rae made an excited squealing sound before jumping up and hugging me over the table.

"You are the best! I'm allowed to offer you an advance by the way, and it's generous because the timeline is so tight."

That would help with paying for repairs for the house, and the new paint job I wanted to do once it was warm enough.

"You're lucky I love you so much." I hugged her back and then grabbed my things. "I have to get going."

"Okay, love you. Reach out if you need a rescue."

We each left a few dollars for our barista and then headed out into the cold. The sky had turned to an ugly gray, dulling the sun and serving as a reminder that I needed to get home and make sure the power was on and things were squared away.

BY THE TIME I had returned home, the power company had come and turned everything back on. I blasted my heater until it felt comfortable to walk on my wood floors without socks, which took a while. Then I tried to shower.

Muttering a few curse words, I tested every faucet in the house, getting the same freezing cold temperatures in each one after several minutes of letting them run.

"Son of a bitch." I put my hands on my hips and looked around, unsure of what to do.

I didn't want to have to call anyone, and it was nearly dusk, so I wasn't even sure anyone would be able to come and look at things until morning. I considered that maybe it wasn't just me, perhaps it was a neighborhood thing.

Letting out a heavy sigh, I decided to ask Colson if his water was also freezing cold, and while I was there, maybe I could casually bring up the tree and see if he admitted to chopping it.

Passing one of the mirrors in my hall, I tossed my hair up in a bun. Only that ended up looking horrible, so I braided it. But the layers made it all messy and annoying. Huffing a frustrated breath, I left it down as I grabbed my snow boots and coat, then headed out my front door.

The sky was streaked with purple, darkening as the last few minutes of the day slipped by. Colson's truck was in his driveway, and I could only hope that I wasn't about to embarrass myself again by interrupting his dinner, or date night. The knowledge, or rather assumptions, about his dating life, ate me alive on a regular basis.

Curling my fingers into a fist, I pushed aside my nerves and knocked. The brisk winter air stung my face as I stared at the basic green wreath that I knew he'd bought from the cub scouts during their Christmas fundraiser. He was a good guy in that way, always helping businesses if he could, tipping, buying local, sponsoring sports teams, so they had jerseys and gear. Right after I moved in, I saw that he bought at least ten boxes of chocolate from the kids who hit up our neighborhood for one of their fundraisers. Where he tucked it all away, I had no clue. Maybe he had a basement full of chocolate, thin mints, and wrapping paper. There were definitely stranger things to have hidden beneath your house.

Lost in my own thoughts, I wasn't fully prepared for the door to swing open or the gust of warm air that hit my face. Or for Colson to be standing in front of me with wet hair, and in nothing but a pair of gray sweatpants hanging indecently low on his narrow hips.

Jesus.

He had so many muscles, and veins…he definitely belonged in one of those contractor porn calendars, or magazines. Did they have those? They needed to have those.

"Nora." He said my name like he'd been expecting me, not like he was confused about why I was suddenly on his stoop.

My tongue felt thick. "Uh…yes. Hello."

Dammit.

Blinking, I tried again. "You showered?"

This was not going as planned. At all.

His face didn't move, not a single muscle along his jaw…he just stared.

"I mean, I know you showered…I saw your bathroom. I was in your bathroom…although, I don't know why I'm bringing that up right now."

Shoot me.

"Was there a reason you came over?" His eyebrow lifted and all it did was remind me that I was the one always tripping over myself for scraps of his attention, or for him to be nice to me for once.

I was so sick of this "fuck off" attitude he perpetually had with me and, after how he'd cared for me last night, it infuriated me to no end.

Sobering, I squared my shoulders and narrowed my eyes.

"Yes. I have two questions for you. The first, do you have hot water? I'm trying to figure out if I'm the only one without it."

I couldn't decipher the varying emotions his eyes suddenly held, almost like his mask lifted for two seconds, or there was a glitch in the Matrix as he shifted where he wasn't supposed to, but something flickered. Something that resembled concern, but he shut it down nearly as fast as he showed it.

"And the second thing?" He bypassed my question completely.

Biting my tongue, I quietly considered him and how I wanted to form my next question.

Instead of asking the burning one in the back of my mind regarding the tree, my brain went haywire and asked something else.

"Why did you really come and find me last night?"

A cold gust of air rushed into the space between us, making him shudder the slightest bit and then search the space behind me.

I wouldn't be going into his house, so I hoped he wasn't about to ask me to.

With a heavy sigh, he finally relented.

"First, I do have hot water."

Okay, well shit. Then that meant something was wrong with my house, again.

"And the second?" I'd figure the rest out, but before I completely froze my ass off, I wanted to hear him explain himself.

His eyes narrowed somewhere above my head while a tick feathered his jaw. "I already explained this last night."

"But how did you know to find me there...were you looking for me? I mean, how did you know I wasn't at my boyfriend's house? Rae said you texted Davis, why didn't you just text me?"

He scoffed, shaking his head. I caught how the top layer of his hair fell a millimeter and now kissed his forehead. It was adorably hot.

"I don't have your number. And you don't have a boyfriend."

Right.

"Okay, well, thanks for the info..." I moved to leave, but his fingers wrapped around my wrist, halting me.

Half on the first step, I looked back at him, seeing his eyes narrow on the contact, as if it surprised him that he'd touched me.

Letting me go, he ran his hand through his hair and swallowed, making his Adam's apple bob.

"Let me get dressed and I'll fix your water heater. It's probably just the pilot light."

I glared at the delicious asshole in front of me, annoyed by the whiplash of him acting like he didn't want to touch me one second and the next, like it was his job to care for me.

I was confused, and cold and with that fogging up my brain, I blinked and slowly shook my head.

"No."

His mouth fell flat, his head lifted the smallest bit, almost like he was remembering something.

"So we're back to this whole thing?"

"What's that supposed to mean?" I asked, feeling defensive.

He rubbed a hand through his wet hair, seemingly ignoring the cold air even with the way it had colored his cheeks red.

"It means you're young, stubborn, and suffer for no goddamn reason and end up causing more work for those who do end up wanting to help you."

"I never asked you to chop up my tree." I breathed out heavily, feeling my nostrils flare.

Colson smirked, leaning into his door frame. "Pride is an unflattering color on you, Nora."

I gave him a sugary sweet smile. "Who says it's not confidence?"

His scoff wasn't encouraging, and neither was the way he scratched along his abdomen.

"Confidence in what? You have no idea what you're doing. You just turned twenty-three and have no life experience at all...so, stop wasting time and let me come over and fix it for you."

His words might as well have been shards of glass for how hard they cut me. My eyes watered as I worked around the lump building in my throat. It was exactly what Jason had told me and the reason he found me so unworthy of staying with. On shaky legs, I gripped the railing to his porch and descended the rest of the steps. Tears burned my eyes as the wind hit my face and I pulled my arms in close.

"Nora! Come on...don't be like that, let me help you."

Not only would I not let him help me, but I wasn't sure I'd ever even speak to him again.

Like hell would I be made into some pathetic charity case for the asshole next door. I'd never be that again...not to anyone.

6

NORA

STANDING under the hot stream of water in my best friend's guest shower was the best feeling I had all week. Aside, of course, from when I was soaking in Colson's tub, but that had been ruined. This shower was a fresh start. It was me taking charge, not relying on anyone but myself for what I needed. Did I *need* a hot shower? No, but I really wanted one, and to see my best friend, so in the end, it all worked out.

I had texted Rae after I left Colson's porch last night, asking if she wanted to do a strategy session at her place, complete with poster board, note cards, and color-coded Sharpie pens. She accepted immediately, because my best friend was a freak for strategy and using Sharpie pens. It happened to work for her to pick me up on her way back home that evening, so I didn't even have to drive my crappy Toyota up the mountain. Not that it would have even made it. Rae had moved in with her grumpy boyfriend, who lived up on the top of Mount Macon, a month or so ago. So now when I needed a sleepover with her, I had to commute.

Shutting off the shower, I considered Colson's weird behavior once more and tried to make sense of it. He had literally come out of the blue with this sudden concern for me, which tossed up a red flag. It should go without saying that I would probably not do well on a blind date, or in any situation where trust is required instantly because I'd ruin it. Immediately.

"Nora?" Rae called through the door, knocking gently.

She hadn't blinked an eye at having me stay over, and Davis hadn't either. He wasn't that bad after everything; he was just sort of growly if you didn't catch him near Rae. She was the sunshine to his cloudy sky, and they were the most disgustingly cute couple that I had ever seen.

"Yeah?" I gathered my hair in the towel and started dressing.

She cracked the door. "Are you decent yet?"

"Pshh like that would stop you," I joked, buttoning my jeans and pulling on my shirt.

My best friend materialized in the doorway with a laugh, her blue eyes bright, and her nose crinkled.

"True, Davis is downstairs, so I thought I'd sneak up here and tell you that Colson just called him."

I froze mid deodorant swipe and looked up at her.

"What?"

Her dark hair was tied up on her head in a messy bun, she wore a big flannel that swallowed her shoulders and hit the tops of her thighs, and thankfully she'd pulled on sweats. Earlier this morning, when I went down for coffee, I found her without said sweats, straddling her boyfriend's lap, while kissing him like she was two seconds from tearing his shirt off. He thankfully had jeans on, and was otherwise decent, but they both blushed and apologized profusely. With a massively immature gesture, I acted like my eyes had been gouged out and hoped we'd all move past it.

"He called for winter tire suggestions, or something *me* related?" I whispered, as though Davis would sneak up and hear us.

She moved closer, fully invested in my secrecy plan.

"*You* related." She smiled coyly. "He asked if you were still here, and then asked if Davis knew if you had a ride home or not."

Why did my heart want to fucking fly like a deflated balloon in my chest?

Colson was up to something, and I didn't like not knowing what it was.

"So…" Rae asked, eagerly awaiting details I didn't have.

Turning away from her, I grabbed my clothes with a heavy sigh.

"He's acting weird, and it's freaking me out because part of me wonders if he's secretly a serial killer. If anyone picked someone to fall in love with and they ended up being a serial killer, you know it would be me."

Rae laughed and slammed her hip into mine as we walked back to the guest room where I had stayed the night prior. Rae and Davis had asked if I would design it for them, so it was like a winter wonderland escape, full of thick throws and rich color.

"Stop it. You have good taste in guys..." Rae winced right after she'd said it because we both knew that wasn't true. I had the shittiest taste in guys, and it was the absolute worst problem to have because I was positive there was no cure.

"Okay, so minus Jason and all his manipulative bullshit...but I don't think Colson is a serial killer, I think he might have a thing for you."

I watched as Rae's eyebrows bounced as if him making a move was something we'd both been waiting for.

Tossing my clothes into my duffel, I laughed at her naivety.

"I know for a fact that he doesn't but even if he did, I want nothing to do with him."

The guest bed was insanely comfortable, and I loathed leaving it, but I packed my stuff so I would be ready to head back in time to avoid being on the mountain at night.

"What?" Rae's eyes grew wide as she pulled her legs up underneath her.

Pulling the towel off my head, I grabbed for my hair products and massaged my curls while I eyed my friend in the mirror.

"He made a rude comment about my age, and how I never know how to do anything." My voice shuddered the smallest bit as the barely repaired heartstrings flailed at the reminder of what Jason had so viciously said three years ago.

My friend's mouth turned down as she watched me work to maintain composure.

"Aw shit, Nora. I can't believe he said that."

Swiping at my eyes briefly and wanting to move past it, I shrugged. "I'm just confused as to why he's suddenly acting like he gives a shit."

Grabbing for a fuzzy throw pillow, Rae pulled it to her chest as she watched me fix my curls. We were both silent for a moment until Rae tilted her head.

"Well, maybe it's his way of telling you he likes you in the only way he knows how…"

Narrowing my gaze on her through the mirror, I asked, "What do you mean? The way he spoke to me last night definitely didn't sound like he was masking feelings."

She sat on the edge of the bed, keeping her eyes on me through the mirror. "I mean okay, maybe not last night, but maybe you're tempting to him, and he isn't sure how to resist you without also taking care of you…I think you should tell him how you feel. Just put yourself out there and see what he says. What do you have to lose? If he's being a dick, then pull the plug, but if he is struggling with how to confess his feelings, then maybe this will push him."

With a call from Davis downstairs, we dropped the subject when Rae jumped up to leave. I, however, was busy pulling apart pieces of what she'd suggested like cheesy bread.

What if he was finally giving in…I mean, maybe…

"Nora, let's get started, I have to get you to the community center by two!" Rae yelled, and I tossed my products on the bed and jogged down to meet her.

"SO, the entryway will be more modern looking." I drew a line with my pencil down the paper, while gesturing at the empty hole in the room.

Rae walked around, her arms gathered in close while she wore a massive coat, beanie, and thick snow boots. The room had been completely gutted, so now it was a freezing shell. We'd walked through the rough draft I had created, and once we'd made our poster board place holders, we'd driven down the mountain and then put things in place in the community center.

Nodding, Rae eyed the space I indicated. "Okay…so show me where you're going to put the receptionist area and how big of a space you're thinking."

Walking over to the area where we'd placed a large poster board titled "reception," I spread my hands out to show the length of the desk I had envisioned. "Right here, and I want there to be enough space for filing cabinets, and at least four desks."

"Four?" Rae raised a curious brow.

"Hear me out." I walked to the corner of the space we'd outlined with chalk. "You wanted this to be a versatile space, and there will be plenty of different departments working in here."

Rae clicked her tongue in disagreement.

"Two desks."

I crossed my arms, countering. "Three."

"Let's put a pin in it, but for now, we'll keep the dimensions somewhat the same. The positioning for the entry and reception looks good, so we'll keep that where it is."

Shifting to the side, we eyed another poster board on the floor, this one was for the bill assistance area.

"This will be attached by a window from this side of reception, out of the way, so when people enter, they have privacy."

"I love it." Rae beamed enthusiastically while jotting something down in her notebook.

"Okay, Davis has texted me like three times, which, for normal people, would be the equivalent of ten, so I need to get going."

I picked up the poster boards from around the room while she punched out a reply to her boyfriend.

Once I collected them all in my arms, I asked something that had been bugging me.

"Did you already contact a construction company? I thought you were waiting on my plans to place a bid?"

Rae helped me gather the supplies and as we walked out, she locked up. Out on the sidewalk, I took in how fast the day had faded.

"Oh good, no more new snow. That means the plowed stuff will have stayed plowed." Rae let out a sigh of relief heading to her jeep.

I followed after her, stuffing all the supplies inside the back seat.

"So, regarding the construction..." She started the car. "I called and chatted with your dad about taking it over."

I buckled, staring over at her as I tried to process.

"My dad?"

"Yeah...is that okay? He already sent a crew to gut it, which was all I needed from him for now. I did ask if he'd consider bidding out the entire project, but he said he had to get back to me. I have two others that I plan on emailing tomorrow."

I wasn't a fan of mixing business with family, but in the small town of Macon, it would be impossible not to. Designing homes, I never had to brush elbows with construction companies. I had a few guys who worked with me, and that was usually enough. This would be an adjustment.

"Is that okay?" Rae asked hesitantly, while maneuvering down Main Street.

I nodded, but my voice came out too high when I replied, "Of course, yeah...I'm glad he's already on top of the gutting portion so we can visualize things."

"Yeah, and the fact that he hasn't left yet is a huge bonus. Hopefully, they'll be here until spring, right?"

I swallowed gruffly. "Right."

Once Rae pulled up in front of my house, I made quick work to get out because I needed to hide whatever expression had leaked onto my face. Without a doubt, if she picked up on a scowl or furrowed brow, she would then come in to interrogate me. The truth was, I didn't want to talk about my parents leaving or how badly I didn't want them to go. I'd miss them, but it was more than that. They were my safety net and had always been there to catch me when I inevitably fell. So if they left...what would that mean? What if my design company tanked, and I lost my house? What if I became homeless?

As desperate as I was for independence, it wasn't realistic that in a dire situation, I wouldn't call them for help.

My thoughts spun in vicious tangles, swooping into my stomach with dread.

Which was why I had been so distracted when I pushed through my front door.

My lights were on, something I failed to notice from outside. My fire was roaring, music was playing, and banging was coming from inside my kitchen.

"What in the—" I set my things down, and stalked toward the sink, positive I was about to find my father fixing something. But it was worse. Much worse.

Tucked under my sink, with a large tool in his fist as he hammered at a pipe, was my grumpy next-door neighbor.

"Colson? What are you doing, why are you here?" Narrowing my focus and stepping closer, I asked, "And *how* are you here?"

He slid out and stood.

He wore a plain white T-shirt, threadbare jeans molding to his thighs perfectly, and covering his blond messy hair was a backward facing baseball cap. Dear, sweet lord almighty. The sight of him in my kitchen, wearing his hat backward, his face smudged with grease, and his abs visible through his shirt was too much.

I was still furious with him for what he said, but that didn't change that I was attracted to him. Which wasn't fair if you asked me. The world should go according to the rules in Beauty and the Beast. You have an ugly attitude then, poof, you're a hairy beast with a limited amount of time to win back the love of your life.

"You're back. Finally." He clipped out the words as though he was upset with me.

Crossing my arms, I guarded the swooping and dipping my heart seemed to be experiencing, hoping my protective arms would hold it all in place.

"Why are you in my house?" I arched my brow in question, unwilling to give in to my pathetic, romantic fantasies that he cared about me in some capacity.

Because I knew better.

"You had no hot water. Now you do." He set the tool down on the counter, then brought his hand up to scratch his jaw.

I was so unsettled by the fact that he was in my space, standing there like he was as comfortable as ever. As though he'd been here a thousand times.

"And all the banging under the sink?"

I didn't know much about construction, or homeownership for that matter, but I knew that my hot water heater wasn't under my kitchen sink.

He removed his hat, ruffling his hair with a sigh. "You had a frozen pipe."

I let out an immature scoff. "And why exactly would you care that I have a frozen pipe?"

I knew it seemed I was being ungrateful, but why was he allowed to treat me so horribly for the past year, ignoring me, and making me feel as though I was insignificant, then start fixing things without asking?

He let out a sound of exasperation, moving away from me and back toward the sink. He pulled up on the handle, but the pipes only groaned in response. Muttering a curse, he moved toward an open tool bag on the counter.

"Colson…"

He ignored me, selecting something else from the carrier, and twisting the top of the metal tool.

Walking around the island, I pulled his arm. "Colson."

"What, Nora?" His blue eyes flashed, his jaw set in a hard line.

"Why are you here?" I repeated, hating how close I stood to him and how good it felt to be in his orbit. Even after his harsh words, his presence was like a weighted blanket, pressing down on all my fears and anxiousness.

"Your pipes—"

Shaking my head, I stepped away from him. "No." I tried again. "*Why* are you here?"

His expression narrowed, his jaw clenched tight and ticked until finally he tossed the tool back into the bag with a frustrated sigh.

"Is it really so crazy to think that I'd want to help you?"

Laughing incredulously, I said, "Yes, it is!"

Stepping closer, feeling myself start to unravel, I yelled.

"I don't need your help. I didn't ask for you to come here!"

"Well, too fucking bad!" He roared back, stepping closer.

We were yelling at one another, it was ridiculous, but I had all this frustration burning under my skin, from his rejections over the past year and what he said on his porch last night. Like an ice pick stuck in my chest, it froze any possibilities that he'd ever see me as anything other than a burden.

Sidestepping his proximity, I tried to push past him. "Well, I don't want your help."

His hand shot out, landing on my hip. It was the most intimate thing between us, even beyond him seeing me naked in the tub. I froze in place with air caught in my throat, my skin burning under his gaze.

"Tough shit." He grumbled before his lips landed on mine.

Too shocked to move, I allowed his chest to brush against mine until he was standing so close, I could hear every rumble caught in his throat.

His hand tightened at my waist as my mouth moved against his. Almost as if there was no other choice but to open for him, his tongue swept against mine, undoing all my defenses. His jaw slid to the side, emanating another rumble. I finally allowed myself to get lost in the feel of him, smelling that delicious spice that filled my lungs with each heaving breath. My fingers linked at the base of his neck, which brought him closer. He tasted me like he was desperate for me…like he'd been waiting for this. In turn, I clung to him hopelessly and desperately as he pushed against me and my ass pressed into the counter.

But I grew too greedy.

Because the second a moan slipped free from me, he froze, and with a rush of air, he briskly pulled away.

Unfortunately, it was behind my breastbone where I felt the tug, and it was about as painful as pulling apart superglued skin. How would he know that his actions would be felt on such a deep level? It wasn't his fault that he didn't have to break into my heart to already own a piece of it.

He had been there, existing, thriving in a place he had no right to be, and now he'd kissed me and pulled away as if he had been caught in the garden of Eden, stealing apples and shit.

I already knew without having to hear a single word that he regretted it.

I closed my eyes, so I didn't have to witness it, and waited until I heard him leave. Not until the front door creaked open and then slammed shut did I finally let myself stare at his bag of tools as if they could explain what had just happened.

7

COLSON
TEN YEARS OLD

DEAR MOM,

Tomorrow is the last day of school and my last day in elementary school. Next year, I'll be a middle schooler, and that's exciting but Dad signed me up for a summer camp.

He said it will be fun, it's on a big lake with cabins and kids my age... it's for two whole months, so I told him that I don't want to go. He got really mad at me...but what if you get better while I'm gone, and come home? I can't miss you coming home, Mom, because I know you will soon. You'll be better and come back to us.

But please tell Dad that I don't have to, so I can be home for it. — Love, Cole

Dear Cole,

My darling, how wonderful that you're out of school and about to enjoy a long summer. Cole, I would love to see you this summer and I am truly hoping that I do come home. The doctors are very hopeful, but please, dear, sweet boy...will you go to that camp, for me?

You see, I was never able to go as a child, and I always saw my friends come back with little necklaces made of wood with their names on it. They'd have pictures and songs they'd sung, camp names that were given to them and lifelong memories made. I want that for you, Cole, and I want to live vicariously through you. So, go, choose a name for me, and make me a necklace and then bring it back to me. I love you,

Mom

THE EARLY RISERS were out and about, already having their coffee down at the diner, and even a few braved the cold to walk their dogs. The sun was out, creating a glitter effect with all the snow, and it felt like we were all holding a collective breath on whether it would actually get warm enough to melt anything.

I bypassed the few people milling about and headed outside of town, needing to hit something and put whatever was happening in my chest to rest. It was a riot of angry thumps and exhausted squeezes ever since I ruined everything and kissed my neighbor.

I tried to push the feel of her out of my head once again and put my truck into four-wheel drive as I drove up the hill leading to Liam's gym. It was a part of the old lumber yard that was in operation for several years until it was finally sold off.

Liam bought it for a dirt-cheap price, then renovated the hell out of the old building. Located about a mile outside of city limits, the distance provided a small semblance of getting out of the city. As small as the city was, Liam's was a local favorite.

I was getting ready to head inside when my phone rang.

Drawing my brows together as I inspected the name flashing across the screen, I let out a sigh and reluctantly answered.

"Dad."

An annoying pause came across the line.

"Colson, I hear that construction company you've been working at is going up for sale, and that you might be putting a bid in for purchase."

Fuck, that meant my brothers had been talking. We had a group chat that we used to keep each other updated as often as possible, a few days ago I had mentioned the situation with my job. That, of course, was if Peter still considered me for the job after everything…considering I'd already fucked up, I was trying not to get my hopes up.

Releasing the grip I had on the wheel, I relaxed into my truck seat.

"Yeah…my boss is retiring."

Not that he cared in the slightest. He only cared about the opportunity to gain something, so this conversation had an agenda.

"What are the terms?"

I thumped my skull against the headrest. "I'm actually about to hit the gym."

I don't want to talk about this with you. I want something that isn't tainted by you.

Just one fucking thing.

"I won't keep you, are you coming for a visit soon?"

No.

"Spring, maybe…"

"Christmas would be better, try to be here the day before so your mother can get things situated."

Pain pierced that same scar tissue that he liked to pull apart every chance he got.

I wet my dry lips and slammed my eyes shut.

"She's not my mother."

His silence was familiar, almost soothing.

"Thought we were past this…"

We'd never be fucking past this.

"Gotta go, I'll talk to you later." I ended the call before I could talk myself out of it and pushed the overwhelming emotions clogging my heart down. Down, down, down.

Then I headed into the gym, where I could hopefully get my ass kicked by Liam.

"YOU'RE SLOW TODAY."

The boxing legend and one of my best friends danced on the balls of his feet as he watched me with a calculated expression.

Thrusting my glove out, I hit air as he moved around me.

"Really slow."

His taunts usually worked, since I didn't want to be slow, especially with a ton of guys watching us spar, but today, my mind wasn't in the ring.

His daughters were on the sidelines too, his youngest, Mila had her eyes fixated on my feet.

"Daddy, he's growing roots!" she yelled toward me, and the room erupted in laughter.

Trying not to let her rather effective comment bother me, I taunted. "Shouldn't she have a babysitter by now, or be in school?"

Liam's jaw clenched, and then a solid punch landed to my side.

Fuck, it didn't pay to rattle him the way he did me.

"Another one quit, I take it?"

"Fuck you, Hanes, why are you so fucking sluggish today?"

Because I fucked up. Likely ruined my chance...the one and only fucking chance to own something of my own without it being tainted by my father.

"Colson, TIMBERRRRR!" Mila cupped her mouth, shouting as loud as she could and in the second I spent looking over at her, my friend landed a hit to my face.

The next thing I knew he was standing over me, with a wince twisting his features.

Mila ran over, and her sisters wouldn't be far behind if she was already on the mat.

"I tried to warn him." Mila said, propping her tiny hands on her knees.

Another face popped into view, dark hair like their father, and sharp blue eyes. "He's better than this...must be distracted." Seraphina, or Seraph as I called her, muttered, narrowing her eyes in a way too calculated for her seven-year-old self.

Maddy, the oldest would be next.

I rolled over, groaning as another shrill voice spoke up. "Ewww, is that blood?"

Liam's eldest didn't like the sight of blood.

I honestly felt for them because this gym was how their dad kept a roof over their heads, but he was doing it completely alone. He couldn't seem to keep a babysitter around and couldn't afford one of those fancy live in nannies…so the girls came here every waking hour the gym was open.

"Come on …let's go." Liam slapped my back, and I heard a few claps and laughs as I made my way out of the ring.

Tearing my gear off, I watched as Mila perched on a stool to my left.

"Daddy says you can get hurt if you're distracted."

This kid was like five and sounded like a better therapist than the one my father assigned to me from the age of thirteen.

"I'm not distracted."

She was a tiny thing, wearing a shirt too big for her, with hair tangled and wild.

"You never get hit like that, so I think you are. Is it about a womaaan?" She drew the word woman out and batted her eyes like the cute little fucker she was.

I laughed and suddenly her sisters were next to her.

"Did he talk about her yet?" Maddy asked, and Seraph giggled into her hand.

I shook my head and poured half my water bottle over my face.

"Talk about who?" Liam added, making his way over to where we were sitting.

"The girl who distracted him," Maddy said, waving her hand toward me.

Seraph added "duh" for good measure.

"There is no woman." I stood and started toward my bag, but the words tasted like a lie. Nora was on my mind and refused to be kept at bay.

Liam laughed, shaking his head. "You heard him, girls, leave him be."

"So you need a place for the girls to go today, or what?" I quietly asked my friend while his kids busied themselves with something on Maddy's phone.

Liam ran a hand over his head, letting out a long sigh.

"Yeah, they apparently don't have school today…something about a teacher work day. Why, you offering to let them hang out with you?"

I'd known Liam for a year, and been around his kids as long, it wouldn't be the first time they watched Netflix at my house or helped me sort my tools. Besides, hanging out with them was usually entertaining.

"I don't have much going on today. I'm between projects…" and I needed to take it easy since I wasn't fully recovered from dealing with Nora's tree.

Someone yelled for Liam's help, and he held up his finger, indicating he needed a second.

"Are you sure? It would only be for a few hours."

Waving him off, I grabbed my bag. "I'm sure. I need help decorating anyway, I'm sure they'd love that."

Maddy must have overheard us because she whisper-yelled to her sisters about going to my house.

"I owe you, man." Liam slapped my back and leveled me with a serious look.

The thing about community and being friends with someone who often needed an extra hand meant you built up your own strength while lending it. For me, it always benefited me to give back, always made me feel brighter inside somehow.

"Okay girls, let's go."

"MILA, PLEASE JUST CHOOSE SOMETHING ALREADY." I stood with my arms crossed in the middle of the aisle, while Maddy and Seraph browsed through the things we'd already put inside the cart. Mila, however, couldn't decide on which frosting color she wanted for her Christmas cookies.

"If I do pink sprinkles, then I can't have this red and green frosting combination," she said, holding two little plastic containers.

Maddy let out an exasperated sigh. "Don't do pink sprinkles, then."

This was the argument we'd been having for ten minutes, and I was over it.

Grabbing all the colors of frosting and sprinkles, I dropped them into the cart and pushed it down the aisle.

"There, now we'll have options."

"Can we get Lunchables?" Seraph begged, bringing her hands together.

I didn't even know what those were, but I agreed and before I knew it, the girls had piled at least six different yellow boxes into the cart.

"Yay, we never get to have those," Maddy said excitedly while holding the edge of the cart, following along.

Liam's eldest was nine or ten, I couldn't remember, but somewhere around there. She often helped keep her younger sisters in check, while also not going overboard with asking for stuff.

"Pick out some other stuff."

It wasn't that I was trying to spoil them, but I knew Liam was hurting financially. Winter meant a slow season at his gym, and he'd just dealt with a ton of legal fees from his ex. I felt bad for the guy and in turn, liked to spoil his kids when I got the chance.

The girls were busy piling ice cream and other treats into the cart when I heard someone clear their throat behind me.

"Excuse me, can I grab the cookie dough ice cream, please?"

The slightest shudder ran down my neck at hearing her voice, followed by a rush of adrenaline in my sternum. This was the first time seeing her after losing my temper and kissing the hell out of her. The memory of how soft her lips felt against mine, and how luscious her tongue tasted as it moved against mine played on a loop like an anthem.

Turning so she could see me, I relished the tiny gasp that escaped her parted lips when she registered it was me standing here.

"Oh…" she whispered while her face flushed red.

I stepped back, so she had better access to the glass door, but remained close enough that she had to brush my arm to get what she wanted.

She gave me a quick smile that didn't feel sincere, her eyes were moving over the tops of the kids' heads, like she was trying to place them with me or figure out a puzzle.

"You guys look like you're having fun." Nora peeked into our cart briefly. "Ooh, those are my favorite kind of sprinkles."

Seraphina piped up first. "Are you a stranger? Dad says we can't talk to them…but if you know Uncle Cole, then it's okay."

"Maybe she's the womaaan." Mila not so quietly whispered to her sisters, who both giggled.

"Girls," I warned, but Nora's laugh pretty much stopped my heart. It was so fucking perfect that I just stared at her with my mouth parted.

"I'm your Uncle Cole's neighbor." She touched the lower parts of Mila's tangled hair.

Maddy interjected, "He's not our real uncle, he's just our dad's friend, and he's babysitting us today, but we like to call him that because it annoys him."

Nora's mouth spread into a genuine smile. "Babysitting?"

I couldn't stop staring at her lips, or the way they stretched over her perfectly white teeth…or how that color of lipstick made my filthy mind conjure up ideas with what parts of my body she could smear that shade of red.

"If you *really* want the cookie dough ice cream, maybe you could come over and help us decorate his house," Mila offered sweetly, with a full-blown smile and everything.

"Yeah, we're baking cookies too!" Seraph added, standing up on the edge of the cart.

Maddy grabbed the roll of sugar cookies. "He said he doesn't know how to make the real ones, so we're just going to make these."

"Our daddy doesn't ever make the real ones either, so we're used to it." Seraph explained, before taking the roll from Maddy and using it as a sword.

"Well, you guys seem like you have a lot going on, I don't want to intrude on anything."

Mila stood on her tippy toes, grabbing Nora's arm. "You're not intuding, you're invited!"

Nora laughed, and I still couldn't pull my head out of my ass long enough to realize I should have been helping a bit more with reining in the girls. But when those aqua eyes landed on me, all I could do was agree with the kids.

"You're not intruding."

With one quick glance at my mouth, Nora took a step back and smiled.

"That's okay, you guys have fun."

It would be better if she didn't come over. Having her join in wouldn't be required to keep an eye on her, and I'd already crossed the line once. It was good that she seemed to understand that.

Mila and Maddy nudged my side as they watched Nora take another step away, and fuck if I didn't see the way their faces fell watching her leave. I forgot how little interaction they had with women outside of school. They didn't have a grandmother that lived close, Liam had no sisters, and their mother wasn't in the picture at all. The prospect of decorating cookies with someone like Nora was probably something they'd be excited about.

"Wait…" I stepped forward, peering back at the girls for a brief second, before setting my eyes on her. "Look…if you're not busy, we'd really like it if you came over. It would mean a lot."

She stared, and it was like another layer peeled back, like she saw right through me. It was uncomfortable and agonizing because I had gotten good at hiding those layers. Someone could get addicted to that sort of connection.

"Well, maybe after I'm done shopping, I have a few things to get, but I'll come visit afterward."

"Yay!" all three girls yelled excitedly.

I gave Nora a small nod, silently thanking her, and then pushed the cart out of the aisle.

WITH THE THREE girls settled in front of the television screen, I popped the cookie sheet into the oven and set the timer. Right as I finished, the doorbell rang.

"I'll get it!" Maddy jumped up, but Seraph pulled her down.

"Not our house, dummy."

"Just keep watching your show and I'll get it." I walked past them, heading to the front door.

I found Nora standing on the other side, holding a paper bag from the local candy store. She had her hair down, wide, bouncy curls all over the place, wearing a pair of tight jeans that tucked into her snow boots and a long overcoat buttoned all the way to her neck.

"Hey." She smiled brightly, a damn sun beam in the middle of winter.

"Come on in." I moved so she could enter.

She handed me the bags, which made our fingers brush against one another. Her wide eyes jumped to mine, but I looked away as if I didn't also feel that zip of energy run up my arm. She followed suit, looking away as she took off her coat and boots before moving in to where the girls were.

"Hey you guys, look what I brought you."

All the girls immediately jumped and grabbed a barstool, folding their knees under them while peering over the counter.

Pulling free four small white boxes, we all watched as Nora popped them open.

"Whoa, what are those?!" Seraph asked, while the other two let out little oohs and aahs.

"These are called hot cocoa bombs, have you guys ever had one?"

Based on how big their eyes had gotten, I knew they hadn't.

"What do you do?" Maddy asked.

Nora turned to me and asked, "Can you grab the milk and a saucepan?"

I nodded, heading to the fridge and the cupboard. Flicking on the burner, I poured the milk in to let it simmer while Nora continued to explain.

"So we get mugs…" Nora gave me another look, silently telling me to grab them. She was getting far too comfortable with bossing me around in my own house without even speaking.

Once I set a mug in front of each of them, Nora had the girls pick out their own ball.

"This one has peppermint with the cocoa inside, and this one will have mini marshmallows," she explained to her enraptured audience.

Once the warmed milk was ready, and the girls had set their ball of chocolate inside their mug, I poured the pot over the cocoa bombs and then we waited.

Each girl had a tiny fist shoved under their chin as they watched their mug. Nora stood next to me, hands braced on the counter as she watched hers. There was a kids' Christmas movie playing on the TV across the room, and with the snow outside it felt sort of magical and shit. Not that I had ever considered feeling magical on Christmas…I hadn't had a good Christmas since I was seven…but this wasn't horrible. Which was probably why I moved to the left, which put me closer to Nora until our elbows brushed.

She didn't seem to notice as I shifted, and my leg touched hers.

Fuck, I felt like a middle schooler trying to get my crush's attention.

"Whoa!" Mila shouted, breaking the silence and my juvenile thoughts.

Seraphina leaned over her mug, dipping her face until it was directly over the top. "It's magic."

Maddy had her knuckles propped under her chin as she watched her mug. "Cool."

I had a stupid grin on my face that wouldn't budge, and when I realized Nora had one too, I understood with painful clarity that this was something I'd want someday. Holidays, Christmas cookies, magic cocoa bombs…and dammit if my splintered heart used the image of Nora, placing her in that dream too.

"CAN WE PLAY CANDYLAND?" Mila asked, holding up the game.

The girls had a closet in the guest room where they kept a few toys and games. Candyland was one of their favorites.

I finished chewing a mouthful of cookie. "Go clear off the coffee table and set it up."

"Yesss." She darted off with a bit of a hop.

Nora came over after washing a few dishes that I hadn't asked her to do.

"Should I head home? I don't want to overstay my welcome."

"No! you have to stay!" Mila paused mid set up, looking over.

I smirked, leaning down to whisper in her ear. "Besides, it's not like you weren't just here, naked in my tub a few days ago. Don't suddenly act like you care about overstaying your welcome."

I saw goose bumps break out along her neck, while her pink lips parted.

"I call yellow!" Maddy called, breaking us out of our little pensive moment.

We turned and followed the girls over to the coffee table, sitting on the floor.

"Colson has to be green, he's always green." Seraphina pulled the green gingerbread man out and handed it to me.

"Just put him at the starting spot," Maddy chided.

"I'll watch you guys play since there's only four," Nora said, sitting with her legs folded, her knee nearly brushing mine.

"Wait...you have to play," Mila said, scrunching her cute little nose in worry.

Waving the green gingerbread at my face and then Nora's, she proclaimed, "You guys can share!"

I leaned over the table, pulling the cards into my hand, which allowed me to inch closer and make my knee hit hers.

"Okay, then we'll share." Nora gave in, glancing at me out of the corner of her eye while focusing on the game board.

The kids drew cards and moved a few paces, Maddy earned a shortcut with one of her cards.

"I always think the princess is in love with the licorice lane guy," Maddy said dreamily.

"He's a bad guy!" Mila shouted, completely outraged.

Nora laughed, grabbing for a card. "Sometimes you can love someone, and they turn into a bad guy."

All three girls stared at her, hanging on her every word.

"Have you ever been in love?" Seraph asked.

Nora flushed red, and I tried to act completely uninterested, but I was definitely interested.

"I was, once."

Maddy leaned closer. "Was it with a bad guy?"

Nora laughed. "He turned out to be one, yes."

Mila jumped in, standing up and half sitting on the coffee table. "What was hims name?"

"Mila." I warned, shaking my head to discourage her from prying too much.

Nora gave a halfhearted laugh. "It's okay, I'm over it now…his name was Jason."

"Ohhh, we have a Jason in our school and he's a bully." Mila jumped off the table and turned to move her piece up the board.

"We're going to name the licorice guy Jason," Maddy said, and each girl agreed with a cute little yell.

Nora was smiling, and that fucking thorn in my chest cut deeper. I tried not to picture this guy who had turned into a bad guy. This person who had earned Nora's love and affection and had somehow ruined it. But my mind was a vicious pool of jealousy and envy as we continued to play.

The evening went on with Nora helping the girls decorate cookies, then she helped hang up a few lights and garland over the mantel. I didn't have many decorations, so the girls went through my garage to see what else they could find.

"You have too much builder stuff in here," Mila said, trying to push aside one of the rolling tool chests I had pulled away from the walls. It wasn't going to budge, but it didn't stop her from trying.

Nora was with us, silently helping unload the few boxes I told them they could look through. But when they got to a box of old photos and I tried to take it from them, the three little ones bombarded me.

"I want to see," Seraphina said, pulling open one of the flaps of the box.

"Who's that lady?" Maddy asked, grabbing one of the images in between her fingers.

Nora stayed quiet, watching everyone's reaction, but I saw her eyes flick to the image and the rest inside the box a few times.

Working around the tightness in my throat and the part of me that wanted to walk away, I explained.

"That's my mother."

The girls stayed silent, aside from Mila's humming, and for some reason it was oddly soothing.

"What's hers name?" Mila held the picture, bringing it way too close to her face to focus on it.

Clearing my throat of emotion as much as I could, I said, "Kathryn."

I felt Nora's gaze heavy on me as the girls seemed to pass over the subtle shift in mood when Liam appeared in the doorway.

"Hey, you guys ready to go home?"

The girls all jumped up, running to their dad, abandoning the box, and thankfully letting me close the flaps once more and put it back.

"I should probably head out too," Nora said, carefully watching my movements before following the throng back inside the house.

"Okay, I'll walk you out."

I sauntered over to Liam and told him I would be right back before Nora had a chance to argue. When I turned around, the girls had their arms wrapped around her waist, saying goodbye. She leaned down and smiled at each girl, promising to see them again.

Then she turned toward the door.

I grabbed my coat and followed her out. The sky was a murky purple with wisps of white fog hanging overhead. The moon was bright and the iced over snow crunched under our feet.

"Thanks for walking me, I'm good from here." She tugged her purse down off her shoulder.

I ignored her and followed her up the steps.

We stood facing one another as our breaths clouded in front of us. Her features faded the slightest bit from the shadow, but her eyes were bright, and the curve of her fuller bottom lip glistened in the moonlight.

"These. Fucking. Lips." I muttered, my eyes dropped and fixating.

I lowered my head, and she didn't stop me when I shoved my hand into her hair, pulling her closer by the neck, until her mouth was mine again.

She tasted like cookie icing and hot chocolate, with something underneath that felt familiar.

Like home.

I shuffled forward, pulling her against me in a tight hold.

She lifted her chin, deepening the kiss, and then opened for me with a sultry moan.

Fire ignited in my core, making me groan in response and cup her jaw while I slid my tongue inside her mouth. She accepted greedily, moving against me at a chaotic pace, until suddenly she was pushing me away.

"Colson, stop."

I pressed my forehead to hers, trying to catch my breath. That's when I realized I was kissing her on her front porch, where anyone could drive by and see.

Including her dad.

"Fuck." I stepped back, exhaling heavily.

Nora gathered her hands in front of her, watching me, with a reserved expression.

"What are we doing?" Her soft voice barely registered over the roaring in my ears.

What was I doing?

This was so wrong, and so off-limits.

"Nothing. We're doing nothing." I met her gaze, shaking my head. "This won't happen again."

She didn't argue.

I paced her porch waiting for her to say something, but she gave me one soft nod and then turned to open her door.

This wasn't how I wanted the evening to go. We'd had a good time, and I had to go and mess it up. I shoved my hands into my pockets and walked back over to my side of the fence, wondering why I'd ever thought I could cross it to begin with.

8

NORA

I CRADLED an old photo of myself as an awkward tween, smiling at the braces that stretched across my teeth and the not so blended makeup line on my jaw. I laughed, shaking my head as I wrapped it with newspaper. The feeling was surreal, almost dreamlike as I went from room to room helping to pack my parents' house. They hadn't yet mentioned when they planned to officially leave but I had an assumption it would be after New Year's, or early spring.

I didn't want to think about it, but I also had to face it. It was happening. Mom had sold her business already, and I knew Rae had been careful with sharing details about what her boyfriend planned to do with it now that he owned it. But bottom line, it was out of my family's life forever. Dad's construction company would be next.

It hurt that neither of them had considered asking if I wanted to buy either business. Not that I had a ton of capital, but I wasn't broke, and I had decent credit. I could get a business loan in a heartbeat. Dad hadn't told me specifically yet who was taking over his construction company, or what he was even asking for that matter, but part of me wondered if Colson would put in a bid, or if he was even able to.

Thinking of him made a fluttering sensation happen in my chest, which

I actively tried to shut down, because after spending the evening with him and seeing him with those girls... it was a sucker punch to my ovaries.

Then there was that kiss...and dammit, the way he chiseled pieces of my heart like a professional stone carver was unbearable. Two scorching hot kisses, with two agonizing rejections.

I didn't need that sort of confusion in my life and while I was mad at him for what he said the other night before my water heater was fixed, I still had a crush the size of Texas on the man. Besides, it didn't mean I believed he'd ever be a viable option romantically. Fantasizing about Colson Hanes was like dreaming you could marry a celebrity; it was all essentially the same exact thing.

Unrealistic.

"Nora!" My mom called from the office.

I set down the pictures I was wrapping and walked down the hall, jamming my shoulder into the door frame.

"Yeah, Mom?"

My mother was kneeling in front of a large box, but as soon as she saw me, she got to her feet.

"Let's head to the garage, your father has something in there I think he wanted to give you."

Furrowing my brows in confusion, I trailed her.

"Okay...is this about his weird license plate collection, because I don't want that."

Once we cleared the garage door, I found my father already inside, pulling down a few jumper cables and the emergency box he kept all his car stuff in. All my life, my father had clear totes he kept kits in.

It was a nice system, one I had mimicked in my own garage.

"Here, honey, you should have these." He pulled out the rest of the jumper cables and windshield wiper fluid.

Shaking my head, I tried to laugh it off. "Dad, I already have that stuff, don't worry about me."

He gave my mother a look and since I'd been around it my whole life, I knew exactly what it meant. He was trying to keep the peace, but wasn't sure how to do it without getting frustrated.

"Well, we think maybe you should just take our box. That way, you know it's all there and it all works," my mother added, likely assuming her gentle tone would keep everyone calm.

"But I have my own box." Because he'd trained that in me. Why was this so difficult for them to understand?

"Nora, don't be difficult." My dad let out a heavy sigh.

Folding my arms over my chest, I narrowed my gaze on the clear tote.

"I'm not being difficult. I'm telling you I already have a box."

"Yes, but I know you, sweetheart." He lowered his tone to a sugary sweet, patronizing level. "It isn't likely that you have the right jumper cables or oil for your car. Just take mine, okay? You know what, I'll keep this all in here because we plan on leaving you the house."

What?

"Did you just say you were leaving me the house?" Because that would be crazy.

My dad let out a heavy exhale, which took me back to being thirteen and feeling like I was inconveniencing him. My mother toyed with looping extension cords, as though she had no idea that her husband had offered me their home.

"It's the smart choice, Nora. It's almost paid off. We'll keep up the mortgage payments, you can sell your house and that way, if anything happens, we'll know you're taken care of."

My face heated, my neck grew blotchy and warm as I worked to get my emotions under control. I loved my parents, but sometimes...fuck, sometimes it hurt to have them in my corner. People always acted like having a corner full of people was a good thing, but it wasn't if everyone there had a knife ready to slide into your back, or a way to cut your tongue out, so you didn't have a voice.

"I have a house, one I bought myself and I—"

"That house isn't safe, the roof is old, the pipes are bad, and you just had a tree fall in your backyard."

I stared at the floor as heat wound around my neck, making my breathing shallow.

"I'll transfer the title into your name in a few weeks." He turned, grabbing for a tarp. Steamrolling me and my objection.

"Dad, I don't want it."

"Don't be ridiculous, sweetie," my mom added arrogantly, "you don't have a reliable place to live, this way we know you're taken care of, and we have peace of mind that you have a home that's safe."

A wave of hurt washed over me, dragging with it a memory so sharp and painful that it nearly stole my breath. I had never blamed my father out loud for Jason. I had never confronted him because that weekend I had arrived brokenhearted and sad, they cared for me, and at the time, I had nowhere else to go. I had to move out, find a new place to live to finish out my last year of college with no money and no way to get into a place on my own. My parents didn't blink an eye at paying for a new place for me, and even drove down to help me move, so I didn't have to face Jason while I did it.

Because of that, all of it stayed buried.

But it was coming back, fresh and potent.

They didn't believe in me and didn't want to worry that I wasn't cared for.

Why couldn't they see that I could care for myself, even if I messed it up occasionally. I could take care of myself.

I didn't need them to do it.

Swallowing thickly, I stepped back and blinked away a few tears.

"I need to go."

"Nora," my mother called, but I was already walking away.

Heading to the front door, I grabbed my things, shoved my feet into my snow boots, and didn't flinch a single time as my mother stood next to me going on and on about how I needed to stop being so prideful, and let them help.

"You're a single woman, living alone. You've got this design business, but it's not going to pay the bills, honey. We just worry about you."

Fuck, that one hurt.

How could she say that? I had won the bidding war on my house because of all the design projects I had taken on while I was still in college. I had savings and active income from my projects; I was good at what I did. I had started my own business, and I was sought after by larger design firms because of my talent. Did she even know that there had been an article done about a local celebrity who'd hired me to design their vacation home? I wasn't hurting for money, and I had done that all on my own.

"I need to go." I reiterated, my voice shaking and in shambles as tears threatened to fall.

Tugging on the door, I ignored my mother's calls. I tucked my arms in close and walked out.

My car didn't do well in the snow, so I had been getting rides and walking as often as I could. It was a hard hit to my pride as my parents watched me go.

Being an only child, I allowed them to essentially do whatever they wanted for me. I was used to it, but after everything that happened with Jason, it put a lot into perspective. I didn't need them to plan my life for me or worry about what I chose to do with it.

The cold wind stung my face as I walked down the street, clearing my parents' neighborhood and making my way to Main Street. Maybe I could stop in and grab some coffee to hold the rest of the way home, to keep my fingers warm.

Right as I crossed the street to do that, the sky broke open and snow began to fall. The snowflakes were so thick, they stuck to my lashes and soaked my hair.

Seeing the coffee shop, I darted toward it, only to see a sign posted on the door.

"Closed due to storm."

Shit, another storm was coming in tonight.

Giving up on the idea of coffee, I curled into myself a bit tighter and continued walking down the road. There was only about a mile between here and my house, which meant ten minutes of walking if I didn't have to worry about slick conditions. I could do that.

Jerking my hood up and shoving my already wet curls inside, I started on my way when a loud diesel truck pulled up next to me. It idled alongside the curb as the passenger window rolled down.

"What in the hell are you doing out in this?"

I turned to find Colson staring at me with confusion, his large torso leaning over his middle console.

Here he was again, telling me nothing was happening between us, then playing savior. I couldn't understand him.

I waved him off. "Just walking."

Moving in the direction of home, I ignored that he was slowly idling alongside me.

"Nora, get in the truck," he finally barked through the window.

His comment from the other day made the stubborn part of me rise. The way he'd kissed me and then told me nothing was going on between us had me walking faster. The sky seemed to think I was being a petulant child because a whirl of wind and snow hit me in the face.

I heard a loud curse, and then the truck stopped trailing me. The wind had picked up, tossing snow in my face, making it nearly impossible to see.

Okay.

This wasn't the best scenario ever...total whiteout conditions, and my dad knew I was walking, which meant he would be on his way to come after me.

Colson was in front of me a second later, the blue of his eyes more intense than usual. His heavy coat was already coated with snow.

Shielding his eyes, he yelled, "I'm either throwing you over my shoulder or you're being mature and getting in yourself."

I wanted to continue to prove my point that I didn't need to be taken care of...but I wasn't an idiot, this snowstorm wasn't a joke and people could get themselves killed, being in conditions like these.

Taking his outstretched hand, I let him lead me to his truck and got inside. I made quick work of rolling up the window. He climbed in seconds later, and the amount of snow he wiped from his hair made guilt tangle in my chest like chewed gum, messy and sticky.

I didn't want to express any gratitude, but I wasn't that girl who was given a handout but swatted it away out of pride.

He had stopped for me and while I still did not understand his reasoning, I was grateful.

"Thank you for stopping."

Once I was settled, he smiled at me, then put his gaze back on the road. "Why the hell are you walking in this?"

I let out a heavy breath. "Long story."

The silence that followed seemed so loud and all it did was make me want to let the tears that had started at my parents' fall free. I was so focused on myself that I didn't realize we had parked in Colson's driveway.

He was already out, and walking around the truck, opening the door for me.

"I'll see you tomorrow," I explained, blinking as more snow coated my lashes.

His silhouette in the snow felt like something from a dream. Broad shouldered, stubble covering his sharp jaw, and tall.

His hand shot out, pulling mine into his as he demanded, "Come inside, let me feed you while you tell me this long story."

I looked longingly over toward my side of the fence. All I wanted was to curl up in my sweats and stuff my face with the leftover pie I'd bought the night prior.

"Colson, you explained last night that there isn't anything going on here, so I think it would be best if I went home." I tugged my hand out of his, but he took a step forward and closed the distance between us.

"There isn't, we're neighbors, and this is a blizzard. You're coming to my house, so I know you're okay. You can fight me after you've eaten."

"Yes, and in a blizzard, all I want to do is change into sweats and watch my show."

He grabbed my hand again, hauling me toward his house. "I'll give you sweats, and you can watch whatever the fuck you want."

I didn't understand why he had this sudden fascination with making sure I was okay, but after walking in that snow, and dealing with my parents, exhaustion weighed on me hard, making my movements lax and compliant as he pulled me up his stairs.

"Okay, just for a little bit."

9

NORA

I STOOD in the guest bathroom, staring at myself in the mirror. Colson's sweats were too long, so I had to roll the waist down, but they were soft and, most importantly, warm. He'd given me a large hoodie to wear too, so I could let my shirt dry. I hadn't realized how wet everything had gotten, but my coat was soaked through, as were my jeans.

My hair was wet, so it was curling, and all my makeup had melted off, save for my lashes.

With a huff, I grabbed my wet clothes and opened the door. Peering to the right, I saw Colson's room, with the door wide open. I assumed he'd gone in to change, but maybe not.

Suddenly, in his bedroom mirror, I could see his reflection. His muscled chest and stomach were visible as he pulled a shirt over his head, and that's when my eyes moved lower.

He had on a pair of green boxer briefs that barely fit the rather large dick imprint that seemed to rest toward the left side of his body. God, he was massive, if that much was visible from here.

He shoved his left leg into a pair of sweats, and I quickly averted my eyes. Why was I spying on him?

Ohmygosh.

Darting out of the hall as quickly as I could, I prayed to sweet baby

Jesus that he hadn't seen me watching him. Instead, I moved around the living room, straightening my clothes out to dry in front of the gas fireplace.

"I was thinking of soup and grilled cheese for dinner...comfort food, what do you think?" Colson asked, walking into his kitchen with ease, like he hadn't seen me watching him dress moments earlier. Maybe he hadn't.

"Yeah, that sounds fine. Can I help make anything?" I asked, letting the sleeves of the hoodie swallow up my palms.

"You can toss everything I hand you into the blender, and then help me butter the bread."

I moved to his side to help him and with everything he diced, chopped, and opened, then I poured and dumped into the blender. Once we'd transferred it to a pot, and the soup was simmering on the stove, I helped butter the pieces of bread.

"So, are you going to tell me about what happened?" he finally asked, flipping the burner on and moving toward our plates. He sucked the pad of his thumb into his mouth, licking off the melted butter, and it was the most erotic thing I had ever witnessed in my life.

Trying not to stare, I toyed with the edges of my sleeves.

"My parents apparently are leaving me their house."

Colson's head swung toward me from his place in front of the fridge, his mouth parted and then he blinked.

"Wait...as in they offered to sign over the house you're living in right now?"

What? Why would he assume that they owned it?

"No...I own my house, which is why I don't want their house."

His blue eyes searched mine from his spot by the fridge, the sound of *The Office* played from the television in the living room, and the blizzard silently flew around outside the window. It was peaceful and warm.

"Wow, I mean...you're only twenty-three, I guess I assumed they owned it."

Watching him grab two beers, he finally shut the fridge and walked back over.

I wasn't sure what to make of his statement...I wasn't that surprised that he assumed they'd bought it, but I hated that he didn't seem to know me at all, and he didn't indicate that he wanted to.

"So, why exactly are they leaving you their house?"

We moved to the table with our beers, grilled cheese, and our bowls of soup. Propping my knee up, I leaned in to pull apart my sandwich and explained.

"You know I've had a lot of issues with my house. It's a fixer upper, I mean, it's still that disgusting brown color from when I first bought it, but my parents think if they move to Arizona, they won't be able to have peace of mind if I'm living here versus over there, where everything has been updated and maintained by my dad. They also seem to think that I don't make any money and will immediately become homeless once they leave."

Colson's gaze flickered between his food and my lips, and every so often his eyes would land on mine in a sad sort of way. Almost as if he was sorry for me.

"Did they ever ask if you wanted to join them in Arizona?"

Taking a spoonful of tomato soup, I tried to push down the hurt around the answer. It was ridiculous that I wanted an invitation, but just the same...it had never come.

"No."

That sad expression returned, arranging his features in a way that made his eyebrows pull tighter and his lips twitch, and all I wanted to do was lean over and kiss it from his face.

I didn't want pity.

"So, you told them no...and what, they forced you to walk home?"

Laughing at his attempt to pull the story from me, I shook my head. "I'm still not so great at driving in the snow. So, I had ridden over with them, but while I was there, I just couldn't be talked to like a child. It drives me insane when they act like I can't manage my own life, or I need to be taken care of."

At that, he stayed quiet, and we finished our meals in peace.

Afterward, we stood at his back door and watched as more and more of our fence line disappeared from the heavy snowfall.

"Maybe I should head home before it gets too dark." I suggested, realizing it was already nearly dark.

Colson made a sound of disagreement with his eyes locked on the storm outside. "Nah, I think maybe you should just stay for a bit...be my drinking buddy."

"Your drinking buddy?" I snorted, taking my hair off my neck in the warmth of the house.

Colson stepped away, his hand grazing my side the slightest bit.

"Yeah...we can play cards," he reached above the fridge and pulled down a bottle of whiskey and then reached into the freezer and produced vodka.

"Ohhh, you mean drink-drink?"

"Drink-drink," he smirked, setting the bottles on the table and then grabbing two shot glasses.

"Where are the cards?"

Lifting his chin, he gestured toward the hall. "Guest room closet."

Spinning on my heel, I walked into the first guest room off the hall. It had a large queen-size bed with a white comforter and puffy pillows. A modest-size dresser sat against the far wall, but otherwise the space was empty. The closet, however, was a large walk-in, and when I flipped the light, my heart nearly left my chest.

Neatly stacked and organized from wall to wall was nearly every single kid's game I had ever heard of. I knew it was for the girls when they came over, but it let me see a different side of him that thawed my annoyance regarding his recent, rather confusing behavior. Smiling at all the extra dolls and barbie toys and a few light sabers he had in a basket, I grabbed a deck of cards and walked out.

"Find 'em?" Colson asked, staring down at his phone.

I padded to the table, sat, and plopped down the deck of cards with a tiny smile.

"Yep."

He looked up and saw what I had grabbed, and those eyes finally landed on me, making me bite back my laugh.

"Go Fish?"

"Yes, sir." I tried to keep from laughing while I pulled out the cards and shuffled.

I didn't miss the way he also worked to keep from laughing.

"Okay, here's the rules, you have to take a shot every time you lose a card."

My mouth dropped. "We're gonna get so drunk."

"You might, I'm fucking awesome at this game."

Handing him the deck, I grabbed for my shot glass. "It's totally chance, you dork."

"Let's find out," he beamed, grabbing his deck.

"IF YOU THINK for one second that I'm giving you my purple fish, you're out of your mind." My cards were dwindling, as were my chances to win. Colson, the glutton, had at least six sets in front of him, and I only had three.

Colson propped his elbows up on the table, his shot untouched in front of him, like mine. We'd both taken a few...okay, more than a few, but I thought maybe I had had a few more than him. My fish blurred a bit.

"You don't have a choice, if I ask for them, you have to give them to me."

We'd moved our game to the coffee table because we wanted to be closer to the fire. The blizzard made the draft by the sliding glass door unbearably cold. But with the new position, we were sitting considerably closer. I could see the tiny flecks of gold in his eyes and the way his upper lip had the smallest scar.

"Then don't ask me for my purple fish," I said, trying to be serious but the way he smirked told me I had fallen short.

"Nora, I can't not ask you when I have two purple fish waiting for the other two in your hand."

Slapping the table, making the shot glass shake, I leaned in closer. "You can ask for pink fish." Pushing my finger into his chest, I added, "Ask me for pink."

The last part of my words came out slurred, but I shook it off.

I wasn't drunk yet, definitely not...just buzzed a little bit.

Colson grabbed my finger and held my hand. "What will you give me for it?"

His question felt all warm and fuzzy, like cotton wadded up inside my chest.

"What do you want for not asking for my purple fish?"

I think a giggle came out of my mouth, but I couldn't be sure.

His eyes were getting red, and he was unsteady in his movements...so maybe he was drunk. What a lightweight.

"I want to kiss you somewhere I haven't kissed you yet."

Wrapping my fingers around his wrist, I tossed my head back and laughed.

"So, you're saying I can keep my purple fish if you let me"—I frowned —"I mean, if I let you kiss me?"

"Somewhere I haven't kissed you yet," he added.

Clicking my tongue, I tilted my head to the side. "Where will you kiss me?"

"Not telling until you agree," he said, leaning so close our mouths nearly touched.

I didn't care about the game or the rules, but I desperately wanted him to kiss me.

Setting my cards down and pulling my hand free, I agreed.

"Deal."

Colson set his hand of cards down and drank his shot. I took mine too, feeling the liquid burn down my throat and warm my belly.

Shifting to his knees, he moved closer to me, placing his palms on either side of my hips. He lowered his head slowly and then his lips were on mine.

I was on my back in front of the fire, my arms wrapped around his neck as his lips traced mine. His tongue delved deeply into my mouth, his teeth tugged my bottom lip, while he made a groaning sound. He traveled further down my chin and neck until he must have realized the hoodie was in the way.

Pulling it over my head, his tongue returned to my jaw, descending until he was tracing the tops of my breasts. He was going to kiss my nipple; I just knew it. I decided I wouldn't mind that at all.

But his head popped up, his eyes on mine, heated and lusting.

I waited and watched and then his thumbs hooked into the band of the sweats I was wearing.

I gasped, sitting up on my elbows to watch.

"What are you doing?"

He moved to sit back on his knees, pulling the sweats all the way off with a heated glare.

"I'm kissing you somewhere I haven't yet."

The cotton in my chest disintegrated into nothing as fire swept through me. I knew I was tipsy, buzzed, maybe even drunk, but the idea of this man putting his tongue on me like that. Fuck, it was hot.

"Yes." I breathed, kicking the fabric away from my feet.

He reached for me, gripping under my ass and pulling me toward him until his tongue swiped through my folds.

I watched, seeing how he looked with his face nestled between my thighs, and then I rotated my hips.

"Fuck." I whimpered, pushing my fingers through his hair to pull him closer.

He acted ravenous for me, licking, and pushing his tongue deep inside me, then he pressed an open mouth kissed over my slit. It was messy, and the way he pushed my thighs apart and repeated the movement had me panting. No one had ever touched me like this. Handled me in such a way that made me feel like I was burning from the inside out.

Lifting up from in between my thighs, he gently swiped his fingers through the wetness he'd created.

"Best fucking kiss I've ever had," he grunted harshly before pushing those fingers inside and returning his mouth to my center. With the pressure of his tongue and fingers...it was too much. My chest tightened as my breathing sharpened and then it hit, rolling through me like a heat wave.

"Colllssson!"

He didn't stop his ministrations, licking my release up with his mouth while his eyes stayed pinned to mine.

"More." I whispered, my chest heaving, my throat dry.

His head came up, his hands landing on either side of my hips as he stared down at me.

"Nora, the things I want to do to you…" He shook his head. "I can't."

"Yes, you can." I wet my lips, sitting up on my elbows. "You can, and you should. Colson, I saw you earlier…in your room… and I'm going to burst out of my skin if I don't get to feel that thick cock somewhere on my body."

He groaned. "Nora. Fuck." Then he pulled his sweats down enough that the tip of his erection bobbed free and the massive, heavy length of him fell to my stomach.

Instantly, my nipples puckered in the cold air, almost in anticipation of feeling his hardness fill me.

Gripping his erection, he dipped his head to watch as he glided the tip of his cock through my folds.

"This is what you needed, Nora? This fucking cock on this greedy pussy?"

God, that mouth. I wet my lips again, trying to catch my breath as I worked to not buck my hips.

"Did you want this cock inside you, or did you just want it to play and tease this pussy?"

Hissing, I tried to grip the carpet at my fingertips, but it was too short. "Fuck me. Please, Colson."

With a few slow swipes of the head of his cock, he groaned erotically while staring down at my spread thighs.

The way he controlled how little of himself he gave, while still consuming so much of me was euphoric. It billowed in my chest like a sail caught in the wind. Arching my back, I swiveled my hips, forcing that tip to move further.

Colson froze with a sharp inhaled breath.

Then he was gone, sitting back on his heels.

I leaned up on my elbows, seeing him fist the rock-hard erection jutting from his hips, the tip of his weeping dick nearly hit his belly button and my mouth watered.

"You need to earn this cock, Nora. Come over here and show me what the back of that throat feels like, desperate for every thick inch. Show me how those pretty lips will look wrapped around me."

Molten heat consumed me, making the ache between my legs insufferable. I needed him, in any capacity, and the image he'd conjured up was exactly the jolt of pleasure I craved. Getting to my knees, I crawled to him and slapped his hand away from gripping his shaft. That large palm moved to the back of my neck, guiding me as I gripped him from the root. Using my thumb to apply the smallest amount of pressure on his column, I lowered my head, taking him into my mouth.

He was so big that he was at my throat almost instantly, making me choke, but I took him like that as long as I could before having to let up.

"Shit, look at the way you take me."

I lowered my head again, sucking him into my mouth while his hips rotated. "Just like that, Nora."

He shuddered above me, as though he was barely restraining himself.

His grip tightened in my hair, pulling me off him, so he could look in my eyes and I hoped he saw how wide my mouth had been stretched from taking his girth.

"So gorgeous. Now, give me your fingers."

Keeping my right hand on his shaft, I lifted my left to his mouth. He took my wrist and then lowered his mouth over my fingers, sucking on the first three. With a groan, he pulled them free.

"Rub your cunt with these while you choke on my cock."

Heat flared in my core and I did exactly as he said, rubbing my aching center as I lowered my head, taking him once more.

He held my head in place as he slowly fucked my mouth, grunting and groaning curses in between thrusts.

"So desperate to fuck this cock with your mouth, and you can barely fit me." He thrust gently, hitting the back of my throat, and with a guttural rasp he added, "Think about how your tight pussy will stretch over my cock when it's sinking inside you."

Rubbing my center in harsher strokes, I groaned and suddenly my lips were freed, and I was being pulled.

His hands went to my ribs as he picked me up and roughly laid me on the coffee table over the card game we'd been playing. I stared up at the ceiling as my hair fell over the edge of the table and my ass hung off the edge, and that's when his hand held my stomach. His face was between my spread thighs, his tongue hovering near my soaked slit.

"When you come, I want it to be on my face." He swiped, spreading my folds with his thick tongue. "You're dripping, Nora, and I'm going to catch every last fucking drop. Now open those pretty lips and let me hear how desperate you are to come."

His tongue moved again, this time sucking my clit with the smallest bite, but he didn't let up. He sucked, and I shattered completely. As I screamed his name, he gripped my hips, pulling me closer to him to lick every drop of my orgasm into his mouth.

"Good, Nora. Very fucking good." He exhaled, moving, and then he slid me closer, so that only half my body was on the table.

Pulling on my hair, he stood over me, gripping his erection in his fist while ribbons of white spilled from him, and holding me in place, he painted my face and chest.

My tongue was out, my eyes closed as I waited for his groans to subside and the hot release to stop pulsating over my skin. Within seconds, he finally sagged back, removing his hand from my hair.

"Holy shit," he exhaled heavily, working to catch his breath.

I opened my eyes, feeling my face and chest sticky with his release. It didn't bother me, when it came to hot sex, my thoughts were always, the dirtier, the better. But I also knew Colson wasn't as young as I was and had likely had way more experience than me. Not that he was comparing, but I wanted him to have me in any way that he wanted me. He made me insane, desperate for any part of him.

"Well, should we shower?" I joked, swiping my thumb through some of the release he'd left behind and sucking it into my mouth.

I knew we weren't ready for sex, which was the real reason he'd pulled back. I was grateful he'd handled that with grace, so I amended my suggestion.

"Or, if you don't mind me using your guest bathroom, we don't have to shower together."

Colson was up, pulling his sweats on as he walked to the kitchen.

Feeling a little awkward that he hadn't responded, I sat up and reached for my things.

"Uh, sure…if you want to hit the guest bathroom, that's fine. I'm prob-ably going to head to bed…will you be okay getting home?"

My head snapped up; my fingers froze over the sweats I'd discarded. I was trying to gauge whether he was joking, but his eyes were lowered, looking at the cell in his hand.

Waiting for him to crack a smile, or joke again, I sat there frozen.

When he turned to grab a glass of water, I realized *I was the joke.*

I could handle a lot, but everything from the night had caught up to me. I felt used, even if I had allowed it, even begged for it.

I felt like he'd played me.

Getting to my feet, I left the sweats where they were and grabbed my clothes that had been drying. Silently walking to his guest bathroom, I washed my face and dressed.

When I emerged from the bathroom, he was still in the kitchen, running a hand over his face.

I didn't say anything as I bent down to pull on my boots and coat.

"You want me to walk you to your door?" Colson crossed his arms over his chest, leaning his shoulder against the arch leading to his foyer. He hadn't pulled on a coat or boots, so I knew it was an empty offer.

Trying not to let the slightest bit of emotion slip through my voice, I replied, "I'm good."

He didn't try to stop me as I walked out.

10

COLSON
ELEVEN YEARS OLD

DEAR MOM,

I'm in detention writing to you. I hit Danner again, but in my defense he's a douchebag. I miss our smaller notes that we used to be able to pass back and forth between Martina going to see you every day. Dad has been working a ton, and his secretary is over at the house a lot now. I don't like it. She even sleeps over. I hate that you're back in there again, after a summer of being home. Why are you back in there? I hate this. –
Love, Cole

Dear Cole,
I'm sorry, honey. I am trying my best to get better for you, but my body is taking a bit longer to get the message. Why are you fighting in school, sweetie? That doesn't make me happy, I want you to be respectful and kind. I want you happy, my son. Surrounded by life. I know your dad works a lot, but try not to forget about the sunshine inside your soul. It was there the day

you were born, and you let it out every time you smile and you think of others. I want you to remember that. Thank you for the beautiful flowers you had delivered. I have no idea how you knew I needed to see those today, but it meant a lot. Please check on my garden, it will bring you joy and comfort on those hard days. – Love, Mom

BEING inside Peter's office felt wrong.

I'd stood inside it hundreds of times over the past year, but this morning, with unwelcome emotions clogging my chest, I didn't want to be here. He'd called me early and asked if I could pop in for a few minutes before I headed to meet Davis.

Peter was busy digging through a few files, before turning toward me with a tired expression, his hair looked lighter too, as if retiring had done the opposite for him, causing more stress. With a singular window that faced the parking lot, and a modest-sized desk in the middle of the room, it was as sparse as ever, considering we were usually working out of our on-site trailers during projects.

"Thank you for coming in, I know you have the day off, so I appreciate it."

I gave him a firm nod.

Sorting a few papers, he looked up and addressed me. "I wanted to thank you for picking up Nora yesterday…it was lucky timing that you were on your way home, but still, I appreciate you taking care of her."

The way my insides wanted to rearrange themselves at the notion that I'd picked her up for him was fucking horrific. He'd called, but he never asked me to take her home with me, and he sure as fuck didn't tell me to touch her.

The only thing I had done for him was hurt his daughter by acting like last night meant nothing to me.

"It was no trouble."

Peter grabbed for his shoulder bag, stuffing folders inside, and pawing through a few documents. He was a fucking mess. Call me an asshole, but the way I resented him right now was too grand for me not to take advantage.

"Nora mentioned you offered her your house."

My boss's eyes bounced up, widening the smallest bit.

I never got personal with his daughter, at least that's what he thought.

"You two talking now?" he chided, putting his eyes back on the various piles around his desk. He needed an assistant, but the dude had too many control issues to hire one.

"Why shouldn't we talk?" I challenged, leaning against the wall and kicking my boot out. I was so fucking exhausted of this game he had me playing, all the goddamn hoops he constantly wanted me to jump through, it was bullshit.

Peter froze, standing from hovering over his work and pinned me with an icy glare.

"You know exactly why you shouldn't, Colson…we discussed this last year."

Pushing off the wall, I tipped my chin. "Refresh my memory, boss…I walked into your office, interviewed, and your daughter came in to see you."

Peter's jaw ticked hard as he glared.

I continued, "I hadn't even met her yet, I hadn't said a single word and you—"

"You didn't have to say anything," Peter rushed out, his eyes narrowing and a vein protruding in his forehead.

His words stopped me, I was trying to push him into explaining why he was so fucking set on keeping me from Nora, but truth be told, I had never challenged him on it. I wanted this place; I needed a fresh start. Leaving my life in Malibu and my family behind, I wanted to carve out a place that molded to my life. So, when Peter said that no one who worked for him would ever be involved with his daughter, I went with it, whittling away at my newfound freedom. But now…I was curious.

"What do you mean I didn't have to say anything?"

Peter rapped his knuckles against his desk, shaking his head in frustration. "The reason I hired you was because I could see in your eyes that you wanted this. You came to me with an MBA, and truthfully, I had no use for someone like you. You'd never built a house, even framed a chicken coop as far as you told me...but I recognized hunger in your eyes. A desire to create something of your own, and make it thrive. So, I hired you and before long, you made it obvious that I'd be an idiot not to make you my number two. You're a natural born leader, Colson, and obviously a savvy businessman. But the way you looked at Nora that day...it was like you'd be willing to accept this job, but for her...you'd leave it just as fast."

Creasing my brow, I tried to make sense of what that meant.

"So because it looked like I would leave for her...you sabotaged any fu—"

He cut me off with a slash of his hand. "It wasn't that you would leave *for* her...it was that you looked at her like there was nothing *but* her ...you looked at her like she was it for you. No job, no person or thing on this planet would ever be enough in comparison."

I had no idea what he was talking about, and yet...

Anger and hurt tangled in my chest like messy patchwork. Why did he get to decide that about me? For all I remembered, I looked at Nora like a normal person. I mean, sure she was gorgeous, and she stopped our conversation when she'd walked in...but how did Peter gather all that extra shit from that one interaction? I didn't buy it.

"I think you saw what you wanted to see, Peter. Nora didn't have the sort of impact you're implying."

Exhaling and finally taking his eyes off me, he expanded. "I take it you haven't ever been in love...or maybe you haven't realized you were, but I have and I know what love looks like and what's better, I know what devotion looks like and you practically tripped into both when you met her."

"Then... why keep her from me? If all that you're saying is true, then why wouldn't you want her to be with me?"

He leveled me with a firm stare, unwavering as he waited...for what, I had no idea but finally after a few tense, silent moments he cleared his throat.

"Because she's too young for you, Colson. She hasn't lived yet. That look you gave her would only shackle her. I asked you to watch out for her because you're her neighbor, and you're my right-hand man. I can trust you, but Macon is too small for her. She's going to spread her wings and if all goes according to plan, you'll be here running this company."

"But what if she wants Macon? I mean, her best friend is here, why wouldn't she settle down here?"

Peter's sigh was loud and heavy as he explained, "She was away from Rae for four years during college. And even after that, Nora wasn't even going to move back here. She did it for us. She has plans, dreams…and anyone who cared for her in any real capacity wouldn't entice her with a cage."

I wanted to tell him he was wrong, explain that he didn't know her the way I did, but the truth was, I didn't know her either and fuck if that didn't hurt to admit. And after last night, she probably wouldn't give me the chance to ask.

Peter walked past me, heading out of his office.

"She's going to need someone to look out for her for now. I hope that person is you, but if not, I'll understand that you're wanting to pull your name out of the running. I have other offers coming in. I plan on making a decision before Christmas."

Without another comment, he walked away, and I continued staring at nothing until my eyes began to burn.

11

NORA

THE SNOW HAD TURNED Macon into something picturesque, with snowdrifts and icicles hanging over storefront windows. Lampposts dusted with white powder added with the holly and lights strung up along Main Street created a replica of every Christmas Hallmark movie ever made.

But it was absolute shit to work in.

"Nora, lift your arms higher!" Rae called from below, wearing white, fuzzy earmuffs, a long pea coat and a disgustingly bright engagement ring.

Lifting my arms so the lights would catch on the hooks Davis had set in place, I ensured the wire was secure.

"Why are you out here, anyway?" I groused, slowly climbing down the ladder one step at a time.

Rae flipped through a few papers on her clipboard while replying in a monotone voice.

"Why wouldn't I be out here?"

Lifting the ladder, I made an unladylike noise as I dragged it to the next section where I had to hang another set of lights.

"Oh, I don't know because you got engaged last night, and you should be off planning your wedding and not here." I tried hard not to let the smallest amount of bitterness through my tone. Just because my evening had ended with my crush painting my face and chest with his release, only to then kick me out of his house, didn't mean I couldn't still be happy for my best friend.

She had loved Davis most of her life, so the fact that he had proposed last night was a big deal. She should be off celebrating, not here, in the town square, working her fingers to the bone, setting up for another big event. My best friend was single-handedly responsible for helping get this town back on its feet, and since then she's tried to maintain and improve on that. It wasn't her job, and yet she'd become indispensable. Now that the businesses were making profits, they were paying her for the ideas she'd think up to generate sales.

The town was having one last hurrah before the cold really set in, and tourism slowed down. All the local shops were opening their booths, and a band was scheduled to set up for the winter carnival. Since my mother wasn't participating this year, I was looking forward to enjoying the festivities instead of having to help in her booth. But it seemed my best friend was planning to rope me back in.

"I'm not planning this wedding until I'm sitting at a table with you, and a thousand notebooks with at least two packages of fresh Sharpie pens. You know I want to use black and gold at least once."

I turned my back and rolled my eyes. I loved her. I really did, but the girl needed to start using Pinterest, plain and simple. She was stuck in the early nineties, and I had no idea how I was supposed to manage all that as her maid of honor. She hadn't asked yet, but it was already assumed. Or was it? Had she asked someone else, did she have other friends?

Right as I was about to ask her if she'd picked someone, she piped up excitedly.

"Oh good, coffee is here!"

Still perched on the ladder, I heard the sound of familiar laughter drawing closer to our little spot in the square. Searching the whitewashed world below, my gaze landed on Davis, wearing a dark beanie and a thick coat, and carrying two coffees. The person next to him wore a forest green beanie over his golden, surfer hair, a brownish gold Carhartt jacket, and like Davis, he carried a coffee in each hand.

I took in the casual way they talked, and their long strides that didn't seem hindered by all the snow, and wondered why Colson was with my best friend's fiancé. Surely, he wouldn't be joining us for the day…maybe he was passing by.

Davis stopped in front of Rae, handing her a coffee while leaning in to kiss her.

His companion bypassed the couple and headed straight for me.

Quickly averting my gaze, I acted incredibly invested in the construct of stringed lights while the man below me came to a stop and tilted his head back.

"You want to come down for some coffee?"

My gut somersaulted at the mere idea of Colson bringing me my own cup as though we were a couple, like our friends. My heart was thumping wildly, likely realizing the trail of red flags he'd left in his wake, and my brain was simply not having it.

"No," I replied evenly.

His head remained tilted as he peered up at me.

"Nora…" He sighed as though I had exasperated him already.

I ignored him because the dude was an asshole. Plain and simple.

He was bossy, arrogant, and always treating me like a piece of luggage he could grab, fill with all sorts of emotional shit, then toss me out of the way when he was done with me.

Well, I was officially done with him.

"So, you're not talking to me then, is that it?" he called in a reserved tone, almost as though he didn't want anyone to overhear us…or like he was ashamed.

I ignored that too because I had no idea how to answer. I wasn't so upset that I truly couldn't speak to the man, I just had nothing to say.

What he'd done the night prior spoke volumes.

And I'd heard enough.

One could only feign interest in stringed lights for so long before they had to climb down and move to the next section. So, with a bit of a reluctant breath, I did just that.

Once my feet were on the ground, my nosy, grumpy neighbor crowded me.

"Look, about last night…" He leaned close enough that I had to tip my head back to see him.

The heat from the coffee pressed into my chest through the opening of my coat, but I felt the burn all over. He was too much this early in the day, and way too much after what happened last night. We needed at least a week before we could go back to acting like nothing happened.

"I was wondering if we could talk somewhere private?"

The audacity of this man.

I spent all night battling tears and hating myself for it because he'd treated me like a complete stranger who'd asked him for the hookup...like he did me a favor but was so reluctant to do so.

Right as I was about to lay into him, someone squealed from behind us.

"It looks like a Christmas movie!"

I peered around Colson's massive stature to see Mila, Maddy, and Seraphina all walking toward us with wide eyes and gaping mouths. Their dad walked up behind them, sipping from a cup of coffee, while looking at his cell. The girls were bundled, head to toe in winter gear, but their dad looked like he was about to walk into a gym, with sweats, a beanie, and a light jacket.

"Oh good, you guys made it." Colson said, stepping away from me and walking to greet his friend.

Rae and Davis walked over, closing our little circle.

Colson rubbed the top of Maddy's head while addressing our group. "Hope you guys are okay with me inviting them along today."

I was beyond confused, which I tried to convey to Rae, who seemed to be purposely ignoring me.

"Of course it is, the more the merrier!" Rae beamed happily.

Her gaze bounced once to me, but it flitted away before I had a chance to convey that I did not agree with, nor did I understand, what was going on.

"Okay, if you need to use the restroom, you better do it now. The coffee shop is right over there, otherwise you'll be going in the snow when we get on the mountain," Rae explained, while everyone talked among themselves. I took the opportunity to pull Rae away by her arm.

"Ow," she whined, but I pinched her for good measure.

"You did not tell me that Colson was coming, or for that matter, his friend Liam."

Rae rubbed her arm, glaring. "I knew you'd overreact if I told you about him, and as far as his friend goes, Colson asked last night if the girls could tag along because Liam has to work."

Why did my stupid heart soften at that?

"You still should have told me." I crossed my arms, being dramatic and immature.

Rae smiled and rubbed my arm encouragingly. "Try to have fun today."

Not likely.

She returned to the circle, and after a few deep cleansing breaths, I did too.

The girls were all excited to see me and all ran up to me as soon as they saw me.

"Hi, Nora!" Maddy said, smiling at me. Her dark hair was tucked under her stocking cap, making her blue eyes pop and her cute rosy cheeks stick out.

"Hi, Maddy."

Seraphina and Mila came up on my other side. "Are you Christmas tree hunting with us today?"

Smiling down at her, I nodded. "I am."

"Yay! I hope you can ride with us."

Oh shit, I hadn't considered how that would go.

Rae was gathering us all back toward the center.

The snow had started falling again, coating our clothes with fat flakes. It was probably a sign not to head up the mountain for trees, I mean, honestly.

"Okay, we're going to head out shortly. We have lunches, hot water, and coffee packed."

I raised my hand like a little kid.

Rae smirked. "Yes, Nora?"

Hating that the focus was on me, I tried to push past it as I asked, "Um, sorry, I just wanted to ask what the ride situation was?"

"Oh, right!" Rae exclaimed like she'd forgotten something. "Oh crap, we're in the truck today, which is a bench seat, so it only seats two comfortably."

"Same with our truck," Davis's friend, Gavin, added needlessly—I hadn't noticed him or his girlfriend pop into our circle, but they had appeared on the opposite side of me, all decked out in winter gear.

I wasn't riding up a dangerous mountain with strangers. I hated feeling like I was at the mercy of everyone in the group. Without even realizing it, my face blushed right as someone's hand landed on my back.

"You're with me," Colson said from behind me, and if I could pull out the arrector pili muscles from my body, so that I wouldn't have to feel any more goosebumps when Colson spoke to me, I'd do it in a heartbeat.

"Yeah, ride with us, please!" The girls all sang in unison, as if I had a choice. I mean, the only real choice now was to abandon the trip and not find a tree.

But I had been planning this trip with Rae for weeks, and honestly, I felt like I had dibs.

Giving them a tight smile, I nodded. "Of course, I will."

Maybe I could squeeze in with the girls in the back seat.

"Okay, let's get out of here. If you get lost or fall behind, it's off mile marker twenty-seven, and then just a mile up, right off the road." Rae spoke to the group while Davis wrapped his hand around hers.

I broke away, following Colson while Mila and Seraphina each held one of my hands.

"Okay, I have a booster seat for you, Mila," Colson said, setting the smaller seat in the back. He bent down and then hauled her up until she was situated. Maddy crawled in beside her, then Seraphina. Then Colson handed them each a brand-new blanket roll, tied with ribbon and everything.

The girls gasped excitedly. "Thank you, Uncle Cole!"

They each undid the tie on their fleece blanket and snuggled up with it in the seat.

"Can we watch 'Frozen' as we drive up?" Mila asked, brushing the soft material of the blanket against her face.

"Of course, I already have it in the DVD player."

He shut their door, and I realized I was just standing there next to the truck, watching this entire thing, enthralled by the way he spoke to the girls, and the way he treated each of them with such tenderness. It was in such contrast with how he handled me, how he spoke to me. He was a rough piece of sandpaper, rubbing against every single part of me with every interaction we had.

Stepping up into the passenger side of the truck, I set my things on the floor and buckled while trying to ignore the man next to me. At least the movie would be playing so that there'd be something that blocked out the silence or any attempts he might want to make to talk to me again.

Once his truck started, Colson looked behind him at the girls. "Everyone have their headphones on?"

All the girls told him yes in unison and a little too loudly from not being able to hear.

Damn his newer truck and all the fancy bells and whistles it had.

We followed Davis and Rae as they headed out of Macon and up the mountain. The weight of the sky seemed to lie on every branch as we drove further up Mount Macon. What was normally a green and lush, scenic drive was whitewashed by the storm. With a graying sky overhead, and a road completely white, tall road markers helped to navigate where the cliff-side started.

The only sound in the car was Colson's engine as he increased and decreased his speed.

"Look, about last night..." he finally said, quietly.

I refused to look at him, so I kept my face glued to the window, watching the vast white landscape as we made our way up the grade.

"I know what I did was shitty. I didn't sleep because of how I treated you. I know you probably hate me, but I wanted to apologize."

"Okay. Apology received." I muttered rudely.

I was being petulant, but my scalp was still tender from where he'd grabbed my hair, and my mouth and throat were still sore from how hard I'd sucked his dick. With a normal healthy relationship, those feelings the day after would be welcome, but after he acted like I had invaded his space? Not a fucking chance.

"Is that the same as accepting the apology?"

Not even close.

The silence grew as I continued to ignore him.

"I shouldn't have taken advantage of you." He seemed to mutter to himself, while shaking his head.

That made my head snap in his direction.

"You didn't. If you recall, I asked you to…" I peered over my shoulders to be sure the girls weren't listening, and whispered, "*go all the way.*"

He glanced toward me and then returned his gaze to the road.

"But you were drunk, and I pressured you to come to my house…"

Scoffing, I adjusted in my seat. "Well…yeah, you were just as drunk as I was, and yes, you did pressure me into coming over. That whole bit is getting annoying."

The dam had burst and I wanted to yell at him for everything he'd done to hurt me.

"You insulted me by telling me I can't do anything on my own, then you kissed me, and then you"—I paused, looking again over my shoulder —"*kissed a part of me that you hadn't ever kissed before*…and then you kicked me out of your house."

"I didn't kick you out."

"You did! I offered to rinse off…together, and you acted like I was a stranger and told me to get out. You didn't even walk me to my door."

I moved my head again, watching the window that had started fogging up.

"You know what…it's my fault." I pointed to myself. "I keep letting you help me, and that's the problem."

"You can accept help from people, Nora, that doesn't make you weak."

Davis hit his brakes in front of us and put his blinker on, which was a relief because that meant we were almost there.

"It is a problem when the person who keeps offering to help tries to kiss you, or make you orgasm, then gives you whiplash by pulling back and acting uninterested."

"What's an orgasm?" Maddy asked from the back seat, and my face caught fire.

Colson held back a laugh as he watched her in the rearview mirror. "*Organism.* Nora said it wrong, and that's an animal, plant, or single-celled life-form."

"Oh, okay." Maddy put her headphones back on and continued watching her movie.

"You're right. I think you should be able to accept help from a friend without the lines being blurred, and I can promise you that I'm done blurring them."

At this point, I was tired of him apologizing. And the fact that he'd taken what happened last night and was now trying to shove it in the friend zone angered me.

I didn't want to be his friend. I wanted him to want me the way I had for the past year. I wanted him to fall for me the way I had stupidly fallen for him.

The silence expanded between us, growing into something we'd never come back from. I could feel it.

So, I did the only thing I could think of.

"I think we should just go back to how things were before you suddenly decided to play savior. Go back to ignoring me and being completely apathetic toward me. I think that was easier."

He didn't respond, and I was too much of a coward to look over and see what expression he was wearing, or if there was anything at all that would indicate that he agreed or not.

A few minutes later, Colson was pulling in behind Davis and putting the truck in park.

Feeling like a dagger had been jammed into my chest, I exited the truck as quickly as possible and made my way toward Rae.

"I'M SO SORRY ABOUT COLSON." Rae apologized for the millionth time as we walked toward the tree line. Davis and Colson were up ahead with the girls, the clearing was beautiful, covered in deep snow, but undisturbed and quiet. Colson had thought ahead to bring sleds for the girls, and the men ahead of us were pulling them behind them, creating this insanely unfair image for anyone with eyes.

"It's fine, there's nothing you can do about the fact that Davis and Colson love each other almost as much as we do." I laughed, bumping shoulders with her.

"I feel like there's stuff you're not telling me about you two. Did something happen?"

Guilt heaved somewhere behind my belly button. Normally I would have already told her about everything, but when she had called me last night, it was to spill that she'd gotten engaged. There wasn't a chance in hell I was going to ruin that moment.

"Yeah, kinda…I mean, I told you about him inviting me with the girls that one day, but yesterday he found me walking home from my parents' house."

Rae lifted her knees to clear the snow, while peering over at me with worry etched into her features.

"Yeah, they are leaving me their house. They'll continue to pay the mortgage while I live there, you know…since I'm broke and have no way of supporting myself."

Rae stopped walking, which forced me to turn and the wind was blowing west, so a gust of snow flurries hit me in the face.

"Are you joking, they actually offered you their house?" Her eyes tightened while her mouth popped open.

Wiping my lashes and face, I resumed my trek forward. "Yep."

Rae made a sound of exasperation, but the distance was closing between us and the men, so I rushed the story to go over everything that happened, including our conversation in the truck.

Setting her gaze on the approaching group, Rae whispered, "I'm not even in the relationship and I'm confused."

"It's not a relationship." I muttered before we were within earshot of the guys.

"Okay, Nora, we're heading up this way to find your tree first," Colson said, acting like nothing had happened in the truck.

Stubbornness stirred within me like a tornado.

"No, I can find my own, thanks."

Colson turned to glare at me.

"Are you fucki—" His gaze dropped to the girls briefly, correcting his cursing. "Are you freaking kidding me?"

I didn't reply because I didn't feel his rudeness warranted one.

"Colson, chill with the tone." Rae cut in, her arm looping through Davis's while her gaze narrowed on the man in question.

With a muscle in his jaw jumping and a scowl cut my way, he challenged.

"You do realize you'll have to cut it down yourself?"

Crossing my arms and staring him down defiantly, I said, "I know how to cut down a tree."

He tilted his head back and let out an exasperated sigh. His annoyance was obvious, but I didn't care.

"Okay, then here." Colson handed me a long axe, not the little hand saw he had, or the chain saw. "Go get your own tree."

Rae's eyebrows rose as she held her hand out and argued. "She most certainly will not. She can't drag the tree all the way through the forest."

"I'm honestly fine, I can get one that's closer to the road."

Colson made some scoffing sound and turned away, pulling both sleds behind him.

I tried not to cave and run after him when little Mila gave me a sad wave, or when Seraphina looked like she might cry.

Fucking hell, had I ruined everyone's day?

I hated this. I didn't want to be around Colson, and why should I be forced to? He essentially took a hatchet to my heart last night and then wandered back this morning to see if I'd accept an apology in the form of a mop, just so he could clean up some of the mess.

Boundaries were good. I was setting one, and that was okay. I didn't want to give the girls any more false hope regarding their pseudo uncle, anyway.

Gripping the handle of the axe as tight as I possibly could, I turned back toward the road. Surely I could find at least one that would be suitable.

As I walked, I could still hear Rae arguing with Davis over the fact that I was chopping the tree alone, which made me feel guilty. I didn't need her to help me, I could do this.

Once I'd walked half the distance back to the truck, I spotted a tree that was a little thin and small but would be perfect for cutting and hauling into the back of Colson's truck bed. I had never axed a tree down in my life, but I chopped wood all the time, how different could it be?

TURNS OUT, cutting a tree down is quite different from chopping up wood. Primarily because the angle is all different, and weird. I was getting so warm with my layers on that I shed them, and then I began swinging like crazy.

I put all the rage and anger from my situation with Colson into the axe as I hit the base, but by the fifth hardy swing, something in my back spasmed and the axe flew out of my hand, landing somewhere behind me.

With a painful shriek, I followed suit, landing in the snow, without my coat, meanwhile the snow fell in heavy clumps again.

Had I mentioned before how much I hated winter? Because this was getting really fucking old.

Although, at the moment, the cold was working as a wonderful numbing agent for whatever it was that I pulled. How stupid could I have been? This wasn't the first time I had done something like this to my back. Once, I carried a large vase when decorating a house, and I threw my back out completely trying to do it alone.

It was embarrassing then, but now...now it was pure, hellfire humiliation.

More and more snow fell on me as I lay there, thinking about my life choices. My face was numb, and as much as I tried to move, it wasn't happening. Not with how deep the snow was, or how bad my back was. Finally, in the distance, I heard the sound of a chain saw being used. Gavin, Davis, and Colson each had one, so there was a small chance that I'd be rescued by one of them within due time.

I secretly prayed that it was Davis who found me first. He would be the only person who wouldn't make it weird, and Rae would be with him. Maybe they could toss me in the back of their truck, along with the tree, and drive me home without anyone knowing what had happened here.

Far off, someone shouted. Then the only sound was the wind blowing through the tops of the evergreens. The snow was burying my stupid body at a concerning rate.

I might have fallen asleep, possibly. But I could hear snow crunching nearby, which caused relief to swell inside my chest. I had no idea how long it took them, but eventually they were close enough for me to hear them say "Shit."

Minutes later, a face materialized over mine, and it was not the face I wanted to see.

"Nora, what the hell happened?" Colson asked as his eyes searched my prone form frantically. His hands were gently wiping snow away, while he lifted my arms and touched my sides and stomach.

My back might be out, but my pride was partially intact.

"A rabid animal came out of nowhere and attacked me…I'm lucky to be alive." I sighed dramatically, as if I had nowhere to go.

Colson must have realized I wasn't bleeding, because he blew out a gust of warm air and stopped prodding my body with his fingers.

"Hmm, that's so interesting…and unfortunate. Just in case that didn't happen, is there any chance you threw your back out?"

I shook my head, which moved some of the fallen snow around. "Not a chance."

Expecting a laugh, or a smirk, he surprised me by stroking my hair and staring at me with a frantic intensity.

"Tell me you're okay, and then tell me you're not going to fight me about being rescued."

Blinking against the onset of flakes, I said, "I'm sure Davis will be coming soon, I can ask for his help."

Clicking his tongue, Colson shook his head. "They took the girls a little further north to show them the reindeer herd."

Dammit.

"You didn't go?" I wasted my breath asking.

It didn't matter, and yet I desperately needed to know why he hadn't gone with them.

He didn't answer, just stared and then let out a heavy sigh before pulling me to his chest. Then he lifted me completely off the ground as though I were made of nothing but air.

"How are you this strong?"

He adjusted me in his arms and walked toward his truck. "I'm used to lifting stubborn women who refuse to accept help, then throw out their backs trying to cut down trees."

Curling into the warmth of his chest while shivers racked my body, I joked.

"You need a new hobby."

He stroked my side, chuckling as we walked.

My stubbornness had finally hit its limits and taken a hike. I'd have to endure receiving help from the man who broke a piece of my heart last night.

Right as I thought we'd head to his truck, he walked past it.

"Why are we going to Davis's truck?"

Shifting me in his arms, he headed toward the passenger side. "We all keep a spare key in the vehicles for emergency purposes. Davis and Rae will bring the girls back in my truck, but I need to get you home."

I was about to tell him it was fine, that I could wait, but as he opened the door and set me inside, a dull throbbing started in my back, followed by a sharp pain that made my breath hitch.

"Relax, if you can. You're tensing up and that will make it worse." Colson brought the buckle across my chest and gently pushed my hair out of my face. "I'm not a fan that you're missing your coat, or that you were lying in the snow without it."

I tried to explain myself, but the only thing that came through my clenched teeth was a painful hiss.

Colson took the hint and ran around the truck, but before we took off, he jotted down something on a little note and ran it back to his truck. Once he returned, we were off.

The trip seemed significantly faster going down the mountain, but it was still too much time being forced into a sitting position. My head had begun to throb, right along with my back, and all I wanted to do was lie flat.

Colson may have talked on the ride, but I didn't remember it. I was so focused on my pain that I closed my eyes the entire trip.

Before long, the truck slowed and stopped.

Then Colson was at my door, carefully pulling me into his arms.

Everything was a blur as he gently laid me down. The first thing he did was bring me a pill with water, which I took without argument. I knew what it was and had used it the last time I was in significant pain. The next thing he did was run a bath, and that's when I realized I wasn't in my house.

I was in his room, on his bed.

"Why am I here?" I asked with a slight wince.

Colson appeared, rolling up his sleeves. "You need Epsom salt, and I think the jets will help you."

Shaking my head, I tried to sort through my thoughts as they grew foggy. "But I just took drugs. I can't be in there."

"You can, I won't leave you."

All my fight was gone, I let him lift my arms, and help me out of my shirt and bra, then watched as he tugged my boots and socks free but refused to watch him peel my jeans down my hips. Even with my eyes on the ceiling, the way his fingers ghosted over my skin made my stomach flicker, like when you find that small flame still licking at the underside of a log long after you assumed the fire was out.

When his strong fingers gripped the waistband of my underwear, he let out a curse as they slid down my legs. It made me think of the night before and how I still had no idea why he'd detached the way he did.

My thoughts fluttered like mist when his arms slid underneath my naked body, and how vulnerable I felt being carried by him. A part of me felt a tether to him, being like this. Like his caring for me wasn't a burden. It was stupid, I knew Colson didn't want to do this, or care for me because he had romantic feelings. I knew he wasn't that person to me, and yet my heart latched on just the same.

My head gently hit the little pillow at the back of his tub as my body sank into the deliciously warm water. His hands left my body but didn't go far as he perched on the edge of the tub.

"This is nice," I said quietly, the pill was already working through me, making every part of me relax. "Don't let me drown, Cole."

I wasn't watching him, but he was there, like a hot sentinel in my periphery.

The strong fingers stroked through my hair as he chuckled. "I won't."

"How come, though? You don't like me, but you keep saving me." My words felt like plastic as they came out, foreign, awkward, and unstable.

His fingers pulled my hair up, off my back. He gathered the curls into his hands and began braiding.

"Who's to say I don't like you?"

It was my turn to laugh, but it came out more like a snort. "Sure, you like me, but refused to be in the same room as me at any given time for the past year, and now you kiss and kick out."

His face became clearer, which meant he'd lowered it, but his fingers were still in my hair. He was so close, I could feel the warmth of his breath on my face, and how it smelled winter fresh.

"Don't you think that if I truly didn't like you, I wouldn't work so hard to avoid you? If I really didn't care, I'd be apathetic toward you. Instead, I had to take extra precautions *not* to be in the same room as you, or to be caught with you while you're wearing sexy workout gear in the grocery store, or letting you see when I noticed how good your ass looked in that tiny robe you wore to check on your garden."

My brain was working so hard to piece together what he was saying, but each word seemed to turn into bubbles in my mind, rotating, shifting, and drifting away.

His lips were hovering over mine with the slightest press, he said, "You're addictive Nora...tempting, alluring, and completely devastating. Of course I stayed away."

That was the last thing I heard before his hands were under me again, lifting me out of the water.

12

NORA

A GROGGY HEADACHE pulled me from sleep.

Blinking at the smothered light leaking in from the large curtains in the room, I assumed it was early morning, that or it had snowed again.

Where was my phone, anyway?

Reaching my hand out across the bed had me wincing in pain.

My back, that's right. I wasn't even home, I was…

"Good, you're awake." Colson walked into the bedroom, sounding pleased.

I couldn't see him from where I lay on my stomach, but I heard him round the bed, and then the curtains were pulled open.

Letting out a hiss, I tried to pull the pillow over my eyes, but Colson stopped me.

"Here, come on, we need to get you up."

I wasn't an invalid, I could move, and I certainly didn't need his help.

Colson came into my line of sight, wearing low jeans that showed the white band of his boxer briefs, and absolutely no shirt. His muscled chest and fifteen thousand abs were on display, completely lickable and so indecent.

Batting away his outstretched hand, I rolled to my back, but I hadn't realized I was naked.

My breasts pebbled, my nipples beading against the frigid air.

Colson stared, but didn't move to touch, or help me cover up. Without being able to lift my chest, I couldn't bend to grab the cover that had slipped off.

"Do you mind getting me the sheet?"

Colson's hand reappeared in front of my face. "I do mind...we need to get you up."

"I'm naked..."

Smirking and moving his hand to mine, he helped me.

"I've seen you naked, Nora."

Having no other choice but to move as he pulled and helped me up, my feet hit the floor and within seconds of trying to stand, I was falling into Colson's chest.

Fuck.

Trying to push off, I gave him a hard glare. "Yeah, but you're supposed to forget what I look like naked because you were mean to me..." Although there was this strange, foggy sensation that last night he wasn't mean, in fact, last night he'd been the complete opposite.

"Nora, I could never forget what you look like naked. You have the most fuckable body I have ever seen in my life."

He helped me to his master bathroom, where the Jacuzzi tub was off to one side, but a shower was on the other. Surrounded by inset stone, the glass door hung from chrome hinges.

"You can't say I have a fuckable body, Colson, that's rude. Can't you quote poetry or something about the bodies you admire? Not mine per se, but one day when you find someone to settle down with?"

Colson pulled on the handle for the shower and turned on the faucet. The warm spray hit the stone floor, and the heat rose, clouding the glass door.

"Who exactly is getting in this shower?" Because it wasn't me...I didn't have clothes, or my hair products, or anyone to help me get dressed. I didn't want Colson to be my nursemaid.

Adjusting the temperature while he grasped my elbow, he turned to smile at me.

"You are."

Shaking my head, I tried to pull away from him, but it made burning hot pain shoot up along my back.

"I took a bath last night, right? I mean, do I smell bad? I don't want a shower right now."

I vaguely recalled him placing me in the tub last night, and saying something while sitting on the ledge, but it was foggy.

"You don't smell, but I figured it would make you feel better."

Shaking my head, I tried again to pull away from him, with no success. Observing my expression, he exhaled irritably and reached to turn off the spray.

"Fine, I'll bring you clothes, and you can dress, then eat."

Then hopefully go home.

He helped me back to the bed where I perched on the edge, and when he came back in with a pair of his sweats and another hoodie, I nearly cried.

I hated him for what he did to me that night. While I could handle casual hookups with men, and not expect them to want to cuddle after sex, Colson had been sending me too many mixed signals for me not to be hurt by his actions.

"I'm not wearing those." I eyed the pile distastefully.

They were a different pair entirely from the ones he'd given me the other night, but it didn't matter.

"Look, where are my clothes from yesterday? I'll dress and go home, Rae can come over and help me, or my mother."

A line formed between Colson's eyebrows. "I called them…"

My stomach flipped upside down as heat infused my face. I hadn't expected him to have already called them. I mean, of course he did. It wasn't like he'd signed up for Nora duty two days in a row.

"Oh." I muttered, unsure what to say to that.

Colson searched my face, which was distracting because he was still shirtless and I could still see the band of his boxers around his waist, that V muscle leading down to his deliciously thick cock was all veiny perfection and, in another world, I'd step forward and lick it.

"Rae can't get away today because she took off yesterday, but she will try and come by for dinner. And your mom…"

I already knew. I just did...she and my dad were acting weird lately and while I didn't understand all of it, a piece of me assumed that they were trying to prepare me for what life would be like when they weren't here.

"Well, if you wouldn't mind helping me to my house, I can stay there. It's really not a big deal to be alone."

"Nora." Colson sighed, rubbing a hand through his hair. It made the strands all messy and disheveled. "Look, I'm between projects right now. I have the time to help you and the proximity, so can you just let me?"

I knew it seemed like I was trying to be difficult, but I wasn't. I was merely preserving what was left of my pride, and the few pieces of my heart that he managed to mangle.

"No, you hurt me, Colson. I don't want to be here with you. I don't want you to take care of me. I want to go home."

His blue eyes were stone as he stared.

I stared back just as hard as the silence between us grew.

Suddenly he roared "Fuck," tossed the pile of sweats out of the way, and paced the room. "Do you think I wanted to kick you out that night? Honestly, with the way I spoke to you, the way I hoarded your presence all fucking night, you think I wanted to do that?"

What was he even talking about? Did he think I was stupid?

"Yes, I do. You basically buttered me up all night, got what you wanted, and then kicked me to the curb."

His tone tipped into incredulous territory as his hands went up. "Got what I wanted?"

Two long strides brought him closer to me, he was raising his voice but only in passion, not *at* me, so I didn't feel afraid. I felt confused more than anything.

But also, if my hammering heart was any indication, I was also feeling exhilarated.

"Nora, what I wanted was to bring you back here, to my bedroom. Throw you on the bed and fuck you. All night. I wanted your face on my sheets, while your ass was in the air and my cock slid in and out of you. I wanted you to straddle me, sliding up and down on my cock as you screamed my name. I wanted"—his voice caught as he looked to the side—

"I wanted all night and then I wanted breakfast with you. That is what I fucking wanted, Nora."

His face had gotten so close, I could smell the aroma of coffee on his breath. It was a good smell, made me want to curl into him like I did when he found me in the snow.

I had so many questions, but words were hard to form, so I just stared.

"I know you hate me. I get it, and I won't try to kiss you, or touch you inappropriately, but please let me take care of you."

My heart swooped and my stomach clenched tight.

Why did it sound so good to be here with him, but also feel so perilous for my tattered emotions? He didn't explain why he'd gone against what he wanted and hurt me the other night. He merely said it wasn't what he wanted, which, as far as liars went, Colson didn't seem to be one.

Complicated, annoying, and prideful, but not a liar.

So it begged the question of what in the hell he was talking about. If he didn't want to kick me out, then why did he?

I had a feeling I wouldn't be getting an answer anytime soon, so I sagged into the bed and gave him a small nod.

"I'll stay."

Heaving a relieved sigh, Colson smiled.

"Let me get you those sweats."

COLSON HAD SET me up in his living room for most of the day, but by dinner, I was ready to be in a bed. I'd called my doctor and spoke with her about my pain. She encouraged use of ice, Epsom salt baths, and pain relief pills as needed. I knew I was mostly up against the clock because the last time my back was hurt like this, it took three days before I could move regularly again.

Rae had checked on me, but I assured her that I was okay at Colson's, so she went home.

My mother never called.

Colson had surprised me with how gentle he was and considerate.

Which, with the way he cared for the girls, shouldn't have been a surprise but was. Anytime I had to go to the bathroom, he'd carefully take my hand and lead me at a snail's pace to the door. He'd actually thought I was going to let him in the bathroom with me while I peed. Hilarious.

I informed him that I would literally rather die than have him see me or even hear me relieve myself.

With anything that I pushed back on, he'd shake his head and give up. I knew as long as I wasn't trying to leave his house, I could pretty much push back on anything. Like taking narcotics. I didn't like being foggy brained, so I chose to rely on Ibuprofen and Tylenol. I'd taken two baths today, both of which he let me have privacy for while I watched an episode of Vampire Diaries on his laptop. It was sweet.

He'd been sweet all day.

And I didn't want to take advantage of him, but I was curious how far that kindness might extend.

"Okay, you ready for another bath?" Colson asked, helping me to my feet.

Wincing, I took each step slow and measured.

"Actually, I was wondering..." My nerves got the best of me.

Colson squeezed my hand as he helped me walk, encouraging me to continue.

We made it to the hall, and I was two seconds away from asking him to just get a blanket and pull me on the hardwood floor.

"Well, would you maybe be willing to massage my back?" I asked hesitantly, then feeling worried, rushed to add, "Not in a sexual way, just a medical way. I was thinking if you applied some pressure to the nerve that's hurting, it could help."

"Of course I can." Colson's tone held the smallest tinge of apprehension in it. I wondered if he was as worried about touching me as I was about letting him touch me.

Once we made it to his room, we stopped on my side...or where I slept the night prior.

Still holding both my hands, Colson faced me and looked down.

"You'll have to get out of this sweatshirt..."

Wetting my lips, I gave him a small nod before reaching for the hem of the sweater.

"Here, I'll help you. Do you want a tank top or—"

Shaking my head, I cut him off. "I was thinking naked, with a sheet over my butt. That way, after the massage, if you use oils or lotion, I can just get in the bath directly afterward."

"Smart."

His hands gripped the hood as he helped lift it off me, then tossed it on the ground. Next, I slowly pushed down the sweats. I had no underwear on because of how many times I had to bathe, so once they hit the floor, I carefully stepped out and tried not to notice the way Colson's throat bobbed.

"How about you start on your back and gently roll to your front?" Colson offered, but it actually hurt more to do it that way.

"Here, just hold my hand while I get on," I said while pressing my knee into the mattress. He held me, and when I wobbled to the side, his hand went to my rib, stabilizing me. From there I put my left hand up by the pillows, and then adjusted so my other knee could come up, and I was on all fours.

"Okay, now for the getting flat part." I muttered, completely unfazed anymore that Colson was seeing me vulnerable and naked. His hand gently gripped my rib cage as I pushed my palms forward and lowered myself inch by inch.

"Ahh," I slipped forward too fast, making my back spasm, but Colson's other hand came under me, catching me so that I didn't fall all the way down.

"Here," he said, helping me until I was flat on the mattress, "need any pillows moved, or anything?"

"Can you just get the sheet and pull it up?" I asked, as my face turned and sunk into the top of my forearm.

Colson didn't reply, but seconds later the cool sheet was slowly drifting up and over my calves, up my thighs until it reached the curve of my ass.

"Thank you."

Colson made a sound, but honestly, I couldn't make it out.

"Let me go grab some massage oils." He left, and when he came back, he lowered the overhead light and flicked on his gas fireplace. It was so cozy and intimate that I instantly relaxed. Especially when I felt his body press into the bed. Somehow, throughout the course of the day, he'd made me feel safe.

"Nora, the position I'm going to need to be in is going to be a little awkward. I'd need to essentially straddle your ass. You okay with that?"

Butterflies shot off inside my belly, swooping and diving into molten lava that had already begun erupting in my core.

I hated how badly I wanted him, and how I couldn't seem to turn that off, even with a back injury.

Swallowing hard, I whispered. "Yes."

As careful as ever, his thighs spread out over my hips, and I could feel his semi-hard erection press up against my rear. I tried not to get worked up about that, I knew he couldn't control when he became hard…and having a naked woman underneath him would be nearly impossible not to get worked up over.

The first drop of oil hit my back in a cool, soothing squirt, and before it had a chance to run off my back, his hands were massaging it into my skin.

It felt incredible to have the tightness worked out of my muscles. I whimpered with pleasure as he applied pressure and traced a line up the center of my spine.

He worked my tissue, adding more oils and massaging his fingertips into my skin as he went, and with each stroke, he seemed to become harder behind me.

My noises continued to increase as his fingers dug deep and worked out stress.

"You're really good at this." I rasped in between moans.

"Good," he said, but his voice was hoarse.

Colson moved his fingers up my neck, applying pressure in long strokes, and then he moved back down my back. I had no idea how much time had passed as I felt myself go in and out as my muscles relaxed.

"Do you plan on staying here," Colson randomly asked, making my eyes pop open. "I mean, in Macon, the town, with your parents leaving. Will you go too?"

I didn't even have to think about that one. "I plan on staying. I can't do superhot temperatures. I realized this when I was in California for college."

"Really?" He laughed, moving his hands up and across my shoulder blades. "Did you go to the beach?"

Shrugging, I thought back to when I lived there. "Yeah, I loved the beaches but I didn't get to go that often and I missed home a lot. I love this area with the trees and mountains. I love hiking when there aren't blizzards."

His light laugh was like a tiny flame flickering in my heart.

"What about you? Did you like Malibu?"

Colson shifted. "Yeah, I like it just fine, but I don't like living near my family. If they moved up here, I'd move away. I mean, probably. Unless I was married and settled down."

Shocked, I made some sound and annoyingly asked, "You want a family?" As if I couldn't picture him with one. But I could.

Easily.

"Yeah, I do, eventually. I want a wife, some kids…probably a dog."

Smiling into my forearms, I agreed. "I want that too someday, kids, a dog…a husband."

Colson paused for a second, freezing his ministrations.

"You don't think it's a prison to be settled? Or are you saying you want that in like ten years?"

Why did he want me to be so specific? It was an odd way of asking his question, but I went along with it.

"I think it would depend on if I met the right guy sooner rather than later. Starting a family is just as big of an adventure as traveling the globe and flying to catch every sunset. If I had to pick between the two, I'd choose the pitter patter of little feet, and strong arms to lie in at night."

He didn't say anything for a long time, and neither did I.

I had no idea why he was asking these questions, but it didn't matter.

Not when his fingers dipped below the sheet.

"Just want to get the lower back a bit better," he said, gently moving the fabric.

I swallowed thickly as his hands slowly rubbed in slow circles. Those fingers kept trailing lower and lower…until he was massaging the top of my ass cheek.

"This okay?" His voice sounded as though it had been drug through glass, and for some strange reason, I wanted to hear it again.

"Yeah."

Colson took advantage, squirting more oil, rubbing and massaging. He swiped left and right over my skin, teasing me like crazy. He was so close to all my intimate places, it made me desperate for his long fingers to dip lower until he was sinking into my heat.

But I didn't say anything, I just let him rub and add more oil. Finally, after the second round of massaging my butt, his fingers dipped inward, along the crack.

He acted like it was normal, and I didn't say anything to stop him.

His fingers swiped up and down the crack, and over the tight hole. I wanted him to linger there, to apply pressure, or do something to make me feel as brazen as I did the other night. This was dirty and naughty, and I wanted to revel in it.

"Can you apply a little pressure right there?" I asked, unsure what he'd say as a response, but it was worth a shot.

He didn't hesitate at all, his thumb covered the hole as he asked, "Right here?"

I nodded. "Yeah, it's tight. Can you apply some pressure, maybe loosen it up?" I realized it was a bad line, so cheesy it probably wouldn't pass in a porno, but I didn't care. I was beyond caring when it came to wanting him.

Again, he didn't skip a beat, he played along, and it made my heart feel light.

"It is tight." He hissed, pushing his thumb in the slightest bit. "I may need a few minutes with it."

I tried not to come on the spot from how good it felt to have one hand massage my ass cheek and the other massage my asshole, but the two together were euphoric.

Slightly applying pressure with his thumb, he twisted his hand until his fingers dipped lower, sinking into my center.

I hissed approval as he said, "There we go."

Fuck, it felt so good.

"You're dripping on my sheets, aren't you, Nora?" He drew his fingers out of my wetness and then plunged them back in. I inhaled a sharp breath at his sudden change and the sexy tone. He sounded like he was two seconds from fucking me senseless.

"Answer me, Nora, are you wet for me?"

I hoarsely replied, "Yes."

"Good girl, I want you wet for me, anytime I'm touching you." His fingers moved, fucking me with brash strokes, pushing in and pulling out. He withdrew, rubbing my wetness along my crack, and applied pressure to that tight hole.

"Nora, do you know how badly I want to fill you up right now?" A wet sound filled the room as his fingers worked my pussy, building my orgasm higher and higher.

"Colson," I begged, moving my hips the smallest bit.

Truth was, I had no idea if he could fuck me, when it came to him touching me, I lost all sense and reason.

"Nora, you need to tell me if I can fill you...because with you on my bed, naked, your oiled skin at my fingertips...I'm either going to fuck my hand until I come all over your backside, or you're going to tell me if I can slide inside you."

Oh my God.

The image was so erotic, my breath compressed.

Swallowing the dryness in my throat, I said, "Yes."

Suddenly, the head of his cock was at my entrance. "You're okay that I enter without a condom?"

I exhaled slowly, feeling the massive head already begin to surge forward. "Yes."

He growled, adjusting himself, and then he began sinking inside me.

My mouth parted as my pussy stretched around him. I'd had him in my mouth, so I knew how big he was, but feeling him stretch me was completely different.

"Oh my God." I rasped, clinging to the sheets.

His hand moved to the dip in my back, holding me in place.

"We're just going to hang out right here, let you feel the tip of my cock while I play with your asshole, and see how fast you come on my cock."

I had never been more desperate to move my hips than I was right at that moment.

But we did as he said, the tip stayed at my entrance, slowly stretching me, while his thumb surged into my hole with more pressure than before.

Feeling both places so full had me gasping, clenching the sheets in my fists.

"Nora, tell me to stop." He groaned, shifting his hips forward the smallest bit, which pushed his erection a few inches deeper.

Right as he did it, his thumb went deeper simultaneously.

I cried out, gasping and trying to catch my breath as an orgasm tore through me.

"That's it, let go." He moved again, pushing in even further.

My mind reeled at the idea that Colson Hanes was pushing his cock inside of me right now, we weren't fucking so to speak, but he was spreading me open.

"Just a little bit more, and you'll have taken all of me." He shuddered before pushing further in.

His hands were on my hips as he held me in place, my face still down on the sheets, my fingers curling into the fabric as he stretched me.

"You're so tight…fucking hell, so"—he inhaled sharply—"so tight."

With one last push, he was fully sheathed.

I welcomed the bit of a burn as we sat like that, thankful he'd relented on my tighter hole because burning in two places at once without the option to actually fuck him wasn't my idea of fun.

"Nora." Colson breathed, shuddering the smallest bit. "I wish you could see how fucking good we look like this, my cock buried inside of you, connected this way."

I made a sound, but I still couldn't think past how full I felt with him being buried inside of me.

His hips shifted the smallest bit, pulling out and then moving forward once more.

Colson gasped, and then bit out, "I'm going to come…fuck, shit." His breathing was labored. He started pulling out when I lifted my hips and clamped down.

"Inside me," I hurried to say and then he was thrusting, filling me so insanely full that when he yelled "fuckkk," I screamed his name, coming for a second time.

Our breaths were heavy as we both sagged into the bed.

"Holy shit." He gasped, then slowly pulled out of me.

"Now we both need a bath."

I smiled into the sheets, knowing he couldn't see me yet.

"Colson," I said softly, trying to get his attention.

He moved until he was lying next to me, his big arm wrapped around my waist.

"Yeah?"

I wanted to say so many things…all the things that had begun building in my chest like little Lego blocks. Building the smallest, most fragile bridges to his heart. But I was still nervous that he'd pull away the second things got too real for him.

So, I simply said, "I get the bath. You can have the shower."

13

COLSON
TWELVE YEARS OLD

DEAR MOM,

    I don't understand what's going on...when I saw you last week, you acted like things were getting better. I'm trying, Mom. I've been trying... but it hurts that you're in there because your mind won't let you be out here with me. I'm pretty sure Dad is doing something bad with his receptionist... I try not to be nosy anymore, when spying only makes things worse. But what am I supposed to do, Mom? When I see you, and you write to me, it doesn't feel like you're depressed. It doesn't feel like you'll hurt yourself. I wish you'd come back for me. I wish I was enough for you. – Love, Cole

    Dear Cole,

    I love you so much, my sweet boy. Everything will be okay. You'll see. I'm getting the help I need, and I'll be home soon. Your dad and I are working it out, don't you worry about it. How's my garden doing? Do you talk to the plants, have you named any of them? I hope you do, talking to plants is therapeutic and can help you process feelings you might not know you're repressing. Stay strong, sweet boy. – Love, Mom

NORA SLEPT CURLED against me all night.

After the massage where I worked more than just her muscles, we took a bath together. She'd joked about me taking a shower, but when I went to help her in, I stepped in first and pulled her to me as we lowered into the water.

She had lain in my arms, soaking while watching her show, and it was oddly one of the most tranquil moments of my existence. The image would stay in my memory forever as a reminder of what it was like to hold the woman I was falling in love with.

It was shit timing to discover it, but the more I thought over what Peter had said, the more I realized I had been falling and dodging this for a while. I couldn't keep pretending like this wasn't what I wanted. I couldn't shove her away or push her off...all I could think about was being near her.

Handing her a mug of coffee, I stared at her while I sipped mine. Her back seemed to be doing much better when she got out of bed and as she maneuvered around my house.

"We still have to put your tree in your house."

Her aqua eyes jumped to mine in surprise. "Someone actually brought it back?"

I nodded. "Davis and Rae tossed it in the back with theirs."

"Let's go." She started toward the front where her boots were.

Walking up behind her, I tugged her to my chest and kissed the side of her neck.

"Just hang on for a second, okay?"

She breathed in deeply. "Okay."

"What if we make a day of it, have the girls come over and help us decorate it?"

She seemed to consider that, but after a few seconds, she pulled out of my arms.

"I would love that...but I missed two whole days of work. I have to get back to it. Can we connect once I've made some headway on my project?"

Feeling the smallest fissure crack open in my chest, I nodded.

"Of course."

We also needed to talk about what we were to one another…I knew the whole relationship discussion was a taboo subject, but I didn't want Nora to have to guess where I was at with things. Having her in my house and having sex made me realize that I didn't want to risk losing her. We were figuring it out, and I wanted the ability and freedom to pursue that.

Peter was right, all I could think of was how easy it would be to give up on the idea of having the company as long as it meant I could keep her. It confused me…I wanted the company more than anything, but after last night…I wasn't so sure anymore.

CLICKING THROUGH MY EMAILS, I was about to close my laptop when one caught my eye. It had been sent a week ago, but I must have glanced over it or missed it. Hesitating, I hovered my mouse over the subject and then reluctantly opened it.

> DEAR COLE,
> I HEARD YOU WERE COMING TO MALIBU FOR CHRISTMAS; I REALLY WANT TO SEE YOU WHEN YOU'RE HERE. I KNOW THE LAST TIME I WAS UP IN PORTLAND YOU COULDN'T DRIVE AND SEE ME… BUT IF YOU COULD FIND TIME FOR ME, I WOULD BE GRATEFUL.

I STARED at the white space under the email where her name should be, or some sort of sign off and scoffed. Still the same bullshit as ever, her trying not to be who she is to me and trying not to remind me who she is. I hated that she was still doing this.

Aside from her email, and frustrating sign off, I hadn't confirmed that I would be attending Christmas. Pulling my cell, I dialed my little brother.

He answered on the third ring.

"Heyyy, if it isn't my long-lost big brother!"

"Nate, why does the family seem to think I'm attending Christmas in California?"

My brother made some sort of chewing sound on his end before replying.

"Dad said you confirmed."

Rolling my eyes, I tilted the phone as I spun in my office chair.

"Why would you assume I did?"

The silence lasted for a bit longer than I was comfortable and then he said, "Because of Mom…I just assumed you'd come back for—"

Sitting up, trying to regulate my heart rate, I cut him off.

"Stop."

I wasn't prepared to talk about her…not like this, so suddenly.

My younger brother's voice was soft as he cautiously pushed on. "Well, if not for her, then would you just come for us? We miss you…fuck Dad, and everyone else. Come visit your little brothers. We haven't seen you in forever."

He was right, it had been well over a year since I had seen them, and our talks were getting sparse.

I had promised that I would go back more often.

Fuck it.

"Fine, I'll come."

"Yesss, you better be ready to surf. Trevor thinks he's the best of us, and I need you to knock him on his ass."

Chuckling, I agreed and then caught up with him about his life before ending the call.

Christmas in Malibu.

Shit.

Snapping my laptop shut, I stood and grabbed my keys.

I'd given Nora the entire day to work. It was time for dinner, and to discuss what we were to one another or maybe we could let things progress naturally without any conversations…

I headed to the market first, grabbing soup, fresh rolls, and a bouquet of bright yellow flowers with specks of gold and red inside. I had no idea what they were called, but they reminded me of her.

Parking in my driveway, I grabbed all the goods and headed across the small gap between the low fence that separated our properties.

Nora's house had a nice tendril of smoke coming from the top of her chimney, and several of her lights were on inside. My stomach somersaulted the way it did the first time I realized she'd moved in next to me a few months back. I remembered how I would come home, see her car in the driveway, and imagine what it would be like to walk over, knock on her door and lean in and kiss her. I used to wonder what she would do if I showed her how many times I left Post-it notes for her in the work trailer, only to have her assume it was one of the other guys who worked there.

She'd been in my head for a lot longer than she would ever realize. My heart was finally processing that it could expel that fucking thorn that had been wedged there for a year and it felt refreshing as fuck.

Before I even knocked, the door swung open, and Nora stood smiling at me.

"Hey!"

I smiled, walking inside. "Hey."

She shut the door, and I took a second to take in her wild curls, the black-rimmed glasses perched on her nose, the slim white tank top, baggy sweats, and thick socks. I had rubbed every inch of her back the night before, and yet seeing her with those tiny straps holding up her full breasts made me want to drag them down her arms.

"What are you—" she started to ask, but I stepped up and pressed my lips to hers, cutting her off. Our mouths moved slow, sensual and hungry. I may have had my dick inside of her last night, but kissing her and feeling those delicate fingers wrap up around my neck and push through my hair was better than anything I could ask for.

"Sorry," I pulled away and then kissed her jaw before heading to the kitchen.

She followed after me, rubbing her arms.

"Wow, you brought dinner and flowers?" She moved to the flowers, gently touching each petal. "These are beautiful."

I set the pint of soup out and turned to grab a bowl from her cupboard.

"Thank you, this was all so thoughtful."

A few minutes later, we both sat on opposite ends of the couch, eating our soup while the news played on the television. I couldn't get over how normal it felt, and unhurried. How ending every day should look like this.

"Can you believe how much snow Portland got this year? It's not even Christmas…they're totally buried." Nora shook her head, watching the screen.

For some reason my stomach tilted with the words I wanted to say to her, but I had no idea where to start…or for that matter, what to say. All I knew was that I liked her, and I really fucking wanted to keep kissing her.

"How was your day, did you get everything done?" I asked, glancing briefly at the bare tree sitting in the corner of her living room. I'd brought it in for her earlier but honored her request not to decorate it until she had a chance to catch up on work.

"I got a lot done, not everything…actually not even close to everything. I ended up having a bad spasm hit my back that had me down for a while. I had my laptop, but I couldn't draw the way I needed to."

"Shit, I wish you would have said something." I sipped my water and set my empty bowl on the table.

"It's okay, I took a muscle relaxer, and it was fine after a while."

She folded her legs underneath her, and watched me spin the cup on my kneecap.

I had no idea how to start this.

Nora cleared her throat and said, "Actually, so I…" She faltered a little bit, making my eyes jump up. "I wanted to talk to you about something."

I moved so I was facing her.

Taking a deep breath, she set her seltzer on the table and brought her hands together.

"Well, I had some time to think about last night, and us…and all the questions I still had around where we stood with stuff."

Perking up, my heart raced at the fact that we were already on the same page with things.

Wetting her lips, she lightly pushed a few curls behind her ears.

"I think the best course of action is to just let things be physical between us. We went a year avoiding one another, and on my end, there were strong feelings, and it seems on your end I have no idea…Either way, it built this tension that finally seemed to force you into my life, still not sure why."

I let out a frustrated breath. "Do you still need a reason?" I was defensive as fuck, but the idea of her finally realizing why I had been forced into her life only meant she'd want me out of it again.

Eyeing me curiously, she moved on. "We obviously are attracted to one another...I think a no strings situation is the best course of action."

For a moment, I stared at her, unsure if I had heard her correctly.

"So, you're suggesting we..."

She shrugged her shoulder. "Hook up, have sex, enjoy each other...but nonexclusive, if you find someone, then you'll tell me and same if I do. But no sleeping with each other and other people at the same time."

I didn't even know what to think...my brain felt like one of those "this is your mind on drugs" commercials, except Nora was the drugs. The idea of her out dating someone else made me feel murderous, but so did the idea of not getting to touch her or hold her anytime I wanted to. If this was the closest I'd ever come to having her, then I would have to take it. Might be the closest I'd ever get.

"What do you think?" Nora asked, toying with one of her curls. Part of me wondered if she was testing me, hoping I'd turn her down and demand more from her. Unfortunately, I couldn't risk saying that and scaring her off. So I dipped my head, thought over all my options, panicked, and then fell back into the same default bullshit mode I had existed in for the past year. I'd continue to shove my feelings down and take whatever I could get.

"Okay. No strings...no expectations."

She watched me, as if she was waiting for something more, but I wasn't in any position to expand, or give her that. As it was, I was barely holding it together. My shitty dinner and flowers made me look like I wanted more from her and were probably the reason she spilled all of this tonight. I'd already fucking terrified the girl.

Finally, she crawled toward me, put her hand on my chest, and lightly pressed. "And no feelings."

Right...that part.

I nodded and cupped her face, pulling her lips to mine.

If she wanted just physical, then that's what I'd give her.

She moved with me, kissing me back, sliding her tongue against mine, and it worked to erase any insecurities I had.

This was enough.

Having her like this, in my arms, where I could kiss her whenever I wanted…it was enough.

MY BOSS LIFTED HIS GAZE, and it seemed to shudder a bit when he saw me.

My mind instantly went to Nora, and whether I should drop the news and tell him that I was falling for his daughter, and while it was no strings fun right now, one day it would be more. His distracted demeanor gave me pause. I'd wait to see what he had to say first.

"Boss." I greeted him and took a seat.

The café was bustling with people, and for some reason my eyes bounced up and darted around the room, looking to see if Nora was somewhere in the fray. That had been something I had tried to stop doing a while ago, it wasn't good that it had started up again. No strings, I tried to remind myself.

"Good morning, Colson. How was your night?" Peter asked, taking a sip of his coffee.

My stomach twisted tight with the memory of Nora falling asleep on my chest the night prior. Instead, I merely shook my head.

"Fine. Same as usual."

"Good, then let's get to business."

My lungs extracted the smallest relieved breath as Peter discussed what had brought us here this morning.

"My wife has put her foot down and wants to be in Arizona before Christmas."

Wait…why the fuck would she do that? What about Nora?

Peter continued, breaking into my thoughts. "So, I'm cutting the cord.

I'm handing all my projects over to you as far as the bids go. I'm not sure I'll get to them until after the holidays."

The barista walked over right then and asked for my order. It was enough of an interruption to allow me to process what he'd said and all that it implied.

"Sorry, sir…I guess I'm confused. Why the sudden rush? I mean, I realize your wife wants to get out of here, but did something happen to make her want to leave immediately?"

All I could think of was what Nora had mentioned the other night about arguing with them, and it not going well.

"My wife has two sisters who moved to Arizona as well, she's eager to be near them and with the last big storm that blew through, she's ready for the warmer weather."

He let out a heavy sigh, worry creasing the spaces near his eyes and mouth.

I didn't say anything although a big part of me wanted to mention they had a daughter they were leaving behind, but it wasn't my place.

"I don't have much time this morning, so first things first. I need you to take over a few upcoming projects."

He bent down and pulled a few folders out of his bag.

"The renovation on Davis Brenton's storefront. I guess he's finally decided what he wants to turn it into. Second"—he set the folder down and opened a rather thick one—"the Rojas house…that's coming up. They want to start in April." I already knew about that project, along with Davis's, but they were both a few months out.

"Then there's the possibility of Nora's building project," he said, shuffling a few papers around inside one of the folders.

The barista brought my coffee over, just in time for me to take a sip and seem nonchalant as I asked, "What building project?"

I didn't like how it felt not to know something about her life. Over the past week, we had grown so close. How could she have not mentioned this yet?

No strings.

Without taking his eyes off the papers in front of him, he replied.

"Nora's designing the new community center. Her friend Rae put her on the job. She'll need to have her mockup done soon to put a bid in with a contractor, but the only problem is, most of the local ones are booked up. So, Rae put in a special request, asking if she could get the plans to me before January, then I'd agree to take on the project as a priority."

"I thought we gutted that building," I said, confused as to how I'd missed the details on this.

"We did. But the plans hadn't been drawn up yet. They still aren't, but I emailed Rae and told her she had to have them in by end of the week in order to get us."

Us meant me. Nora would be working with me if Peter was handing it all over.

Taking another sip of coffee, I took my time responding. Because I'd been so adamant about not interacting with Nora for so long, even taking on a girlfriend for a while, which wasn't even real, but it worked to convince my boss that his daughter didn't mean anything to me—I wasn't sure how to converse about Nora-related topics. Unless, of course, I wanted to push my boss like I did the other day.

"So, with you leaving…" I muttered, wiping my hands on my jeans.

Why the fuck was I so nervous? He'd already asked me to watch out for her. Now he was telling me I'd be working in close proximity with her. It was fine. We'd agreed to no strings attached, so why did it make me so edgy?

My boss sipped his coffee, peering down at the papers in front of him.

"You'll take that over if it goes through. Can I trust you to bid it all out properly, while remembering what we talked about the other day in my office?"

Silence settled between us, but it wasn't comfortable. It was tense, tight…about to snap.

Peter cleared his throat, setting his cup in front of him, while his eyes lowered to the table.

"Colson?" His left eyebrow raised as his eyes swung back up to meet mine.

My chest burned as the desire to tell him that I didn't need his permission hung like hot air, right there in my lungs.

The memory of when I'd met Nora came back again with clarity. For the first time I felt as if someone had pried open my chest and reached inside it, cradling my heart. Nora had looked at me with so much feeling, so much life, that it was impossible not to watch her every move, and every single rise and fall of her chest as she stood off by her father, smiling. Existing.

Taunting.

Tempting.

She saw me in a way no one ever seemed to, and I was addicted to it.

Just a few days ago I was ready to flip him the bird where his daughter was concerned, but she had pulled back…so where did that leave me? It left me with a company that I wanted to buy.

Tipping my chin up, I nodded. "Yes, sir."

Peter watched me, his gray eyes moving back and forth over my face, until he finally clenched his jaw and let out a sigh.

"Good, then I'll leave you to it and be in touch about the bid."

He closed the folders and slid them across the table to me, while our barista came over to collect our cups.

"So…Christmas?" I asked, curious if Nora would go with them to Arizona or spend it with Davis and Rae. She didn't seem like the type to be away from her family during a holiday that big.

Peter grabbed for his wallet tucked into the pocket of his jeans. "Yeah…Lilly wants to spend Christmas on a cruise ship, then come home to warm weather and zero snow…so our ship leaves from Seattle on Christmas Day and returns two weeks later."

"What about Nora?" I blurted, hating that I couldn't keep my fucking mouth shut. He was already making assumptions about my feelings toward his daughter. Any extra concern would be fuel to the flames.

So, to be safe, I added, "Only because I won't be here and you asked that I keep an eye on things with her, and if we're both gone…" I let my voice trail off, hoping to cover my blunder.

My boss thumbed through his wallet, his eyes down until he finally let out another cement worthy sigh.

Flicking the cash on the table, he responded, "I think this will be a great opportunity for her. We'll see her when we get back and do a small celebration before we leave."

Oh.

I swallowed and pushed my chair back, standing.

"Okay…well keep me posted on what you need from me."

Peter turned toward me with a pensive expression. Holding his cell to his ear, he barked out a few demands to our foreman, Tyler, and then he hung up.

"Actually, Colson, I could use your help prepping our house."

"Oh, are you selling?" I asked, trying to cover the fact that I was just being nosy. I remembered that they had offered it to Nora, and I knew she wouldn't take it.

Peter focused on his cell again and distractedly said, "My daughter is going to take it, she just doesn't know it yet."

14

NORA

THERE WERE plans scattered all over my kitchen table.

I had removed all the chairs, so that I could walk laps around it while I worked to get a different perspective. If this didn't work, I'd tape them in a different order on my wall and stare at it for an hour.

The process was annoying, but it always worked.

"What are you looking for, exactly?"

I jumped. "Shit, Rae, I totally forgot you were even here."

She slowly chewed her popcorn. "Sorry, it's just that you've been walking around that table forever and I've been trying to be quiet, but I can't take much more."

Moving one of the papers, I examined it in the light.

"The reception area isn't working for me. I need it closer to the front door, and there should be bathrooms here, in case the homeless need to access them, but don't want to interrupt anything."

Rae walked closer, still snacking.

We hadn't talked about anything but these plans for two days straight and it was wearing on me. While my back had gotten better, I was still trying to be careful with it.

"I agree." Rae nodded, looking over the plans. "Okay, the last thing we need to go over is the flooring."

I finally slumped onto my couch and stared at the fire that had been going all day.

"Why don't we take a break and go down to the diner? My dad just made your favorite pie."

Perking up at her suggestion, I set down the plans.

"The berry crumble one? Because you always think I like that lemon flavor, and I don't. I hate it, and yet, you've effectively used it to lure me to your parents' diner several times. I'm not falling for it this time."

She slumped next to me, holding the metal tin of popcorn.

"It's the berry one, I promise!"

"Okay, fine."

Ten minutes later, I was walking into Mac & Millie's, the local diner, owned by Rae's parents, Roger and Millie.

Once we sat down, her dad brought us over pie and ice cream.

"Okay, you need to spill Colson details ASAP." She dug into her pie, her engagement ring catching on the Christmas lights. It was still strange for me to see that on her. Because of the community center, we hadn't even had time to talk about it.

"You sure you don't want to talk wedding ideas first?"

Her blue eyes went wide and for a single second, I thought I had her, but she lifted her fork instead. "Nice try, now spill."

Darting a quick look around to ensure we wouldn't be overheard, I leaned forward.

"So, I did what you suggested…"

She licked the fork clean before it registered with her.

"You were honest with him about how you feel?"

Nodding, I scooped the vanilla ice cream and smeared it over the top of the pie, then broke and shook my head.

"No, I'm lying." Dropping my fork, I confessed. "After the back injury thing, we had a really good day. I mean like falling for him so hard type of day, and that night…well things got physical, but before the physical stuff, he started asking me questions about my plans and stuff."

My best friend's mouth dropped.

"Oh my gosh, so he cared for you all day, asked about your future, and thennn he. . ." Her eyebrows jumped suggestively.

Smothering a laugh, I nodded with a little groan. "Rae, he's like Ice Barbarian huge for real. We didn't even have sex like real sex and I'm sore."

"You didn't have sex...then how?" She trailed off with her brow puckered.

Leaning into whisper, I explained, "He just...sort of stretched me by going all the way in and then he...you know." I sat back, grabbing my fork again.

"Finished." She bent forward, whisper yelling, "As in, he finished inside you?"

I nodded, keeping my eyes on my plate so she'd move past this.

"Nora, you are the queen of not letting guys finish without being wrapped. How could you let him..."

"Because he's Colson, okay?" I snapped, hating how defensive I was.

Rae leaned back with a warning look. "Girl, fine...you're an adult. You know what you're doing, but I also know you absolutely are too far gone for this man to be letting him spread his seed without buying some property first."

Her eyes narrowed as her fork clanked to the plate. "Unless...did he declare his love, ask to be your boyfriend?"

This was where my heart stuttered to a stop, thudding pathetically slow at what had occurred.

"No, he didn't." Toying with a blueberry in the cobbler, I took a deep breath and explained, "I suggested we should be casual...have no strings attached sex."

Rae's face fell flat, her mouth turning down and her brows following.

"Nora Petrov, you did not."

I nodded sheepishly, knowing my best friend was going to verbally kick my ass.

"Tell me he didn't agree."

"He did."

We both inhaled collective sighs as the bustle of the diner drowned out our silence.

"Do you think he's just doing it because you said it first?"

I had considered that it was possible that I had shot myself in the foot by saying it first, but...

"He has to know with how he's treated me over the past year that I'm on defense...and if he wanted to change his play, he would have to be the one to do it. He would have to make it abundantly clear how he felt because every time I have, he's made me feel like an idiot."

She gave me a sad nod, then dug back into the flaky crust of the pie.

"So, how far will you take this?"

Shrugging, I watched a flurry of snow fly around outside. Across the street was a tiny shop, all closed up with brown paper covering the windows. I knew Rae's fiancé owned it now, but for as long as I could remember, it had been my mother's. I used to come into Rae's parents' diner, sit here with her while we did our homework, or help her journal about her larger than life and completely impossible crush.

Which happened to be Davis, the man she was now engaged to. It was all simpler back then. My parents were my entire world, my everything... and now they were leaving soon, and I honestly didn't feel like I had them at all. Which only made this test with Colson that much more painful. Part of me preferred it though, it was easier to handle heartbreak when you knew what you were gambling. But going in blind? That was something I didn't know if I'd ever be able to do again.

"We can date other people, and we can have no strings-attached sex. We're having fun."

Rae watched me carefully, finishing her pie until she finally pushed it away.

"I asked how far *you* were willing to take it."

I didn't know.

"I think it might depend on him, he's been silent for two days and I refuse to make the first move. So, if he's over it, then it's done."

"But..." My best friend narrowed her eyes. "If he shows up tonight and asks for hot and heavy sex, you'll say..." She held her hand out, encouraging me to continue.

"I don't know, probably yes. The man is talented with his tongue."

Slapping the table with her palms, she angrily scolded me. "No, Nora. The answer is no, you will not."

Rolling my eyes, I argued. "But why?"

"Because you're in love with him, you've been in love with him…you forget that I found your Pinterest Wedding board that you had created for him. You can't do no strings, because you have nothing but strings with him. You're tied to him emotionally, and letting him stick his dick inside you, then go on a date with someone else will kill you."

Feeling frustrated at how right she was, I slid out of the booth and tossed a few dollars on the table. "Let's go visualize the spaces at the community center before it gets too dark."

Rae followed but not without a warning. "We aren't done talking about this."

I knew she was right.

The point of me telling him how I felt was to see if he was being genuine with the whole savior act, or if it was more of an obligation to him. Which now that I hadn't done that, I had no idea where he stood. I knew this had an expiration date, but I couldn't explain it, there was some place deep within me that wanted this tiny piece of him. Even if it was the only thing I'd ever get.

ONCE RAE and I were finished with the community center, and she had left, it allowed me the opportunity to process the fact that Colson hadn't stopped by. I had heard him leave in the mornings, but now that my life wasn't tied to his in the way of needing heat, a tree removed, or assistance with my back, we sort of seemed to slip back into the way things were.

Maybe he was already done with me…

It was too frustrating to think about, so finally calling the workday to a close and emailing the finishing touches to Rae, I put on Vampire Diaries.

I was right in the middle of settling into the couch when someone knocked on my front door. Assuming it was my best friend who had probably gotten my email and hadn't left town yet because she was a workaholic, I huffed an irritated breath.

Refusing to get up again, I snuggled deeper into the cushions and yelled, "Just use your key!"

When the lock turned a few seconds later, I pressed play, thinking my assumption was correct.

"Hey," a deep, very un-Rae-like voice said from the entryway.

My head spun so fast, I might have given myself whiplash. Colson appeared in dark jeans, brown work boots covered in snow, and a gray flannel that buttoned all the way up to his throat. He had a day's worth of scruff along his jaw, and his eyes looked tired. All I wanted to do was jump up and hug him, ask how his day was and why he'd stayed away from me for two days. Instead, I shoved all that way down and asked, "How do you have a key to my house?"

Colson smirked, dipping to unlace his boots.

"You don't have one to mine?"

Already annoyed with him, I returned my attention back to the screen. "I don't even have your cell phone number, why would I have a key?"

Walking over in his socks, he dropped right next to me on the couch.

"Well, I stole mine...figured you had done the same thing when you broke into my house."

That was an option? I wasn't the type of person to invade someone's privacy like that. I just broke in like a classy person.

The show played, fire cracked and popped, and we both seemed to fall into a pensive silence, until he gently grasped my hand.

"Haven't seen you in a bit."

Watching the show, as Caroline attempted to pull everyone together for yet another Decade dance, I tried to seem completely unaffected by the way he toyed with each of my fingers. He drew shapes into my skin and traced the dip between each finger.

Finally finding my voice, I explained, "I've been busy with work."

And obsessing over the fact that you've been ignoring me.

"Same," he shot back, while watching the screen.

The way heat followed his touch made this whole hand holding thing way more erotic than it should be.

"Honestly, I thought I scared you off."

He turned toward me, a megawatt smile on his handsome face. "You... how?"

No idea, but you left, so it had to be something I did.

"Maybe I was too much for you to handle." I lifted my shoulder briefly, going for nonchalant.

Tugging on my hand, he forced my body to dip closer to him as he leaned over. His lips were at my ear, slowly kissing the edge, down along the lobe.

"I haven't even begun to handle you, Nora."

Feeling the heat from his breath on my neck, and a different kind of heat stir in my lower belly, I tilted my lips to where they were at his ear.

"Prove it."

"How's your back?" He stroked my face, pushing away my hair gently.

I kissed his jaw tenderly. "All better."

He moved, taking my hand with him until I was up.

"Where are we going?"

His lips ghosted over my jaw for a second before leaning back. "I need to shower...just got off work."

Weaving my fingers into his hair, I closed the gap between us and pressed my lips to his.

Soft and gentle at first, the kiss turned urgent as his hand moved to my waist, and an insatiable hunger seemed to overwhelm his frenzied movements. We moved back, step by step, until we hit the hallway, where he pressed me against the wall and trailed sloppy open-mouthed kisses down my jaw and neck. His rough fingers tugged at the buttons on my shirt. In turn, I undid each of his and then pulled his undershirt over his head.

Returning my lips to his chest, I licked along the hardened muscles, up to his throat where his Adam's apple bobbed.

His hands were granite at my waist as our mouths came back together, hungry and desperate, moving our jaws to the side to get a deeper connection. His taste was fire, burning and changing me in ways I'd never recover from. There would always be an imprint of him every place he touched and tasted.

His hands came up under my ass, lifting me and forcing my legs around his hips. My arms locked around his neck as he carried me down the length of the hallway until we got to my bedroom. Tossing me on the bed, he stared down at me with an expression no one has ever worn while looking at me. Colson viewed me as though I had been misplaced, and he'd just finally recovered me and now he'd do anything to ensure he never lost me again.

It was hungry, devouring, and tender all at once. It undid a latch in my heart that had slammed shut long ago.

Sitting up on my elbows, I watched as his hands moved to the waist of his jeans, and he unfastened the copper button, then slowly dragged the zipper down.

"Nora."

My eyes bounced up to meet his once more.

His smile was seductive and dark as he commanded, "Take off your clothes."

The zip of energy that traveled up my spine was something I'd never felt before...I had never been so insatiable and eager to touch someone, or to have them touch me.

Moving my fingers clumsily, suddenly nervous, I pulled and tugged until my jeans were down my hips far enough that Colson could drag them the rest of the way. Then, reaching behind my back, I unclasped my bra, freeing my aching breasts and exposing them to the cold air.

Colson continued to watch, his large palm covering his growing erection that his boxer briefs could barely contain. The sight spurred my actions as I peeled down my panties, kicking them to the side.

"Now, spread yourself with your fingers. Let me see you."

My breath hitched, because goddammit, no one had ever talked to me like that.

Fire lit in my core, making the ache between my legs grow as I lowered my fingers to my mound. Tracing a line over smooth skin, feeling it pebble, then trailing down my slit, I used two fingers to spread myself wide.

"Fuck." Colson hissed, freeing the head of his erection, smoothing his hand over the weeping tip, and then skimming the rest of his length. My mouth went dry as I stared at how the veins along the side of his shaft bulged, and the entire length of him was granite for me...because of *me*.

"Wet your fingers, Nora." He ordered, stepping closer to the edge of the bed.

I complied, bringing my fingers up to my mouth.

His raspy voice grated, making the slickness between my thighs intensify. "Now slowly fuck that pussy."

My fingers worked in a slow rotation over my clit, causing breaths to skip and hitch inside my chest. The way his eyes devoured the space between my legs, the way he spit on his cock, gripped his shaft, and stroked in slow, measured movements had my hips bucking against my hand.

We stayed like that, tethered by the heat mounting between us. His eyes darkened while he watched my fingers. I lowered my gaze as he lubricated his shaft, then ran his hand along the smooth expanse.

"Do you feel ready to stretch around my cock?" His knee pressed into the bed, his strong fingers hovered over my mound, covering mine until he was moving them slower and pressing deeper.

My voice was husky as I made a sound of acceptance. I was feeling too much, and he hadn't even entered me yet.

"Let's find out." He braced the space next to my head and gently pulled my kneecap, spreading my legs apart.

"Condom?" he asked, rubbing the tip of his cock through my folds.

Hitching my leg higher, I shook my head. "I'm on birth control." This was the conversation we should have had the other night when I let him enter me and fucking finish inside me, but with him…I knew it was stupid and dangerous, but I had on blinders when it came to him. All my inhibitions were gone.

Bending down to kiss me, he whispered, "I haven't been with anyone…" Hesitating a second, and pushing back my curls, he added, "since I met you."

Searching his gaze, I wanted him to explain himself. He'd said he had a girlfriend, he—

Without waiting for me to wrap my mind around his statement, he slowly sank into me, inch by inch, letting me adjust as he went, just like he had the other night.

My mouth opened, as the sensation of him filling me overwhelmed my senses.

"Colson." I rasped, gripping his biceps as he held himself up, watching his length disappear inside me.

"Look at how perfectly you take my cock." He groaned, going deeper. "You're so fucking tight, Nora."

Scraping my nails down his chest, I moaned loudly. Considering I hadn't been with anyone since Jason, I *was* pretty fucking tight.

"Wait." I gasped. "Just…wait." It was too much, the sharpness of him stretching me too painful. Even though he'd been inside me a few days ago, he hadn't fucked me, so everything was still too tight.

With a furrow of his brow, he immediately pulled out.

"No, I just need a second." I reached for him, but he was already back on his knees.

"Turn onto your stomach, Nora. That cunt needs to be stretched by my fingers and milked of at least one orgasm before it can take my cock."

I had never…I couldn't even grasp the filthy language or what to do with it.

Flipping to my stomach as he requested, I pressed my fingers into the comforter, feeling the cold air kiss my skin.

"Here"—Colson touched my hip—"lift up."

Going to my knees, he stuffed one of my pillows under me, which propped my ass up.

"Nora…"He groaned. "What are you doing to me?"

His hand worked my ass, skimming up and down my skin, touching… prodding and groping with a few muttered curses.

I liked that he was enjoying himself as he played with me.

But it didn't last long, suddenly cold air hit me and while my ass cheeks were spread wide, three of Colson's fingers plunged inside my center.

"Oh." I tried to turn my head, but Colson slapped my ass cheek, and then dove deeper with his fingers, working me through and moving his thumb up to my hole, where he gently applied pressure. It was so hot that I ground my hips against the pillow, chasing the friction I needed. Every time I thought he'd let up, he only seemed to increase his ministrations, fucking me with his fingers until I was coming so hard, his name left my lips on a smothered scream.

"Now you're ready to take my cock." Colson flipped me, leaving the pillow in place, so that it cushioned my hips. Without waiting for me to catch my breath from the orgasm that had ripped through me, he pushed his length all the way inside of me until he was fully sheathed.

I watched as he struggled to control himself, his eyes going as wide as mine.

And then we both moved. "Fuckkk." I whimpered, lifting my hips.

His grip came down hard on my waist, holding me in place as he rotated forward, driving his cock impossibly deeper with each thrust.

His lower abdomen tightened, and the muscles contracted as he thrust forward. As if he couldn't get close enough, he lifted my leg, pushing it back so he had a better angle.

"Goddammit, Nora, fuck…" he roared, moving his hips faster. His thumb came down on my clit, flicking and massaging it while he fucked me senseless. The sensations were too much for me to contain.

"Yes, yes, yes," I repeated, as he pumped faster. He was muttering something filthy; my name was thrown in there through gritted teeth as he chased his own release. Then he pinned my hips to his tightly as he pumped and shuddered, finishing inside of me.

I tried to catch my breath, but the orgasms had pulled too hard at every part of my body.

Finally, Colson pulled out and sank to the bed next to me. He twisted to his side and pressed a kiss to my shoulder, then pulled me closer to his chest.

Counting to ten in my head, I allowed myself a few precious seconds to take this and keep it against my heart, where no one would ever know I tucked it.

Then I moved.

Getting off the bed, I headed to the bathroom, turning on the shower.

While it heated, I ran a wide comb through my hair, then tied it up in a bun on top of my head and stepped into the billowing steam.

My shower was more of a stall, not exactly the gorgeously spaced one like Colson had in his master. So, I wasn't expecting the door to open or for Colson to join me while I was washing my body with my loofa.

"Tight in here." He muttered, while smiling at me in that devastating way that made his sharp jawline more noticeable. I wanted to cup it with my palm and feel his eyes land on me in that way I was starting to realize was rare and only for me.

Turning my back to him and my face toward the spray, I merely hummed my agreement. I continued washing, feeling him at my back, until his arms came around me, drawing me to his chest.

"I can feel you pulling away from me." His nose skimmed my ear, his lips following in a sweet kiss.

Leaning into him with the water pouring down on us, I brought my hands up to his forearms that were around my chest.

"I thought this was part of our deal…no strings."

Humming his own response, he spun me around until I was facing him.

With his chin dipped, and those blue eyes focused on me, I could feel another latch unlock inside my chest.

"Let's chill on the no strings aspect…if our roads go separate ways, then they go separate ways…but I'd like to think we have at least a few strings keeping us together."

I wanted nothing more than to be a ball of yarn that Colson got tangled up in, but I needed to guard my heart more.

So, keeping emotions aloft, I gave him a kiss on the lips, followed by a warm smile. His hand came to my neck, where he cupped it and pulled me in again…and we lost ourselves once more to the heat burning between us.

15

COLSON
THIRTEEN YEARS OLD

DEAR MOM,

Why aren't you taking any visitors? I have come two weekends in a row and have been turned away each time. Things are bad here...Dad's been acting stressed...look, Mom, this is really important... Please, just for a while don't accept any letters or calls from Dad. Okay? I know you might need some time to feel better, but just...don't talk to him for a bit. – Love, Cole

Dear Cole,

Silly boy, they just got the dates mixed up on visiting days. All is well. I'm perfectly fine, sweetie. How's my garden? Are you still watching over it for me? Can you show me a picture of it the next time you come to see me? Your father and I love each other honey, very much...don't worry, in fact I am calling tomorrow to see if he can come talk to my doctors. I think it's finally time for me to come home.

NORA BUSIED herself in her kitchen while I watched her from over the brim of my coffee mug. She had her hair pulled back into a loose braid, with curls escaping and framing her face. A white shirt covered her shoulders, dipping down to barely kiss the top of her breasts, and then flowing around the dark jeans at her hips. She was stunning.

I had a difficult time not watching her every move, even when she cared for her plants, making that invisible knife twist inside my chest. It was one that had been there since I was a kid whenever I saw someone care for plants or a garden, because while they were experiencing and enjoying the life their plants brought, all I could think about was death.

"Don't your mornings usually start earlier?" Nora asked without looking up from her plant. I smirked, knowing she was going to keep pushing on this tenuous relationship we'd made with one another.

Taking another slow sip, I merely smiled. "No…I have the day off."

Swiping her thumb over the screen of her phone, she focused on it while humming.

Shoving off from the counter, I stepped toward her and grabbed her cell phone out of her hand.

"What has you so focused this morning?"

"Just leave it." She argued, crossing her arms which pushed her tits up, momentarily distracting me.

I leaned forward and pressed my lips to hers to quell this new spark inside my chest every time Nora managed to rob me of breath. The fact that I *could* kiss her now was something I still hadn't gotten over.

Scanning the screen of her phone, I saw that she was on a local dealership site. "Are you in the market for a new car?"

Heaving a sigh, she tried to grab her phone again, but I moved it higher.

"Yes…okay, I'm going today to go look at a few four-wheel drive options. I don't want to be at the mercy of other people having to get me around anymore."

I clicked my tongue as if that was ridiculous. Once she'd given up and moved to rinse her mug out and wasn't watching me, I put my number in her phone and then handed it back to her.

"Great, let's go."

Giving me a stern expression, she walked off toward her living room, where her purse and coat were. She huffed out a sigh.

"No, thank you. I'll catch up with you later."

Grabbing my boots, I laughed while shaking my head. "You're adorable."

"Colson, seriously...this is more of a boyfriend thing to do, and we don't need to blur those lines any more than we did last night."

After our shower last night, I didn't ask to sleep over. I crawled into bed next to her and pulled her to my chest and fell asleep. She wasn't wrong...we were blurring lines, and tying strings where we vowed not to have any. But I knew it wasn't just me. She tried to pull away and put on a mask that she didn't want this, but the way she kissed me and let me hold her told me she did.

"You're not going alone, so you might as well accept it."

Inhaling a deep breath, Nora finally smiled at me before opening her door. "Fine, you can come, but fair warning, I will not respond well to anything being mansplained. Got it?"

Putting my hands up, I swore. "Got it."

"TAKE A LOOK AT YOU, I haven't ever seen anyone look so hot in one of these." The fuckface car salesman complimented Nora in a flirtatious tone. He had one of those hairstyles where he pushed the front of his hair up with gel, like he was fourteen instead of what I assumed was twenty. The second we walked through the dealership doors, he was salivating over Nora.

Keeping my head low, I didn't say anything, but I was getting pretty fucking tired of his comments. When we'd arrived, Nora introduced me as a friend, which gave Cooper the fuckface a green light to shamelessly flirt.

Nora hopped out of the massive Toyota that was way too much truck for her and beamed up at the idiot who had held his hand out for her. Dude was tall, I'd give him that, but that was about all the qualifications he had to even exist. My eyes narrowed into slits when she placed her hand in his, accepting his help down.

Fuck. This. Shit.

"I don't think I could see myself handling something that big," Nora explained, while moving away from the massive vehicle.

I snorted, pushing off the side wall and said, "You didn't have any problems handling something that big last night."

I laughed, but Nora's face turned about five shades of red.

"Excuse us for a second, Cooper," she said sweetly, and then pushed me until we were walking away and concealed between two massive trucks. Snow coated every single car on the lot, which made today a shitty one for car shopping.

"Are you freaking kidding me?" She hissed, darting her gaze around.

I shrugged my shoulders. "What?"

Her breath clouded in front of her face. Her pink lips were puffy and her lashes were dark, framing her aqua eyes in a way that made it difficult to look away.

"That was wildly inappropriate, and honestly, I'm over it. You've done nothing but scoff, sigh, clear your throat, and click your tongue at every single vehicle I've looked at." Her chest heaved up and down like this was something that upset her.

I narrowed my gaze at the way her tits pressed against the material through the opening of her coat. I'd had enough of this.

Turning to the side, I gripped the handle to the nearest door and gestured with my head.

"Get in."

Wild aqua eyes searched mine. "No, I'm not getting in."

"I just want to talk and get a few things straight, there seems to be a misunderstanding between us because it felt like you were totally fine with cockface flirting with you."

"Cockface, really?" She linked her arms together.

"Yeah, the guy who's been tripping over himself to please you and impress you every goddamn five seconds. Not to mention touch you every chance he gets."

Bringing her fingers to her nose, she inhaled. "That's not even…"

"So then talk to me, get in and talk to me and I promise that I'll leave or behave whatever you prefer."

Raising a dark brow, she challenged, "You're serious, I just talk to you in the back of this Tundra, and you'll stop?"

"I promise you. I just want a chance to talk to you without cockface around."

"Oh my gosh, stop, that's not his name nor is it remotely funny." She trailed off, climbing into the back seat of an extended cab truck. The back seat was about as spacious as my own, with a bit less head space.

I crawled up after her and then shut and locked the door.

Our knees pressed together as our bodies faced inward, and she took a deep breath and relaxed into the seat.

"Okay, what do you want to talk about?"

"Nothing, I just wanted to apologize. I know I've been acting a little weird. I'm not doing well with how strong he's been coming on to you."

"Well I—"

I cut her off. "I'm not done apologizing."

Her eyes held defiance as she watched me, but she let me continue.

"Want to know one of my favorite things about winter?" I asked, slowly taking off my coat.

Nora watched me, still pissed.

"I know it's cold and miserable for almost everyone else, but I like it."

"What does this have to do with—" Nora tried to cut in, but I pressed my fingers to her lips.

"Still not done."

She rolled her eyes and finally relaxed into the seat.

Reaching over to her, I undid the large round buttons on her pea coat. She watched, dipping her chin and bouncing her eyes to mine.

"Colson, what are—"

I pushed the coat off her shoulders and then shifted her so she could lie on her back.

"Colson!"

Ignoring her, I continued, "I love that during the winter, and with how frequent these storms have been, none of these car dealerships have the time to clear the windshields."

I pushed her shirt up until it crowded her neck, and I could see her white bra holding up her tits, which were rising and falling as her breathing increased. Her eyes were on me as I slowly lowered myself between her parted legs.

"No one can see us, Nora. But honestly, even if they could"—I raised up and leveled her with a heated look—"it wouldn't stop me from apologizing."

With her lying flat on her back down the length of the seat bench, I kissed her belly and unbuttoned her jeans.

"We can't," she said, already pushing her hips up like she craved my touch.

Hooking my thumbs into her jeans, I pulled them down her hips, and her black thong went next until she was naked and exposed to me.

"We can...and we are," I kissed her smooth mound, while looking up to watch her expression as my tongue darted out and swiped through her folds.

Breathing heavily, Nora's fingers wound through the longer strands of my hair gently, almost in a caress, like she wasn't aware of the tenderness she was exhibiting.

Raising her hips, I went slow and took my time to savor this moment as I leisurely licked through her center and sucked on her sensitive nub. I was beginning to catalog and look forward to the different sounds that Nora Petrov made while writhing underneath me. Her hips rocked, chasing friction as I fucked her pussy with my tongue, and when her moans grew louder and her breathing more erratic, I pulled away and sat up.

"Come here." I demanded gruffly while I pulled her up and then turned her, so her ass was on the middle console that was folded down in the front, her legs spread wide as her feet landed on the seat where I was still perched.

"I like this view." I smiled, watching her glistening pussy as she sat in front of me. I pulled my cock out of my jeans and stroked it up and down.

"Touch yourself, Nora. Let me watch as you fuck your fingers."

Her mouth parted as she blinked, searching every window, but each one was covered in ice and snow.

"Do it." I commanded her.

Letting out a breath, she moved her hand down the length of her body and gently circled her clit.

The way she looked, perched in front of me like a meal I could devour, would stay with me for life.

"Now bring that pussy over here and sit on my cock."

She moved off the console, taking my hand for help, until she was straddling my hips. Her knees stretched wide as she lowered herself onto me.

I watched as she sank down, inch by inch, slowly taking me as she was able, without too much pain. I knew she was still acclimating to my size, so I let her adjust. Finally, once she had taken me fully, she groaned.

"Holy fuck." Her fingers dug into my shoulders as she looked down at where we connected.

Then it was as though someone had thrown a match into a barrel of gasoline. She moved, and I gripped the back of her neck, marking her with open-mouthed kisses.

I tugged her shirt free of her neck and then pulled her breast free so I could suck on her nipple.

"Colson." She gasped.

Her hips rotated at a brisk pace, rounding and pushing down on my dick at a frenzied pace.

Gripping her waist, I pulled her against me as I sucked on her breast.

We moved, writhing against each other as our breathing fogged the windows. Her hand went to the roof to aid her in pushing against my length. Her tits bounced as she moved, and it was the most glorious thing I had ever watched. I had never in my life been this lost for someone, or desperate. I sure as fuck had never fucked someone in the back of a vehicle that I didn't even own.

Needing her mouth on mine, I pulled her chin down. She lifted herself up the slightest bit so she could swivel her hips forward, rotating them in a way that pulled my cock out of her, and then she lowered herself, consuming it with her pussy again.

"Colson, I need you deeper, this seat...I can't."

I moved my ass to the edge, allowing her knees more space, and for her to sink even lower on my shaft and the way she moved against me...fuck.

"Oh God. Fucking shit." She clamped down, claiming her orgasm with sultry moans.

"Nora. Fuck."

I managed to rasp out, letting her tight cunt swallow my cock and every drop of my release. Her hips slowed, her fingers came to my shirt as she caught her breath.

Our foreheads finally touched as our breathing evened out, and that's when I realized Nora was smiling.

A smile I hadn't ever seen before, it made her eyes brighter, and a small dimple pop along her cheek.

I stroked her hair, tugging on the ends so I could have a better view of it.

"Are you done being mad at me?"

She laughed, then pulled back so she could cradle my face in her hands.

"Were you really jealous of that guy?"

Loving how it felt to have her touching me, I leaned into it.

"Not him...just the way you seem to react to it. I didn't like that. And I don't like him touching you, even if it's just your hand."

She considered me, brushing her thumb over my lips while humming.

"That might be a problem for us."

Swallowing harshly, I watched as she stared at me, and something seemed to shift between us. Like when a glacier slid into the ocean, it was noticeable and a big fucking problem. We were right back where we were the other night. Did I want to admit that I didn't want other men to talk to her, or her to allow them to? Did I want to be introduced as a friend? Fuck no...but I also didn't want to lose her.

Besides, aside from a label separating us, there was a shit-ton more. Namely, the shit I was carrying around from her father.

When she found out that he asked me originally to help her, I knew it would hurt her. If it wasn't handled properly, she would take it wrong and walk away from me forever. But I ran the risk of losing her either way... and for now, I was too selfish to give her up.

16

NORA

AFTER COLSON and I cleaned up, using a few Kleenexes from my purse, I realized the truck we'd snuck into was kind of perfect. It wasn't too big, but big enough that I felt secure inside of it, and it wasn't so tall that I couldn't get in easily without help.

So, once we exited, I planned to track Cooper down and tell him I had finally found the one. But we quickly realized that Cooper was waiting a few cars down from where we were. The snow had stopped falling, but the black asphalt was wet, and he stood wearing nice slacks, a blue button-down and a brown coat...his slick shoes were not enough to keep up with the temperatures outside, so why the hell was he just standing there?

Approaching him, I tried to pretend like nothing happened, but Cooper glared at us both with his bony elbows sticking out as they banded over his chest.

"Hey, Cooper," I said, tucking a few loose strands of hair behind my ear.

His eyes narrowed as he tracked the movement.

"You guys realize cars aren't soundproof, right? And I was two seconds from calling the police..."

Guilt hit hard, forcing a flurry of red to smother my face. I was not about to admit to having sex in a vehicle that I didn't own.

"I have no idea what you're talki—" I started, but Colson put his hand to my back and stepped forward.

"We were under the impression we were allowed to test drive the cars," Colson said with a completely straight face. "Or are you just mad that you weren't there with us as we took it for a spin?"

Cooper's scowl worsened as the tops of his cheeks and ears turned a harsh red.

"Our mistake."

Seeing the effect he had on Cooper, Colson smirked and continued, "Now, after testing the back seat, she would like to buy it."

I perked up, loving that he was here and handling Cooper cockface for me. And it wasn't like anyone had caught us, or had seen us, and unless he was right next to the car, there's no way he actually heard us. Besides, he was getting a sale out of it, so at least this wasn't a total waste.

Going through the motions, Cooper remained irritable but seemed to do everything by the book, including trying to match the price I requested. By the end of an incredibly long yet satisfying morning, I drove a new-to-me truck.

It had seat warmers, a heated steering wheel, and a self-start button. I didn't hate that it also had a great memory already inside of it. I'd never forget the way Colson's head dipped between my thighs with that hungry expression, or the way his tongue darted out and swiped through my folds.

I shook my head, knowing I had to stop tying myself emotionally to Colson. This no strings attached plan had a billion invisible strings that I had pulled around my heart, while attempting to loop his in too. I didn't do it consciously but every time I pulled away, it was as though he pulled on a string, forcing me closer.

It wasn't healthy, and the more space we created between one another, the better.

Since I had traded in my previous car, I pulled directly into my drive-away and parked. Colson unbuckled next to me and twisted his body in my direction.

"Where to now?"

I loved having him in the car with me...or truck, that was going to take some getting used to. But him in my space, in front of my house, it was another looped string around my heart.

Which meant I had to pull away before I got hurt.

"I have to change, and then I have a meeting."

Colson gave me one of his megawatt smiles, the one that I knew if I googled him, I'd find on some eligible rich bachelor website. I had no idea why the man was here in Macon, but his face belonged in Hollywood.

"I have a meeting too, but maybe we can catch up later?"

"Yeah, I don't know my plans yet, but I'll see you later." I exited the truck and started toward my door when he followed and suddenly tugged my hand.

Turning on my toes, I barely had a chance to see what had replaced the usual hunger he had when looking at me. I wouldn't acknowledge the adoration that I caught when he stepped into my space.

I couldn't.

His lips landed on mine, gentle and slow until I was opening for him. His large arms came around me, hugging me until I heard his whisper, "I can feel you pulling away again."

I wasn't sure what to do with that because we'd agreed, no strings.

Yet, he kept saying I was the one pulling away as if it were a bad thing. Like he was just standing there with a rope, ready to tie this shit together, but he'd agreed.

If he wanted more with me, he would have said it.

Turning my face so that my lips landed against his neck, I squeezed him back and then stepped away.

"I have to go. I'll talk to you later."

He stayed rooted in place, and when I gave him one last glance before closing my door, I saw the sad way his eyes dipped and mouth turned down…it did something to my chest. Making it sloshy and unstable. Unpredictable. He couldn't look at me like he cared if I pulled away.

It was precisely why this entire arrangement had to come to an end.

BUSTLING into the community center in a pencil skirt, thermal lined tights, and high-heeled boots, I appeared as an entirely different person.

Gone was the frumpy jacket, snow boots, and frizzy hair. I was in business mode, something most people didn't get to witness often, but when I signed contracts or talked to the people who had to execute my vision, I showed up in armor.

"Oh my God, Nora! That lip color is divine on you," Rae called from her spot on the floor where she was measuring something.

"What are you doing?"

I was suspicious because all the plans had been finalized with nothing to modify until we talked to the contractor.

Rae blushed, letting the tape slide back into place. "I just wondered if we were too generous on the kitchen."

Shaking my head and clicking my heels toward her, I grabbed her pencil and measuring tape. "The plans are perfect, leave it alone."

"Fine. Fine."

Tossing them into the bag, I ignored how cold my toes were growing and tried to gauge the rest of the space, ensuring nothing else had been changed.

"Where were you today?" Rae asked, shuffling papers as she came up next to me.

I explained my new truck and how Colson had helped me pick it out. I left out that he made me orgasm in the back seat.

"Ooh yay, now you can come visit me more often without worrying about the roads. I hate that you haven't been up as much."

"I feel like if we increase how often I sleep over, Davis might get annoyed." I snort laughed because I was up at her house at least three times a week as it was. Usually sleeping over at least once during that week.

She waved me off. "He loves you."

I shivered in my jacket and thermal tights, even with the shelter of walls in place, the temperature was below twenty degrees inside.

"He may love me, but he's still going through some stuff…" I hated the sad expression that had claimed my best friend's face. Davis had just learned some terrible news about his family and was working through it.

Right as I was about to ask how he was doing with everything, an entire group of men shuffled in through the temporary front door. Wearing those thick-soled boots like Colson, and warm flannels, the contractors filed in, one by one, around the empty space, while Rae and I waited next to one another.

I recognized a few guys from my dad's crew, which meant that this bid likely had gone to him. It made sense, considering he'd gutted the place, but I didn't think he'd want to take on another project this close to leaving. I kept watching for my father's head to tower above the others like it usually did, but once the crew assembled, it was Tyler, the lead foreman, who talked with Rae about specifics.

I tried to focus on what they were talking about, but I was having a hard time. Why was my dad's company taking on a project this big? I considered whether plans may have changed for him and my mom, but I hadn't spoken to them since that day when things blew up.

Dammit, they hadn't even left yet, and we were already drifting apart.

"So, can you sign off on all this, then?" I tuned in, hearing Rae ask Tyler.

With a mop of messy brown hair, shoved under a ball cap, he looked like he was about eighteen or so, not nearly as experienced as I would have liked the lead person on this job to be.

"No, I'll leave that up to the boss."

I was about to step up and ask him where my dad was when the front door opened again with a cold gust of air, and a shiver ran down my arms. That's when a familiar pair of blue eyes landed on me, creating a fluttering sensation ripple behind my belly button.

"Colson." Rae greeted the man who now stood next to me.

He addressed my best friend, but his pinky touched the inside of my palm, making my heart jump in my throat.

I almost stepped away to break the contact, but then he stepped closer... it was a small adjustment no one would notice, but I felt it everywhere.

Then again, I had gotten so used to hiding in the shadows and watching Colson from afar. I always felt his presence, even when he wasn't watching me, or near me. It was as though he'd always been there, in my periphery... waiting for some proverbial green light to touch me.

"Nora."

His eyes undressed me as he moved from my toes, slowly up my tight, black skirt, to the white capped sleeve shirt I had tucked into it, and then to my hair that was mostly tamed with loose curls.

Feeling the weight of his gaze, I shifted on my feet. His stare left a blazing trail of heat everywhere but my toes. Those were solid blocks of ice, and incredibly uncomfortable in my cute high-heeled boots.

Finally turning his attention back to my best friend, he explained.

"I'll be leading things for the project, Rae. I just need to get the budget nailed down and walk through the space."

My head snapped up from where I was staring at my toes, wondering if they were bleeding or broken under the layer of leather. Had I heard him correctly?

He'd be taking on the project? If that were true, then that meant we'd have to work together. Suddenly, my attempt to get space from him seemed futile.

"Okay, if you want, let's get started. I don't know if you need the whole crew here. I think just you and Tyler would work for this meeting." Rae eyed the other twelve or so men who were scrolling their phones, waiting.

Colson nodded. "Sorry it was a bit last-minute. We're shuffling leadership a bit." He turned his head toward the group of workers and said, "You guys go grab some coffee or some grub. We'll go over everything in about thirty."

Once they were gone, Tyler and Rae led the way to the farthest corner of the space. When I followed, I could feel Colson behind me. Slowing our steps, his chest brushed my back as his hand grabbed my left ass cheek and squeezed. Tyler and Rae spoke about the architecture of the building while Colson whispered in my ear, "I want you at my house tonight, wearing this skirt."

I inhaled a sharp breath, trying not to react, but the fire in my core was fast and primal. The mere idea of being with him tonight, of going to his house and letting him touch me...hold me was so tempting. But we couldn't keep doing this...blurring the lines.

If he didn't want more with me, then he'd have to survive with less.

"Okay, Nora, go ahead and start painting a verbal picture for them." Rae paced to the side, tucking her clipboard in close to her chest.

Stepping away from Colson felt like chipping a piece of rock. I didn't even know why. I felt so settled nestled into his chest, when I had to leave, I didn't like what it did to me.

"So, in this space, it's pretty self-explanatory." I indicated the space with my hands and held up the plans as everyone followed along with me.

I tried to share the vision I had that went along with the plans each person had a copy of, but as I explained every detail, my words faltered. Because through every single explanation, Colson's eyes never left mine.

He never once looked down at his papers, or at his phone. And every time I seemed to accidentally look at his lips, he'd smirk as if he knew how flummoxed he was making me. The entire situation was infuriating.

Why was he here, anyway? Dad could have at least spearheaded his company projects until he sold it, which from what I understood might be soon. Mom had mentioned they were considering selling it to a California based company that had offered quite a bit of money to keep the name and even all the employees. I'd have to call them tonight to figure out what was going on.

Finally, we were done with the walkthrough, and Colson was busy asking Rae questions about the timeline and budget when I made my way toward the exit. I pulled my coat on and turned to lean against the wall while I waited for Rae. I used the time to devour Colson's broad shoulders and muscled back, which were visible through his shirt. It made me think about how they felt under my fingers while he fucked me the other night.

I didn't like the way it felt when I looked at him because when my eyes landed on any part of him, whether it be his strong hands, his calloused fingers, or the way his hair looked after a shower...all of him looked like he belonged to me. Like he was already mine.

"Nora?"

I blinked, and Rae came into focus.

"All done?" I bent down, reaching for my laptop bag while trying to recover from zoning out.

Rae nodded. "Yeah, but I think we need to talk about the flooring. Colson mentioned a few things about the cost. I didn't know the supplier had changed recently." She rubbed her forehead and let out a sigh. I knew this was probably weighing on her pretty heavily, Rae had gone from helping the town boost business with storefront aesthetics and vendor fairs and now she was in charge of the entire renovation on the community center. It was a big undertaking, that plus a wedding. I wasn't sure how much more she could take on.

"Let's go brainstorm. It'll be okay." I tried to reassure her by rubbing her arm through her coat.

"I am so glad the holidays are coming up." She pushed open the door and headed out into the frosty air. "I'm taking the whole week off, because Davis surprised me with a trip. I wanted to spend our first Christmas at his house with all the snow and everything, but after the blizzard last week, I'm over the cold."

I couldn't believe Christmas was already a week away. I hadn't even asked about plans or what my parents were doing. They had packed up all their stuff, so maybe they'd want to come to my house. I needed to talk to them, which meant my little fun fest with Colson wouldn't be happening.

"That does sound amazing." I muttered distractedly and stopped in the middle of the sidewalk. "You know what, I forgot something inside, where are we going for this session?"

Rae paused and hitched her bag higher on her shoulder. "Uh…diner? I want pie."

"Okay, head there, I'll meet you in a few."

I turned, my toes gave out a painful squeeze in my boots as I ran up the steps and tried to locate Colson. He was on the phone, asking his crew to head back. I took the opportunity to step closer and put my hand on his arm. As soon as he was off the phone, he twisted.

"I—" I opened my mouth, but he was suddenly moving.

Darting his eyes around the space, seeing that Tyler was on the phone off to the side, he grabbed my hand and tugged me toward one of the class-rooms that still had a few load-bearing walls up.

Pushing my back up against the wall, his hands landed on either side of my head.

"Did you come in here to cancel tonight?" he asked, searching my face.

His blue eyes were so intense, so full of something that I was too scared to consider real.

Swallowing, I tipped my head back. "I have to—"

He didn't let me finish. His lips landed on mine, hungry and desperate.

My hands were up, gripping his shirt as he cradled my jaw, savagely invading my mouth with his tongue and sucking it into his. I was breathless, kissing him, trying not to get lost in him, while knowing it was no use.

His hand traveled down and around me, groping my ass while he let out a gruff sound.

"If you don't come to my house tonight, I will come to yours. Either way, you're letting me peel this skirt off your body…"

I tried to catch my breath as his mouth moved down my neck and to the tops of my breasts. "I have to call my parents tonight."

"Call them from my house after you soak your feet. I can tell you're uncomfortable in those boots. They're sexy as fuck, but I know they hurt your toes."

His tub did sound amazing…

He nipped at my ear. "I know you want to. Come on, have a sleepover with me."

"I think"—I blinked, hating that I was the one that had to confess this —"it's starting to confuse me, Colson, I—"

"There's nothing to be confused about. I want you in my bed tonight."

His lips moved to my neck, where he began kissing and sucking, teasing.

"Fine." I pushed at his chest. "I'll come over."

"Good." He gave me one more quick kiss and then pushed away from the wall.

"I'll see you tonight."

I watched him go and shook my head. I needed to get a backbone because without it my heart was completely exposed, and I was going to end up hurt.

17

COLSON

FOURTEEN YEARS OLD

DEAR COLSON,

My name is Mary and I'm one of the nurses that cared for your mother.

I know you called several times last week regarding your mother, worried she wasn't accepting visitors. I have a feeling your father didn't give you much information…Unfortunately it's not my place, but…I know that today is your birthday…I only know because your mother had made a birthday card for you. I kept it out of her personal effects when your father came to pick up her things. I could lose my job if anyone finds out, but your mother meant a great deal to me. She was my favorite patient. And she would have wanted you to have this.

I hope you find some peace in reading it. – Mary

Dear Cole,

My sweet boy, you're fourteen and I can't believe it. I remember when you were just four and loved bringing me flowers from the garden. You loved my garden, Cole. You used to ask if we could sleep in it, while we watched the stars and a few times we did. I don't know if you remember that…but I do.

I know I've missed so much of your life...I know you probably don't forgive me, and I know that one day we'll get over it. We'll make it better. You'll see. We just need time, sweetie. Don't worry about me, I'm strong, and so are you.

Your father explained about his plans with Sherrie...and the child... I know you were worried about how I'd take it, but there's nothing to worry about. I'm fine.

I had a feeling about this when I saw Sherrie pregnant at his office those few years ago.

It doesn't matter. What does matter is you have a little sister, and I want you to be strong for her.

It's not her fault...or your fault that he fell in love again. I don't hate him or hold it against him. He couldn't stay married to me forever.

Don't worry about me, I'll be fine.

I love you, make a wish for me, and let's dream about tomorrow.

Be the best big brother ever.

Love, Mom

IT WAS JUST after five when I saw Nora's new truck pull into her driveway. Not that I was waiting...I just happened to be in my office, going through emails. The reason I had been sitting here for longer than normal after going through my emails is because two more had come in from *her*.

DEAR COLE,
DO YOU KNOW YOUR PLANS YET, OR HOW LONG
YOU'LL BE IN TOWN?

I STILL HADN'T REPLIED to her first correspondence. I wasn't sure what I was supposed to say to any of them…especially the next one I clicked on.

> DEAR COLE,
> I GET THAT YOU HATE ME…I REALLY DO, BUT CAN I GET YOUR CELL NUMBER? I NEED TO TALK TO YOU, IT'S SORT OF IMPORTANT. I CAN WAIT UNTIL CHRISTMAS IF YOU DON'T GET THIS EMAIL, BUT IT'S CRUCIAL THAT I SEE YOU. PLEASE.

THE KNOCK on my door had me closing the laptop screen and walking away. I'd think about that later, for now I had a black pencil skirt to deal with.

"How come you haven't made yourself a key yet?" I joked, swinging the door open for Nora.

She still looked as gorgeous as she did earlier, even if she had tamed those wild, gorgeous curls. She had reapplied the lipstick that she had on when I'd walked in earlier, and I was already imagining that color smeared along the base of my cock.

"Long day?" I kissed her cheek as she set her things down.

"You promised a bath for my toes," she said, sitting on the entryway bench.

Bending low, I carefully pried the high-heeled boots from her toes. "Why are you wearing these? It's like twelve degrees outside."

Wincing in pain, she watched as I gently rubbed the arch of her foot.

"They're cute with this skirt."

My smile turned diabolic. "About this skirt…we need to get you out of it."

Picking her up, and hearing her let out a thrilled squeal, I tossed her up onto my shoulder while running down the hall.

"Colllssson." She shrieked as I entered the room and tossed her on my bed.

"Don't move." Standing, looking down at her as she smiled up at me, my heart burst. This was getting too real for me. If she walked away or…

I pushed the fear down and walked into the bathroom, leaning over the tub to fill it for her.

When I walked back to the bed, Nora had unbuttoned her shirt and was lying there in her white bra and pencil skirt. Her hair fanned out behind her, while her deep purple lips spread in a sensual smile. The way her dark lashes fanned the tops of her cheeks had me bending low and kissing her gently there.

She fit under me so perfectly.

"Do you know how beautiful you are?" I whispered, slowly dragging my finger down her face and tracing it along her collarbone.

She parted her lips as I kept placing small kisses on her face.

"When I first met you"—I pressed my lips gently to her eyelid—"it was your eyes that stopped me."

I moved to her nose, and then her chin. "And those curls... fuck, that hair drove me wild."

I kissed lower, right above her heart where her chest kept rising and falling in quick succession.

"Then you kept showing up on all our work sites, and you'd wear these cute as fuck outfits. I remember two occasions where you wore this skirt."

I moved lower, licking between her cleavage and up along the swells of her breasts. Her fingers tangled in my hair gently, rubbing in a caress.

"You would bring coffee for all the guys, and in my mind, I would make up this story that you saved me for last because you wanted that few seconds of eye contact. Do you remember all those times I'd stare at you while our fingers would touch? Some days, I waited all day just to see you come by."

I knew I had to stop; this was crossing too many lines, but I couldn't seem to.

"Then you moved in right next to me and at first, I thought it was your dad playing a joke on me. I honestly assumed he'd bought it and put you there to tempt me, but now I realize it may have been fate."

Her breathing was ragged, her stomach was dipping as my lips trailed a line down to her belly button. Swirling my tongue there and holding her ribs, I placed a gentle, sweet kiss against her pebbling skin. I let my mind wander for two seconds, thinking what it would be like to do this someday, with her...while she was swollen with our kid. I'd kiss her belly every night, I'd run her baths and take her shoes off.

Looking up at her, I admitted how I felt. "That first time you smiled at me, that's when you had me."

"Colson," she whispered, bringing her hand to my jaw and pulling my face up. She had tears in her eyes, one went rogue, running down the side of her temple.

Our gazes clashed, and there were three words on the tip of my tongue, she seemed to struggle to say something too as she opened her lips.

"Colson, I—"

The sound of water splashing made both our eyes go wide.

"The bath!" Nora gasped as I jumped up and ran.

"Shittt." I stepped through the overflowing water and turned the faucet until it stopped.

The water had spread to every corner of the bathroom, soaking the bathmats and circling around the toilet.

"I'll go get towels," Nora said after peering in the doorway.

She darted away as I reached for the two hanging and a few left on the shelf. Throwing them down, I mopped up the water. Nora walked back with a huge pile in her arms.

We laughed as we cleaned up the mess, but the confession on the bed had gotten tangled in my rib cage, threatening to tear it completely apart and expose my heart.

I had to protect it.

I'd said too fucking much.

"Here, the bath is still good, come on over."

I held out my hand to her, and she stepped closer while her arms dipped back, peeling off her shirt.

Turning her so she faced away from me, I deftly moved my fingers over the back of her skirt until I had the zipper and pulled. Excitement thrummed in my sternum as I carefully bent her forward. I had waited all day for this moment, to see her ass peeking out from the open fabric of her skirt. Nora peeked over her shoulder as the zipper parted and then laughed.

My face fell.

"What are these?" I rubbed the material with the pads of my fingers, confused why her thong and ass wasn't currently filling my palm.

She smirked, her chin on her shoulder, her lips spread wide while she wiggled her ass.

"Fleece tights."

With a sarcastic laugh, I roughly pulled the material down her hips and then stopped at her thighs. She made some sort of squeaking sound as she tried to catch her balance by falling forward and grabbing the counter.

She couldn't move, and I finally had total and complete access to her.

She sucked in a quick breath as I stood behind her and ran my hand down her back, adjusting her so that her chest was bent over the counter.

I didn't waste any time getting her prepped, or wet. I didn't let her orgasm or tell her to play with herself like usual.

I stared at her round ass and lightly slapped the cheek. I repeated the process, then pulled my cock out and lined myself up.

Then I thrust forward.

Nora gasped, gripping the edge of the counter.

I pulled out the slightest bit, wrapped her hair around my fist and then thrust again.

I realized me taking her like this, how rough I had entered her, and the way I held her hair, it contradicted the sweet sentiment I had shared in the bedroom, but that was calculated on my part. I had shared too much, gotten too real...and it was going to scare her off if I didn't rectify it and remind her that it was just physical.

"Such a fucking tight pussy." I grunted in between thrusts. "Look at how well you take this cock."

She made a whimpering sound, gasping for air as I exposed her neck, pulling on her hair.

In the mirror, our bodies reflected an erotic visual as her breasts pushed against the cups of her bra, jolting every time I drove into her. Those aqua eyes were half open, watching me as I watched her. Her left hand lifted from the side, and slowly drifted down to her clit and while we fucked in the mirror, I watched her rub circles into that pink center.

But that would have her coming too soon, so I reached around and slapped her hand away. Her eyes grew wide as I let her hair go and gripped her by the hips and pulled her away from the counter.

"What are—" I kneeled down and tore the leggings and skirt from her legs, freeing her.

"Take off your bra," I gritted out, moving to the tub.

It was still plenty hot, so I finished stripping and settled inside, resting my head against the pillow.

Nora watched me while a line formed between her dark brows.

"Come here." I held out my hand, inviting her into the tub.

She did as I said and dipped her toe into the steaming water. She kept her eyes on my fist, where under the water, I rubbed my cock until she lowered herself while lining up with my tip. Her knees went wide as she sank down, inch by inch. Even with the water, it took her a few seconds to adjust completely. Once she did, her hands landed on my bare chest, and her eyes locked on mine.

I flashed her a carnal smile and pulled on the ends of her hair, tilting her head again.

"Now fuck me."

Parting her lips, she did as I said, rocking her hips. Water sloshed as she moved but I didn't care, we'd already made a mess of the room.

"Don't hold back, Nora. Fuck me like you want to milk this cock for every drop of pleasure that your pussy always gets. Show me how greedy you can be."

Her movements increased, she gripped the base of my neck as she took what she wanted from me, rotating and grinding against my hardness. She moaned, making sharp crying sounds every time my cock hit her G spot, and while she fucked me, I savored her tits.

The water splashed over her breasts as they bobbed and bounced. I pulled them into my palms and sucked the hardened nipples into my mouth as she threw her head back and moaned.

I let her breasts go to pin her hips with my hands, thrusting in harsh strokes.

"This, Nora…fuckkk." I bellowed, finishing inside of her.

Sinking against me, she nestled her head under my chin as she slowly caught her breath. I traced lines into her back softly...gently stroking her arms around my neck as she clung to me.

We stayed like that until I finally lifted her hips, and she freed my softening cock, but I returned her to my lap where I could hold her against me. I wanted to stay like this...just holding her, stroking her back while toying with pieces of her hair. The bathroom was a mess, we hadn't lit candles, the overhead light was on and brash against our skin as every single towel I owned save for two were on the floor to mop up water.

It was ridiculous and not romantic, and yet it felt real. The most tangible thing I had ever held between my palms.

Growing up, I always assumed relationships had to look perfect in order to last. My parents, from what I could remember, always smiled and doted on each other when we were in public. But behind closed doors there was always a lot of yelling and crying. The house was a disaster until our maid would come and clean up Mom's outbursts. I remembered helping one time and my mother took my hand, leading me away from the mess while tears streamed down her face.

She smiled at me like she didn't know mascara ran down her cheeks, or that her lipstick was smeared. She would take me to her garden and tell me to make sure it looked presentable...things didn't last unless we made them look worthy of care. Maybe that was why Nora was such a mindfuck to me. She never seemed to care about those things, her hair could be frizzy and wild, or tamed and relaxed. She could have it matted to her face from a workout, or tucked under a hat while she worked in her garden. Her house was the ugliest one on this block, and yet she was the most substantial person I had ever known.

Maybe it wasn't about the exterior, but what was built inside that made someone worthy of being cared for.

"I have to go call my parents before it gets too late." Nora suddenly broke into my thoughts.

I kissed the side of her head and helped her up.

"You call, I'll go start dinner."

NORA WALKED AROUND in one of my larger T-shirts that stopped at the tops of her naked thighs. She paced the living room while I sautéed chicken. She'd already spoken to them about the weather and her business at the community center and then the conversation switched, and I felt the tension in the room.

"Since all your stuff is packed, did you and Dad want to have Christmas at my house?" Nora asked, toying with the ends of her hair.

I added garlic and cream to the chicken, flicking my gaze up a few times to make sure she was okay. There was silence, and then Nora stopped pacing.

"What do you mean a cruise?"

Fuck, that hit hard.

I knew, and I hadn't warned her, and that fucking shitty thorn in my chest resurged. I tried to drown out the guilt with the notion that it wasn't my place to interfere, and Nora and I had just recently started getting along.

"But—you can't just leave…" Nora sunk to the couch; her shoulders caved in as she held her cell to her ear.

"So you're leaving before Christmas, going on a cruise and then when you get back you're heading straight to Arizona? What happened to spring?"

Her voice was cracking, and it made my chest physically hurt.

"Don't worry about me…No, Rae is leaving too. I'm an adult now, I can stay home for Christmas on my own, it's not a big deal…Yes, Colson does live right next door." She turned to look at me.

I froze on the spot.

Fuck.

Shit.

She didn't know that I wasn't allowed to be with her. She didn't know and if she said…

"Well, no, I don't know when he's leaving. But does it really matter?"

My heart practically jolted out of my chest. The chicken was burning, so I flipped the burner and set the dish aside.

"No, you can't talk to him, I'll ask him. But you guys are officially off the hook…It is late, I'm here because we…"

Her gaze snapped to mine, likely gauging what I wanted her to say.

"We're…well, honestly, I have no idea, but it's casual."

My eyes closed slowly.

I didn't know what hurt worse, the fact that the company was gone, or that she didn't seem to know if we were a thing.

"Colson looks like he might pass out, so I'm going to go. Merry Christmas, call me when you're in Arizona." She ended the call and ran over to me.

"Are you okay?"

I blew out a long and heavy breath, bracing my hands on the counter.

"Yeah…I just think your dad might want to kill me now."

She smiled at me, cupping my jaw. "I promise he won't. He talks about you all the time. I swear he loves you."

"Yeah?" I said for her benefit, but I knew better. He liked me as an employee, a VP but not as an option for his daughter.

Gripping her wrist and pulling her closer, I pressed my lips to hers briefly and then asked her something completely insane and something that I probably shouldn't.

"So it sounds like he mentioned my plans?"

Nora popped a piece of chicken into her mouth, keeping her eyes down.

"Yeah, they seem to think I should crash someone's holiday in order to survive. I'm an adult and will be perfectly fine on my own."

Right…why was I so nervous to ask this?

"Well, about that…I don't really like the idea of being away from you for a week and if you're going to be alone, then why not come with me?"

Her eyes snapped up again, surprise evident in how wide those aqua orbs had gotten. Her lips parted as she stared, and then she blinked.

"Sorry…did I hear you correctly?"

Smirking, I tried to push away the nerves. "Yeah, come to California with me."

What was the worst that could happen? She'd meet my shitty family, we'd have sex, I'd show her how to surf, we'd have sex again, and she could meet my brothers. The more I thought about it, the more I was beginning to like it.

"What do you think? Want to spend Christmas on the beach?"

Her long stare and flushing face weren't the best sign...maybe I'd ruined this entire thing by asking.

Fuck.

18

NORA

I TUCKED the blankets under my chin and closed my eyes, trying again to fall asleep.

The house was at the perfect temperature, no lights were on, so that wasn't bugging me. I hadn't had any sugar past seven.

I loved Colson's bed…and well, Colson himself, which was something I was finally comfortable admitting in my head at least.

So, why couldn't I sleep?

I moved my toes, stretching them under the blankets. I was sore from earlier, but the bath helped ease any discomfort. Still, his fucking monster dick was on my shit list right now. After dinner, he had tried to start things again, and I shut him down.

A girl needed to rest.

So, we went to bed, and I have just been lying awake.

Colson finally turned toward me and let out a loud exhale.

"You're very loud when you can't sleep."

I tilted my head on the pillow and stared at him in the dark.

"I literally haven't said or done anything but stare at the ceiling."

"It's this." He put his hand on my chest. "I can tell when you're upset or breathing harder than normal. When worry slips in and ties up your heart, I feel it tighten around mine too."

I grabbed his hand and brought it to my lips, kissing the pads of his fingers.

"I think I'm struggling to wrap my head around what you offered."

I could tell his eyes were still closed as he stroked my arm.

"What?"

"Your offer, the one where you said I should go with you for Christmas."

"Oh. That." He let out another sigh, moving to his back.

"Yeah…that seems big."

"It's not." He clipped out.

I hated when he did that, downsized something that felt significantly large.

"You're taking me home to meet your family for Christmas, won't they ask who I am to you?"

"No."

Fuck, he annoyed me.

It was my turn to let out a sigh, which must have made him realize he was frustrating me.

"Nora, my family is fucked-up. They want to see me once or twice a year so that we can be photographed together, or so they can brag about their latest accomplishment. Trust me. They don't care who I'm currently fucking."

Ouch.

My voice was a little wispy as I asked, "So you'll introduce me as the girl you're currently fucking, then?"

His snort wasn't encouraging.

But he moved closer, his chin dropped to the hollow of my neck as he pulled me into his arms.

"Nora, if I knew that it wouldn't scare you the fuck off, I'd introduce you as my girlfriend, but I'm trying to play by your rules."

"My rules?" I asked, pulling out of his arms.

He sounded exasperated.

I didn't care.

"Yes, you're the one who asked for no strings attached…did you forget that?"

Oh no, he did not just act like I was the one who wanted this. I jumped out of bed and flicked on the light.

"Fuck, Nora." Colson groaned, covering his eyes.

I crossed my arms and paced the room.

"I need you to explain. What do you mean that I'm the one who wanted that?"

"I have bedside lamps…"

Ignoring him, I asked again.

"What did you mean?"

"Fuck…" He lifted his arm and dropped it on the bed. "I showed up at your house with flowers, and dinner, Nora, and somehow you drew the conclusion that I wanted something casual?"

Wait…

I had completely missed that. I mean, he'd been taking care of me with my back, and the pipes…I just thought it went with his savior complex.

Stepping closer to the edge of the bed with arms linked, I stared down at him.

His hands were over his eyes, and the blankets pooled around his waist, revealing his muscled chest. It made me think back to all the sweet things he'd said before the bath. The confession. I had tossed the entire thing away as a move to fuck me, especially because of how brash and rough he was with me directly after said confession.

"So you wanted…" I faltered, too nervous to throw it out there and risk rejection.

Finally, he sat up, glared at me, and answered.

"Strings. Lots of them, Nora. A tie for every fucking thing you do and say. Preferably you tied to my bed, naked, so I can do lots of wicked things to you. Now please turn off the fucking light."

He plopped back down and the last latch in my heart opened, releasing a set of wings. My entire chest swelled, feeling my heart take flight.

He wanted strings.

With me…

"Why didn't you say that then, and why did you confess all that to me then get rough in the bathroom?"

He groaned from under a pillow, then sat up. "Because I didn't want to scare you off, and I was so worried that you wanted no strings that I tried like hell to pull back any that I might let show. I was worried you'd walk away."

My heart flipped because while he didn't say it…his sentiment felt an awful lot like love.

"Nora…please." He muttered, tugging the pillow back over his face.

Turning on my heel, I flipped the light off.

"Now come back to bed."

I did as he said, crawling in and pulling the covers high. He pulled me to his chest, intertwined his legs with mine, and whispered in my ear.

"You're a ridiculous kind of crazy, baby. But you're *my* ridiculous kind of crazy." He kissed my jaw and then said, "Now go to sleep."

And I did.

"OH MY GOSH, THIS TREE!" I gasped, tilting my head back as I stared at the largest decorated Christmas tree I had ever seen. It was lush with white lights, golden and red bulbs, silver and golden beads, and ribbons tied around it. My designer heart soared.

Rae stood next to me and let out a soft but happy sigh. "Isn't it gorgeous?"

"I haven't even decorated my tiny one yet."

Which reminded me that we needed to have the girls over to help us, but it was just a few days until Christmas, and Colson and I were leaving for California. It was why we were up at our friends' house, visiting them before we took off.

Davis and Colson were talking on the back porch while fresh snow fell, and the dogs played in the yard. Rae had invited us up for lunch, considering dinner would put us on the mountain at night, and my anxiety couldn't take that.

"Okay so…" Rae said, flicking her eyes to mine as she headed back into the kitchen to prep lunch. "California…Colson…spill."

I spent the time cutting vegetables, explaining what Colson had told me the night prior.

"So, he ended up confessing first, then?"

Taking the salad plates from her, I set them on the table and tried to push away the blush creeping along my neck.

"Yes, it seems that way, doesn't it? I just hate this...I felt broken. I completely missed all the signs, and even when he was practically confessing his love to me last night, I assumed he was trying to get laid."

Rae's eyes softened sympathetically. "It makes me feel the tiniest bit better that I'm not the only person who missed signs and well, you still can't top my crazy with the way I stalked Davis..."

"It's not like I want to...but I think that what happened to me before ..."

"It messed with you," Rae added for me.

I nodded, hating the truth.

"Well, meeting Colson's family is a big deal, so keep your guard up. Has he told you very much about his past, or any of them?"

I thought that over and realized he hadn't, but it wasn't like I had asked.

"Umm, I know what I've read on the internet..."

"That's the other thing." Rae walked over to the cupboard and grabbed two glasses and handed them to me before grabbing another two. "His family is rich and kind of famous."

That didn't bother me anymore...at least I didn't think it did. "Being rich and famous doesn't really faze me, people are people."

Rae lit a candle in the middle of the table and flicked her eyes to mine.

"Okay, but you haven't asked him personally about what you might have read. Don't you think you should know about his parents and siblings, like on a personal level, as in should you bring anything, or will they expect you to sleep in separate rooms?"

Dammit, she was right.

Slumping into a chair, I blew out a breath and set my chin in my palm.

"So how do I ask without trying to come across as nosy?"

Rae grabbed her white wine and settled next to me.

"Just ask...or don't and form your own conclusions when you get there."

Yeah, that could work.

Davis opened the door, carrying a glass pan with steaks and a few pieces of chicken. He was laughing at something Colson had said to him, with a devastating smile and a set of eyes that searched for Rae the moment he stepped inside. The way they gravitated toward one another still made me swoon. My best friend had found her person, and the way he treated her set the bar fucking high for the rest of us mortals who didn't have grumpy mountain men who worshipped the ground we walked on.

However, Colson's gaze did exactly what Davis's had, that smile grew and then he dipped and pressed his lips to mine in a quick but sweet kiss. As our first form of public affection, I wasn't entirely sure what to do with it.

I grabbed his hand under the table.

Colson drank a beer while Davis and Rae explained the details of their wedding that was coming up in a few months. They wanted a quick ceremony up here where they lived, with a small number of guests. Davis asked Colson if he'd be a groomsman, Rae had finally asked me to be her maid of honor by sliding a gold bracelet my way and telling me I better start planning.

"I already have an entire Pinterest board created for you," I assured her with a hug.

On the way back down the mountain, I asked Colson a few questions about his family like Rae had suggested.

I looked over at him, feeling nerves shudder under my skin. "Is there anything I should know about your family?"

He laughed, looked over and smiled, then put his eyes back on the road.

"What do you mean, exactly?"

Shit, already off to a bad start.

Shifting in my seat, I tried again. "Well...we're staying with your parents, right?"

"My dad, yeah," he clarified with a tight jaw.

"So, your mom isn't in the picture, then?"

I wanted to tread carefully with this question because of how solemn and closed off he seemed when the girls had pulled that box of photos of her out.

He adjusted his hand on the steering wheel, but the muscle in his jaw kept jumping, until he finally muttered. "No."

Okayyy...

"Um...so, do you get along with your siblings, or are there any black sheep of the family I should watch out for?"

"I'm the black sheep." He looked over again, but his stare was heavy. "I get along fine with my brothers."

That was good. Right, no drama with the brothers meant things were good.

"Do they know you're bringing me?"

Slowing down, he put his blinker on and turned his steering wheel before he smiled at me.

"Yes, they know."

Okay. This whole conversation felt great...just fucking wonderful.

I looked out the window, feeling defeated. I was going to have to show up and make my own conclusions.

I saw him glance over again out of my periphery. "So, Liam texted me...he mentioned having a training session that was booked last-minute. I know he could use the money, so I'm going to have the girls come over. Would you be okay with me bringing them over to help decorate your tree?"

Smiling at the mention of the girls, I looked back over.

"Of course."

At least we wouldn't be stuck brooding over this awkward as fuck conversation.

19

COLSON

SIXTEEN YEARS OLD

DEAR MOM,

This feels stupid...but my therapist said it was a good idea.

Feels fucking lame, though. Because I'm not reading it to anyone, no matter what that guy suggests, and you'll never see it.

So, what's the point?

I don't even know what to tell you...maybe that I'm graduating early. But don't be proud of that. I'm graduating so I can get away from Dad, and his new family. Don't worry, the boys have fallen in famously with them. They're one big happy family, I'm the one with the issues.

I'm the one who remembers my dead mother.

I'm the one who keeps yelling and screaming at everyone because I feel like no one else does.

I blame him. I can't not blame him, Mom, and I know you'd tell me not to. I know you'd tell me to let it go and focus on something else, but I don't want to.

And I don't want their family. Not Sherrie. Not her...

I don't want any of it.

So, I hope you're in heaven, loving your garden. Maybe one day I'll find someone who makes me feel sunshine the way you always did. Maybe one day I'll find another garden to nurture with someone who wants me like this. Broken and bruised.

   I'll dream about tomorrow, Mom.

   Love, Cole

THE NEAREST AIRPORT was two hours away, so Nora and I had to get on the road soon, but I had to make a pit stop at the office first. Peter apparently had an emergency.

Like fuck did I believe he actually had a crisis, but by going in, I could finally put to rest all the shit I knew he wanted to say about what Nora had said the other night.

The office parking lot was empty, save for Peter's truck, and considering Christmas Eve was tomorrow, all our projects were on hold. Snow still covered the sidewalks, the top of the building, and all the empty spaces. The sky was dark and graying, but at least the forecast was clear, so Nora and I could leave for Portland on clear roads.

I parked next to him, hopped out, and hustled inside.

Peter was at his desk, like last time, but now there were no pictures of his wife or Nora on his desk, nothing on his walls. The desk was completely empty, which made me think we could have met somewhere else, or even talked about this on the phone.

"Peter." I greeted my boss.

His graying hair seemed even lighter, and his eyes seemed darker as they focused on me from behind his glasses.

"Colson. Thank you for making the time to come before your flight."

Settling into the seat across from him, I asked, "Don't you have a cruise to catch?"

He brought his hands together in front of him and inhaled a sharp breath.

"No, actually. After our conversation with Nora the other night, we realized that we needed to stay here for Christmas. For her."

Well, here the fuck we went.

Rubbing at my jaw, I tried to keep the "fuck off" vibe out of my tone as I said, "Well, Nora is coming to California with me."

Peter stood, shoving his chair behind him.

"What part of me not wanting you two to be romantically involved do you not understand?"

I slowly got to my feet because like fuck was I going to allow anyone to yell down at me.

"Sir, with all due respect, Nora didn't realize you'd be here, so I offered for her to accompany me as my guest."

Peter's eyes narrowed. "And is that all she is to you? A guest?"

I waited, unsure if I wanted to do this…but after closing my eyes and taking a deep breath, I ripped it off like a Band-Aid.

"No. She'll be introduced as my girlfriend."

"You prick." Peter seethed.

I ground my molars together, not wanting to fight with him, but needing to stand my ground.

"I love her, Peter. I'm in love with her…you know this, fuck, you knew it the day I met her."

"And I told you this can't happen."

I shook my head incredulously. "And I listened to you and almost ruined everything with her. I stayed away from her for a year, Peter."

"You stabbed me in the back…took an assignment and twisted it to fit your own agenda."

Gripping the back of the chair, I dipped my head and laughed.

"My agenda? Are you fucking serious? I wanted this company, Peter. I worked my ass off, I wanted to be the first in line to buy it from you. That was my agenda. That and falling for my next-door neighbor—"

"She won't be your neighbor for long," Peter said, like he knew a secret that I didn't.

I decided to ruin that for him too.

"You're right, I plan on asking her to move in with me around the new year."

"Why did you want this company, Colson?" He tilted his head as though he were truly curious. But Peter had heard about my family…he knew about my father.

"I want something that's just mine...something I can build, leave to my family if I ever have one. Something that isn't tied to my father in any way."

"And you're willing to give all that up for a twenty-three-year-old girl who can't even decide what her favorite flavor of ice cream is?"

She seemed to like mint...didn't she?

"I wouldn't have to choose, Peter, if you'd accept the fact that I'm with her."

He shuddered like I'd slapped him.

"You said it yourself, the Hanes name is poison. I don't want her near it."

I spread my hands. "I don't speak to my family but a few times a year...she won't be affected by them. I promise you that. Still, at the end of the day, this is her life and she needs to live it."

Peter slammed his hands down on his desk. "You can't do this. She'll change her mind. She needs wings, not someone who comes home every day with concrete on his clothes."

"Why is it okay as her father to have this job, but not the man who wants to settle down with her?"

My boss scoffed. "You'd understand if you were a father. Any parent wants their kid to have better. I want her to be taken care of, swept away. I want her to see the world. If she marries you, you'll put a kid in her right away and she'll be stuck here. You'll work some construction job, and she'll resent you for the life you kept her from."

Done with hearing any more, I shoved off from the chair and backed up.

"If you do this...if you choose to take her with you for Christmas, you're pulling your name from the bid officially, and, Colson, something tells me you're going to want to have your name on that list after you realize who else has put theirs on it."

Dipping my brows, I turned back toward him. "What does that mean?"

"I'm not showing all my cards, but I am telling you, once you realize what's at stake, you'll be calling me."

I gave him one last look before walking out of his office.

NORA WAS ready to go when I got to her house, her two small suitcases were in her entryway as she ensured all her plants were well watered, her shades were shut, and her cupboard doors opened under the sink and in the bathroom, in case we had another bad freeze.

"All set?"

She beamed at me excitedly, wearing dark skinny jeans, a teal shirt that matched her eyes, and a pair of high heels.

"Yeah, just let me make sure my truck is locked up."

As she grabbed her key fob, I gripped the handle to one of her suitcases, ready to haul it out, but guilt got the best of me.

"I just saw your dad…" I waited for her to turn toward me, see my expression, and realize something was wrong.

But she didn't speak up or interrupt me.

"He mentioned that they decided to stay home for Christmas…to be with you."

She grabbed her coat from the hook by the door and shoved her arms through.

"Huh… well, they never said anything to me."

Shifting on my feet uncomfortably, I asked the one thing I didn't want the answer to…because if she turned me down and I didn't get to have her for Christmas, it would kill me.

"Well, I don't feel right taking you from them if they—"

She stepped up to me, smoothing her hands along my jaw.

"Colson, my parents wanted to show me what it was like not to have them…I hope they have a great Christmas, but I'm going with you…that is, if you still want me."

Breathing a little easier, I wrapped my arms around her and pulled her tight.

"Of course, I want you."

"Good, then let's catch our flight." She smiled and dipped to grab one of her suitcases.

On the plane, I checked my phone before switching it to Airplane Mode, and realized I had another email.

DEAR COLE,
I HEARD YOU'RE BRINGING SOMEONE WITH YOU
THIS YEAR...I GUESS I DON'T KNOW HOW TO FEEL
ABOUT THAT. MAYBE EXCITED...BUT PLEASE
UNDERSTAND THAT I NEED TO TALK TO YOU WHEN
YOU GET HERE. IT'S REALLY IMPORTANT. MORE
IMPORTANT THAN PISSING HIM OFF.

AGAIN, I hated that she didn't sign it.

It always made me feel like she was trying to remind me of who I had made her out to be in my life.

No one.

Nora's hand closed over mine. I rested my head against the seat and closed my eyes.

This was probably going to be a shitshow, but at least for the first time in my life, I didn't have to face it alone.

20

NORA

THE WEATHER WAS sunny and gorgeous when we landed at LAX and drove along the coastline to Malibu. Colson was reserved and quiet but he covered my knee with his large palm and we relaxed in the back seat of a luxury town car.

Apparently Colson's father, Oliver, had ordered it to pick us up. I had no idea what to expect being around his family, but seeing the town car parked with Colson's last name scrawled onto it was basically the coolest thing that had ever happened to me.

Colson, of course, didn't act fazed whatsoever.

As we drove, I tried to appreciate how beautiful the white-capped waves looked underneath the sapphire sky, but my nerves got the better of me. Colson seemed to have flipped some sort of switch emotionally. His hand remained on my thigh, but his gaze was distant. I was gathering that he didn't like coming home often, especially from the little he'd said about them when he mentioned he only saw them once or twice a year and their reunions were usually shallow.

It left me feeling apprehensive... but as I looked over and Colson tightened his grip on my leg, I decided not to worry.

After driving for close to an hour, we circled a massive butte with the glistening ocean directly off the sheer cliffside. Once we crested the top, we drove past two massive mansions that had privacy gates, security, and a plethora of other systems in place that screamed expensive and important.

When the nose of the car finally turned down a drive, with its gate wide open, I had expected something modern…maybe a mansion that looked like something I had seen in a movie or on a magazine cover. But the car pulled up to an older, almost rustic-looking house. Red brick sprawled up the length of three stories with large, gaping windows. The roof was black, same with the front door, and there were at least three chimneys jutting from various places along the ridge.

Behind the house was a steep drop, and what seemed to be one of the best views of the entire Pacific Ocean.

The driver opened my door, and I gingerly stepped out, conflicted by the way it felt to have the sun setting while the sea air whipped through my hair in gentle waves. I was so used to feeling the bitter cold and snow. In fact, I wouldn't even know it was December save for the Santa and reindeer display off to the side of the walkway. It was all set up nicely, and I was sure once the sun had set, lights would wink on, making it a marvelous sight.

A gentle hand guided at my back as Colson encouraged me to walk.

Swallowing my nerves, I strolled forward, realizing the doorman would handle our luggage. Before Colson could knock, or push through the door, it swung open and a woman in what looked like her early forties greeted us. She had big brown eyes, with long, lush lashes, perfectly shaped brows and glossy pink lips. She was stunningly perfect, without a single wrinkle or hair out of place. Her sheer dress was shimmery and golden, her high heels were tall, opened toed, revealing perfectly manicured feet.

When she smiled eagerly at Colson and went in for a hug, a part of me wanted to shove my hand in front of her face and tell her to back off. Especially when Colson gripped my hand and froze in place.

"Sherrie."

His tone was ice cold, telling me all I needed to know about this woman.

We did not like her.

"Cole, oh my God, it's been so long. I can't believe you're here." She fussed, going in for another attempted hug. He didn't release my hand as she wrapped her arms around him, and he never once lifted his arm to hug her back.

Getting the message, she finally stepped back and cleared her throat.

"So, you have a guest this year?"

Her brown eyes looked me up and down, as though I was the trash her expensive sea breeze had blown in.

Colson pushed me forward.

"My girlfriend, Nora."

Oh hell, he'd done it. He labeled us, and my heart was not prepared.

Jutting my hand out, I introduced myself.

"Nora Petrov, nice to meet you."

Sherrie's eyes widened the smallest bit, then flicked to Colson.

"Petrov? I feel like I've heard that name before." Her brows pinched like she was trying to figure it out. "Well goodness, where are my manners, I'm Sherrie Hanes, welcome to our home."

She moved to the side and walked us into her house, which nearly stole my breath.

Cherrywood floors sprawled beneath our feet, polished so well it nearly reflected the grand chandeliers hanging in the foyer. Yes, the entryway was large enough to have two. A grand staircase with the same wood crawled all the way up to the third floor. The banister was wrought iron, giving the house an older feel.

"Cole, we prepared two rooms for you because we weren't sure of your relationship with Nora. If it's okay, we'll keep that arrangement."

Colson kept pace at my back, showing no emotion or giving any indication that what she'd said bothered him, until then.

"No. She'll sleep in my room."

A shudder ran down my back at his terse tone. He did not like Sherrie, and it made me curious about their relationship.

"Okay, perfectly fine. I know if it were me visiting my boyfriend's family, I would want to show a little propriety, but times are changing, aren't they?"

She tried to joke, but her dig landed exactly where she wanted it to. That paired with the cold tone and robotic way Colson acted, made me snap.

"Don't worry, I have manners. When we fuck, I'll be sure no one hears."

Sherrie's eyes popped open, her mouth dropped, gaping like a fish.

Colson snorted, turning it into a cough to cover it up.

I didn't care. Anyone who thought it was okay to talk to their guests the way she did didn't deserve propriety.

"Right. Well, Colson, you know where your room is. I'll let you two get settled, then we will see you at dinner at six."

Sherrie spun away, a cloud of perfume and irritability leaving in her wake.

Colson tugged my hand, guiding me toward the staircase. We walked up, Colson trailing behind me with the luggage. I wanted to help, but he kept pushing me forward.

"Here," he said, gesturing with his head toward the hall once we'd cleared the second floor. The windows on this side of the house were open, letting the breeze in from the ocean. I moved to them so I could see the view from the back of the house.

"Oh my gosh," I breathed, watching as the sun set on the horizon. The water roared in the distance below, crawling up the cliff.

"This is beautiful."

I gently touched the pane of glass, loving how the windows seemed to let in the whole sky.

"This used to be my mother's favorite spot…in the house at least," Colson whispered from behind me.

I snapped my head around, hating the wince he tried to hide, and the tick in his jaw that jumped before he walked past me, down the hall.

I had so many questions, but I could tell it was a topic that was buried in his heart, guarded by a thousand thorns and brambles.

Trailing after him, he opened the last door in the hall, which revealed a spacious room surrounded by windows. In the center of the room was a massive king-size bed, covered in thick feather down comforters and at least ten pillows bordered the headboard, and two white nightstands stood on either side of the bed with matching lamps.

"This is nice," I tilted my head back, taking in the nice crown molding around the top of the ceiling, the chandelier dripped with tiny crystals, but added a classy ambiance to the room, with the white accent rugs and cozy chairs that faced a quaint fireplace, it all went together perfectly.

"Go see the balcony." Colson laid our suitcases down and gave me a smile.

I walked to the glass French doors that I assumed were large windows and pushed them open.

The breeze tangled my hair and blew the scent of the sea across my skin. I closed my eyes and let it have me, relishing how good it felt to be on this coastline again. I hadn't hated my time in California. I had missed home, but I enjoyed my time on the beaches, feeling that warm bay air caress my skin and leave my hair wild and untamed.

Strong arms came around me, pulling me to a firm chest as Colson settled his chin on my shoulder.

"I like having you here with me."

Grabbing his hands as they circled my waist, I settled into him.

"Even if I piss off Sherrie?"

He laughed, nuzzling my neck. "Because you piss her off. I can't stand her…I like that you stood up to her."

"There's something ugly in her heart. I can tell."

He sighed, lifting his head. "That seems true, at least from what I know of her."

Turning in his arms, I toyed with his hair.

"How long has she been your stepmom?"

His eyes landed on mine; worry was woven into every fleck of blue.

"Sorry, we don't have to talk about it…" I tried to recover.

He swallowed, his throat bobbing as he continued to watch me.

"It's just…I turn into a bit of an asshole when I talk about it."

Rubbing his arms, I tried to put him at ease.

"Well, I can handle it. If you need to be an asshole to get it out, then be one."

I love you. I love you. I love you.

Internally I screamed it at him, but I couldn't get myself to say the words out loud.

His forehead fell to mine, and we stood there with the sea air billowing around us, the sun setting, the lavender and orange streaks turning to a murky gray.

"She was my father's secretary a long time ago, closer to your age when she started working for him. She was involved with our family a lot back then. Coming to holiday dinners, birthdays, and when my mother would get sick…she'd be here helping."

I pieced things together, not needing him to fill it in. She was the other woman, and now the Mrs. Hanes that the public saw. I had never thought to do a google search on Oliver Hanes, or his wife. Now it made me curious what happened to Colson's mother. He'd mentioned sickness, so maybe she had cancer, or something else similar to that.

"I hated her then…I always felt uncomfortable having her here. I always saw the way my dad looked at her. The way he'd play with her hair when he'd walk past her or pinch her ass when he thought no one was looking. He was obsessed with her…and if my mother hadn't been in the picture, I wouldn't have held it against him. As an adult, I can look back and see that he'd fallen in love with her."

"But your mother…" I whispered, unsure if I was overstepping.

Colson rubbed my arms, but stepped back.

"It's getting cold, why don't we head inside."

He pulled me by the hand without waiting for me to answer. I gave one last look at the horizon, curious how many times Colson had come out here and watched his days end, or how many new mornings he had to witness… and how painful each of them were for him, considering how much pain he showed whenever his mother was brought up.

COLSON AND I BOTH SHOWERED, separately.

I knew he needed space, so when I offered to go first, and he let me without trying to join, I knew he was trying to deal with whatever demons had come out to fight with him since arriving here.

I did my makeup and worked smoothing product into my hair before drying it.

Once I was done, I straightened and then curled a few strands, leaving my hair wavy. With my hair and makeup done, I slipped into a black dress that dipped modestly, revealing the tip of my cleavage, wrapped around my hips in a tight, sensual way, and then fell to the floor, leaving a long slit up the side.

Walking out of the bathroom, while putting an earring in my ear, I didn't realize Colson had stopped buttoning his white shirt.

Our gazes clashed momentarily. I smiled, finishing with my earrings, but his hungry stare wouldn't stop caressing my curves.

I could feel the heat crackle in the air, even without his hands on me, he was fucking me with his eyes. Raw and hard.

My breathing hitched as I walked toward my shoes, but when I stood, he was there at my back. His lips came to my shoulder, and slowly he lowered the strap of my dress.

"Colson, we have to go to dinner," I said, feeling my heart jack hammer at his touch.

He growled something unintelligible and gripped my ass through my dress.

"We don't *have* to do anything." His lips marked my jaw and up near my ear, where he swirled his tongue around the shell.

This was his house and his family, so if he wanted to go down late, then we would. Hell, it would drive home the point I had made to Sherrie.

"You have two choices," Colson whispered in my ear, pulling my hips against his erection, "either I thrust into you again, like I did in the bathroom that night and just let your pussy adjust..." He lowered the other strap of my dress, making it pool at my waist.

"Option two?" I asked breathlessly.

He slid my hair to the side, away from my neck.

"You get on your knees and use that tongue to get my cock nice and wet, so it's ready for you."

I turned, looking up at him through my lashes, and felt his thumb press into my lower lip.

Then I slowly lowered to my knees.

My fingers worked the button on his soft slacks, pushing them down and freeing him from the confines of his boxers.

His hands picked up my hair, cupped the back of my skull, gently pushing me closer to his bobbing cock.

Gripping the base with my hand, I licked up along the shaft, wetting the entire monstrous size of him. If he was going to fuck me, he was going to be lubricated.

His hiss and the way his hips jumped forward told me he liked the way I licked him.

"Wrap those lips around my cock, Nora. I need you."

The way his eyes blazed with heat had me opening for him and taking him as deep as I could go.

"We have to get it nice and wet, baby, which means you're going to have to choke a few times," he pushed further into my mouth, hitting the back of my throat until I couldn't breathe. Saliva pooled in my mouth, and I felt it drop down his shaft as he pulled back and strings of spittle left my mouth, clinging to him.

He groaned and repeated the process, pushing my head down until I was choking, sucking him into my mouth, licking and being reckless with how messy my chin and lips were getting. He pulled back again, and I tried to catch my breath as more dribble left my mouth, soaking his cock.

"One more time, and then you'll be ready to take me."

I gripped his waist as he pushed his swollen cock to the back of my throat, and while I stood up on my knees, I worked his hardness by bobbing up and down as fast as I could, but he wanted me consumed, so he pushed me down, gagging me until I was nearly suffocating then he pulled me off and lifted me up.

With his cock bobbing, he shoved my dress aside from the slit, and then pinned me against the bedroom door.

"You're not wearing any underwear?" His voice gritted next to my ear, aligning himself while holding me in place.

My arms went around his neck as he plunged forward, spearing me with his thick length.

"Colson," I gasped as I always did because even after how many times he'd stretched me, every time seemed to feel like it was the first.

"Shit, I'm already so close." He pressed his forehead to mine.

I wanted him to come, to lose himself, so I kissed him, biting his bottom lip until he was hissing and fucking me hard against the door.

It creaked and thudded behind me with every thrust of his cock.

"Yes!" My head slammed against the wood as he slowly wound me up, and I spun faster and faster. "Yes, yes, yes!" I cried in sync with every hard thrust.

"Where are your manners, Ms. Petrov?" Colson tsked, gripping my ass cheeks in his palms before pulling out of me, his tongue circled my pebbled nipple, sucking and pulling as he thrust back in.

I lost it.

"Colsonnn!" I screamed, knowing the whole entire house was probably hearing us, but I didn't care.

I wanted him completely and after hearing about Sherrie's insertion in their lives, I didn't want her to be comfortable. I wanted her to hear our passion and hopefully remind her of how she must have made a much younger Colson feel on far too many occasions.

"Yes, baby. Fuck." Colson spat, while pumping briskly, until he held me still, and he released a string of curses.

Once he'd caught his breath, he slowly let me down.

"Put some underwear on," he whispered, kissing my forehead.

Quirking a brow, I asked, "Why?"

"Because I want you to go to dinner with my release between your legs."

Fuck, that was hot, but impractical.

"That's how UTIs happen, so no. I will be going to relieve myself." I moved past him, but he gripped my wrist and then slammed my back against the door.

"Just tonight." He cupped my sex, toying with the mess he'd left inside me, which was already dripping down my thighs. He touched it and rubbed along my pussy, shoving his fingers in and out of me.

I tilted my head back and tried not to get turned on, but fuck.

I liked this dominant, bossy side of him, and I liked him treating me like this.

"Is your pussy that greedy that it needs another orgasm?" He rasped, closer to my ear.

My breathing was shallow as he continued to shove his fingers inside me, slowly fucking me while his release spilled through his fingers and dripped down my legs.

"Why can't you just obey me, Nora? I guess you need to be taught a lesson if you're going to ignore me."

Why did it make me so insanely hot when he talked to me like that?

He gripped my neck and pulled me away from the door, throwing me on my stomach across the tall bed. Lifting my dress so my ass was on display, he spanked me hard.

I hissed and dug my fingers into the plush comforter.

"Now you're spilling all over the bed, aren't you? It's going to get all over your dress, and I'm not going to let you change."

My hips bucked, writhing, begging for his touch.

His fingers spread my pussy from behind, and I could feel his release still inside me. He toyed with it, making another mess when his wet fingers moved to my tight hole, where he started coating it.

Humming, he continued doing that, bringing as much of his release as he could to that tight space and circling his finger. Then, using the lubrication, he pushed his finger in.

I inhaled a sharp breath.

"Maybe I should stretch this hole around my cock, let you go to dinner with my release dripping from your ass and your pussy."

His monster dick in my ass? Hell fucking no.

I wiggled, trying to renegotiate the terms of this punishment kink when he hissed and gripped the globe of my ass. "Calm down."

I did as he said and he spanked me again, which only worked to turn me on.

"I was kidding, you'll wear my handprints on your ass, and I'm going to fuck you one more time so that you're consumed and dripping."

I made some sort of sound when another slap echoed through the room, and then he was lining himself up again with my center and thrusting inside.

"Get on your hands and knees, Nora." He ordered, still inside of me.

I did as he said, realizing my dress was ruined and probably my makeup and hair too.

I didn't have time to adjust or wait, as he pulled out and then slammed his hips forward, entering me once again. I yelped, grabbing the comforter as tightly as I possibly could, but his thrusts were too forceful.

Especially when he gripped my hair and pulled it back.

"Just like this," he said, pumping his cock in deliciously deep strokes. "Are you going to be a good girl and stay wet between those thighs, wearing my release to dinner, or do I need to finish somewhere else and let you walk in with proof of who you belong to smeared all over that beautiful face?"

He slapped my ass again, and I hissed in pleasure.

"Answer me, Nora."

"I'll be a good girl," I said breathlessly as he continued to barrel into me. Leaning forward, he squeezed my breast while thrusting.

He was so deep, and the pressure on my scalp with the way he pinched my nipple was so much. I moaned, pushing against him.

Finally, he rasped. "Good girl, now come on my cock."

I whimpered, falling again into another mindless orgasm.

He grunted, holding me by my stomach, finishing inside.

When he pulled out, he dipped down to kiss my spine.

"Let's go eat, beautiful."

He moved to my suitcase, pulling out a pair of cotton underwear, then brought them over to me and helped me with each leg.

Once they were pulled up, he pressed his fingers into my knees, while watching my center. His cock was covered in our mixed releases, still semi-hard; his eyes were dark. He looked like a dark king, salivating over his war prize.

"Fucking perfect, look at that...you'll carry me and"—he pulled his cock into his boxers, still coated with our mess—"I'll carry you."

Then he kissed me, hard. Biting my lips until they turned puffy and red, then he moved.

"You're mine, Nora. All mine."

I stared at how his face had contorted into something I had never witnessed, and realized that this was all about *that* look. The ownership of having something that was just his...

I stowed away the questions I had surrounding that and got up.

"Don't fix your hair…you look perfect."

And like I just had sex.

But fuck these people, if Colson needed this, then I would give it to him.

I slipped my toes into shoes, pulled up my straps and did exactly as he said.

21

NORA

THE DINING ROOM was opulent with six windows on the south side of the house, and in each one, someone had placed a lit candle. With the garland and holly draped above each pane, it gave a regal feel to the space.

"Ah, there they are." A man sitting at the end of the long table stood and walked over to us. He had Colson's eyes and hair, although his was thinner and much lighter. Otherwise, he was fit, and while he did look older, maybe in his fifties, he was rather attractive.

He slapped Colson on the back while eyeing me salaciously.

"Who do we have here?"

His eyes dropped to my cleavage and traveled over my dress and down to the rather long slit. His gaze made me want to pull on a heavy trench coat to remove anything for him to look at.

"I'm Oliver Hanes, Colson's father." He reached his hand out for me to shake.

Colson brought his hand to my hip, gently nudging me behind him as he walked past his father.

"Everyone, this is Nora, my girlfriend."

He settled into a seat and pulled me down next to him. I still wasn't used to that introduction, but it helped ease some of the awkwardness as the eyes around the table widened with curiosity.

Three other men sat at the table across from us. Each looked relatively younger than Colson.

"Nice to see you big brother, glad you could…finally join us." He bit his lip, trying to hold back a laugh.

"Brock." Colson sighed, exasperated.

The seventeen-year-old looking kid snickered.

Which garnered another warning from Colson. "Trevor, don't even think about it."

The last one raised his glass to us and added, "Seriously though, we miss you, asshole."

"Nate." Sherrie scolded him with a glare that aged her by about ten years.

Colson's brother glanced at the woman, but didn't seem to give her any credence.

"Very funny, let's move on," Colson said.

Trevor snapped his fingers as if he had just thought of something. "Nora, do you surf?"

I gave him a warm smile. "Actually, I did learn when I went to college here a few years back. I'm not very good, but I had an instructor, and he seemed to think I had promise."

Colson's hand tightened on my thigh. The guys across from me all seemed to give each other a secretive smile as they smothered coughs.

"So, Nora. You live in Oregon then?" Sherrie asked, sipping her wine.

"Yes, in Macon. I'm Colson's next-door neighbor." I attempted to be civil, but couldn't suppress a bite to my tone.

Sherrie flicked her gaze to me, then Colson, and then set her glass down. "Well, how charming."

I wasn't sure what to say to that, so I sipped my water and tried to focus on the décor.

In front of us, the spread was beautiful, with white and gold plates and crystal glasses. But there was no food. I looked around, a tad confused, and unfortunately my gaze collided once again with Sherrie's.

Wincing, she shifted in her seat. "Sorry, we weren't sure how long you two were going to be, so we had the kitchen staff stay late and keep everything warmed up. I suppose I can let them know you're here now."

Bitch.

I shoved the knee jerk reaction to apologize deep-deep down and instead stayed quiet.

Why wasn't anyone else talking?

Sherrie glared, then pushed away from the table and walked away.

Damn, this sucked, I hated feeling like I was the reason everyone had been waiting to eat dinner. Not that anyone seemed to be put out by it, but still. How incredibly rude.

Colson's hand landed on my back, rubbing circles in soothing strokes, but as soon as I sat back, Oliver's eyes were on me. I felt like a snake had slithered around my neck, cutting off all the circulation.

"So, Colson." Oliver started, and I could feel the hand on my thigh move higher, almost as if he was trying to calm himself. "Tell me where you've been working again?"

"I work at Petrov Construction. It's actually owned by Nora's father."

"For now, he's selling it." I added, although I wasn't sure why.

Oliver looked intrigued as he leaned forward.

"Really, now that is interesting. So tell me, son, did you put in a bid?"

I peered over at Colson, but he remained unfazed.

I had never asked if he had plans to try to put a bid in for the company, but last I had heard, it was a different company who had offered to buy it.

"Okay, dinner is ready and—oh good!" Sherrie came out, beaming while staring somewhere behind us. "You made it!" My head swung around to see a young woman near my age standing in the archway of the dining room.

The woman hugged Sherrie briefly, but her gaze stayed glued to the man at my side. I turned to catch his reaction, but his eyes were on the woman as well.

Oliver leaned back in his chair, watching his son...not the newcomer.

The woman made her way to the table, slowly.

She wore a smart yet flirty business suit that seemed to age her past her twenty-some-odd years, she had silky dark hair which I assumed she got from Sherrie, but she looked like Colson...they had a similar eye shape, and the same nose...which reminded me of Oliver's.

Oh my God.

"Hey, Cole," she said tentatively, carefully pulling out the free chair next to me.

Colson didn't reply.

Servers filtered out of the kitchen, wearing nice ties and aprons. They moved meticulously as they set trays of food in front of us and refilled everyone's glasses. I was slightly geeking out; I had never been waited on like this outside of a restaurant or big event. "Thank you." I tried to catch one of the servers eyes, but I was met with a grim expression.

Awkward.

I faced forward, digging into the delicious meat and potatoes, seeing the woman next to me push her food around.

Feeling self-conscious and not sure if I was supposed to hate her or not, I finally gave in and turned to her.

"Hi, I'm Nora," I whispered.

She lifted her head and returned my smile, with a bit of what seemed like relief.

"Haley. It's nice to meet you."

"You too."

"Yes, my gosh. Where are our manners?" Sherrie said, back in her seat at the head of the table. She sipped her wine and then cleared her throat.

"This is our daughter, Haley."

I watched the guys across from me, keeping to themselves, two of them had cell phones they were looking at from under the table but none of them seemed to notice or care that their little sister had arrived.

Although…as I looked at the youngest, he was clearly younger than Haley.

"Only girl," Haley said, filling in the silence.

I chewed my food slowly, absorbing and trying to arrange everything like a million-piece puzzle.

"So Colson was just telling us about potentially bidding on Nora's father's company," Oliver said, making Colson's eyes dart over.

I could feel Colson's body coil tight, his hand cinching the dress on my thigh in his fist.

Haley butt in, talking while she chewed. "Oh my gosh, I forgot to tell you guys about this guy that totally hit on me today. It was the worst!"

"Haley, not now, we're talking." Oliver scolded her sternly.

"Colson, tell us—" Oliver started again, but Haley interjected, speaking over him.

"The guy was like all over me." She put her hands out in front of her. "It was so gross. I was like, 'dude, stahhhp.'"

Silence followed, Sherrie's gaze bounced to Oliver and then to Haley.

"Haley, honey, I think your dad is trying to talk to Cole."

"Oh, stupid me…" Haley shook her head and drained the rest of her glass.

Oliver cleared his throat and opened his mouth, but Haley made a sound again.

"Buttt, here's the thing," she interjected, pointing her fork with a speared potato toward the room. "He was sorttta hot, so do you think I should have given him a shot?"

Oliver's hand came down in a hard slap against the table.

"That is enough, Haley."

"Haley, it's fine…" Colson finally addressed his sister, and I wanted to pinch his leg because why did it take him so long to say something to her? She was over here doing the Lord's work, trying to stop Oliver from asking Colson annoying questions, and no one was throwing her a line.

"You know what," Sherrie said, slowly standing from the table, "I think we should go out on the veranda and have some hot cocoa. The lights are really beautiful right now, and we have the chimineas going."

"Mom, no." Haley quickly responded, freezing with her fork in her hand.

Oliver, Brock, Trevor, and Nate all stood. "Hales, stop it. You're embarrassing yourself." Trevor snidely commented.

I slowly slid out of my chair, my heart desperately trying to reach out to Haley, unsure why she was so uncomfortable.

Colson was behind me as we all headed toward the back of the house, but Haley turned, trying to catch Colson's eye.

"Cole, don't…you can't go out there," she whispered, but Oliver brought up the back, putting his hand on Haley's shoulder.

"Come on, dear, let's go prep the cocoa."

I watched as Haley's eyes begged for us not to go outside. I slowed my steps, my gut telling me to heed her warning.

Colson didn't, he pushed me on.

"Come on, I want to show you my mother's garden," he whispered, encouraging me to walk.

Tugging his arm, I whispered in his ear, "Maybe we shouldn't. Haley seems worried."

He shook his head. "Haley is a spoiled brat who likes attention."

Oh. Well, that wasn't the impression I got at all...but okay.

We exited, stepping down through French doors. Candles glowed inside lanterns that lit up the walkway to a massive paved patio. Lights were strung up overhead, and as Sherrie mentioned, there were four little chimineas set up facing patio chairs.

"Wow, this is..." I looked up, staring at the beautiful night, but Colson had stopped walking.

I turned to see what had stopped him, but his eyes were over to the right, where there were no lights.

It looked as though a separate batch of concrete had been poured over a large square, and all that was set up on it were two sun loungers.

I turned, gently tugging Colson's arm, but he refused to move.

Oliver walked out behind us, clapping Colson on the back as if nothing was wrong.

I stood off to the side, seeing this was a tense moment between them.

"Come on, Cole, let's have some hot cocoa."

Colson swallowed, his eyes watering. "Where is it?"

His voice cracked and my chest mirrored the sentiment.

Oliver acted like he didn't know what his son was talking about, but even I had noticed that there was no garden out here and that patch of weird concrete seemed like the perfect place to put one.

"Where's what?"

Colson inhaled sharply. "Where is my mother's garden?"

I flicked my gaze over to Brock, Trevor, and Nate. They all had their heads down, but didn't say anything.

Sherrie was the one who stood, her heels clicking along the stone as she faced Colson head-on.

"I paved over it. I sit out there now getting a tan. That spot is the perfect place to catch the sun."

No.

She couldn't...that was too heartbreaking, even for a twat like her.

"You let her do this?" Colson asked his father, his eyes watering.

He looked like he was waiting for his father to make this right...to fix it...as though he was a young boy looking to his dad for protection.

"Son, your mother has been gone for a long time. There wasn't a reason to keep it."

"Not a reason?" He scoffed and right then Haley came out, looking worried with her green eyes wide, her lips thinned.

Colson noticed her and pointed his drink at her.

"How about her? Is she reason enough? Or her?" He pointed at Sherrie. "Was the fact that you caused my mother to kill herself not enough for you?" he screamed, throwing the glass in his hand against the wall.

Tears coated my lashes, mirroring Haley's as silence swallowed the patio.

Sherrie had her elbow tucked across her chest, her expression annoyed...even bored.

"Colson, that's enough," Oliver warned.

"No, it wasn't enough then when you were fucking your secretary in our home throughout every one of our mother's episodes. It wasn't enough that you had cheated on her with that whore or then, on the brink of her getting better, you pushed her over the edge by telling her you were not only marrying the very woman you cheated on her with but that you also had a child with her!" Colson screamed, his neck bulging in rage. "None of that was enough for you?"

Sherrie spoke up, her face turning red. "She was never on the verge of getting better, Colson. You're delusional if you think that."

"Don't"—he rasped in a deadly tone—"you don't get to talk about her."

Brock stepped in, arguing, "Cole, come on, man...chill. She was our mom too, but you're freaking out over nothing."

Trevor and Nate hung their heads.

"You don't remember her garden and how that was the only thing that made her happy?" Colson asked, tears blurring his eyes.

"Son, nothing made her happy...she was depressed. In and out of mental hospitals for most of their lives...and yours. You were the only one who wrote to her, but you have to understand that the letters she wrote back to you"—Oliver shook his head—"she wasn't in her right mind. The image she presented to you was different from what the doctors told me. Sherrie helped keep us together, and while I did slip up when Haley was born, I did everything I could to shield your mother from that."

Fuck, becoming an adult sucked because it put things that framed your entire childhood into a different perspective. Sometimes that perspective was more painful than the original image.

Colson had finally had enough; he raked his hand through his hair and walked past everyone. Haley went after him.

I was on her heels, while everyone else stayed out on the patio.

Sherrie had to know what would happen when Colson saw that garden paved over. On principle, she was a bitch for doing that without warning him.

"I need to talk to you, Cole!" Haley yelled, trailing after him as he stalked off. "Colson, pleasssseee."

He finally spun on his heel and yelled at her.

"I know, Haley! I got all your fucking emails. Did you not get the hint? I didn't respond to a single one. I never do. I don't call on your birthday. I don't answer when you call on mine. I don't care about anything at all in your life. Why do you keep trying with me?"

Haley had tears streaming down her face as she pulled her arms in close to her chest.

"I'm your sister, Cole. Whether you want to admit that or not." She said feebly with her lip trembling.

He lowered his face until he was her height.

"You're a reminder of the worst day of my life. My mother literally killed herself the day she found out you existed."

"Colson!" I ran up, grabbing Haley's shoulders.

She was shaking, sobbing as Colson seemed to finally realize I was there witnessing all this.

He blinked and faltered back a step, then briskly walked away.

Haley wiped at her face, pulling out of my arms.

"It's okay…can you just go check on him, please?" She hiccuped.

Her green eyes were red and irritated as I tried to gauge if she was okay.

"Are you sure?"

She laughed. "I've been dealing with this my entire life. I know he's in pain because he just found out they did this. Go see if he's okay."

Giving her a nod, I did as she suggested and left her standing there as I went after Colson.

22

NORA

COLSON WASN'T in our room when I went up.

As badly as I wanted to make sure he was okay, I knew he needed space.

So, I showered, washing away all signs of our time together from earlier, then I pulled back the sheets and crawled into bed. I stared at the ceiling, trying to process everything I had heard tonight.

Poor Colson, to have your mother ripped away from you like that and then to have to call the person somewhat responsible for it your stepmom, would be so difficult.

While I had no idea what he'd gone through, or who Haley really was...she didn't seem like she deserved to be treated the way he had treated her.

I desperately wanted to call Rae and ask for her advice on how to handle this, or what to say. I had never seen Colson angry like that. It reminded me of how earlier he'd mentioned that he became an asshole when his mom was brought up...and how I told him I wouldn't be scared off if he was.

Pulling my cell out, I brought up his number and shot him a text.

Please just tell me you're safe...

The text bubbles moved like he was going to respond, then they stopped...until a few seconds later.

I'm safe

I hesitated, not wanting to push him, but needing him to know that I was here.

Are you close?

Colson: ...

I SMIRKED at the airdrop location of the house that he sent through.

Where?

Colson: The guest room of propriety...reserved to keep your honor intact.

I smiled at the phone.

My honor was ruined a long time ago

Colson: Ouch...please don't make this night any worse by talking about your exes.

None of them ever put my honor in question, you're the only one I let do dirty things to me.

Colson: ...

Did you shower?

Yes

Colson: ...

> Are you mad at me?

> Colson: Please don't ever question that. I'm not mad at you, Nora. I could never be mad at you. I'm ashamed of myself. I hate that you had to see that tonight. It's fucking embarrassing.

> Come here. Please.

> Colson: I think I should be alone for a while.

> I made you a promise earlier...you can't scare me away.

> Colson: Not even if I treat you like I did earlier tonight?

> Not even then...also I liked it earlier, so please repeat it again sometime. Just not tonight, I already showered.

> Colson: ...

I watched his dots appear and stop, only to reappear again, until finally I heard the door open. In the darkness, I heard him lock the latch and then move to the edge of the bed.

"I don't deserve you."

Leaning up on my elbows, I tried to make out his features.

"Does anyone really deserve anyone? We're all a mess."

He moved, pulling his shirt off, pushing his slacks down, and then crawled in next to me. The second I felt his arms come around me, my heart seemed to settle.

His breathing hitched as he tucked me under his chin, and I ran my fingers over his rib cage.

"I know you have questions," he whispered, running his hands up and down the length of my back.

I considered that, unsure of which one was burning in my head at the moment.

"Why are you so mean to your sister? She seems to really care about you."

Twirling a lock of hair around his finger, he exhaled heavily.

"I can't seem to get past what she represents in my life...Sherrie had been my dad's secretary for a long time, all of us can remember back when she was just out of college, perky, young and eager to help her boss. Mom was having a few challenges then...she had Nate and Brock so close together that her postpartum depression is where everything started. She had pills at first, but Dad realized she needed more acute help."

I hated that I didn't know this about him. I'd been walking around in the dark with Colson leading the way, only to finally have him flick the lights and show me how much carnage he had in his life.

"So, she admitted herself?"

Colson nodded against my head. "I found out when I was older that if she checked herself in, then she could check herself out. But if she had an incident where the hospital had to be involved with any lifesaving maneuvers, then she wouldn't be released back to us until they believed she wouldn't be a harm to herself or others... Her first attempt was pills."

I held my breath, trying not to crumble as he explained. I had never dealt with anything remotely close to this...it made me feel ill-equipped and young.

"That was when she needed longer visits. I used to write to her all the time. Our maid would go back and forth, exchanging our notes...and in every one she would talk about her garden...that place used to be our spot. We'd go in it every time she felt sad. We'd even sleep out there sometimes."

"So, she must have gotten better for a while, right, because there's Trevor...and he's what, seventeen?"

"Yeah, she did. She was better for a while. She'd only go in sometimes for a week, then home for a few months. When she got pregnant with Trevor, she'd already had so many visits. Sherrie had been around at that time so when she got pregnant, we were all happy for her. We even met her baby...we just always assumed she had a boyfriend or a husband. We never realized it was our dad, or that the baby was our sister."

That would have been so hard to adjust to losing a mother and then having to accept that you have a new sibling and stepparent.

"How old was Haley when she was finally introduced as your sister?"

"She was six. Trevor had just turned three."

"For six years, your dad kept her from you guys?" My voice was high, my tone incredulous because... how unfair.

"Dad said he tried to do the right thing, knowing if he told us, then we'd tell Mom, and he knew Mom couldn't handle it. The longer my mom stayed in there, the more I agreed with him. I even told him he could file for divorce papers, as long as he didn't explain about Sherrie or Haley."

"But he didn't." I guessed.

"It was like he suddenly had the key to hurt me. I was only fourteen years old at the time, and we'd been arguing a lot. He wanted me to go to some school in Europe, I didn't want to. I begged him not to tell her, but he did it anyway. The next thing I knew, we were being told she had found a way to—"

His voice broke, and I didn't want to hear any more.

I turned in his arms, wrapping my arms around him as he pushed his face into the crook of my neck.

"He took the only thing that was just mine."

Connecting the dots, I finally understood.

"Which is why you left and moved to Macon."

"I moved back to Macon..." he said, voice cracking and breaking. "It was our winter home, but I moved to Macon and attended high school there after Mom passed. Dad allowed it, as long as I kept my grades up, but it only lasted two years. Then he had me back in California. Which I guess was still better than Europe, except California reminded me of Mom."

"This was her home." I guessed out loud. Colson nodded against my head.

"It made me want to reject the one thing he wanted me to accept..."

Kissing his brow, I answered. "Haley?"

He nodded, kissing my shoulder.

"I know it's not her fault. She just represents *them*...and I hate them."

I'd tackle that issue tomorrow, but in the darkness of the room I let myself break with the man I'd fallen in love with, not even realizing all this time he had a darkness ebbing at the fringes of his life, and it made me want to dig into his heart deeper, find some place that I could thrive. Because darkness or not, Colson Hanes was mine now, and I wasn't letting him go.

23

COLSON
ONE YEAR AGO

DEAR MOM,

I can't believe I'm still writing these to you...but maybe that therapist knew what he was talking about. I don't see one anymore...sometimes I think maybe I should. I don't know...I honestly don't even know what made me want to write this to you today. I guess it was because I met someone ...

She's my boss's daughter...and the second she introduced herself and I shook her hand, I knew she was different.. I don't know, Mom, do you believe in love at first sight? I'm twenty-seven years old...I don't really believe in this stuff, but she made me think it might be possible.

I always thought you and me would talk about this stuff someday...I don't know, but I can't stop thinking about her.

Her name is Nora.

Nothing will probably come of it, but you never know, right?

Maybe I can get to know her, and she'll give me the time of day.

Maybe you can send a little prayer for me or talk to the big guy up there...or however that works.

Anyway, I love you, Mom.

I'm still dreaming of tomorrow.

Cole

NORA'S HAIR was too straight.

I knew she'd done it the night prior for dinner, but I was hoping overnight that the curls would come back, and I could wrap them around my fingers. It was early and sometimes when I couldn't sleep, I'd play with her curls…almost as a way to deal with my anxious thoughts.

She was the best form of therapy for me.

Her strong heart, big enough to fit all my fucked-up issues inside of it and still find room to be generous and kind. Her tenderness from the night prior pulled at my gut. I had warned her that I could become an asshole, then she went and saw it for herself…and she didn't run.

I'd always known my aversion to facing my mother's death and the reality of her mental state wasn't healthy. I never talked about it, and the only thing I did in the form of dealing with it was to write to her every now and then. But that didn't mean I was actually processing the pain, so there were pieces that were left unattended and festered.

Like Haley.

Rubbing the sleep from my eyes, I tried to push all the stress away. The pain of what Sherrie had done…of what Haley heard me say…what she'd been hearing from me for the past fourteen years of her life. I liked her, was even nice to her when she was little, back when she was just Sherrie's little girl. The second she became my sister, that all changed…and not because my dad was a fucking cheater, but because her existence led to the end of my mother's.

It wasn't her fault.

I knew that…logically, but it hurt so badly, and hating my father wasn't enough, not when he didn't give a fuck either way.

But Haley wanted my love, so not giving it to her allowed me some form of control.

I knew I needed to change…especially now that Nora had witnessed my toxic behavior, but it was going to take more than this visit to shift all that shit around.

I couldn't think of it anymore.

I had to stop, so I turned on my side and stared at Nora.

She was still sleeping, even as streaks of light crept inside the room from the sheer blinds. So, being selfish, I woke her.

When Nora slept, she liked to pull the blankets up from the end of the bed and have them loose around her feet. Keeping the sheet tucked around her chest, I slowly moved the blankets aside from her waist. She wore a pair of cotton panties and one of my T-shirts, and the sight of her asleep in my bed, wearing one of my shirts was too fucking much.

My heart thundered in my chest with the need to explain what she meant to me.

First, she needed to be awake.

I moved to my stomach in front of her, pulled her underwear down her hips, and then lightly pushed her right leg to the side. Advancing forward, I slipped my arms under her and around her hips, then slowly licked along her slit, through her center.

She tasted like crushed rosebud, musky and sweet, and that taste belonged entirely to me.

"Colson." She rasped with sleep heavy in her tone. She gently pushed her fingers into my hair, while adjusting her legs as though she was slowly waking.

I sucked and licked, loving how her hips lifted off the bed. My arms caged her in, my hands came together over her stomach as I continued to suck her clit into my mouth. She was losing herself as she gasped and muttered curses under her breath. Her hips swiveled and rocked against my face until I felt her shudder against my tongue. With a sultry moan, she tugged on the ends of my hair and that's when I let up and slowly lapped up her orgasm, needing every single drop.

Not finished with her, I got to my knees and grabbed her by the backs of her thighs, until she was aligned perfectly with my engorged erection.

Gripping my cock by the base, I pressed the head into her soaked center, loving the way her eyes dipped to see the two of us connect.

Before I went any further, I paused, making sure I had her attention.

"Nora."

Her gaze lifted, watching me.

Her eyes were always beautiful, but even more so reflecting the sunrise breaking into our room. And the way she observed me…the way she seemed to see through my armor, all the iron pieces I had pulled around me to keep the hurt out, it was my undoing.

"I love you," I whispered, sinking slowly into her.

Her lips parted on a silent gasp as I filled her.

"I've loved you for a long time…probably longer than I even realize, but you need to know"—holding her knee, I gently pulled out and kept her gaze—"you're mine."

I thrust into her in a long, deep stroke, pulling a moan from her.

I repeated the movement, pulling out and thrusting forward.

Our gazes locked as she moved her hips with mine, and I saw the smallest tear slip down the side of her face. I bent forward, fitting myself in between her open legs, and pressed my lips to hers.

Her hands came up to hold my jaw as we fucked slowly.

"I love you too, and I've been yours for longer than you've deserved." She smiled.

Her lips met mine as our hips lifted and pushed against one another. I drew out both of our orgasms as long as I possibly could, until with our heads pinned together, we finished at the same time.

With heavy gasps, we stayed pinned together while we both caught our breaths.

"That wasn't a bad way to start the day," Nora joked, pressing a quick kiss to my nose.

I got to my elbows and kissed her again.

I couldn't stop kissing her. Our lips moved sensually slow, nipping and teasing one another until I finally pulled out of her, and got up.

"You're not going to make me wear your jizz all day again, are you?" Nora slid to the edge of the bed and gingerly placed her feet on the floor.

Pinching her ass, I smiled over my shoulder at her. "Not today, go shower. I'm going to go downstairs and see if I can get some breakfast to bring up here."

Watching me from her spot near the bathroom door, she dipped her dark brows.

"Colson, find Haley please. You need to make things right with her."

I gave her a nod, ducking my face.

I knew she was right, but I still wasn't entirely sure how genuine it would be if I went to her. I could apologize, though. I could start there.

Pulling on some jeans, and a shirt, I padded downstairs, assuming I'd see my brothers watching something on the TV, or goofing off in the kitchen, but no one seemed to be around.

An entire breakfast spread was laid out in the kitchen, with bagels, yogurt, orange juice, and fresh berries. From the amount Sherrie had prepared, you'd assume she'd opened a fucking bed and breakfast.

Grabbing an orange juice, I spun on my heel and started for the library, looking for Haley. She was a reader, so I knew she appreciated hanging out in the elaborate collection our dad had.

As I passed the office, I heard my dad.

"Colson, good you're up. I need to talk to you about something."

Talking business with my father was always a bad idea, but I would rather get it out of the way. Nora and I were only staying for the day and tomorrow, then we were heading back home. The only reason we were staying after last night was because, although these pricks paved over my mother's garden, this was still her home. There were still places that reminded me of her, and I needed to be around it.

"What?"

I sat in the chair that faced his rather obnoxious desk.

He'd been hinting at something all night about my job, and it was either to make it seem that I was only dating the boss's daughter to get in with my boss, or he was trying to get at something with the sale of Peter's company.

My dad was in casual clothes, which for him meant he looked like he was about to go play golf. He wore a collared peach shirt with khakis and loafers. It was Christmas Eve, dude could afford to dress down once a year.

"I just wanted to extend a professional courtesy to you regarding the bid on the Petrov company."

My confusion must have reflected on my face, because one of his shit-eating grins slowly spread across his pasty white face.

"Oh, your boss didn't tell you?" He settled into his chair, drawing a cigar out.

Sherrie hated when he smoked in the house, but only because my mother used to. Once upon a time, my father's secretary cared about my mother, or at least she pretended to. But the two tag-teamed Oliver into quitting his ugly habits of drinking and smoking, for a while at least.

"After you turned the bid down by bringing his daughter here, he reconsidered my offer."

"What the hell are you talking about?" Peter wouldn't have done that. There's no way he would have sold the company to my dad, not when he'd preached about my dad being poisonous.

"Well, considering you're my son, Peter and I have gotten close, professionally speaking of course, and well, we talked about the offer you had on the table." He shoved his hands deep into his pockets. "It was assuming you'd leave his poor daughter out of our dirty family affairs of course."

"Interesting choice of words." I narrowed my eyes on the man I knew as father but had more than proven was my enemy.

"You lost the bid. It's going to me, so I suppose I'll be your new boss."

His smile was conniving as it disturbed his normal scowl and deep-set jowls.

"Like fuck are you getting that company." I stood to leave.

My dad's voice trailed me.

"You're too late, I already have it in motion. You made the wrong choice bringing her here. Now you don't have a shot."

I entered the hallway right as Haley came out of the library, her face withdrawn, her brows dipped as she tried to piece together what we were talking about.

I half turned to my dad. "He's not selling to you...he would never sell to you. I just need to talk to him."

My dad stepped closer. "How strange that you were willing to risk it... knowing it's the only way to be truly free of me. You'd be out of your trust fund money and own something not tied to me in any capacity. That company was your way of standing on your own two feet."

"Fuck you!" I yelled right as Nora rounded the corner.

Her eyes were huge and worried.

My stomach swirled with fear and the anxiousness to talk to Peter. He wouldn't sell to my father. He had to be bluffing.

Haley walked closer.

"Colson," Haley interjected, trying to insert herself into our conversation.

My dad swung his gaze to her, sneering at her interruption.

"Haley, not now."

Nora focused on Haley, her gaze going soft and a line forming between her brows as though she wanted to know what the interruption was.

I ran upstairs with Nora trailing.

Nora followed me. "Colson, what happened?"

I couldn't explain it until I had a chance to clear it up because there was no way. No fucking way.

"Colson, talk to me, what's going on?" Nora asked again.

I had to get out of there.

Pushing through the door, seeing our bed still tossed from our sleep and time together this morning, I ignored it and the look that Nora gave me when I ran up here.

I had to talk to Peter.

I had to stop this; he wasn't going to sell to my fucking father.

Not this.

"Colson." Nora pressed on the door, walking inside.

My head stayed down as I tossed my clothes into my bag, stray socks, boxers. I moved to the bathroom.

"Colson!" She tried again, but I couldn't focus on her right now.

Toothbrush, deodorant, hair shit. I swiped it all into my suitcase.

"Can you grab my cell and open the airline app, see if you can pull up a last-minute flight for us?"

Nora scowled, her arms linked over her chest and her mouth set in a firm line.

"Not until you tell me what's going on..."

Heaving a sigh, I gave her a quick glance. "I promise I will explain it, but we have to get out of here."

I ignored the fact that she looked so good in her leggings and tank top, with freshly showered curls spilling down her back in waves.

"Are we in danger?"

Zipping my suitcase, I shook my head. "No."

"Is someone hurt back home?" she questioned, stepping closer.

"No, it's nothing like that, Nora. I just need to get back home and I promise I will explain everything on the plane." I pulled the case shut and set it on the floor.

She stared at it, then glanced at her suitcase, which was still open by the closet. "Well, I think you need to talk to Haley first. Whatever this is, it can wait."

Shaking my head, I grabbed my charger and phone base.

Nora watched, but didn't move to gather her things. "I'm serious…she has something important to tell you and she said you've been dodging her."

"I'll call her." My eyes were on my cell since Nora hadn't grabbed it.

"I'm not going with you unless you talk to her."

My head lifted at that.

"What?"

Her shoulders lifted, like she wasn't sure what other options she had.

"You need to talk to her…and you're not telling me what's going on, so I'm not leaving with you until you take two seconds and explain, then listen to her."

I didn't have time for this, and I wasn't about to be told what to do, not when it came to this fucking family. Nora didn't know them like I did. Haley was using a manipulation tactic, that was all.

"Let's talk about this later, on the plane, preferably."

"No." She stood her ground.

Fuck.

Nora would understand later, but I absolutely could not allow my father to sign those papers.

"You're an adult, Nora, I'm not going to play this game with you. I don't want to talk to Haley, so I'm not going to. And I already told you that I will explain everything once we're on the plane, but I need to go. If you really want to stand on some moral high ground and not get on a plane with me, then I love you and I'll see you in Macon when you come back."

Grabbing my suitcase, I pecked her on the cheek and then walked past her.

24

NORA

WELL, that backfired pretty fast.

I understood Colson had something happen with his father and it was bad enough that it made him want to rush out of here, but whatever it was, he could have taken two seconds to explain it to me. Honestly, as much as I loved him, I wasn't a doormat. And for the life of me, I could not understand why he was throwing this relationship with his sister away.

My heart broke for her, and no matter how hard I tried, I couldn't just leave her. If I was the only link to Colson, then I'd do whatever I could to help her. Which apparently included finding my own way back to Macon.

It was Christmas Eve, Sherrie was gone, the three boys were out drinking or so Haley said, and Oliver was nowhere to be found. Great family.

Really fucking awesome.

I stood in the doorway of Haley's room and watched as she packed a suitcase.

"Knock knock."

I'd given her some space earlier because she and Oliver had gotten into a screaming match. I only heard bits and pieces, deciding to stay in the room until all the yelling had finished. I had no idea what I had gotten myself into, but my gut said I was doing the right thing by staying. It was awkward as hell, but I still felt like it was necessary.

Haley looked up from her luggage and smiled.

"You're still here."

Pushing forward, I slumped onto her bed, watching as she packed her room.

"What are you doing?"

She grabbed pictures off her wall, putting them into a cardboard box.

Her hair was a sleek sheet down her back, hints of red blending into chestnut, her freckled skin was showing through her tank top.

"I'm leaving. Something I should have done a while ago."

I popped my left leg over my right watching as she packed her bedroom into various boxes.

"How old are you?"

She seemed much too young to be saying things like "a while ago."

Huffing a laugh, she said, "Twenty. How old are you?"

"Twenty-three."

She nodded, keeping her head down as she gripped her rather expensive Mac.

"Look, I know he hates me, but I really need to talk to him, and the only way I'm going to be able to do that is if I see him face-to-face. I'm not living here anymore. I don't know where I'll end up, but I know I need to stop in your town and talk to him."

Putting her hand to her hip, she turned to face me.

"So will you go back with me?"

"To Macon?"

She nodded, softening her green eyes, in what looked like hope.

"Of course."

"It'll take like seventeen hours' drive time, I think, but if we take shifts…"

I stood from her bed. "Easy peasy."

"Are you sure? You don't even know me."

Toying with the edge of her comforter, I let out a sigh.

"I know, but I believe you love your brother and I love your brother, so I think we'll be okay."

She nodded again, but her eyes watered.

"He hates me."

"He hates the circumstance, not you." I moved so I could rub her shoulder.

Before long, she was in my arms, and we were both crying over the boy who had flown back to Oregon without us.

HALEY and I set out for Macon on Christmas morning.

She privately spoke with her parents, or at least I assumed she did. She was an adult who didn't have to tell them if she didn't want to, but I assumed she at least told her mother where she was going.

Haley had the twin to my new vehicle, except hers was a rugged SUV, made for driving in the snow. It was going to be perfect for Macon, and since frivolous things like gas money weren't relevant to an heiress, it made the perfect road trip vehicle.

She also liked to drive really fast.

Like thirty-above-the-speed-limit fast.

By the time we pulled into Macon, we'd shaved two hours off our expected drive time.

It would have been more, but I hogged time behind the wheel, trying to increase my odds of staying alive.

Colson had texted and called, but I wasn't ready to talk to him yet.

"Oh my gosh," Haley whispered, plastering her face to the window as we pulled into the city limits of Macon.

Slowing to stay within the city speed limit, she got her fill of all the holiday decorations.

"This is the cutest freaking town that I have ever seen!"

"It's fairly adorable." I muttered, seeing the sunshine on Mount Macon, which the town was propped up against. It made the entire town look magical.

"So, if you want to head to your house, we can drop you off and I can look up a hotel."

Turning the vehicle down Main Street, I clicked my tongue.

"I have a guest room, and a pretty nice guest bed, at least according to my best friend. But anyway, it's yours for as long as you need it."

Twisting toward me, she asked, "Are you sure?"

"Of course, I'm sure." I veered onto my street and slowed.

Colson's truck was in his drive, making my stomach somersault.

Pulling up against the curb in front of my house, I put the car into park.

"Oh, and by the way"—I unsnapped my buckle as my neighbor's door opened and that messy head of golden hair poked through—"my neighbor is your brother."

Colson darted off the porch in bare feet, heading toward us.

I was out the door, but I didn't race to him, and I tried not to care that when he was close enough, his hands shoved into my hair, or that his lips urgently claimed mine.

I was upset with him, but there was still that part of me that felt tied to him, as if those strings we joked about not having had been tying us together all along. When I was close to him, I craved him, and so I caved and kissed him back.

Pulling away to catch his breath, he pinned his forehead to mine.

"I'm so fucking sorry."

"We'll talk about it later," I said, then turned.

Haley gently shut her door, watching us.

Colson's hand dropped to mine, tangling his fingers through mine as he turned to see his sister. They didn't move or speak, they just watched one another.

"You're not wearing socks or shoes...and there's like fifteen feet of snow." Haley mused, pushing her purse up her shoulder.

I looked down, realizing she was right.

"Colson, get inside. Oh my gosh." I pushed his shoulder.

"Okay...um, Haley can we catch up later?"

My heart thundered in my chest at his inclusion of her. She gave him a small nod before he kissed me and jogged toward his house.

"So...you guys are neighbors..." Haley said, following me to my porch.

"Yep...it's recent."

She nodded, letting out a little laugh.
"Right."

HALEY WAS SETTLED into my guest room, but we both realized how awkward it was that she was staying with me and not right next door, with her brother. I asked if she wanted to come over with me to his house, but she had said that she was too tired, and would try for tomorrow.

I left her clean towels and then explained that I'd be next door for a little while with Colson.

I didn't knock on Colson's door, assuming he knew I was coming over. When I pushed inside, I noticed he had all his lights off except the ones on his Christmas tree, and the few strung up around the room. Holiday music played from his television, and there were a few presents under the tree.

Setting my things down, I slowly made my way to the living room and settled into the couch.

Moments later, Colson came out, rubbing a towel over his wet hair.

"Hi." He leaned down to kiss me.

"Hi."

He hadn't put a shirt on yet, and just had a pair of sweats hanging on his hips.

I hummed while he leaned in for another kiss.

"This is nice," I said once he pulled back and moved to the kitchen.

Grabbing two mugs, he came back and set them down in front of us. I noticed the chocolate balls sitting in the midst of heated milk, slowly melting.

"I got you the peppermint one."

My smile garnered a few tears because he'd remembered.

He saw them and rubbed his hand up my leg. "It's Christmas, and I feel so insanely shitty that you spent the entire day on the road…that was never my intention when I took off. I'm so sorry."

Reaching forward to grab the cocoa, I kept my eyes down.

"Yeah, it did suck…and what you did was pretty shitty, and I fully expect you to make up for it with back rubs, and orgasms, but I am actually glad I came with Haley. I have a feeling about her."

He let out a long sigh, reaching for his mug. We both watched the fire flicker against the glass while the music played overhead.

I peeked over at the tree, seeing the gifts.

"Are any of those for me?"

Smirking, he set his cup down and jumped up. "One is for you."

"And the rest?" I raised my brow in confusion, because who else was this man shopping for?

"Seraph, Maddy, and Mila."

My God, this man.

"I love you." It came out as an exhale, but I felt it in every fiber of my being.

He stopped where he was, crouched next to the tree, and stared at me with so much hunger and adoration that I nearly melted on the spot.

"I love you too."

He grabbed a small, wrapped gift and brought it over, placing it in my palm.

Watching him settle next to me again, I tugged on the string and then lifted the top.

A silver key rested inside on a box of white fluff.

"Oh…a key."

Colson smiled. "To my house."

For two seconds my heart soared, rising on the wings of assumption that he was asking me to move in with him. But right as that thought entered, it plummeted to the ground.

"Just so you can be kept safe, in case your tree falls, or you run out of hot water or something."

What?

Why was he making it seem like the key was only used for emergencies? Why did I need more than that, though? This was still so new, what we shared in California didn't mean that he'd jump to bring us closer…it just meant we knew more about each other. It was a nice gift…really it was. Shaking the weird feeling, I leaned over and kissed him.

"Thank you."

It was quick, cold, but on his end…not mine.

He rubbed my shoulder, toying with my hair as he started a movie.

I rested against him, watching without seeing, the entire time wondering why we weren't talking about why he'd left me in California.

Finally, halfway through the movie, I sat up.

"Are we going to talk about California?"

His brows arched like he had no idea what I was talking about. Then it was like it finally registered and he dismissed it like it had never happened.

"Yes, I'm so sorry, it was just a big misunderstanding. I overreacted."

The movie played but my focus was completely on the man next to me.

"Okay…but I still want to know."

Colson played with my hair, letting out a sigh. "Your dad was going to sell his company to my dad, and I guess I freaked out because of the issues I have with my dad. I didn't want him to win that bid, so I rushed back to talk to your father."

Feeling a little confused, I sat up so I could see him better.

"Why would your dad even know that my dad's construction company was for sale?"

He tilted his head. "I told my brothers…"

That still didn't make sense to me, so I shook my head. "You told your brothers it was for sale because you might lose your job? Why did you bring that up to them unless you planned on putting in your own bid? And if you were planning it, why not tell me?"

Pausing the movie, he shifted to see me better.

"I had mentioned it to them because it was in the line of what we were already talking about, and I guess they let it leak to my dad. Honestly, I have no idea how he found out."

"But you wanted to put in a bid?" I clarified.

Dipping his head, his wet hair shifted, a little piece falling over his brow. "Yes. I did. I have wanted his company since the day I started. It would be something to own, to have that's just mine. It would allow me to use up the last of my trust fund, severing the last tie to my father. I know I could just spend it to spend it, but I want a legacy I can pass on to my own family someday…but something that has nothing at all to do with the Hanes name."

My heart softened, realizing how important this was to him. Our relationship was still new, so I understood on some level why he hadn't shared it. So, I cupped his jaw and brought his face up.

"Did you get the company?"

He smiled, his devastating jaw glinting in the firelight. "I'm in the process of getting it, but yes, he agreed to sell it to me and not my dad."

Relief swelled in my chest, happy that he was going to get his dream.

"Okay, good. I know we're still newish, but is there anything else I should know?"

Colson leaned in to kiss me. "No. Well, I mean..." He rubbed his neck, the muscle in his jaw tensing. "I was offered the bid first, but I walked away from it when we went to California, which was why I freaked out hearing that my dad had gotten it."

"Why did you walk away from it?"

His eyes were soft as they landed on me. "Your dad wanted a promise from me that I wouldn't be involved with you romantically."

I laughed, feeling slightly frantic with disbelief that my father had interfered again.

No. Fucking. Way.

"Excuse me, he said what?"

Colson leaned his elbows on the tops of his knees as he tilted his head toward me. "Your dad hasn't wanted us to be together from the beginning, so seeing an opportunity..."

"He took it." I finished for him.

I sat there for a few moments processing all the information...confused and heartbroken. But it still felt like there were pieces to this puzzle that Colson wasn't sharing. I watched him for any sign of deception because my gut twisted and screamed that there was something more that he wasn't telling me. When he didn't elaborate, I extended some trust.

"I'm so sorry he did that. I'm not surprised, but I am sorry. I'm glad you were able to stand up to him."

Something flickered in his eyes, and my chest felt hollow. What wasn't he telling me?

Sinking back into his side, he resumed the show.

"Let's just put it behind us." He pressed a kiss to my forehead and pulled me closer.

Colson remained silent as his hands rubbed my back in slow strokes.

I should have known something was wrong when we kissed goodbye that night, and he didn't ask me to stay.

25

NORA

AFTER TOSSING and turning all night, I woke early and went for a jog.

Which ended the moment I opened my door and realized how cold it was.

Instead, I checked my laptop, drank coffee, and went through my emails.

Haley slept in, which was fine...I wasn't ready to face her anyway, not with this weird sensation buzzing under my skin.

I needed to go see my dad, but I didn't like feeling like I was sticking my nose into something that had been resolved and no longer had anything to do with me. But I couldn't stop thinking about why my father would accept Colson's bid when he'd already told him he'd be forfeited for taking me to California.

Pulling out my cell, and closing my eyes, I dialed my dad, but after a few agonizing rings, it went to voicemail.

Which meant I had to talk to him in person.

Grabbing my keys and leaving a quick note for Haley, I darted out the door.

My truck maneuvered the streets easily enough as I slowly made my way over to my parents' house.

Parking and exiting the truck, I made quick work of the stairs.

The lockbox secured around the golden handle gave me pause, but didn't stop me from rapping my knuckles against the door.

After a minute or so, it was obvious that no one was home.

Okay…they must have left.

My gut instinct was to double check my dad's office one last time to make sure I wasn't totally off course, but they were supposed to leave for a cruise, so our little conversation might have to wait.

The sky over Macon was a bright blue, with the sun shining on all the snow that had dumped over the past few weeks. It was finally a clear day without any clouds, which gave me hope that maybe the snow might hold off for another week.

A few minutes later, I was pulling into my dad's office parking lot, feeling a zing of anticipation and relief that his truck was parked in his usual spot.

Walking in, the silence wrapped around me and held me in a viselike grip.

Dad was in his office, typing on a laptop, while the copier ran behind him.

"Nora?" His eyes took me in, worry etched along his face and seeped into his eyes.

Like déjà vu, the same emotions bubbled up as when I came home after I realized my father had had a hand in destroying my future, but I fell into the security of his arms regardless.

I was furious with him, but I was also confused, which ultimately was why I rounded his desk.

His long arms wrapped me up as he pressed a kiss to the top of my head.

"Hi, Dad."

"How was your Christmas, sweetie?"

Pulling back, I sat down in the simple chair across from his desk.

"Weird, uncomfortable…I missed you guys." It was all true, parents didn't stop being your parents even when they broke your heart. They continued to be who they always had been.

He let out a sigh, taking his glasses off. "We missed you too, kiddo. Next year, let's be sure we're together." He smiled at me reassuringly and I tried to return it. Regardless of where I was or who I was with, I wanted to be with them for the holidays, but I had to know that he wasn't trying to sabotage my future again.

"So what brings you by?" my dad asked, breaking into my thoughts.

He returned his gaze to the laptop screen, then turned to grab a stack of papers from the copier.

"Oh, just some weird stuff that happened in California…"

A deep line formed between his dark brows. "Oh, that… I'm sorry you got messed up in all of it. I tried to keep you clear of the Hanes."

That made my ears perk up.

"What do you mean you tried to keep me clear of it?"

Dropping the pile of papers in front of him, he flicked his gaze to me, licked his thumb, and flipped through pages. "Well, originally I had asked as a favor that Colson not get involved with you romantically…that was the deal anyway, he wanted to put a bid in for the company, and I needed to know I could count on him to watch out for you after we left, without worrying that he'd take advantage. I had to see how serious he was about not trying to date you."

My breathing slowed, which was a clear indication that I was two seconds from a heart attack.

Acting unfazed, I cleared my throat and asked, "When was this, exactly?"

My dad didn't look up as his brows wrinkled in concentration.

"Oh…the day your tree fell, I think. I remember there was an issue, and I was angry that he hadn't helped you."

The day he found me in his tub and didn't get mad that I was there… the day he hunted me down in the diner and helped me light a fire.

All of it.

The savior routine… it wasn't because he liked me…it was because he was trying to buy the company. My lungs seized like someone had plunged something sharp into them.

"So…who did you end up selling to, Oliver made it seem like he was a candidate."

Heaving a sigh, my dad pulled a sheet free from the pile, looking it over.

"No, I can't stand that man or what he stands for. I ended up selling it to Colson after we renegotiated the terms."

My chest was two seconds from collapsing, as though those latches that had unhitched were flapping in the wind.

"What terms?" I said around a thick ball of nerves stuck in my throat.

I had to hear them. I had to know.

My father finally paused his movements and leveled me with a stare as if he assumed I knew.

"Part of the final purchase agreement was that he wouldn't be romantically involved with you in any way. It's a legally binding stipulation in order for the transfer of sale and ownership to go to him."

There was so much...so many things invading my chest, making it hollow out, making my voice weak and feeble.

"He wouldn't agree to that." I barely managed to say through a cracked set of lungs and a barely functioning voice box.

With one tiny lift of his wrist, my father handed me the page he'd pulled out, and there on the bottom was Colson's signature.

I snatched the paper from my father's hand, reading every word on the page, to confirm that this wasn't some joke or elaborate scheme.

Tears clogged my throat as I tried to speak, but nothing but a sob worked itself free.

"You can't..." I tried and failed.

Anger surged forward, so potent, so raw that tears blinded me as everything from Jason and now Colson came to the surface.

I ripped the paper, and then I reached for the whole pile.

"Nora!"

My dad tried to stop me, but it was too late. I was ripping and tearing everything in sight.

"How could you do this again?" I sobbed, my chest ached, my fingers were numb to several paper cuts bleeding along my fingers, but I didn't care.

My father stared at me like I was a deranged fool.

"How could you, with Jason, and now..." I couldn't even say his name, how could he have signed, how could he give me up?

"You deserve better, Nora, and if I have to break your heart so that you find the right one to hold it, then I will."

"No!" I cried, throwing the shredded paper at him.

"You don't get to decide that for me, you can't choose these things for me and put an impossible choice in front of these men that I loved. I loved Jason, I wanted to marry him."

"And you found Colson, because of me… now think of who you'll find after Colson."

He thought he was helping me. He thought…

I couldn't breathe.

"These men are given simple choices, and the day you find the man who picks you out of everything offered to him, you'll know he's the one."

I wasn't hearing him anymore, not really. I had no idea what sounds I was making, but my chest was burning.

"Nora, calm down." He soothed, trying to calm me, but it wouldn't work.

My heart was shattered. All I could see was Colson's signature on that line, a few paces above it, said he agreed not to ever enter into a romantic engagement of any kind with me.

I sank to the cold floor, hiccuping as sobs worked through me and tears streamed endlessly.

"Call Rae. Please call Rae. I can't look at you and I don't ever want to speak to you again."

"Honey, you need to breathe. I think you're having a panic attack."

I couldn't focus on his face, or even his voice. Black dots danced in my vision, which made me angry. I hated that this hurt so much. I couldn't breathe around the crater in my chest.

Another man I loved had fallen for it.

Choosing that I wasn't worth it.

I closed my eyes and then I finished breaking.

I COULD HEAR RAE TALKING.

And I knew that Davis had carried me into the house. I had no idea what time it was, or why she'd brought me home, but I didn't want to be here, or anywhere close to Colson.

Sitting up, I slowly gathered myself enough to start packing.

"Hey…you're up," Rae said from my doorway, she held her elbow like she wasn't sure what to do with me.

I didn't know what to do with me either, so that was fine.

"Thank you for getting me." I rasped, my voice raw.

She moved closer. "Of course. Your dad didn't say much, just to get you home."

I laughed sardonically at that.

"What happened?" Rae's voice was small as she settled on the edge of my bed, watching me grab clothes.

Slamming a drawer, I tried to make my voice work without sobbing.

"He gave Colson an ultimatum to buy the business."

Rae's eyes searched mine, and I knew she understood all the things I wasn't saying.

Her head shook as she whispered, "He didn't agree. Tell me Colson didn't agree."

My gaze moved past my best friend, and that's when I saw him, hovering near the doorway.

His voice was low and tainted with pain as he made his way into my room. "I agreed on paper, but only because it was bullshit, Nora. He was going to be in Arizona, I could fight the stupid shit in court. I had a plan."

Colson walked in, trying to defend himself.

I shook my head, while Rae got up from the bed to block his path.

"I think you should go, Colson."

He ignored her and stepped forward, pushing his hands into my hair as he cupped my jaw.

"No, it wasn't real…I just…" He hesitated, his jaw working and tensing. "I couldn't let him have it."

Pushing him away, I cried. "Well, congratulations, your father doesn't have the company, but you lost me in the process. I hope your dream is everything you hoped it would be."

His brows came together, as if he couldn't process what I said, then his mouth twisted.

"No, I didn't lose you."

He grabbed for me, but I pushed him away again. "Leave, Colson, and give me your key. Yours is still at your house, by the way, because I saw right through that bullshit."

His eyes closed, and I knew I was right.

"I panicked...I needed time, but I still needed you close until I figured it out because I can't lose you, Nora. I won't lose you."

"You already did!"

My voice was sharp and loud, I knew Haley was in the house, so was Davis...I had no idea who else, but he wasn't hearing me. Now maybe he would.

"No..." he whispered, tears coated his lashes as he shook his head, "please, no...I just...I messed up, let me fix it. I already gave it up, Nora. The first time he—"

His pause nearly made me laugh.

"The first time he asked you to watch out for me. The real reason you were suddenly nice to me, and couldn't seem to leave me alone? When you said you were just being a good neighbor? Yeah, he told me about that too."

"Did he tell you that I wanted to be with you a year ago?" Colson stepped forward again, the muscles in his neck straining as he pleaded with me.

"Nora, I've wanted to be with you, I've been in love with—"

"Stop, Colson. Just stop because all I hear you saying is that you let my father decide for you, and I refuse to be with any man who would allow that. Not ever again."

"Nora..." He strained again, but I moved to the bathroom and shut the door, locking it.

I heard him yelling something, but then Davis intervened, and I wasn't sure how they got him out, but eventually they did.

I finished packing my things, and thankfully Davis and Rae stayed, helping me load it all into my truck. I couldn't run into Colson again; it would hurt too much.

"I'm so sorry about all this," I said to Haley, hating that I left her in the lurch.

She shook her head, waving me off. "Don't worry about me. I'm sorry my brother is such a mess."

Nodding my head and swiping at my tears, I handed her a key.

"Would you mind housesitting for me while I'm gone? You said you didn't have the next place picked yet for where you would go, and you need to talk to him...so please stay here until I'm ready to come home?"

She nodded and then wrapped her arms around me.

"Of course, I will. Davis mentioned a gym that I might like, so I'm going to check that out and treat this as a sort of vacation."

"Good."

Grabbing my purse and snagging my favorite plant, I headed toward the door.

"I'll text you to check in with you."

Haley walked out with me, my eyes stayed down, refusing to look over at his house.

"Okay, take all the time you need to."

Opening my door, and tossing my bags in, I gave Colson's porch one glance, just one.

He was standing on it, white air clouding in front of him as he watched me. His hands strangled the railing as he dipped his face, that muscle in his jaw jumped and the sight made my stomach swoop.

He'd done this.

He broke it.

As I climbed in and my door was still open, I heard him yell my name.

Then my door slammed shut, and I put my truck in reverse.

26

NORA

RAE'S GUEST room was dim with the blackout curtains drawn shut.

I preferred it that way, and honestly, I had no intentions of getting out of bed at all. Except I didn't plan on staying with Rae and Davis…and the idea that I might be crashing here was probably stressing them both out. Davis was insanely private, and as nice as he was to me as Rae's best friend, I knew it was hard on him to have people in his space. Especially as he worked through some tragic family stuff that had recently happened.

So, reluctantly, I pulled the covers back and got up.

The house was quiet as I lugged my overnight bag with me down the hall to the guest bathroom. Turning the spray extra hot, I stood under it for a little longer than necessary, but my face felt like old leather from all the tears I had cried last night, so it felt justified. I massaged my hair, washed my face, and waited until my skin was tinged pink.

Finally, dressed and somewhat ready for the day, I went downstairs.

Rae was sipping coffee at the table; her laptop was open, and a million papers were spread in front of her.

"You never use your office." I clipped, heading to the coffee machine.

Since Rae moved in, Davis had transitioned to something fancier than his old Keurig. A large pot with an attached frother for milk, that I never learned how to operate, sat in its place.

She slid out of her chair and walked up behind me. "I do use it…just not in the mornings when he's off doing deliveries and I'm alone."

I grunted something unintelligible.

She watched me, softening her tone. "How are you feeling this morning?"

I settled into one of the chairs at the table, watching her backyard as the snow slowly fell and the sun glittered on every piece. Up here, on Mount Macon the winter had hit about a million times harder than it did in town. Which was why it always stirred up vacation vibes when I stayed over at their house.

"I'm sad," I said, watching the snow drift over their hen house and goat pens. None of the animals were out, but it still was peaceful as the snow floated everywhere like tiny pieces of gold.

She tucked her chin in, likely unsure of what to say.

"So…you're taking a break from being neighbors with Colson…where are you going?"

I shrugged, and I knew the next thing out of her mouth would be an invitation, but I would never do that to my best friend, so I rushed to add.

"I think I want to go somewhere…maybe I could rent a small camper trailer and travel to Montana or something…"

Rae hummed from her spot near the sink before shoving off it.

"But…the fact that you'd die in that scenario because you don't know how to drive with a camper trailer on the back of your truck tells me that maybe you should shoot for something else."

Slumping in my seat, I griped morosely. "Dammit. You're right, I totally would get stuck or something and be eaten by wolves."

I thought over some other ideas. "What if I stay in a cabin for a while… up here, all alone. Get some perspective. The community center should be good for a bit…there's enough for them to go on. All my other projects are in the initial stages, so I won't have to travel anywhere. I have savings…I think it's exactly what I need for a while."

Rae settled in across from me, propping her knee in checkered flannel pajamas.

"You whisked me away when I needed it, so if you need to stay here, you know you can."

"Thank you, but I think I need to be alone…" I swallowed around the small truth I needed to acknowledge. "I've tried so hard to prove that I'm independent, buying my own house and doing everything on my own, basically being the opposite of everything I was accused of being, that I never stopped to think about what I wanted. All this time, I have been crafting this image that I wasn't weak, that I didn't need people. When really, that wasn't what this was about at all…"

Shaking my head, I tried to sort out what I was trying to say, but it was all a mess in my head. I needed some space to figure it out.

"Can you make sure that Colson doesn't find out where I am?"

My best friend's eyes softened. "Of course. I think Davis plans on talking to him, but yeah, we'll keep that a secret."

Which meant Davis would end up knowing. I guess it didn't bother me if he did, as long as his friendship with Colson didn't get in the way of my privacy.

Rae clicked around a few things on her laptop and then slid it toward me.

Images of private cabins tucked away in the snow next to a frozen lake reflected on the screen.

"Davis did all the light fixtures and ironwork at this resort. They have cute, secluded cabins and Davis gets an insane discount because he's not just a vendor, the owner is a friend of his."

Taking the laptop from her, I clicked through the images. The cabins were furnished, with massive fireplaces, precut wood, cute kitchens, and log beds.

"I don't want to abuse the discount, but if it's not any trouble, then I would love to use it."

Rae waved me off. "It's no trouble at all. Let me call Davis and ask what we need to tell them, and we'll get it all set up."

Giving her the best smile I could muster, I nodded and watched as she dialed her fiancé.

THE NEW FOUR-WHEEL-DRIVE vehicle was already proving to be the best purchase I ever made. The trip further north up the mountain was a breeze and uneventful as I followed the GPS on my phone into the Point Macon Resort's parking lot.

Checking in was a bit crazier as an entire school of kids had checked into the ski resort, but when it was finally my turn, the staff was incredible. The owner came out to greet me personally because of my connection to Davis, who had told this man God knew what about why I was staying here. But they offered me a spa package at no extra cost and gift cards for their market and restaurant, so I decided it didn't matter.

I took them up on the gift cards by stocking up on goods, and at the restaurant I ordered a meal that I could devour later.

Once I was ready and had my room key in hand, I got back into my truck and followed the small map around the rather large loop.

The whole resort was mostly inside the lodge, with rooms and varying balconies that hung on all five levels, but pushing past the outdoor pool and tennis courts, I saw more and more private cabins and fewer guests. Before long, I ventured off on a small side road, into a dense tree line.

The frozen lake sat undisturbed to the left, surrounded by tall evergreens and frosted with fresh snow. Clearing a small hill, I closed in on a lone cabin resting at the edge of the lake.

It was modest, but well-kept, and the logs looked freshly sealed. After parking in front of the small porch, I gathered my luggage and swiped the key across the small access pad.

The door opened to a cozy room, with pine floors running under my feet and beautiful throw rugs softening the space. A beige two-seater couch faced a large fireplace which had a fresh set of wood ready to be lit. The kitchen butted against the living room and was large enough for maybe two people to move around in, but it had a gorgeous view of the lake.

Down the hall was one bedroom, which had a massive king-size bed, with a log frame and quilt beautifully stitched with deep red and blues.

Another fireplace stretched along the wall, facing the bed, and at the back were French doors that led out to a hot tub.

Setting my things down, I tried to ignore the silence...but it was so loud, screaming all the things I had shoved down. My insecurities taunted me that this secluded getaway would do nothing to help me get over the heartache shattering my chest. What I wanted was to scream at Colson, have him hear how badly he hurt me, but I didn't want to hear anything he had to say in return.

What I needed to do was come to terms with why I had been trying to prove to someone that wasn't even in my life anymore that I wasn't spoiled when that someone had decided I wasn't worth the effort or time.

I had a few things to sort, and while I sorted, I was going to enjoy my time alone...at least as much as I could.

27

COLSON

SIX MONTHS AGO

DEAR MOM,

I still don't know why I write to you every time I feel like this…

When it comes to Nora, it's this feeling that I've never had before, like every time she's near me, my heart might explode.

Is that love?

Did you ever feel it with Dad…? I hate that I never asked while you were alive…and that I only talked about such shallow things with you…it isn't fair that time provides perspective and appreciation for experiences. I want to know about what you went through in life…what it was like for you to fall in love, and what I'm doing wrong in my own life.

I wish I could call you and ask you for advice and how to get Nora Petrov off my mind.

She shows up on our work sites, bringing coffee to everyone, and every time she does, she saves mine for last. I like it because it gives me a few seconds longer to look at her, to hold her gaze, and last time, I grabbed the cup in a way that made our fingers brush.

It was stupid, but I haven't stopped thinking about it.

My boss doesn't want me around her. I let his objections have a place in my head…they just never make it to my heart. I want this job to work out, this place...I want Macon because it's free of Dad, or anything he's touched.

I'll try to go home to make sure the boys haven't messed up your garden. I'm sorry I haven't gone back as much as I should, but you know why I can't.

I love you, and I'm still dreaming of tomorrow.
Cole

MY FINGERS ITCHED to grab a pen and a piece of notebook paper.

I wanted to write to my mother, my own form of catharsis bullshit, which helped me process my feelings.

But every time I thought of what I would write, my fingers would curl into a fist, and I'd punch the heavy bag in my garage.

I could not write to my dead mother that I lost the only woman I had ever loved. The one I spent a year telling her about...the one I had cowardly let slip through my fingers all so that I could have one fucking thing not tainted by my father.

I punched the bag, watching it swing at my pathetic attempts.

My hangover wasn't doing shit for my performance today, and if Mila saw it, she'd be shouting all sorts of shit at me right now.

The scraping sound outside my garage door picked up again, for the third time today, and enough was enough.

Dropping my gloves, I pushed the button to open the bay door.

The light assaulted me first, so I blinked harshly, then the wind swept in and reminded me it was the tail end of December, and fucking freezing.

But there she was, again.

Stomping over in my slippers and sweats, a raggedy tank top was on my chest, and I was pretty sure it had stains from my whiskey and the chili I'd eaten from the can earlier, I knew I didn't look particularly great.

"Hey," I shouted toward the sprite figure in the driveway next to mine.

Her head spun, the earmuffs covering her ears were Nora's I was pretty sure, which made my anger spike.

"Why are you out here shoveling again?" I yelled across the drive, "This is the third fucking time today, Haley. You wanted my attention, fine, here it is!"

Raising my arms high, I challenged her, not even feeling the cold on my skin.

Her sharp green eyes narrowed on me as she dropped the shovel. It was also Nora's.

"Don't drop her shit!"

She stomped closer. Good, we needed to finally have it out.

"Why are you still here, why are you in her house?" I droned on, her form getting a little blurry as she got closer. Was I still drunk?

Shit, how much had I had?

Directly in front of me, my little sister glared, setting her narrow chin high.

"Nora told me I had to stay on top of it, or else it would freeze and get all clumpy. She used a more intelligent word, but I can't think of it at the moment."

"You talked to Nora?" I stepped closer and nearly lost my footing.

She shoved my chest and then coughed.

"God, you stink."

"You stink," I mimicked childishly. Did I stink? Fuck, I was drunk.

Haley tore her gloves off and let out a heavy sigh.

"To answer your question, idiot, you keep ignoring me every time I knock on your door. I was thinking of breaking in through the back at some point, but thought I'd try annoying the shit out of you first with the scraping."

She continued to push, helping me back into the house and jamming her fist into the garage opener so that it closed.

"Nora broke into my house once."

"Really?" She held my elbow. "Step up."

I did as she said, clearing the stairs into my house.

"Yeah, she broke in and stole my tub."

Haley pushed my shoulder until I was falling back onto the couch. How were we already in the living room?

"She stole your tub, huh?"

"Yeah, because I was a prick and didn't offer to help her."

Haley moved around in the kitchen, clanking pots and turning on the water.

"Well, are you done being a prick?"

A glass of water appeared in front of my face, along with a pill bottle.

"Drink, take these. You're not doing anything for anyone being drunk and mean."

I took the glass and popped the pain reliever into my mouth, swallowing it down.

She watched me with a hawklike gaze. "Don't you have a job? You haven't left the house in three days."

That whole thing.

Fuck.

I thought back to my conversation with Peter three days ago.

After Nora left, I was a mess. So I drove over to his office and stormed into the building. When he saw me, he was still trying to pick up all the tattered pieces of paper that had been torn up.

"I'm out." I had gritted out with anger lacing my tone.

Peter stared but didn't say anything.

So I continued.

"You talk about her needing wings when really you clipped them a long time ago. You want her in your cage, you want to control her future. You don't give a fuck about her leaving and being free."

"You don't know what you're talking about." Peter scoffed, shaking his head.

"That's why she won't speak to either of us? Because I don't know what I'm talking about?"

I moved forward to the desk and slammed my hands down.

"Here is what I know. Your daughter is beautiful and brave. She knows exactly who she is and what she wants in life. If she wanted wings, she'd have them, but she wants roots. If you knew her, you'd realize that. She's not too young, she's the perfect age for me. She's the only person I've ever met that can see the entire picture and think calmly, critically, and allow the pieces to fall into place. She works harder than half the guys on the crew, and she doesn't need anyone to take care of her. It's a privilege if she lets you, but she doesn't need it."

I tried to calm my breathing but the realization I had lost all that and she was gone ripped through me on such a painful wave I almost wanted to punch Peter.

"I officially withdraw my bid. If she ever forgives me, I'll never do anything to lose her again."

Now, thinking back on the mess I'd made of everything, I pulled one of the couch pillows over my face and groaned.

Haley must have stayed put because she asked from the same spot, "Well, what happened?"

Shifting position on the couch, I realized she'd taken a spot on the coffee table.

"I quit my job and pulled out of the deal."

Her eyes stayed level, and her mouth thinned into an apathetic line. "Bravo, brother. Do you want applause?"

Her fake clap had my molars slamming together.

"Fuck you."

"No, fuck you." She shoved my leg with her boot.

"If you had talked to me like I asked you to, then none of this would have happened. Well, some of it would because you're an idiot and offered to help Nora while conspiring with her father."

"Your point?"

I gingerly left the couch. I needed coffee, or something because a migraine the size of Texas was invading my scalp despite the pain reliever I took.

"Dad's broke."

I paused, my hand hovering over the coffee pot.

She moved behind me, closer to the counter, and continued as I poured.

"His company is tanking, I don't know if you've looked at the shares, but it's a mess."

I turned toward her, my eyes narrowing.

"Then how did he offer to buy the company?"

"He didn't have the money to buy the Petrov company. He was going to use my company...the one he'd set up in my name, and put me as CEO of, at least on the tax forms that's what it said. Legally, I have complete control over the money in the business."

"And you were going to do what with that information?" I sipped my coffee, letting it burn my tongue.

She removed her earmuffs and jacket, likely realizing I wasn't going to kick her out.

"I was going to buy the company out from underneath Dad, and then sell it to you."

Well, shit.

"He's not a threat anymore, Cole. He's going to sell the house. He wants to try and disappear so he can live on an island without paying back shareholders."

That one hurt.

Just the house, not leaving. They were fucked if they thought I cared about that.

"Do the boys know?" My brothers were assholes, but they were my siblings...a sentiment I finally extended to the girl in front of me.

She shrugged. "They treat me like you do."

Which meant they didn't listen to her.

Propping my elbows on the counter, I cradled my head. Fuck, it felt like it was splitting in half.

My heart was caving in on itself too, and somewhere in the middle was this budding affection for my little sister. She deserved so much more than what she got with this shitty family. All this time, I made assumptions about her motives based on who her mother was and none of this was her fault, and yet the burden of the whole family landed on her shoulders.

"Just so you know, I'm done with them. My car has everything I own inside of it, and once Nora comes back, I'll be moving on."

That couldn't be right...she couldn't just go and live on her own. She was only twenty years old and had a shit time of things so far. No, I couldn't let her do that.

"Look, Hales...I'm so sorry." I lifted my head to look her in the eye. "I've been a shitty brother, and you deserve so much better. I don't expect you to accept this, but I would like the chance to start over with you."

She was quiet, her eyes low while she drew circles on the counter.

"I don't want you to do this out of some place of feeling guilty, or manipulation. I'd rather live on my own and away from every last Hanes on the planet than be a pity project."

I reached forward, pulling her hand into mine.

"It's not pity...it's remorse. I fucked up my life, Haley...with you, and with Nora. It's all a mess. I need to fix things, not make them worse. I want to get to know you."

As she gave me a small nod, someone knocked on the front door.

I hadn't even made it to the hallway before it burst open and Seraphina, Maddy, and Mila were running inside.

"Uncle Cole!"

Liam closed the door a second later, giving me an apologetic look.

"Did we have plans?" I asked, rubbing a hand down my face, watching as the girls all ran to the guest room, finding their toys.

Liam walked up, his dark hair was askew and under his leather jacket he had on a nice black button-down shirt.

"Sorry, I texted you a few times..." Liam's eyes bounced from me to Haley in confusion.

"My phone has been..." I trailed off, not sure where it was, or when the last time was that I saw it.

Liam settled in the kitchen, close to where I was standing, his eyes still on Haley.

"Sorry, Liam"—I put my hand out—"this is my little sister, Haley. Haley, this is my friend, Liam."

Liam shoved his hand out, and Haley slowly accepted it. "Nice to meet you."

I frowned at their touch, confused as to why Liam lingered so long.

"So, you headed somewhere tonight?"

Liam blinked like he'd just remembered and pulled away from my sister. "Yes, is there any way at all you can babysit for me? I have, uh"— his gaze swung quickly to Haley, then settled back on me—"a date."

"Well, I would, but I'm not in very good shape, man..." He knew about Nora, because the second place I went after I lost her was to his gym, and I stayed there until he kicked my ass out.

His face shuddered. "Oh shit, man..." His hand moved over his hair.

"I'm so sorry. I—shit, I knew I shouldn't have even agreed to this stupid date."

Haley hopped off the stool and made her way around the counter.

"Well, I'll be here too, do the girls like makeovers?"

"Yesss." All three girls screamed at once from the living room.

Haley beamed. "There, I'll help Cole tonight. Go, enjoy your date, have fun."

With the way Liam trailed my sister's every move, I was practically pushing him out the door to go and indeed enjoy his date.

"Okay, well, thank you…" he said, giving his girls a quick wave and one last glance at Haley before exiting.

Haley's smile couldn't be matched. "Okay, I need to run next door and grab all my makeup stuff, I'll be right back."

Haley grabbed her boots and ran outside.

I made my way to the girls and sat down on the floor in front of them.

"Uncle Cole, when is Nora coming back?" Mila asked, tipping her head back so that her hair moved out of her eyes.

My chest cracked, and tears clogged my throat again because it had been three days, and I hadn't seen her or heard from her. I hated not knowing where she was…and yet all I could do was wait.

"Really soon, sweetie. Should we make her a card?"

All the girls jumped up in excitement at that, running to go find craft supplies. I stayed rooted in place, thinking over how I'd ever get her to talk to me again.

28

NORA

NO ONE ever talks about how boring self-discovery can be.

In the midst of sadness and self-pity, I found myself doing yoga, taking walks along the lake, and catching up on work...but it was all boring as hell.

There were a few things I had investigated, such as my complete and utter obsession with mint ice cream, but only the green kind.

I realized I needed therapy, which was a powerful epiphany and one that led to a series of online sessions with a licensed therapist named Geraldine. She listened as I explained and then she suggested I write letters to all the people in my life that made me feel like I had to stand on my own two feet in order to feel valid or worthy in any way.

I wrote Jason a letter, where I called him a coward, and went into great detail how bad in bed he was, now that I had Colson to compare him to. That unfortunately led to a downward spiral where I questioned whether I'd ever find sex as good as it was with Colson again.

That call went to my best friend Rae, not my therapist.

Rae listened to me wail on the phone while I paced the length of my cabin for an hour. I owed her an entire pie for that conversation because she had to hear me talk about Colson's monster dick and how much I missed it.

But afterward I woke up feeling a thousand times better.

The next letter would go to my dad, but instead of burning it like I did with Jason's, I mailed it.

To their new Arizona address.

It wasn't the nicest note, and I definitely didn't hold back. I explained how badly he'd hurt me by taking too many liberties with my life and how that would no longer be happening because I would not be including him in mine until he agreed not to ever interfere with any aspect of my future. I didn't bring up either of the men that he'd played like a violin because men would come and go in my life, but I wanted my father to understand how I needed to be treated going forward.

The third letter was currently tucked inside my pocket, because it was going to Colson.

On my way down the mountain, I stopped at Rae's to check in on her.

Pulling her front door open, she looked like she hadn't slept in days. Her hair was a rat's nest, and she was in the same pajamas I left her in days ago. Surely, she washed them in between days, but still.

"What happened to you?" I shut the door, following her inside.

Rae waved her arm up in the air, grabbing for a carton of orange chicken. "Oh my gosh, I have so much to catch you up on."

"Um, I hope the first item on your list is how you got your hands on Chinese takeout all the way up here."

"Davis brought it home from town." She dug into the carton with her chopsticks.

Her kitchen table shed light on her situation.

"Whoa."

"Nora, everything is falling behind, I'm stressing out."

Every inch of her table was covered in papers and plans.

"What happened?"

Setting her carton to the side, she pushed her glasses up her nose. "So, there have been a few developments."

"Okayyy." I sat down, pulling on a few pieces of paper to try to make sense of what was going on.

"Colson quit...so your dad's company sort of dissolved or something, but there's no one working on the community center, and all the other bids are months out, so Davis and I have been trying to come up with some idea on how we can get it done and stay on track. Meanwhile, Davis is trying to open his new storefront and there's a lot going into that. I'm just..." She slumped into her chair, trailing off.

"Rae, why didn't you tell me all this was going on?"

Her eyes were a dead giveaway, and I knew it was my shitstorm of a life...but still.

"I'm your best friend, you should have told me. Not let me go on and on about losing my sex life."

She laughed into her hands, and before long she had to wipe tears from her eyes.

"Why are we trying so hard, Nora? This is all bullshit. I was a simple nobody a year ago, up in New York and you were a cool college graduate, living at home. How did we get here?"

I laughed with her, bringing a piece of paper up to cover my face.

"We're not mature enough for this."

Davis walked in on us while we pretty much unraveled into fits of laughter and tears.

He shook his head, cracking a small smile while he grabbed the carton of food from Rae.

"Okay, okay..." I blew out a breath. "Want me to reach out to my dad and ask what's going on, or talk to anyone?"

"Your dad is on his cruise, officially," Rae answered, gathering a few papers into a pile.

I narrowed my eyes. "How do you know?"

"Because at present I'm your voice mail service and your parents wanted to be sure you were alive. I relayed that you were, and they told me they're on their cruise until the middle of January."

Of course they were. Dad got to do a shit-ton of damage and then go on a cruise.

Oh well, he'd get that letter the second he got back.

I knew Rae wasn't going to ask me to talk to Colson, but he was the next logical choice for how to get someone started on the community center project.

"Okay, I'm going to head back home and see what I can do to help from there. I'll call you later." I stood, heading over to give her a hug.

"Nora, you don't have to do what I know you're thinking of doing."

Taking her face in my palms, I squeezed her cheeks until she laughed.

"Yes, I do, and it will be okay."

Because it was time I started doing things for myself, not worrying about what anyone else thought.

THE SNOW HAD MELTED, and even with the tiny snow flurries now and then, thankfully it wasn't sticking. Which meant the roads were clear, and the sky was a gorgeous blue. Haley and I had been in touch throughout my absence, and while I was gone for nine days, we only talked once or twice.

Never once did she bring up Colson.

Pulling up to my house, I saw that her SUV was missing, so I'd have the house to myself for a while. It would give me some time to figure out how to talk to Colson.

Once I parked and opened my door, I heard the sound of a latch clicking and looked up.

I immediately wished I hadn't.

Colson's eyes were red and tired. His face was ghostly white, his hair skewed and messy, and it was clear he hadn't shaved a single day since I left. In plain jeans, and a dark Henley that gaped open at his throat, he stood on his stoop, watching as I pulled my suitcases out.

His jaw worked as he pushed his hands into his pockets.

"Do you"—he cleared his throat nervously—"do you need any help with those?"

As angry as I was, seeing him as worn and beat down as I felt emotionally softened my stubborn streak.

"Yes, actually."

He moved, striding down his steps, and the closer he got, the more aware of his scent I became. My nose wanted to dive into the crook of his neck, and I desperately wanted to feel his arms around me.

I had never felt this way before with anyone. My heart was physically trying to exit my chest just so he'd hold it again.

He opened the door to my back seat and stood there staring.

I knew what he was seeing, and my throat worked around a sob as I envisioned us back there in that car lot, making love as he fought against his feelings.

As I fought against letting mine through.

Feeling a surge of emotion hit my chest, I stood there with the doors open and blurted, "You said you wanted strings…" My brows dipped as I tried to work out his intentions and if they were all false. "Why say that if it was an act?"

He shifted his feet, his dark boots crunching the small rocks that had been left in my driveway, and his blue eyes caught mine, revealing a storm of emotions.

Brewing, manifesting, and tearing through pieces of him.

"It was never an act—not a single moment with you was an act. Your father did ask that I look out for you, help you…but none of it was an act, Nora, and trust me, he never encouraged me to get romantic with you. That went against everything he wanted. So, when I kissed you, that was me." He had gotten closer; his breathing was coming out harshly as he hit his chest.

"When I took you home, put you in my bath, and took care of you, that was me." He hit his chest again, advancing closer.

His lips were a breath away from mine as he whispered, "And when I fucked you, Nora…when I held you in my arms and finally let you fill the space you'd claimed a year before"—he pressed closer, whispering at my ear—"that was me. All of it was real. It was just overdue."

I was going to fall into him and let him kiss me. I could feel it. But all that would do is patch the gaping hole between us, and we'd keep falling through it over and over again until it was repaired.

So, pulling myself together, I grabbed the letter from inside my pocket and when my hands landed on his chest to push him back, the letter poked him.

"I wrote this for you. If you could read it, that would mean something to me."

His hand moved over mine, holding it to his chest. I refused to look into his eyes.

"I'll read it." He stepped back, and then he grabbed my suitcase. "And I'll hold on to this for you when you're ready to come and talk."

"But, I—" I tried to speak up, but he was already moving, taking my suitcase with him up his porch and into his house.

A spark of something flitted inside my sternum.

He hadn't pushed me away. He hadn't given up or left. Part of me assumed he'd leave if he couldn't have his dream, but he was still here and, based on the way he just devoured me with those eyes, he wanted me more than ever.

29

COLSON

THREE MONTHS AGO

DEAR MOM,

There's been this house sitting vacant next to me for as long as I've lived here. It's a shit stain brown color, and an eyesore in the neighborhood. I loathe looking at it every day, but today the pending sale sign came down.

At first, I wondered if I was being punished, and then I considered that maybe you had indeed shot a prayer up for me because my new neighbor is Nora Petrov.

She's still off-limits to me, according to my boss and honestly, Mom, I'm not proud of how I've behaved around her. I don't think she likes me very much, and I don't blame her. I've had to push her away, so much so that I made up a fake girlfriend. It's a long story, but I think she sort of stripped for me or something, anyway I walked in on her and I froze... totally panicked and blurted that I was dating someone.

How pathetic does that make me on a scale from one to ten?

I'm feeling like it was a ten. She's stopped coming to the work sites, I feel like I never see her anymore. But maybe now that she lives next to me, I'll finally have the chance to talk to her...or get to know her.

I don't know, but send up another prayer for me. This will either be the best or worst thing that's ever happened to me.

Love, Cole

I READ Nora's letter three times.

Call it overkill, but I didn't want to miss anything, and it wasn't a hardship, considering the letter wasn't that long.

I watched the clock, seeing that it was close to five, and getting dark. She still hadn't come over to talk, or to get her suitcase. That was a cheap shot, but I still took it because when it came to Nora, I was desperate.

She'd deprived me of her presence for nine fucking days, and I was losing my mind.

The first thing I did when I came back in the house was shower, shave, and clean my house.

It was a disaster, and Haley had said as much every day that she'd been over to see me. We'd shared dinner nearly every night this week, except for one where she mentioned she'd offered to meet someone about a job.

I had no idea what that meant, but the next day she seemed all giddy and happy. Today I texted asking where she was and she sent a smiley face with her reply, "work."

I, however, was still unemployed.

Which I wasn't sure how all that would land, but I'd be okay for a while.

Pushing the letter back by the edges, I looked at it one more time, making sure I understood what she'd written.

COLSON,

It's taken me a few days to understand this piece of myself...to truly wrestle with it, tame it, and accept it.

But I have.

In doing so, I realized there are stubborn parts of me that have pushed you away and then punished you for not pulling me back in.

I realized that I didn't know myself, and really if I had, then I would have just come clean with you long ago and told you that I liked you. I would have let you in instead of always being a sharp shard of glass, ready to cut you the second you got too close.

My behavior doesn't excuse yours, not by any means, it merely explains my own.

I know I need to grow up, figure out my desires, hopes, and dreams.

For five days I have sat here thinking of what I wanted to say to you, and all I can think of is that I don't want an end.

I want a beginning.

A real one.

Without lies or fake bravado. One without falling trees and break-ins. One without our masks.

I just want you, the real you that's still hurting after losing your mother.

The real you that detests your father but goes home to visit regardless.

The real you that loves your friends and has a soft spot for three little girls who you mean the world to.

I love you, Colson.

Loving you has been the realest thing that has ever happened to me. It's been the scariest and most freeing feeling I have ever felt.

You should know about Jason, and why this deal with my father hurt so much. I'm not telling you so you can compare, but only so you can understand, because when we start over, you should know all of me and what makes me tick. This piece is a big part of what broke me.

And since I plan to be fully put together for you and with you, you need to know. So, here you go. Here's my story...

I PULLED ON THE EDGE, realizing I had no idea how badly this fucked-up scenario would have hurt her, but when I read about that fucking asshole, it felt like I'd pierced my own goddamn chest with a knife.

Of course, she was hurt. I was the second man she'd loved that had essentially fallen to the demands of her father and hurt her.

The fact that I had given her up on paper...fuck.

Just fuck.

I needed to talk to her.

Finally, after I was about to walk over, she opened my front door without knocking.

My eyes snapped to her form in my entryway, and my breath hung suspended in my lungs.

"You read it."

Swallowing, I dipped my head and nodded.

She moved forward. "Good. So, a few things…"

Her tone was all business, no emotion whatsoever. I didn't like it.

Her hips pressed against the counter as she searched my face.

I wanted to touch her, it was a burn under my fingers so raw and so strong that I reached forward and placed my hand over hers.

The air finally left my lungs when she didn't pull away.

"First, I'd like a letter from you. I know, it's circa Ross and Rachel: we were on a break. But humor me."

I nodded because that was easy.

"Done."

Her face flushed the smallest bit when my hands enveloped hers by intertwining my fingers with hers.

"Uh…" She cleared her throat. "Second thing, can you go back to work, or help Rae figure out how to get the community center done? She's scrambling, and I feel like it's all my fault."

Oh shit, I hadn't considered what would happen to the center once I quit.

"Tyler and the guys aren't there?"

Surely they were still on the job, why wouldn't they be?

Nora shook her head. "Dad's company dissolved, or at least that's what I heard. Everyone lost their jobs, and all the projects he had are on hold until he can figure something out."

"But…" My face fell, trying to piece all that together. "I'll volunteer… I'll pay the guys out of my own pocket to finish, don't worry."

She shook her head. "No, that's not what I want. I was hoping you could talk to my dad, see if…" She searched my face and then paused. "You cut ties with him?"

I nodded.

"I loved working for him, Nora, but he played me from the very start.

He's a part of your life, and since I have no intention of not being in your life, I know that we'll have to reconnect at some point, but I can't work for him again."

"Then work for me," Haley said, walking in through the front door, slamming it shut with a wince.

"Sorry, that's still so much lighter than Dad's. I'm not used to it."

Nora turned and pulled her hand from under mine to hug my little sister.

"Are you guys...?" Her eyes bounced from mine to Haley's.

Haley walked over and tucked herself under my arm.

"We're family...and"—she looked up at me for confirmation and I smiled back—"I'm staying in Macon."

Nora's jaw dropped. "Oh my gosh, that's amazing!"

"I have a job lined up too, which I'm excited about. It'll be really new for me."

I shifted, and Haley slipped out from under my arm to sit on the barstool.

"Yeah, explain this working for you thing..." I raised my brow at her.

"Well, I tracked Peter Petrov down and spoke with him on the phone."

Nora and I glanced at one another.

"He's on a cruise...and unreachable," Nora explained as though she'd tried to reach him but couldn't.

It pissed me off that her dad left with things so shitty between them.

"Yes, well, every cruise ship has a captain and point of contact for emergencies. I can be very persistent when I want to be."

Nora glanced at me again, biting back a smile.

"So what happened?"

Haley folded her hands in front of her. "I bought the company. While my dad thought he'd use our names on these fake companies for his own purposes, I was busy investing my trust fund and allowing my money to make money. I own several franchises around California and Oregon. Peter and I came to an agreement. He requested that I make sure you have a job if you want one...he even suggested I make you partner because you're such a great asset."

I hummed, unsure how to feel about him saying that. It felt too soon to give it any levity.

"So, this is your new job, then?" Nora asked.

Haley shook her head, "Oh no, not even close." She laughed. "I'm handing things over to Cole completely. I want nothing to do with the company, in fact, he can buy it if he wants…but it's his to run, he's the boss."

I let that settle in my chest as my eyes searched for Nora's, knowing there was no chance I could enjoy getting what I thought was my dream when I had finally realized she was it. Nothing else.

"Congrats, Colson. I'm happy for you," Nora whispered softly.

I was about to tell her that I wasn't happy for me, that I'd turn it down if it meant she'd give us a shot. Her letter indicated she wanted a beginning…a start.

Leaning in close, I pressed a kiss to her cheek.

"A nice beginning."

She stilled and then pulled away.

"So, Haley, what's your new job then?"

My sister excitedly tapped the counter.

"I'm going to be a nanny! Doesn't that sound so exciting?"

Oh fuck.

Nora laughed, and my gaze swung from her to a confused Haley.

"What?"

"It's nothing—"

"I'm going to let you guys talk, I have to get back." Nora cut in, waving at Haley as my sister's gaze stayed withdrawn and confused.

"What, Cole…what aren't you saying?" Haley asked, but my mind was on Nora.

I followed her outside, down my steps, trying to get her to stop.

"You made it seem like the job thing for the community center was number two…what was supposed to come after that?" I asked, trailing Nora to her driveway. The night was crisp and cold against my face and like ice inside my lungs.

Nora kept walking.

"Nothing, I just…"

Once she was at her door, I tugged her hand and stopped her.

"What do I have to do?" I begged her, my eyes searching her face in the shadow of her porch. "Your letter mentioned a beginning for us. I want that, what do I have to do to make that happen?"

She shrugged, tears welling in her eyes.

"I don't know...I—" She ducked her head, then lifted it, and finished. "I need your letter first, then we can talk."

"Okay," I hurried to agree, and let her arm go.

Once she was inside safely, I walked back to my side of the fence and got to work.

30

NORA

THE LETTER? I banged my head against the door after I shut it because I was an idiot.

I didn't care about a letter, but I was too terrified at the notion of letting him back into my life.

Especially after he'd gotten his dream without sacrificing anything to have it. I mean, he'd quit his job, and without any way of knowing that this would happen…so there was that. And technically he didn't own it, and it was tied to a Hanes. I mean there was some poetic justice in that, but I was still feeling petty about it.

Pushing off the door, I wrangled my suitcase into my room, realizing too late that I had forgotten my larger one inside Colson's house.

"Shit."

I pinned my hands to my hips and shook my head.

This whole day was bat shit crazy and upside down.

I needed my stuff, and at this point I fell onto my bed, staring at the ceiling because I wasn't sure what to do. If I went back over to his house to get it, I'd have to see him again and that was already so painful that it made me want to gouge my eyes out.

Then there was Haley…

I shot up from the bed, my eyes going wide as it finally hit me.

I could text her and tell her to bring my suitcase back over.

Right as I pulled my phone out to text her, the front door opened.

"Oh no, you have to go back and get my suitcase," I yelled from my room. She didn't reply, but I heard something rolling on my hardwood floors, which meant she'd grabbed it. Jumping up, I rounded the corner,

"Oh my gosh, you must have read my—"

Colson walked with a folder in one hand, and in the other, his fist gripped the handle of my luggage.

"Thought you might need this," he said softly.

My heart thrashed in my chest at seeing him in my house, remembering that I needed the bag.

Fuck, it was too much.

Tears started, and I couldn't make them stop.

He stalked closer, step by step.

"Please don't cry, baby." He let my suitcase go and brought his thumb up to my cheek, swiping at my tears.

"Here, this is for you." He handed me the blue folder, and then straightened.

I carefully took it from him, curious when I went to crack it open, his hand came down on mine.

"You can't..." The air left him in a rush. "Not while I'm here, at least. These are the most vulnerable things I own, and it's like peeling back a layer of my soul and showing you how pathetic I am. I don't want you to read these, but I feel like you need to."

I quirked a brow. "Your letter..."

He gestured to the folder. "Everything I could ever say is in there. If you still need space after you read them, I'll understand. You can have as much time as you need, I'll wait. But I need you to know, Nora, that you acted like you weren't sure who you were in your letter. Or that you've recently discovered yourself, and that's not at all how I saw you. You remind me of spring, you thrive in all the right conditions, baby, even spring, in all the ways it thrives and brings life, stays buried during winter. Struggling during a harsh season isn't in any way a reflection of who you are as a person. I love you, Nora. You're exactly who you should be."

He pressed a kiss to my nose, and then my lips, and turned to leave.

I stood there watching, frozen in place with tears trailing down my face.

MY BEDSIDE LAMP cast a glow in my bedroom as I curled up under my blankets and poured through the folder.

The first page I pulled free was crumpled and dated over a year ago.

When I glanced at who the letter had been addressed to, my heart nearly seized.

Dear Mom...

OH MY GOD.

Carefully and slowly lifting them from the folder and flipping through each one, I saw that these were letters he'd written to her...about *me*.

I flipped to another one.

Dear Mom...

AND ANOTHER,

Dear Mom...

AND EACH AND every one was about his growing crush on me. By the third letter, it didn't seem like a crush, but something more.

Dear Mom,

Tonight, I crashed a dinner party at Nora's house. I wasn't even invited, how pathetic is that?

My friend Davis had to invite me because he saw me in the backyard, watching while I sipped a beer. I was wallowing in self-pity because earlier that week, Nora had made a comment about having a boyfriend.

We went back and forth plenty about that stuff, but she had no way of knowing how deep it hurt when she threw her barbs out. Or how badly I wanted inside her world. She gardens Mom, did I tell you that? I feel like I did, but every time I see her out there, catering to that little patch of dirt, I fall a little bit more in love because I feel like she was made for me. Like you helped pick her just for me, knowing I needed someone in my life who knew how to harness the sun, and produce life.

Just like you always did.

I ended up making Nora mad at this dinner party. I kind of hate myself right now because no matter what I do, it seems I'm always messing up. One of these days, I'm just going to blurt out that I love her and I have no idea what she's going to do.

Send a prayer for me, Mom...I could use it.

Love, Cole

TEARS CLOUDED my eyes as I continued to read about the times he'd seen me but was too stubborn to be nice, and how that had become our normal way of communicating. The more I seemed to hate him, the angrier he became...like a vicious cycle he couldn't break.

Then there were letters closer to the end of the pile that made my breath hitch.

Dear Mom,

My boss offered to consider my bid for the company over the other offers...but he wanted to know if he could count on me to help with Nora.

Mom, I'm so confused. How do I go about this because Peter knows that I've been in love with Nora since I started working for him. Yet, he's asking if I can help without being tempted by her?

I'm going to fail this test, Mom. I know I am, but I'm worried about the fallout.

What if she likes me back...what if she wants me the way I want her?

I don't know what to do, but I know that I won't be able to resist her.

Send a prayer up for me. I'm still and always will be dreaming about tomorrow.

Love, Cole

THE LAST ONE robbed me of breath, and I knew I wouldn't be able to keep this stubborn façade up with him.

Dear Mom,

I messed it up. Nora's gone...I don't know for how long, but all the cards were on the table and she flipped the table over. She wants nothing to do with me.

When you died, there was a part of me that I had assumed died with you. I knew, internally, that I just walked around with half a heart because my mother took it with her to the grave.

But with Nora, for the first time ever, I felt like maybe that empty half could grow back. Like I could be whole again.

She makes me better, Mom.

She also makes me feel like I can hurt and grieve, but with her there, it won't consume me...not like it used to. She was my tether, and while I know it's my fault, all of this is my fault, I'm still selfish enough to want her.

I need her, Mom.

I want her future, I want to see her walking down the aisle toward me, I want to see her pregnant with our kid, I want her in my house, decorating for Christmas, I want her creating gardens wherever we live, and I want her breathing life into every dead place I've been existing in.

I don't know how to get her back, Mom, other than just staying and waiting.

I love her, so send a prayer up for me, Mom.

Help me get her back—that's my dream for tomorrow.

Love, Cole

I TOSSED THE BLANKETS OFF, feeling my heart break and mend all at once.

There was no chance of me sleeping after that. I had to see him.

Glancing at my phone, I realized it was after midnight.

I had showered, unpacked, caught up with Haley and basically done everything in my power to hold off reading these letters, and now I was paying for it. I thought I'd want to sleep on it, whatever it was I would read. Assuming it was his attempt at apologizing or justifying what he did…but this.

I couldn't.

I grabbed my coat and phone. Then tiptoed through the house, grabbing my boots.

Once I was bundled up, I exited through the back door.

The sky was violet with white stars smearing the inky expanse. The snow had frozen over after nearly melting all day, so it crunched loudly as I walked.

The build up near our fence was enough to climb, but once I'd made it to the top, I ended up sliding on my butt the rest of the way down.

Colson's yard was as dark as his house, and I belatedly realized he might lock his doors at night, which was smart...but not so great for me.

Still, I had to check.

Quietly creeping up the stairs, I pulled on the handle and, like the first time I had broken in, the door slid open in a silent woosh as I stepped inside. Securing the door behind me and locking it this time because, safety. I stepped out of my boots and took off my coat.

The warmth from the house enveloped me, and I immediately felt at ease.

Padding down the hallway, I crept into his room, seeing his sleeping form snuggled under the sheet.

Stripping out of my clothes, I slowly slid in next to him and closed my eyes.

Even if he didn't wake up, this would be enough.

My breathing calmed as I relaxed into the pillow and tried to rest, but seconds later, he turned toward me.

"You honestly think you could be in my bed, and I wouldn't know?"

My eyes popped open, seeing him hovering over me. I smiled and touched his jaw.

"Nora." His rough rasp was my undoing.

I lifted on my arm and pressed my lips to his, softly. Carefully.

He watched me as I pulled back, almost as if he didn't know if he could move, and then I went in again, gripping his face while I claimed his lips.

Whatever he'd been holding back finally snapped.

He groaned as he pulled me to him, viciously taking my lips in his, kissing and marking me in a starved manner.

Our movements were quick, desperate as our lips slid to the side, deepening our connection, and he pulled me on top of him.

My kisses turned messy as I trailed down his neck, to his chest, marking my way down his muscled torso, until I was licking the trail to his boxers. Without wasting time, I pushed the material down and freed his monster dick from the pathetic confines that his boxers provided.

He was thick in my fist as I licked up the shaft.

Colson lifted his torso, watching as I took him into my mouth. I had only bobbed my head twice on his weeping tip when he hissed and pulled me up.

"I need you, Nora. I need you right the fuck now. So, either slide down on my dick or get under me, so I can bury myself inside of you."

Greedy and needing to claim him in some way, I lined myself up with his erection and slowly slid down his length.

He let out another hiss as he grabbed my hips. "Yes, inch by fucking inch."

Once he was fully sheathed and I was spread wide over his hips, I rocked forward.

"Colson," I whispered, as my fingers dug into his chest and his hands came up to hold me.

His eyes landed on me, and though it was dark, I could make out that stare, the heavy lust and need that covered them.

"Nora."

We moved at the same time, he slammed my hips down while thrusting up into me, and I rocked forward, fucking him in slow strokes that, with each one, drew out my own pleasure with silent gasps and an arching back.

I rode him, swiveling my hips in tandem as he thrust and thrust and thrust.

"Fuckkk." He groaned, holding me against him while he found his release. Without wasting a single second, he flipped me until I was under him.

Then he buried himself in me once more, pinning his forehead to mine, as he moved in slow, powerful strides.

"Nora, tell me you're mine, tell me this is real."

Gasping for air, I tangled my fingers in his hair. "This is real."

Kissing my neck, he groaned.

"And mine, swear you're mine."

He rocked his hips, hitting that spot deep inside me that had me crying out.

"I'm yours, and you're mine." I added, "Forever…"

He froze over me, staring down.

It made me marginally nervous the way he watched me as if there was a problem, but his length remained hard and erect inside of me.

Then, on a guttural rasp, he said, "Don't tempt me, Nora. If you offer me forever, I'll take it."

I stared into his eyes, realizing how badly he needed this. The letters, now etched into my heart and serving as a way to better understand him, had me tracing his eyebrow and down his nose.

"I promise you, Cole. You have it. My future, my forever, all of it."

His lips landed on mine, starved for as much as he could take, his hips moved once more, and I was soaring.

Crying out my pleasure and need for him, and he groaned his own.

Connecting with him in this way, with him spilling inside of me…now that we'd made these vows, felt so much deeper than any other time we'd ever fucked before.

Having him like this was more intense, knowing he was claiming my body, my heart and soul all at once.

It wasn't enough. His lips found my neck as he marked my skin, and I pressed my rear into his growing hardness. His hand cupped the globe of my ass, stroking and massaging until he was thrusting into my core from behind. His previous releases were still inside me, spilling down my legs, but I didn't care. My head went back to his shoulder as his hand came around to my front, holding my stomach.

We didn't need words this time as he pulled out and thrust forward, fucking me senseless. My tits bounced as his frenzied movements shook the bed and left my mouth gaping in shock. He had never fucked me this hard, and when his orgasm finally ripped through him, it was my name that fell from his lips.

Catching my breath, and feeling him sag against me, I turned and kissed him hard.

Then I whispered in his ear.

"Again. Fuck me again."

WE ENDED up in the shower, his sheets completely destroyed and on the floor after so many rounds we lost count.

Our mixed releases were all over the place.

I couldn't get enough of him, but out of sheer exhaustion, he pulled me into his arms, like he was worried I'd try to slip away.

"You wrote to your mom about me," I whispered into the darkness of the room.

His warm breath was soft against my neck. "Yeah…"

We waited in silence for a few moments until finally, I broke.

"You loved me, all this time, you loved me."

His embrace tightened. "I didn't know it was love, Nora. I just knew I couldn't get enough of you, but I was so worried you didn't feel the same way and that I'd get fired, so I buried it with insults and trying to get under your skin."

I laughed, rubbing the hair on his forearm.

"You were already under my skin…I made a secret wedding board for us a long time ago. Rae found it a few months ago and ruthlessly teased me about it."

I could feel his chuckle reverberating down my spine.

"You have to show it to me."

Clicking my tongue, I tried to shake my head.

"That's bad luck, Colson."

Stroking my hair, he kissed my ear as he asked, "But marriage, you want that someday, then?"

I hummed my response, then added. "I'd be happy with a few kids too. And Macon?" I asked him, curious if he'd want to settle here or go back to California at some point.

He squeezed me tight. "Macon…but starting tomorrow, I think you need to move your stuff over here."

Laughing into his arm, I kissed it. "Deal."

I fell asleep knowing this was exactly where my future would begin.

31

NORA

TWO MONTHS LATER

MADDY AND MILA were staring at me through dark sunglasses. Seraphina had hers pushed up into her dark hair, while she devoured her ice cream cone.

"Nice shades, ladies." I mused, adjusting my own shades on my face.

The sun was warm against our skin as bits and pieces of winter melted away. We all knew this was false spring, every year around this time we were treated to sunshine, warm weather, and the temptation to take off our winter tires. Newbies always fell for it, but we knew better.

"Haley bought us these, aren't they glamorous?" Maddy asked with a dazzling smile.

I raised my eyebrows, feigning shock. "The most glamorous that I've ever seen."

"She's from Cawifornia. She knows dees things." Mila said in her cute little five-year-old way.

Haley was off near the cotton candy booth, talking to Jeffery Ackers. Colson and I hadn't failed to notice how often he hung around her, or how now that Haley rented my house from me, he was over all the time with flowers and coffee.

We asked if she liked him, but she'd always shrug as if she didn't know. Colson disagreed with my other theory, which was fine, but because

I was curious and nosy as fuck, my gaze slowly moved to the left of the massive barbeque, which was where Liam stood… and sure enough his eyes were on Haley and Jeffery.

I counted down in my head. By the time I got to one, his jaw ticked.

"Every time." I mused to myself.

No one seemed to notice that Liam had a hard time keeping his eyes off of his new nanny, and while Colson brushed it off saying he was just watching the girls, I specifically watched for the times when she wasn't near them. Like now.

"Well, what do you girls think of the new community center?" I asked, taking in the big celebration around us. Rae had planned all of it of course and even with snow on the ground, the people of Macon wouldn't be stopped from gathering and having a great time.

Seraphina wrinkled her forehead. "Isn't it for old people?"

Rae, who was on the other end of the bench, choked on her coffee.

Mila added, "Yeah, Daddy said it's for old people."

I watched my best friend as she slapped at her chest.

"I heard there was an entire room dedicated to kids, with painting, floor mats for exercise, and foam pits for playing."

The girls perked up.

"Really?"

"Yes, really," Rae finally recovered enough to add.

Her eyes met mine in a panic. "Do you think everyone assumes it's a senior citizen home?"

"Of course not."

They totally did but with enough time, they would know all the things it offered. I could tell my friend was already trying to find different ways to market it to the public, so they knew it wasn't just for senior citizens.

The building had been completed in record time. With Haley as the new owner, and Colson taking it over as the new boss, it was like everyone blinked and the entire thing was done. They were here five days a week, Colson tackled what he could on the weekends, and I would stay to help him as we caught each other up on how our week had gone.

I had moved in with him, but we didn't spend our time together talking about work.

When we were together, we didn't do much talking at all.

We were very much in the honeymoon phase of our relationship, which to Haley's dismay meant she'd walked in on a few traumatizing moments where Colson was doing unholy and unmentionable things to me. One time in particular I think I was on all fours, on the counter and we both screamed so loud that Colson tripped and fell backward, completely naked. He complained that he might have broken his dick. I laughed for two days straight.

After that, Haley made a big show of knocking and ringing the doorbell a million times before entering.

She seemed to enjoy nannying, although she seemed completely oblivious that her boss was the hottest man alive, excluding Colson of course. Liam was all toned muscle, hard jawline, and dark hair shaved closely on the sides of his head, but left longer on top in that way that made girls go stupid. He honestly could pass for a rock star when he wasn't wearing gym gear.

But he was also twelve years older than Haley, so maybe she didn't see him like that.

Although Jeffery Ackers wasn't that much younger than Liam and she didn't seem to have any issues accepting his flirtations.

"You are way too invested in her love life," Rae whispered next to me, pulling my gaze away from Haley and how she patted Jeffery on the shoulder then walked away.

Poor guy.

"She's just so clueless, it's cute."

"You are honestly going to have to reel it in because if you say anything at all to her, you will ruin it," Rae warned, and I knew she was right.

"Fine."

Turning toward my best friend, I smiled and shoved her shoulder.

"You ready to get married?"

Her face took on that same dreamy state that it always did when we talked about her wedding.

"I can't believe it's a week away."

"I can't believe you are literally engaged, moving in, and getting married to Davis all in less than six months."

"The heart wants what it wants." She shrugged.

"Can we be flower girls?" Mila asked brazenly.

Rae looked at me with a twinkle in her eye.

"I think that would be fun...and I think you girls might be doing a lot of that here pretty soon."

My eyes widened as I shot a look to Colson. He was laughing at something Davis said across the yard.

"Do you know something?" I gripped her arm.

She pulled it away. "Owww, Nora. OMG."

"Spill." I reached for her again, but she got up and laughed at me.

"Nope, not now. You need to learn to control yourself."

"I will tackle you, Raelyn Jackson."

"It's almost Raelyn Brenton to you, ma'am, and how soon will it be Nora Hanes?"

She stopped all of a sudden, and her mouth gaped as she stared at me.

"Oh my gosh, Nora, your dad is going to lose his shit when he realizes his baby girl will have the last name Hanes."

I snorted, she cackled, and soon we were being shushed by two elderly women.

Colson hadn't even proposed yet, but we always made jokes about my impending marriage.

My dad had finally received my letter, and when he asked if he could come to Macon to talk, I told him yes.

I didn't, however, warn him that my house was now shared with Colson.

That was a fun little perk and I relished how uncomfortable it made him to sit on Colson's couch, and be offered a drink from Colson's fridge, and the cherry on top was when Colson sat close enough to put his hand on my thigh. No, he didn't have a private audience with me, everything he said, he said in front of Colson.

Down the road I knew we'd get there, but I was still so hurt over his control, that it was something we had to build up to. My mother wasn't happy and had been staying with her sister for a while until they figured out where this need to control me stemmed from. She had reached out, offering to host both Colson and I for a weekend at their house in Arizona. We hadn't decided yet what weekend to go, but we both agreed that we would. She had also withdrawn the offer on me taking her house here in Macon. She wanted a place to stay when she came to visit, and was even considering making it her second home so that she was only gone during the winter.

"You know my dad will likely not even attend when he realizes it." I joked to Rae as we both got up and held our hands out to the girls to follow us.

Maddy held her sister's hand as Mila latched on to mine, and Seraph hung on to Rae.

"Come on girls, I want to show you the kids' room and how very un-old-person-like this place can be," Rae said, heading toward the center.

We all fell in line as I glanced behind me, seeing Davis and Colson track our movements. I smiled at Colson, feeling my heart warm in my chest, and the way he smiled back and left his conversation to head over made my belly swoop.

I didn't know when he wanted to make me his wife, but I wasn't in a hurry. We were exactly where we needed to be.

Together and surrounded by our friends.

The End

EPILOGUE

Colson

4 Months Later

A ROGUE OCEAN breeze shifted the sheer curtains Nora had picked out for this floor. They were my favorite of all the ones she'd picked. Each floor had its own theme, but this one...my mother's favorite spot, she'd decorated it all for me.

I told Nora I wanted whatever color she picked to match her eyes.

The aqua fabric had the sun bleeding through it, casting a glow over the hardwood.

I shoved my hands into my pockets and looked down right at my mother's garden and smiled.

"There he is." Nate mused, tipping his head back with a drink from his flask.

Trevor came up next, slapping me on the back. "You ready for this?"

I turned towards my brothers, smirking at the sight of them in suits.

"I've been ready for this for a while."

Their shoulders shook with laughter.

Nate twisted the cap on his flask. "Well, we have to find your best man…any ideas where he might be?"

"He's been with me most of the day…maybe he went to check on the girls?"

Trevor furrowed his brow, "last I saw he was talking to Haley…they looked like they might be in an argument or something."

Fuck. I didn't need to be worried about whether or not my little sister was going to lose her job right now. Liam couldn't keep a nanny or babysitter to save his life, I had no idea why my sister would be any different. Regardless of what Nora seemed to think…Liam and Haley argued too often for her theories to be correct.

"If I find him with his hands near our baby sister, I will lose my shit. Your wedding or not, I will kill him." Trevor warned, stealing Nate's flask.

Nate and I both laughed, shoving his shoulder.

"Liam is a fucking boxing legend, you idiot. And he'd never cross that line with his nanny…not to mention our little sister came here with a date."

The sound of music starting up from below made my heart slam into my ribs.

It took me back to that first time I had brought Nora here, and how much brokenness I had felt that night. How she saw me through the worst of it, how she gave me a chance to prove to her how much I wanted this… how much I wanted her.

I planned on reminding her every single day.

"We're going to go find Brock," Trevor slapped my back and the two of them left.

I had no idea how much time passed as I stared down at the place where I'd marry Nora, the arch covered the expanse of my mother's garden, the cement that had been poured over it was gone, so now it was tilled, fresh soil. Over the top of that soil was a raised platform, where I'd stand, along with our bridal party and the pastor.

There was green ivy, white gauzy fabric woven through the arch, along with big white flowers. I had no fucking clue what they were called, but I remembered when Rae and Nora talked in great detail at our kitchen table over which ones to order. The designer in Nora had come out in full swing and was showing up in every precise detail.

I knew I'd go down first, but a small part of me wanted to just stay here, a few doors down from where I had stayed with Nora that night...a few doors down from where I first confessed to loving her. From the place where I realized that she wouldn't run from how broken I was.

Part of me wanted to just have her come up here, marry me in the privacy of this hall, in my mother's favorite place.

But I wanted to marry her over that soil even more. To flip the middle finger to Sherrie and my father. Fuck knows where they ended up, they left as soon as Haley had discovered that the house didn't even belong to him.

Apparently, my mother left me the house; it was supposed to go to me on my twenty-fifth birthday...my fucking father never said a word.

"Colson, it's time." Liam walked in, straightening his tie.

I turned to look at my best friend and realized he was clenching his molars which made his jaw tick.

I gripped his shoulder, distracting him from fixing his tie. "You good?"

Liam wouldn't look me in the eye, which made my concern over Haley losing her job rise to the surface. I wanted to ask but I knew this wasn't the time...not the day.

My friend finally gave me a smile. "I'm good...just had an issue with the girls, but I'm fine. You ready?"

I knew he was bullshitting me.

Liam got that look in his eye when he wanted to hit something. I saw it when we sparred in the ring.

I'd deal with his bullshit later.

Walking past him, I took the stairs one at a time feeling my pulse race each step of the way.

The ocean air was balmy and felt good against the summer sun. It was nearly six in the evening, but the heat from the day was still heavy in the air. The breeze ruffled the white gauzy material woven in between the ivy and flowers. I stared at the backs of the guests' heads who were seated in rows of white fold out chairs, set up along the grass.

The preacher was already on the raised platform waiting, my guys followed me as I stepped up and got into place. There off to the side were two people holding a violin and a cello, their strings moving in a beautiful rhythmic melody.

My breathing was a mess of panic and excitement as I listened to the crescendo rise, and I realized this was happening. It was real.

It made me think back to when I had asked Nora to marry me a few months ago.

We had moved the fence line between our properties so that her original garden could be expanded on my side. It was something that had bridged our worlds together and one day while she was covered in dirt, wearing a hat over those big curls, she smiled up at me, holding a berry that had grown.

She was so insatiably happy over something she'd produced; over something she'd done—it tore me open in a way that had me sinking into the dirt next to her. Then after tucking a curl behind her ear, I simply said.

"Marry me."

She was so stunned that she'd flung herself at me, knocking me back into the dirt and kissed me senseless, covered in soil. It was fitting now marrying her over the start of a new garden.

Mila, Seraph, and Maddy began walking down the aisle, tossing more of those white flowers out of their baskets. They wore beautiful dresses, a pale-yellow color that seemed to match the bridesmaid dresses.

Haley walked behind them beaming down at their heads. Her hair was curled, she had darker lashes than she normally did and that with the little gold flecks on her cheeks, made her look like she'd stepped from a fairytale.

I smiled at her as she crossed in front of me, but her gaze lifted and stuck to the man standing next to me. It wasn't a smile that graced her lips though…it looked more like a sneer.

Liam cleared his throat behind me and adjusted his tie.

I couldn't focus on that, not when Rae cleared the aisle next, her gaze staying on her husband, Davis, who stood next to Liam. Then the tune changed, the melody of the violin and cello slowing and thrumming with base. It made my stomach swirl, and my heart slam against my chest.

A flash of white, and she stepped out.

My heart thundered; my lashes coated with tears as my eyes betrayed me.

Shit.

Her curls were wild, tossed up some gorgeous way that left tendrils floating around her face, and her dress fell off her shoulders, dipping into an elegant v, showing off her delicate collar bone. Those aqua eyes stayed on me as she walked, and the guests stood. Her father held his elbow at an angle, and her hand rested inside it. Seeing him walk her toward me made me smirk for an entirely different reason.

Fucker had come a long way over the past few months.

He even looked like he was fighting a few tears as they walked, but if I had to guess it was merely because she'd chosen me over his ridiculous idea of freedom and choices that were never hers.

The closer she got, the more my hands began to shake.

She slung a wide smile my way with that same purple color staining her lips, that I loved so much.

She was really doing this.

She'd chosen forever with me.

Her father helped her step up the raised dais, and then her hand was in mine, and everything seemed to melt away.

Her eyes locked on my blue ones, and my breath hung heavy in my lungs.

This was it.

Our forever.

Nora
5 years later

THE OCEAN ROARED below the cliff, but it was in steady competition with the happy squeals echoing through the air as my sons played tag. I was currently tending to a patch of soil that was supposed to be yielding sweet potatoes but hadn't yet. I had no idea what I was doing wrong, but this was the summer I'd figure it out so we could harvest this fall.

We spent every summer here in California, staying on the estate, and liked to donate whatever we yielded here to a local soup kitchen before we headed back to Macon. A chime came from my phone, forcing me to take my gloves off. Pulling it from my overalls, I smiled.

> Colson: when are you coming back inside?

I slid my fingers over the screen rapidly.

> Me: the boys are playing tag

> Colson: so let them, have Haley go out there … she said Jamie just woke up from a nap and wanted to play outside.

I considered it…

> Me: what exactly would we be doing once I go inside?

> Colson: you'd help me in the shower…I haven't had you in two days…Haley keeps monopolizing you at night with that stupid show.

> Me: First of all, it's not stupid…and secondly; fair. But I don't want a quickie…I want to orgasm at least once before you insert your mc into me.

> Colson:…you know I hate when you type the initials

> Me: and you know I hate when I have to spell out the whole word….

> Colson: Monster Cock. Not that hard, baby…
> sorry—it in fact is currently getting hard. I'm
> thinking of how you begged for this monster
> cock to fuck you so hard you wouldn't be able to
> walk the next day.

> Me: a massive, miscalculated request…

The boys made a giggling sound behind the sunflower patch, which made me smile. They were planning something. That was where they went to conspire against the world.

> Colson: Come up here, Nora. I'm already fucking
> my hand thinking of your lips wrapped
> around me.

I was already getting worked up just thinking about it.

> Me: Deal…coming right now, start the shower.

STANDING, I dusted my knees and called for the boys.

"Kane, Tarryn!"

The twins popped into view, their big blue eyes beaming with giddy excitement. They both had lighter hair like their father, but they had my curls.

"Come on, we need to go inside and get Aunt Haley."

Tarryn reached into his pocket with his little fingers, grabbing a piece of paper.

"Wait!" he rushed in a frantic pout, "first, we have to mail our letters to grandma."

Kane started feeling his pockets until he pulled a paper from the back of his jeans.

"Yeah, our letters!"

The boys had begun drawing pictures for their grandma, and after they realized their dad wrote letters to her, they wanted to participate as well.

So, I'd set up a mailbox in the garden, and whenever the boys had a letter for grandma, they'd walk over and place it inside. Colson would collect them, and then tape each one into a photo album that each of our sons would get when they were older.

But every time those letters made my husband smile, and every single summer that we came and stayed here, it was like a piece of daylight pierced his heart and breathed fresh hope into his lungs. This place was slowly healing him. Our life, our marriage and boys…they worked to knit those tattered and torn heartstrings back together.

I loved when he saw what his sons would create, and the fact that it was now a tradition whenever we came to visit made my heart burn bright.

"Okay, let's mail them and then go find Aunt Haley."

I followed after them as they began running barefoot through the soil, then when they found the rusted mailbox with leaves growing all around it and a few sunflowers, they tugged the metal flap down and shoved their little fists inside, leaving their notes behind.

I smiled as they both ran back towards the house.

I took a second to watch the sun beat down on our little world and thought back to how I'd been tempted by my neighbor into a fulfilling and meaningful life.

One that I couldn't be more grateful for.

Saving the Single Dad is available for preorder now!
Want to read what happened when Haley ran outside, right after Liam left for his date?
Click Here, and enjoy a few deleted scenes from Tempting the Neighbor and a few sneak peeks of Saving the Single Dad, coming this spring.

ALSO BY ASHLEY MUÑOZ

ACKNOWLEDGMENTS

First and foremost, this book wouldn't be possible without the support and help of my family.

Babe, thank you for stepping in and being so understanding about my deadline, and knowing when I needed grace, and how to deliver it and for always being willing to create new things in our home for me to love...no matter how many times it doesn't go the way I initially thought it would.

To my children who came to my office with blankets, ready to snuggle in and watch baking competitions while I typed and typed and typed, thank you for understanding and for always loving me.

To my sister Rebecca, the owner of The Hook, you absolutely saved this book. Your willingness to walk alongside me as I wrote each chapter, providing feedback and essential comments regarding the development of characters and their arcs was so essential to me reaching the deadline and having this book publish on time. I am eternally grateful for you.

To my incredible beta readers, Amy Elizabeth, Kelly Drudy, Melissa McGovern, and Casey Ragghianti, I could not have done this without you. I know some people say that but, in this case, it's never been truer. The initial feedback early on in the story, and the completed read-through as I continued to produce chapters were so helpful in creating this book. Your support, encouragement, and love for my story were absolutely everything. I can't thank you enough, and I hope I have you on my team forever.

To my incredible PA, Tiffany Hernandez. We've been through it all, and I know this season wasn't an easy one for you, but I am so honored to call you my friend, and to have you in my corner. To all the rest and everything in between.

To my publicist, Sarah Ferguson. I am so grateful to have you, and you're so insanely talented at all you do, I am so honored to have you on my team, and for your help on literally everything I throw at you. Thank you for being so excited for me and for always being my friend. And to the entire support staff at literallyyourspr, I am so honored to have you working with me and to have all your help.

To my agent, Savannah. Thank you so much for all your dedication and hard work that you put into my books and all my series.

To Dawn, and that day we met back in AP English when our friendship forged. I'm so glad I still have you and thank you for inspiring so much of this book and being the amazing designer goddess that you are.

And to my Book Beauties, thank you for loving my stories, and for loving me. I appreciate all your support and look forward to so much more.

ABOUT THE AUTHOR

Ashley is an Amazon Top 50 bestselling romance author who is best known for her small-town, second-chance romances. She resides in the Pacific Northwest, where she lives with her four children and her husband. She loves coffee, reading fantasy, and writing about people who kiss and cuss.

Follow her at www.ashleymunozbooks.com

Join her Reader Group: Book Beauties to stay in touch